SORCERY FOR BEGINNERS

A SIMPLE HELP GUIDE TO A CHALLENGING AND ARCANE ART

BOOK I
OF THE
CODEX ARCANUM

BY

EUPHEMIA WHITMORE, PH.D., M.L.S., D.D.S.

WITH MATT HARRY

ILLUSTRATIONS BY JULIANE CRUMP

Published by Inkshares, Inc., San Francisco, California
www.inkshares.com

Edited by Staton Rabin and Adam Gomolin
Illustrations by Juliane Crump
Cover design by M.S. Corley and interior design by Kevin G. Summers

Paperback ISBN: 9781942645689
eBook ISBN: 9781942645696
Library of Congress Control Number: 2017940875

First edition

Printed in the United States of America

For Wade Werner, eighth-grade teacher
and my first writing mentor.

Thank you for setting me on my own
path to a challenging and arcane art.

CONGRATULATIONS!

If you're reading this, you have been selected.

You are now a candidate to fight in a war that has waged for centuries. A war between soldiers and spell casters. Guns against magic. Science versus sorcery.

You see, around five hundred years ago, sorcery began to disappear from the world. Steam engines and computers took the place of enchanted farm tools and spell books. Magical seers were replaced by Google. Science became the primary system of belief, and the secrets of spell casting were forgotten.

But sorcery isn't gone.

The energy used by spell casters—the same power that can transform matter, control the elements, and compel creatures—is still out there. It is waiting to be harnessed, like a wild unicorn running through a wood. We need only to find an innocent maid, lure the horned beast into a net of finely woven gold, tie ourselves to its back with unbreakable chains (preferably ensorcelled silver), then hang on like grim death until it grants us a wish. Easy!

But perhaps you're intimidated by such arcane procedures. Perhaps, with your World Wide Webs and cellular pocket phones and instant everything, you find it difficult to absorb the intricacies of a three-thousand-year-old art.

Happily, there is a solution. This book is the first in a series designed to teach the modern young person ancient and complicated studies in a fun, entertaining manner. Complex ideas are broken down and explored through illustrations, instructions, and informative sidebars in three delightful categories:

SORCERY FOR BEGINNERS

Throughout this book, you'll find many terms relating to sorcery. These sections discuss, analyze, and reinforce magical concepts, so that novice spell casters may improve their skills.

ENCHANTING DETAILS

If there's an interesting fact about a non-magical person, place, or thing, this is where you'll find it. Just don't quote us.

BEWARE THE EUCLIDEANS

These sidebars include everything you'll need to know about the history, identification, and avoidance of magic's most dangerous foe.

Most importantly, *Sorcery for Beginners* is no longer presented in a dull, textbook-style format. Instead, spell casting is introduced through the absolutely true tale of one young magician-in-training named Owen Macready. By his example, readers will learn the three aspects of all enchantments, the Twelve Basic Incantations, how to duel with more experienced magic practitioners, and the true power behind all great sorcerers (hint: it's not power).

By reading onward, you are electing to join the battle. To learn sorcery and use it responsibly. To defend magic from those who would suppress, destroy, or subjugate the arcane arts. If that sounds like too much work, go no further.

Still here?

Then let's begin.

Volume One

On the FINDING
and USAGE of
MAGIC SPELL
BOOKS

PROLOGUE

RUSSIAN RUNNER

Snow fell on ST. PETERSBURG as the young sorceress ran for her life.

It was a January evening in the Russian city, just past 1:00 a.m. The city's colorful buildings and onion domes glinted in the cold light of a nearly full moon. At this hour, the streets were mostly empty, save for the occasional late-night piroshki seeker or insomniac. Had anyone looked out their frosted bedroom window, they would have been surprised to see the running young woman for two reasons: 1) the girl was without a jacket

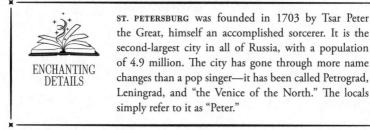

ENCHANTING DETAILS

ST. PETERSBURG was founded in 1703 by Tsar Peter the Great, himself an accomplished sorcerer. It is the second-largest city in all of Russia, with a population of 4.9 million. The city has gone through more name changes than a pop singer—it has been called Petrograd, Leningrad, and "the Venice of the North." The locals simply refer to it as "Peter."

or hat, which was highly unusual for anyone in St. Petersburg at that time of year, and 2) there seemed to be nothing and no one chasing her.

Still, she ran. She was a pale Russian teenager of fourteen years, tall for her age and reedy, like an icy cattail caught in a winter storm. She wore a blue-and-white gingham blouse with a dark navy ankle-length skirt, the hem of which was coated in slush. Large, round eyeglasses slid down her nose as she ran. A wispy blond braid swung wildly across her back. Her breath came in frantic, icy puffs. Clutched to her chest was a wadded-up quilt.

The sorceress didn't break her stride as she glanced over her shoulder. The streets were empty, the air hushed with snowfall. And yet she must have seen something, because a ragged cry of fear broke from her throat. She attempted to increase her speed, turning down a narrow cobblestone alleyway. The leather heel of her shoe slipped on a wet stone, but she managed to keep her balance and continue moving.

At the far end of the alleyway, she skidded to a stop. Her exhaled breaths created great clouds of vapor, obscuring her face. With one hand, she removed her glasses and wiped the condensation on her quilt. Then she scanned her surroundings.

Directly before the sorceress was Palace Square, a massive, open area the size of five soccer fields. The square's only defining feature was a forty-seven-meter-high red granite spire, known as the **ALEXANDER COLUMN**. Behind that was the Winter Palace,

ENCHANTING DETAILS

Unveiled in 1834, the ALEXANDER COLUMN is a monument to Russia's defeat of Napoleon two decades prior. The main column is composed of a single piece of stone that weighs 661 tons, and is set so well that no attachment to the base is needed. If only modern creations were built so cleverly.

a gorgeous eighteenth-century building of white and azure, accented at symmetrical intervals with gold paint. With its current dusting of fresh snow, it looked like a particularly large and expensive wedding cake.

The young woman had no time to appreciate architecture, however. Her desperate eyes scanned the length of the square until they landed on what she'd been running to this whole time—the blue-and-white symbol of a Russian police outpost.

She took a deep breath and sprinted straight toward the glowing sign. She made it only ten steps into the square before her foot caught a patch of ice and she fell to the ground. The bundle in her arms unfurled, sending a heavy rectangular object skidding across the snow-dusted stone.

It was a book.

A thick tome of yellowed parchment, bound in rich brown leather and stamped in gold lettering. The kind of book one usually sees locked in a glass case at a museum, with a tiny placard explaining how old and rare it is. Even in the dim light of Palace Square, it was clear this book was even more old and rare than any of those.

The young woman got to her feet, desperate to retrieve her treasure. She had barely taken a step when a circle of white light illuminated the book. A spotlight. It shone from a helicopter, hovering fifty meters above the square.

SPOTLIGHT ON SPELLCRAFT

There was a *whizzing* sound, and black nylon ropes hit the ground. The sorceress watched, terrified, as three men in dark military garb descended from the helicopter. In their hands were M5 automatic rifles, the sort favored by particularly bloodthirsty mercenaries. On each of their right shoulders was a white-and-black insignia—a compass and a flaming torch bisected by a squat cross. The cross was similar to those she'd seen on the shields of medieval knights, but these men were knights in the same way that African lions are a kind of house cat.

They touched ground, forming a line that blocked her way forward. One of them spoke: "I don't get the running. You knew we had a helicopter."

The sorceress ignored him and ran for the book that lay between them. The mercenaries lifted their rifles. The young woman bent the fingers of both hands into three complicated positions, then gave a single clap.

A crack of thunder echoed across the square, rattling the windows of the Winter Palace. The concussive blast knocked the three adults right off their feet, as if they were little more than paper cutouts in a gale-force wind. Their weapons went flying. They hit the ground several meters away and lay still for a moment, dazed.

The sorceress tossed aside the quilt and ran forward, scooping up the book. She continued toward the police sign, which was still several hundred meters off. The mercenary closest to her rolled sideways, his fingers clutching for the slushy hem of her skirt. He managed to grab ahold of it, pulling the fourteen-year-old to the snowy ground. She kicked at him, but her desperate attacks were no match for his battle-hardened strength. He lunged forward to take the book from her—

The young woman's fingers sketched a few more patterns in the crisp air. She placed a hand on her adversary's chest, whispering a single word: *"HEDFAN."*

The man's feet went up into the air as if tugged by an invisible rope. He let go of the sorceress, frantically scrabbling at the wet cobblestones. His body continued upward, rising farther from the ground as if he were filled with helium. He floated by the Alexander Column, and as he passed the angel statue that stood atop it, he managed to grab ahold of the cross held in the angel's hand. The mercenary hung there, upside down, shouting to his companions for help.

SORCERY FOR
BEGINNERS

HEDFAN is Welsh for "fly." Many older spells had this kind of simplicity—if you wished to manifest something magically, you simply asked for it. Modern sorcery is more focused on getting permission and being clear about one's intentions before casting anything.

By then, the young woman was back on her feet and two dozen meters farther down the square. So focused was she on the glowing blue police sign, she had failed to notice that a second mercenary had gotten to his feet and was sprinting toward her. Only when he was two meters from her did she hear the slap of his boots on the wet stone.

The sorceress spun to face him. She tucked the book under one arm and swept her fingers through the air in a series of movements. Then she stretched a hand toward the man's face and spoke a sentence in gasping French: *"Vous êtes bloqué par une forêt de cannes de bonbon."*

A swirl of smoky, colored light burst from her hand and wrapped around the man's head like a silk scarf. Red-and-white candy canes suddenly sprung up before him, jagged and enormous and blocking his path. The soldier skidded to a stop, looking for a way through the peppermint forest. But his search was in vain for two reasons—first, the candy cane obstacle extended infinitely to either side, and second, there was no forest. Everything he saw existed only in the fog before his eyes, a three-dimensional, picture-perfect **GLAMOUR**.

SORCERY FOR BEGINNERS

A GLAMOUR is a targeted hallucination created by magic. Glamours can incorporate sight, sound, and even smell, if the magician wishes to show off. They can be cast on both objects and people. A glamour will remain in effect until dispelled by a sorcerer, or the target realizes that what they are experiencing is not real. For this reason, it is not a good idea to cast glamours that encourage touching.

The young woman spared no time to appreciate her spell-craft; she turned and kept running. She was only fifty meters from the police outpost now. Once she made it to the door, she and her book would be safe. Her pursuers wouldn't dare risk violence so close to a law enforcement—

Thwipp. A zipping sound cut through the hushed air of Palace Square. Something knocked the book out from under the young woman's arm and sent it spinning to the ground. The sorceress came to a stop. Her heart pounded from her recent exertions and from the object she saw buried in the book's spine, mere centimeters from where she'd been clutching it to her chest.

It was a bullet.

BULLET TIME

Slowly, the young sorceress turned, raising her hands in the air. Twenty meters behind her, the third mercenary pointed his M5 rifle at her heart. He was bigger than his two companions, and had a feline, predatory grace. Keeping his gun steady, he pulled off his combat mask to reveal a handsome face with strong cheekbones and a shaved head.

"This is fun and all, but it's getting toward my bedtime," he said. "And there's no way for you to escape."

The young woman shivered. For the first time in an hour, she realized how truly cold it was. "Please," she said in slow, heavily accented English. "Do not shoot me."

The bald man kept his gun up and drew closer. "A week ago, we asked you nicely to hand over the book. Then we offered to buy it. Now it's a demand. Give it to me, no tricks, or I will be forced to—" He broke off, pressing a finger to a hidden earbud. "But, sir," he said to the unseen commander, "I can get it without further—" The voice on the other side of the earbud interrupted him with an order. "Yes, sir. Understood."

The Euclidean breathed deeply. He tucked his rifle into the hollow of his shoulder. He was only ten meters from the young woman, the barrel of his gun aimed at her heart.

"No, please!" the teenager said, her voice wavering in terror. "Take the book. It is yours. Do with it what you like. I will tell no one, I swear."

The bald man spread his hands. "Sorry, kid. Orders are orders."

He pulled the trigger. The muzzle flash illuminated his face. The young woman shut her eyes in a death-expectant wince—

And time came to a halt.

Snowflakes stopped in midair. The bright flare of gunfire stayed fixed and still, like the petals of a glowing flower. Even the bullet froze in place, a pointed gray blur in the air between the mercenary and his target. The silence was immediate and shocking.

Only the sorceress still had the ability to move. Noticing the world around her had been placed on pause, she cracked open a single eyelid in surprise. Somehow, someone had actually stopped time and saved her life. She began to laugh in relief, when another voice broke through the quiet.

"Exactly what sort of idiotic plan was this?"

Performance Review

A woman stepped from the shadow of the Alexander Column. She was in her sixties or seventies and quite attractive, with an elegant, regal quality about her. Her silver hair was swept back and pinned above her pale forehead. A pair of silver-framed spectacles sat upon her aquiline nose. She wore a trim, high-necked blue blouse, a smart dark gray jacket, and a maroon skirt that went to her exquisite ankles. If Shakespeare's Juliet could teach a few torches to burn bright, this woman could make the entire sun blush with envy.

Inclement weather can be as great an obstacle to spell casting as your enemies.

"Ms. Whitmore," said the young woman. "Thank you for saving me. I had . . . troubles."

"'Troubles' are what occur when you spill a teapot or misplace your house keys," the woman named Whitmore said crisply. Her melodious voice was ribboned slightly with a British accent. "Relinquishing an incredibly powerful guide to sorcery to the very people dedicated to its destruction—that is a *disaster.*" She looked at the frozen mercenaries with disdain. "I have been observing you for the past hour, and still I cannot fathom what your harebrained intentions here were."

"I . . . uh . . ." The sorceress trailed off. Her voice sounded meek in the deafening quiet.

The elegant woman walked forward, leaving a person-shaped hole in the suspended snowflakes. "This time-enchantment I've cast will maintain itself for quite a while, but I do have other candidates to monitor, you know. Speak up."

The young woman cleared her throat. "I was going to the police. For help."

"With sorcery?" Ms. Whitmore laughed, a full-throated, musical sound. "They are lucky to catch ordinary criminals. They would not know where to begin with these well-funded, highly trained murderers." She shook her head at the bald mercenary, who stood like a statue not two meters from her, his face illuminated by gunfire.

"I thought . . . perhaps they could . . . arrest them?"

"To catch a mouse, one actually needs the cat to be on-site. This police outpost has been closed since 7:00 p.m. Their hours are right there on the door."

The young woman's face burned with embarrassment. "I should have planned better. I apologize."

"Not much good in that, is there? Now I shall have to begin the selection process all over again. And meeting new people is so tedious. But I'm afraid there's nothing else for it." Ms. Whitmore held out a perfectly manicured hand. "The book, if you please."

The young sorceress picked the tome up off the ground, cradling it protectively to her chest. "But . . . you said it was mine."

"It *was* yours, but you failed to protect it, now didn't you? Come, don't deny it. Had I not stopped the clock, you would have given one of the rarest, most magical texts in the world right over to these dolts, and then been shot. Or perhaps vice versa, but the outcome would have been the same: the secrets of our **THREE-THOUSAND-YEAR-OLD ART** in the hands of our greatest enemies. And all because you did not 'plan better.'"

She gestured with her fingers, but still the young woman refused

SORCERY FOR BEGINNERS

Technically, sorcery is much older than THREE THOUSAND YEARS. Since humans descended from the trees, magic has been passed on through oral tradition and memory. Three thousand years ago is simply when someone had the bright idea to write some of it down.

to relinquish the book. "But I know so much. The spells . . . I have learned nearly all of them."

"You knew the rules. I was quite clear about what would occur if you failed. No, I simply must continue the search for a new candidate." Ms. Whitmore sighed, softening her voice a bit. "Look at it this way—you will be no worse off now than before we met."

Tears welled in the young woman's eyes, and she shook them away. "But I will. How can I forget . . . that I experienced all this . . . magic?"

"On that, you need not worry." Gently, Ms. Whitmore took the tome from the sorceress, tucking it under her right arm. Then the older woman's long fingers began to trace complex patterns in the air, leaving behind sparkly, golden trails. "Everything you have encountered in the last few weeks—the book, these men, even sorcery itself—none of it will concern you after tonight."

"You are wrong. These things, for the rest of my life, I will remember."

In answer, Ms. Whitmore opened her hands. Cupped in her palms was a glowing orb of golden light, roughly the size of an American quarter. It rose into the air like a soap bubble, made a quick orbit around the young woman's head, and then came to a stop in front of her.

"No," said the older woman, a bit sadly. "No, I am afraid you won't."

Then the golden orb shot forward, vanishing into the young woman's skull.

✸ ✸

Chapter I

Mystery Spot

Six weeks later and half a globe away, one of Ms. Whitmore's "new candidates" sat in his father's car, looking glumly out the window. He was an American white teenager of thirteen years, and he did not yet know what the future had in store for him. At present, he was more focused on the large city they were driving toward.

The metropolis sat in an area where none should be. It was bordered on all sides by low, jagged mountains. The ground beneath it was dry, hard-packed sand, terrible for growing plants or retaining water. The temperature of the area was known to fluctuate wildly, between triple-digit daytime heat and bone-chilling nighttime cold. The air was so dusty, it discouraged breathing.

And yet the young man had been told that over two million people lived there. It was a bustling hub of activity, with airplanes coming and going at all hours of the day, automobiles of every shape and size clogging the main avenues, and tacky buildings soaring into the skyline.

Why? the teenager wondered. *Why would anyone choose such a gross spot to found a city? What would make them spend the money needed to keep the place running? Why would anyone stay in such an isolated, awful, sun-scorched location?*

He would have been shocked to hear it, but the answer to all his questions was the same: magic. The land beneath the city, the rocks, the trees, even the surrounding air, all functioned as a focal point for MAGICAL ENERGY.

Despite the young man's misgivings, the place was clearly flourishing. Every year it drew millions of visitors. The best of everything was shipped there from all over the world. The buildings were in a constant cycle of destruction and renewal. Each day, fortunes were made and squandered, lives were transformed, and people faced the worst of their inner demons. It was a quintessential American town.

Have you guessed its name yet? No?

The city was Las Vegas. And it was to be Owen Macready's new home.

SORCERY FOR BEGINNERS

There are places all over the world that act as focal points for MAGICAL ENERGY. The Giza Necropolis of Egypt, the temple of Angkor Wat in Cambodia, and the city of Machu Picchu in Peru are but a few. In these locations, any spells cast are greatly amplified. The ancients recognized this, but instead of keeping such knowledge secret, they built massive structures on the sites, which was kind of like putting up a sign that read FREE TREASURE INSIDE! on the front of one's house. It's no wonder they are all ruins today.

MUCH ADO ABOUT OWEN

Owen was a skinny, unassuming teen. He considered himself, in almost every respect, to be quite average. He had average brown hair, average brown eyes, and was an average height for his age. He wore average clothes, had average hobbies, and was possessed of an average personality. And that was all fine by him.

You see, Owen had learned in his thirteen years that being ordinary was far easier than being extraordinary. Extraordinary people might go on adventures, or date the most attractive girls, or play professional sports, but doing those things also took large amounts of talent, bravery, and, most annoyingly, effort. In every story he'd heard about successful people, at some point it was revealed how tough they'd had it. How many obstacles they had faced. Yet somehow, these heroes had found it within them to spite the odds and keep going. To Owen, that sounded like far too much work.

Instead, he was content to coast through life. He didn't go the extra mile, didn't work into the wee hours, and he absolutely

A Portrait of the Candidate as a Young Man

never took a stand. As a result, he had a solid group of acquaintances. He received perfectly acceptable marks in school. And (most importantly to him) he had lots of time to play video games on his computer. His existence might be unremarkable, but it was stress-free.

Little did he know that, before the month was out, he would be offered one of the most extraordinary, difficult opportunities in the world.

Whether he survived it would be another matter.

The Wrong Good-bye

There was another reason Owen didn't consider himself to be special. Four months earlier, the teenager's parents had separated. His mother, Eleanor, a former wild spirit who still listened to punk-rock music and had a half dozen tattoos, had never been comfortable in the suburbs of **CLEVELAND**, Ohio. The city was too conservative, she said in her many late-night arguments with Owen's father. It was too cold, too depressing, too square. Even the animals she treated—Eleanor Macready was a veterinarian—were boring. Just once, she wanted to work on a Komodo dragon or a capybara. She wanted excitement

ENCHANTING DETAILS

CLEVELAND is actually a lovely city, filled with artistic venues, enjoyable nature spots, and some truly unique sights, such as the Rock and Roll Hall of Fame. Unfortunately, any love for the city's sports teams will result in nothing but heartbreak.

in her life. Purpose. Finally one night, Owen's father, Marcus, a compact, balding man with a few too many pounds around his midsection, said loudly that if she wanted to experience such things, she should leave.

Both he and his son were stunned when she took him up on the offer.

She packed a bag that very night. Owen, who had been pretending to play video games during the screaming match, sat before the dim light of his bedroom computer, listening as his father apologized, then guilt-tripped, then pleaded with his wife not to leave. The whole time, Owen's mother said not a word.

Finally, around 10:30 p.m., she entered her son's room. "Owen, honey," she said. "Have I ever told you about the orangutans?"

This question was so random that it almost made him turn from his computer. But he refused to give his mother the satisfaction. Instead he shrugged, continuing to play his game. Eleanor sat on the bed behind him. "The thing is, there are less than seven thousand of them left in Sumatra. The people there need help to keep them from going extinct. Lots of help. Especially from veterinarians. So I've decided to go and lend a hand. It won't be easy, but doing anything special takes work."

Owen said nothing. "Not that I don't consider you to be special," she continued hastily. "I mean, I love you, but you're gonna be fine here. You're strong and stubborn and smart when you want to be, but the orangutans, they *need* me. And I need to be someone other than your mom for a while. There's someone else inside me, someone who wants to make a real difference in the world, and I need to find her. Do you understand?"

He shrugged, keeping his eyes on the computer. Onscreen, his berserker Viking was laying waste to a horde of monsters. At this moment, the violence felt supremely satisfying to him.

His mother laid a hand on his shoulder, but he jerked away. "Can you pause that for a minute so we can at least say good-bye?"

Perhaps had she not asked, he would have done so. He'd have hugged her tightly, told her he could be special too, begged her not to abandon her only child for a group of orange primates. At the very least, he could have said a proper farewell. Instead, he tapped his keyboard, annihilating a cluster of orcs.

Eleanor sat behind him for several more minutes, staring at the back of her son's head. He couldn't be sure, but he thought he heard her sniffling. Finally, his mother rose from the bed.

"Guess this is it, then," she said, her voice breaking. "Bye."

She kissed Owen on the crown of his head. Then she walked out of his bedroom and shut the door. It wasn't until he heard her car pull away that he allowed himself to stop the game.

By then, of course, it was far **TOO LATE**.

SORCERY FOR
BEGINNERS

It may seem cruel, but young people who endure traumatic moments such as this one often make better spell casters. Perhaps it's because a happy and content existence leaves little motivation to improve oneself.

Running on Emptiness

Eight weeks later, Marcus Macready announced he'd accepted a job out of town. Owen was not surprised. His mother's departure had left an emptiness in the house, a damp, omnipresent fog that filled every room they walked into. The furniture, the wallpaper, the knickknacks—all of it was a constant reminder that Eleanor was somewhere else in the world. And rather than stay with her son and her husband, she had chosen to live with apes.

What did surprise Owen was the location of their new home.

"Las Vegas?" Owen said, not bothering to keep the distaste from his voice. *"Why?"*

"Lots of construction in Vegas," his father said as he cut and chewed his rubbery, microwaved steak. Marcus was a building engineer. He had gotten more bald since Eleanor had left, and there were dark circles under his eyes. "Lots of job opportunities. They just built a new school there that's supposed to be top-notch. It'll be a fresh start for us, bud. A chance to break out of this . . . funk."

He hadn't asked Owen's opinion, hadn't given him a choice in the matter. He'd simply decided they were moving to the desert. *Vegas is cool*, he'd said. *Vegas is exciting*. Vegas would make them forget Rocky River, Ohio.

Except it didn't. Now that Owen was looking upon their new home for the first time, a metropolis in the middle of nowhere, he was struck by a crushing loneliness. All those people and houses and brightly lit casinos in that brutal, isolated landscape—to him, it smacked of desperation. It was as if they'd built the whole place on a massive sand skillet, and everyone who lived there was pretending to not notice the increasing heat.

Owen and his father moved into a brand-new house in a cookie-cutter neighborhood south of the Strip. The suburb was called Henderson, and it was right on the edge of the Mojave Desert. Their home was so similar to the others on the block that Owen had to write his address on his backpack so he wouldn't walk into the wrong house.

Because Marcus was new, he was assigned the swing shift at work. He'd be out of the house from noon until two o'clock in the morning, sometimes six days a week. Owen and his father would barely see each other. Sadly, neither of them seemed to mind it too much.

SPRING'S FORWARD

On his first day at his new middle school, Owen was given a card with his assigned locker number and combination written on it. He headed in the direction where the office administrator pointed, but it wasn't until he was far from the office that he realized the locker number had been scrawled so hastily, it was nearly illegible. He stopped in the hallway, debating if he should turn back or attempt to puzzle it out on his own.

"Ahoy there! New guy. Yes, you."

Owen turned. A tiny African American girl of about twelve years old sat at a card table, her thick hair pulled into braids.

Her warm brown eyes were framed behind funky purple glasses, and when she spoke, he glimpsed a mouthful of braces. She stood, revealing a quirky patchwork skirt beneath her purple polo. Owen wouldn't know it until later, but her full name was Perry Spring.

"You look lost," she said, walking over to him.

"No, I'm just trying to find my locker." He showed her the slip of paper from the principal's office.

"Ah-ha. The execrable penmanship of Mrs. Macklevore strikes again. That appears to be . . . ten-oh-six. Or ten-sixty-six? Either way, your destination is the same. Down that way, sail on past the gym, hard-a-starboard, and you're golden. I'm Perry." She stuck out a hand. On her index finger was an oversized grape Ring Pop.

"Owen," he said, giving her a brief handshake. "Well, thanks."

"A moment, Owen. Perhaps you'd care to repay my chivalry by making a small contribution to Ye Olde Cause?"

She nodded back toward her card table. A colorful poster board sign was taped to the front edge. *SCA Fundraiser*, it read in puffy purple paint and silver glitter—*Send us to WAR!*

"What's—?"

"You haven't heard of SCA?" she asked, pronouncing it *ska*. "Society for Creative Anachronism? Folks dressing up as knights errant and as medieval lords and laying waste to each other on the field of battle? It's high-caliber, Excalibur fun."

In fact, Owen had heard of such groups. They were renowned to be populated exclusively by nerds. "Right. Cosplay stuff."

"Cosplay is what children do on Halloween," she sniffed. "Our aim is to re-create all the best aspects of the medieval experience—cooking, warcraft, calligraphy—and none of the bad things, like dysentery. We're raising money to attend the Grand Fracas in August. That's when all the shires from the western kingdoms get together and do battle. So . . . wouldst thou purchase a Snickers or two, good sir?"

She jiggled a box of candy bars. Clearly, this girl cared not a whit what anyone else thought of her. Owen fished a crumpled dollar bill out of his pocket. "Here you go. Fare-thee-well and all that."

She pocketed the buck, following him down the hall. "You're a fan of **OLD ENGLISH**? Runic letters, et cetera?"

"Not really. I've played a few medieval video games."

"Then you should join us. Do it for real!"

Owen had never been the most popular boy in school, but he knew aligning himself with a group of Ren Faire geeks on Day One would be tantamount to social suicide. "Not really my thing. But thanks for the directions."

ENCHANTING DETAILS

OLD ENGLISH is an early form of the English language that was used by residents of Great Britain between at least the mid-fifth century and the mid-twelfth century. Its alphabet was comprised of runic letters and pre-dated Latin. To read it is to be amazed that the Brits ever learned how to communicate.

He waved, leaving Perry behind with a disappointed look on her face.

Over the next few days, Owen quickly settled into a routine. He biked to school, put forth a bare minimum of effort in his classes, biked home, warmed up something resembling food in the microwave, and spent the evening either playing computer games or watching movies online. He felt fairly confident he could get through the rest of eighth grade in this fashion, and perhaps even the entirety of high school. His only worry was that, before he graduated, he might perish of boredom.

Less than two weeks later, however, Owen would find himself beset by a variety of perils, and boredom would be the very least among them.

CAUGHT IN CANDY

It was a Friday afternoon in late February when Owen first encountered sorcery. School had just ended, and he was walking to get his bike. It was chained up near the building's western exit, but when he got there, he found the doorway blocked by orange cones and a large amount of cotton candy. The pink, sugary substance filled the hallway. It poured from the air vents and collected against the walls in six-foot-high mounds. Several students had gathered to watch two beleaguered janitors attempt to wrangle the mess. They'd reach for a handful, and it would duck between their legs. They'd shove some into a trash can, and more would spill out of the vents. For an **INANIMATE OBJECT**, the stuff had very strong ideas about being captured and contained.

"Can't . . . go . . . this way!" one janitor said to Owen as he struggled to pin a mound of spun sugar that continued to squirm farther away. "Use the . . . gym exit."

Then the school employee ran to free his coworker from a swarm of sugar tentacles. Owen sighed and started toward the opposite end of the building. He had downloaded a new video game the night before and was eager to start playing it. Hoping to save some time, he cut through the school gym, which was dark and empty at this time of

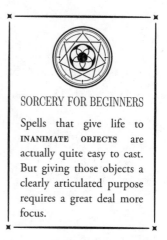

SORCERY FOR BEGINNERS

Spells that give life to **INANIMATE OBJECTS** are actually quite easy to cast. But giving those objects a clearly articulated purpose requires a great deal more focus.

day. Everyone had been forced outside to take part in various extracurricular athletic programs, or as Owen viewed such activities, torture.

The light in the equipment room, however, was still on. Voices drifted from the slightly open door. As Owen passed, he saw something inside that made him pause. Three large eighth-grade boys had cornered a small Indian American kid against a metal bin filled with red rubber dodgeballs. The leader of the menacing middle schoolers was probably fourteen years old. He had orange hair cropped into a short Mohawk, a thick layer of muscles more suited to a high school senior, and a good eight centimeters' height on everyone else in the immediate area. His skin was pale and translucent, the purple veins underneath making him look like a stinky European cheese. His orange-freckled fist was drawn back as if he was about to deliver a devastating punch. Sensing he was being watched, the older boy turned and made eye contact with Owen. A slow, cruel smile split his face.

Bully for You

Normally, this would have been the perfect opportunity for Owen to avert his eyes and move on. But for whatever reason, whether it was the obvious fear on the younger kid's face, or the sight of such overwhelmingly unfair odds, this time Owen stayed where he was.

"You got a problem?" Orange Mohawk said. His name, Owen would learn later, was Bryan Ferretti.

"No," said Owen. Standing up to bullies was not exactly in his wheelhouse, so he hadn't spent a lot of time crafting witty comebacks.

"Then get out of here, new kid. You're interrupting a business transaction."

Owen glanced at the Indian American boy. The silent plea for help in his eyes told Owen this encounter was far from businesslike. "Um, the thing is," Owen said. "I need some equipment from in there. A, uh . . . dodgeball." He pointed a finger at the metal bin behind them.

Now, what happened next was not technically his

*As evil creatures go,
only werewolves are worse than bullies.*

doing. It was certainly given form by his actions, but the power to accomplish it was, let's say, temporarily gifted to him by an interested third party.

The second Owen gestured, a rubber ball flew out of the bin. It collided with the back of Bryan's head, caromed off the equipment room wall, and smacked into Owen's outstretched hand.

Everyone else looked at the dodgeball bin in surprise, then over at Owen. *Why does everything have a mind of its own today?* thought Owen. *First cotton candy, now dodgeballs. What's next, my own homework attacking me?*

Bryan rubbed the back of his head, his eyes bright with anger. "You should've kept on walking, new kid."

The young man took a step back. "Sorry. I don't know how that—" Owen let go of the ball, but instead of dropping to the floor, it rocketed across the room, smacking Bryan in the forehead. The bully fell backward into the metal bin. The container tipped over and out spilled the dodgeballs, covering his body and tripping up his **CRO-MAGNON** cohorts.

The Indian American boy saw his chance and ran from the room. "Thanks!" he said to Owen before exiting the gym at something near the speed of light.

Owen looked back into the equipment room. Bryan rose from

ENCHANTING DETAILS

The term CRO-MAGNON is a nickname for early human beings (aka *Homo sapiens*, aka cavemen). Most likely smarter and more attractive than this lot.

the pile of dodgeballs, a round red mark already forming on his forehead. *Not good.* "Grab him," he said to the Cro-Magnons.

The two words propelled Owen into action. He sped through the dark gym, pushed his way out of the exit doors, and jogged down the corridor just in time to see the last bus pulling away from the school. As his bike was on the opposite end of campus, he had no choice but to evade the bullies on foot. Hearing the gym doors squeak open behind him, Owen took a deep breath and ran.

Run Free or Die

It was not much of a chase. First, Bryan and the Cro-Magnons had their bikes chained right outside the gym. Second, Owen was unfamiliar with the area. He tried to lose his pursuers, but a mere four blocks from the middle school, in a retail area that included nail salons and chain restaurants, the bullies skidded to a stop right in front of him. Each of them sat atop his bicycle, smiling in anticipation.

"You made me look stupid back there, new kid," Bryan said. "And I ain't stupid."

Had Owen more pluck, he would have mentioned that using the word *ain't* was fairly strong evidence to the contrary. Instead, the eighth grader kept walking. *He can't do anything too bad to me*, Owen reassured himself. *We're in a public setting.*

He was, suffice to say, not very familiar with the behavior of sociopaths.

The bullies followed him. "What, you think you're tough, new kid?" Bryan said. "Huh? Do ya? Huh?"

To punctuate each question, he rammed his front tire into the back of Owen's legs. The last time was so hard, it left a black mark on his calf. Angry, Owen kicked the bike away. Bryan was surprised for a moment, then the sly smirk returned to his face.

"You gonna fight us all by yourself? Ain't no lucky dodgeball gonna save you this time."

He was correct. And so, Owen contemplated his options:

1. *I could stand up to these jerks. Sure, I'll probably lose, but my story will live on forever.*
2. *I could run and escape to fight another day.*
3. *Who am I kidding? There are three of them, and one of me.*

He ran.

He only made it a meter or two before a big, beefy hand grabbed the back of his T-shirt. Too late, Owen remembered his pursuers were on bikes.

"Get his arms and legs," said Bryan.

The Cro-Magnons seized Owen. Bryan squatted over him, his upside-down face leering like a jack-o'-lantern with a Mohawk. "I have to make an example out of you, new kid. Something that will remind everyone at school what happens when people disobey me." He motioned to his cohorts. "The ice chest," he ordered.

The Cro-Magnons lifted Owen off the ground. There was a convenience store only a few meters from them. Just off the main entrance was a large metal cooler, the kind used for storing big plastic bags of ice that people only buy for barbecues and then forget to use. Tittering with anticipation, the Cro-Magnons started to carry Owen toward it.

The young man struggled. "Hey!" he screamed. "Somebody, help—"

But Bryan clapped a sweaty hand over his mouth. His fingers smelled of grime and rusted metal. The maniac smiled, waving his free hand to a passing car. *No problems here. We're just fun-lovin' boys hazing a good buddy.*

They were less than a meter from the cooler now. Owen tensed every muscle in his body, kicking and straining, but the teens were stronger. Their hands held him like iron clamps. Owen tried to bite Bryan's fingers, but the bully smacked his teeth away.

They slammed Owen against the metal container. Bryan made sure no adults were watching, then opened the freezer doors. A blast of frigid air billowed out. The inside was dark and smaller than the trunk of a car.

"Gonna be a tight fit," said Bryan. "Hope you ain't claustrophobic."

He nodded, and the Cro-Magnons began to shove Owen into the chest. He fought madly, kicking and punching, but Bryan socked him in the gut. Owen wished for someone to see what was happening, for a police officer to drive past, for a meteor to strike the parking lot right behind them. As they slowly crammed him farther into the metal container, all these thoughts boiled down to a single, shouted word:

"*HELP!*"

Now, most cries for help are limited by the scientific fact that sound waves can only propagate so far through space before they fizzle out. There are some, however, so fraught with desperation and need, they can echo halfway around the world. Owen's shout was one of these. It traveled through the city like an air-raid siren, reaching the ears of anyone inclined to offer magical assistance. It helped that one such person had been observing Owen all afternoon.

Unfortunately, even sorcerers need time to prepare.

So at first, the only response to Owen's cry was Bryan punching him in the mouth. The young man tasted blood, and his body went limp. The Cro-Magnons took the opportunity to stuff Owen fully into the ice chest. They were about to shut the doors when the young man's call for help was finally answered.

WHOOOM.

A loud, concussive sound erupted from across the street. It was as if a massive elephant foot had stomped on the ground. A shockwave of hot air slammed into the convenience store, setting off every car alarm in the parking lot and knocking the bullies to the asphalt. They lay there for a moment, dazed.

That moment was enough.

Without sparing a thought on the **EXTRAORDINARY PHENOMENA** that had just saved him, Owen kicked himself free of the metal container and ran around the side of the convenience store.

ALLEY OOPS

The boy found himself facing a long, narrow concrete alley. Behind him, Bryan and the Cro-Magnons were regaining their senses.

"What was that?" groaned one of the bullies, clutching his head.

"Who cares. He's getting away!" Bryan said, scrambling to his feet. "Come on!"

Owen, meanwhile, sprinted down the alley as fast as he could go, only to see a chain-link fence blocking the exit ahead of him. He was trapped.

Unless . . .

There was a dumpster beside the barricade. A daring person might leap over the fence from atop the dumpster and make it to the other side. Owen wasn't particularly daring, but he was terrified.

SORCERY FOR
BEGINNERS

Human beings are incredibly adept at ignoring EXTRAORDINARY PHENOMENA, even when they occur right before their eyes. Ghosts, monsters, and magic (especially magic) have all been explained by laughably trivial things such as eye problems, swamp gas, and even too much eggnog.

Owen placed his hands on the dumpster, hearing the smack of Bryan's boots draw close behind him. Owen pulled himself atop the garbage bin fairly gracefully. A glance backward told him the sprinters would reach him in seconds.

Owen didn't think. He simply pumped his legs, leaping from the dumpster and kicking off the fence with one foot. There was a single, blissful moment of weightlessness—

Then his sneakers hit the concrete on the other side and he rolled with, not exactly poise, but something that was a distant relation of it.

It was Owen's turn to grin. He didn't know how exactly he'd managed to leap over a seven-foot fence, but if they wanted to follow him, they'd have to make the same difficult jump.

Bryan, however, simply walked to the fence. He scowled, grabbed the metal links, and began to pull himself to the top. Owen paled. He'd quite forgotten there was another way over the barrier.

He bolted down the alley, hearing Bryan's boots hit concrete less than two meters behind him. Owen rounded the corner, finding himself across the street from yet another strip mall. Hearing the *slap* of the bully's rubber soles draw closer, the young man ran straight into traffic. One car honked its horn, but he made it across the street without dying. He ducked behind a brown sedan, peering back at the alleyway.

Bryan emerged, scanning the street for his quarry. He looked down the busy avenue, glanced at the strip mall across the way, then his gray eyes settled on Owen's hiding spot. He jogged straight toward it.

Cursing softly, Owen checked the stores behind him. A nail salon, a laundromat, a magic store, and a place where children could make, bake, and paint cheap clay crockery. All terrible spots in which to hide from a lunatic.

A fifth store looked promising, though. In fact, the boy was surprised he had not noticed it straight off. It was set back in the corner of the strip mall, its windows filled with books that blocked any view to the inside.

Also, it was at least ten stories tall.

The top of it stretched far above the surrounding rooftops, each level a different style than the one below it. There was a section that looked like a castle, one that resembled a mosque, and one that boasted flying buttresses and stained-glass windows. The ground level was a bland, nondescript storefront that would be at home in any Las Vegas strip mall. It was the most bizarre building on the block, but then again, the city was filled with bizarre buildings, among which were a pyramid, a duplicate of the Eiffel Tower, and a smaller-scale reproduction of the New York City skyline.

Owen looked closer. An ornate, wood-carved sign hung above the door. **CODEX ARCANUM**, it read. **Purveyors of the Exotic, Rare, and Unusual. E. Whitmore, Proprietor.**

Good enough, thought Owen. Keeping himself low, he crab-walked toward the shop. Bryan was facing the opposite direction, waving over one of his bike-riding goons. Now was Owen's chance.

He ran the last meter toward the bookstore, yanked open the door, jumped inside. A tiny chime tinkled as the door shut. Owen peered through a space in one overcrowded bookshelf, seeing Bryan's cohorts join him in the parking lot. They seemed to look right at him, but then their eyes moved on. They argued about Owen's disappearance for a minute, then split up, riding in two different directions.

Owen exhaled in relief. *I'll just wait here long enough to make sure they're really gone, then sprint back home and not leave the house for a week. Maybe two.* Perhaps by spring break the bullies would forget he'd ever existed.

Suddenly, a voice spoke behind him. It was careworn, filled with wisdom, but sharp as a dagger:

"Welcome, candidate. Do you wish to join our ranks?"

Each level corresponds to a different location around the globe.

Meeting Ms. Whitmore

Owen turned. The words had been spoken in a melodious British accent that projected authority and intelligence. It belonged to the elegant woman who, six weeks prior, had stopped time in St. Petersburg's Palace Square. Today she wore a tasteful red blouse and tartan skirt. Her silver spectacles glinted mysteriously.

"Speak up," the enchantress said. "Are you here to become a defender of sorcery, or have you entered my store for some other purpose?" She paused, waiting for Owen to break his stare. "Or has the education system in this country grown so poor that they've ceased teaching language altogether?"

"Actually, I'm, uh . . . hiding?" said Owen, unable to think of a lie.

"Hiding." The woman nodded. "Well, you've chosen a most excellent spot. People avoid this place as if I were selling plague."

*When storing magical texts, tasteful interior design
is as important as shelving space.*

Owen inspected his surroundings for the first time. The store was filled floor to ceiling with bookshelves. They rose several stories into the dark upper reaches of the interior. The crooked pathways between them were barely a meter wide. Green-shaded banker's lamps cast yellow pools of light at seemingly random intervals. The numerous books on the shelves absorbed both light and sound, making the building as dim and quiet as a tomb. And the smell . . . Well, if you've ever inhaled the woodsy perfume of an antique text, there's no need to describe the majestic aroma that now wafted through Owen's nostrils.

"What is this place?" the boy asked. A stupid question, but we must remember, he had just been running for his life.

"Don't tell me you've never been inside a bookstore! I knew it. At long last, I have lived to see the end of human culture."

"Of *course* I've been in a bookstore," said Owen, offended that she thought him so ignorant. "Just not one so . . . crowded."

"Ah. Well. The Codex Arcanum serves several purposes, one of which is a bookstore, but another, and more important, is a recruitment center. And I am the head recruiter." She extended a pale hand. "Ms. Euphemia Whitmore."

"Owen," said the boy, shaking her hand uneasily. Her skin had the feel of cool, delicate paper, but the fingers were surprisingly strong. She held his hand tightly as her sharp, ice-blue eyes looked into his. Her pupils appeared to grow larger and larger in the murky light of the store. It was as if two black whirlpools were swirling all about him, tugging and teasing out the deepest thoughts from inside his MIND—

And then his hand was released. Owen blinked. Had the sun outside changed position? The shadows certainly seemed longer.

"So . . . what are you recruiting for?" he asked.

"For war, of course. A secret war, that has been waged for more than five hundred years. A war to keep sorcery and the other arcane arts from falling into the hands of the Euclideans."

SORCERY FOR BEGINNERS

The spell used by Ms. Whitmore here is Menno's Mental Manipulation. As it requires looking deep within a human MIND to determine its intentions, it can only be cast by a very high-level sorcerer.

"Euclideans?"

"Our greatest foe. They wish to take our knowledge and destroy it, so that magic may perish from the world. They think it evil."

She beckoned him deeper into the store. "For centuries, the volumes you see here have helped trained aspiring sorcerers to fight the Euclideans. We have out-of-print books, illuminated manuscripts, and even some carved stone tablets."

She turned a corner. Owen followed, but the older woman had vanished.

A LITERARY LABYRINTH

"Hello?" Owen called out. His voice was absorbed almost immediately by the books. "Ms. Whitmore?"

"The pages of our books possess energy," she said from several aisles over. Owen followed her voice, taking one turn, then another. "You must feel the weight of them in your hands, examine them with your own fingertips. You must inhale their scent."

There she was, turning down the end of a long aisle. Owen jogged toward her, the tomes looming over his head. Whitmore rounded the corner—

And again, she was gone. The store must have secret passageways, Owen decided. He pressed on, the aisles becoming more precarious now, twisting sharply this way and that. The ground seemed to undulate under his feet, like swells on an ocean of concrete. Strange titles caught his eye: *The Book of Kells* . . . **THE GREATER KEY OF SOLOMON** . . . *Malleus Maleficarum* . . . Several times he had to hop over piles of bound texts.

"There are some books," Whitmore's voice continued far in the distance, "that are more magical still. **GRIMOIRES** that gauge the reader. Stories that diverge based upon your desires. Manuscripts with minds of their own."

ENCHANTING DETAILS

One of the most famous books of magic in history, THE GREATER KEY OF SOLOMON was not actually written by the well-known biblical king. It dates back to the fourteenth or fifteenth century and represents a rather pedestrian example of Renaissance-era magic. The name Solomon was most likely used for marketing purposes, just like modern-day athletes are used to sell shoes.

SORCERY FOR BEGINNERS

Books about magic, or GRIMOIRES, date back to a time before, technically speaking, there were even books. The first collections of sorcery and spells were recorded on tablets, scrolls, even the occasional stone pillar.

Her voice was practically gone now. Owen increased his speed, ducking underneath a low overhang—

And he nearly collided with Whitmore. She stood straight and tall, as if she'd been waiting for him the entire time.

"Of course, the term *book* is a bit pejorative," she said. "Most of the magic texts that surround us have been copied from other sources and bound for ease of transport." She traced a finger down the spine of a wide red leather tome, then fixed him with her piercing gaze. "Would you like to see one?"

A Tome to Remember

Owen suddenly realized how dark it was in the back aisle of the bookstore. He had left the sun far behind, and the only illumination came from a green-shaded lamp high overhead. Whitmore stared down at him, the light and shadows making hollows of her eyes and cheeks.

"A . . . magic book?" Owen asked.

"There's one just down there." She pointed a long finger at the shelf near the boy's feet. "I believe you'll find its contents rather . . . illuminating."

His eyes followed the imaginary line of her finger. One spine on the shelf stood out to him. Unlike the surrounding volumes, it was bound in bright, plastic-coated paper. Owen crouched, tilting his head to read the title. The letters squirmed as if he had water in his eyes, but when he blinked, they were in clear printed English.

"*Sorcery for Beginners,*" he read, looking up at Whitmore. "You wrote this?"

She gave a not-so-modest shrug. "My talents are legion."

"So what is it, like, a how-to guide for magic tricks?"

"Tricks, young man, are for charlatans and All Hallow's Eve. That book teaches the art of *real* magic. An art, thanks to the Euclideans, that is little practiced anymore."

Dubious, Owen slid the book off the shelf. It was a paperback done in the style of an old-fashioned textbook, with magic-related graphics on the cover. He flipped through the first few pages, glimpsing figures of hand positions and diagrams bordered by strange symbols.

"I thought you said it was ancient."

"Looks can very often be deceiving," she said coolly. "Some even change depending on the viewer."

Owen skimmed a few more pages. "No wands?" he said jokingly.

The bookseller scoffed. "True magical energy is harnessed through **SOMATIC COMPONENTS**—the physical, practiced movements of a human body."

"Neat," Owen said, unenthusiastically.

"You're not the practicing sort. Very well," she said, holding

SORCERY FOR BEGINNERS

The SOMATIC COMPONENTS of which Whitmore speaks are most often finger and hand positions, but can include dance steps, facial expressions, even the specific motions of a sorcerer's hair follicles.

out a hand. "Best hand it back and return home to your new video game."

The boy hung on to the book, wondering how she had guessed such a thing. "It's just, you know it's not real. Sorcery, I mean. It only exists in, like, books and movies."

"Oh, its presence may have decreased in the world," she agreed, "but that does not mean it's gone."

Owen was unconvinced. The older woman tapped the book's cover. "You don't believe me? Read the dedication page."

Grudgingly, Owen opened the book to the second page. It was blank, save for the following words:

For Owen, who does not believe in magic

He looked up at Whitmore, surprised and impressed. "How'd you do that?"

Her smile could have eclipsed the *Mona Lisa*'s in the mystery department. "I told you, books are magic. And that one more than most."

"Prove it," Owen said. "Make it do another trick."

She frowned. "Simply being unable to replicate an extraordinary phenomenon doesn't mean it did not occur. One could argue, in fact, that's what made it extraordinary in the first place. But without such proof," she lamented, "learned men and women have discredited entire schools of magic. And so now, young people like yourself do not look to the universe for answers, but instead to Wikipedia."

Owen shrugged, putting the book back on the shelf. "Ooookay. Good luck with all your codexes arcanum. And maybe think about adding a few windows in here."

He started back down the aisle, in the direction of what he hoped was the front door. He was just about to turn the corner, when an object dropped at his feet with a heavy *thwack*.

It was *Sorcery for Beginners.*

He turned to look at Whitmore. She appeared not to have moved from her position.

"The plural of *codex*," she said, "is *codices*."

"Nice toss," he said back to her. "But I'm still not buying."

He stepped over the book, continuing on his way—

Thwack. There it was at his feet again.

Owen looked back at the old woman. She still hadn't moved, but the *Mona Lisa* smile had returned. "It appears you are meant to join our fight," she said mildly.

"I'm not a fighter," Owen replied, kicking the book back down the aisle. It slid several meters, stopped, then REBOUNDED as if tied to an invisible rubber band. It bounced off the toe of Owen's sneaker, falling open to a page toward the back.

SORCERY FOR BEGINNERS

Clearly, Ms. Whitmore cast a SPELL OF ATTRACTION to link Owen and the book. This medium-level charm magically binds two objects together and is frequently used by sorcerers to avoid losing their wallets and car keys. But take caution: the charmed objects will do anything to come back together, even burrow through the earth itself. This is why the bookseller removed the spell once it served its purpose.

"Perhaps you are, only you've never been battle-tested," she said.

Owen bent to pick up the book, his eyes drifting to the text on the open page. Again, the words squirmed in a funny manner, but when he blinked, they were in plain written English:

A Spell to Rewrite History

Beneath the title was a description of the spell and an accompanying list of instructions. But the bottom of the page was what made his breath catch in his throat.

A series of three illustrations demonstrated how the spell should work. Instead of generic drawings like the ones on the cover, though, the first panel showed a young man sitting at a computer, his mother behind him.

The two bore a striking resemblance to Owen and Eleanor.

This was no trick. Even if Whitmore had known he was coming, there was no way she could have known what had happened four months ago, much less printed a drawing of it, bound it in a book, and placed it at the back of her store on the off chance he'd come in to hide.

The old lady seemed to understand what he was thinking, gently nodding for him to continue to the next panel. It depicted a close-up of Owen reading the spell from a book. In the third panel Owen was sitting with his mom and dad on the shores of Lake Erie, watching a sunset. They were back in Rocky River, his parents were no longer separated, and it appeared as if the move to Las Vegas had **NEVER OCCURRED AT ALL**. It was what the boy had wished for every day since his father had driven him into the Nevada desert.

He looked at Whitmore, astonishment and desire battling for dominance on his face. "How much?"

SORCERY FOR BEGINNERS

Next to love spells, enchantments to affect time are among the most sought after. But novices must be wary: fiddling with time can spoil the endings of anticipated films, unexpectedly alter history, or even erase one's whole existence.

THE PRICE IS WRIT

"$19.95," the bookseller said, ejecting the drawer on an old-fashioned cash register. Their walk back to the front had been surprisingly short. Owen supposed that with all the twists and turns, the store only appeared to be larger than it was. Or it could be the whole place was enchanted. He wasn't confident of much at the moment. He took the emergency twenty-dollar bill from his canvas wallet and handed it to Whitmore.

"Your five cents change, and—" She held up a parchment-colored bookmark; the Codex Arcanum logo was embossed upon it. "In case you need to find us again," she said, slipping it inside his purchase. "All sales are guaranteed to work provided the owner applies himself, but sometimes people have . . . questions. Remember, we're here to help."

She handed him the book. The boy reached for it, but she pulled it back with quicker reflexes than he would have expected.

"By purchasing this volume, you are taking an oath to join our ranks. To learn the spells in this book and defend sorcery from those who wish to destroy it. But most importantly, to make sure this text never falls into the hands of the EUCLIDEANS."

Owen blinked. "And those are . . . bad guys?"

"Have you not been listening? They are our worst enemies. Our adversaries for over five hundred years! If they were to acquire this information, they might use it to enslave the world!"

The young man nodded, eager to leave. "Yeah, yeah, yeah, I got it. I won't give 'em the book."

BEWARE THE EUCLIDEANS

One surefire way to spot a EUCLIDEAN is to look for their initiation tattoo. Every new member is required to have the order's insignia permanently inked somewhere on his or her body.

"Do you swear it? Because if they do get ahold of it, the consequences—"

"Yes, I swear they won't get anything," Owen assured her. He was beginning to think the old lady was a bit batty.

"Very well," she said, releasing her hold on the book. "You are now the custodian of a sacred art that dates back three thousand years. Once you have learned the contents of this volume, you will be given a final examination before you can receive your Sorcery Learner's Permit."

"Super," said the young man, who had no intention of taking any tests, battling in secret wars, or safe-guarding much of anything. He only wanted to return home and figure out how to cast the Spell to Rewrite History.

"Congratulations, Candidate Macready," she said cheerfully. "I wish you luck."

He was confident he had not told her his last name.

Beginning Beginners

CONGRATULATIONS!

If you're reading this, you have been selected. You are now a candidate to fight in a war that has waged for centuries.

So began the first page of Owen's edition of *Sorcery for Beginners. A bit intense for a kid's instruction manual,* thought the teenager, *but at least it's not stuffy.* He put a pillow between his back and his bed's headboard, settling in for a long read. When he'd arrived home, he had decided not to waste time making dinner, instead grabbing a strawberry Pop-Tart and a can of Mountain Dew. Now comfortably barricaded in his bedroom, Owen took a bite of the high-calorie, chemical-filled toaster pastry. His father wouldn't be back from work for at least six or seven hours, so Owen had plenty of time to pore over his new purchase and fill his body with junk food.

The first few pages contained more warnings about responsibility and dedication and using magic for good, but Owen wanted to cast some spells. He **SKIPPED AHEAD** to the first lesson.

Basics Training

Lesson 1: The Basics of Spell Casting

Many people think learning to use magic takes a long time, possibly because so many wizards and witches in stories are scary older folk. But this couldn't be further from the truth. SORCERY can be used by anyone who has the will and discipline to master it.

SORCERY FOR BEGINNERS

Responsibility and dedication and using magic for good are actually very important lessons, which is why this edition of *Sorcery for Beginners* uses these text boxes to ensure that novices cannot simply SKIP AHEAD to the "good parts" without at least feeling guilty.

So probably not me, thought Owen glumly. His grades were middling—Bs and Cs for the most part—and he'd shown no aptitude for creative pursuits such as music, writing, or drama. In athletics, he was hopeless. The only activity in which he showed any proficiency was playing video games. And even those required him to make frequent use of online strategy guides and cheat codes.

SORCERY FOR BEGINNERS

This is a bit of a simplification. Yes, the average person may be able to cast one or two entry-level enchantments, but gaining a true mastery over the complex nature of SORCERY is a lifelong pursuit that takes wisdom, patience, and plenty of hard work. Roughly .00000006 percent of the populace become full-fledged sorcerers. But you'll never know if you're one of them unless you try!

I know what you're thinking, the book continued as if it could do exactly that. **"I'm just a normal kid with average grades; I'm not talented enough to be a sorcerer."**

"That's exactly what I was thinking!" Owen said aloud. "But how can you know that? You're just a book."

Correction: I am a magic book. Why do you think the writing style is so informal? Why do you think the "Spell to Rewrite History" drawings looked exactly like you? Your thoughts are reflected in my pages. I'm a mirror for your mind.

"So if I thought of any question—anything at all—you'd respond to it?"

Try me. Think of a question, and I shall answer it.

I gotta come up with something unexpected, Owen mused. *Something so impossible, so bizarre, there's no way Whitmore could predict what I'd think of next. That'll prove sorcery's not real.*

You have your question? Now turn the page.

Owen did.

The next two pages were blank.

He was disappointed, but not particularly surprised. How could a book have known what he was thinking, unless it was really, truly magic? Real magic didn't exist, no matter what kind of clever tricks Whitmore and her speedy bookbinding might come up with. Besides, Owen had thought of a question so weird, even he didn't know what the answer would look like.

But then, ink began to appear on the blank pages. Lines arced across the creamy emptiness. Cross-hatching sprouted like blades of grass. Shading smudged itself into existence. And before his eyes, the answer to his question took shape.

On the left page roared a menacing Tyrannosaurus, its stumpy arms augmented by huge, muscled limbs that had been

Magic has been used to create sillier drawings, but not many.

stitched onto its body in the style of Frankenstein's monster. The beast threw a stunning right-handed roundhouse into the following page, where jagged teeth and gears flew from the maw of an enormous metal-plated shark. There was only one question the drawing could answer.

"Who would win in a fight between a Frankenstein-ed T. rex and a robot shark?" breathed Owen. The book *was* magic. There was no question of that now.

He turned the page.

Presto! Now can we move along, please?

"Sure," said Owen. "Sorry. It's just . . . I have thirteen years of non-magical experience to get over."

Apologies are for those who can't cast spells.

THREE IS A MAGIC NUMBER

Now, continued the book, Let's go over some basics of spell casting. All sorcery has THREE ASPECTS:

1. **Energy**
2. **Components**
3. **Focus**

"Great. You gonna explain any of those?" Owen said impatiently.

Patience. For a spell to work, all three aspects must be perfectly in sync.

ENERGY is what you draw upon to create magic. It is around us at all times, unseen but powerful.

SORCERY FOR
BEGINNERS

Unseen ENERGY is nothing new. Radiation, microwaves, and wireless fidelity (Wi-Fi) are all invisible, but highly useful. Magical energy is just like these, only it can be used for far more interesting pursuits.

"Like Wi-Fi," said Owen.

> Correct. And some things—people, objects, even places—have more magical energy than others.

"Disneyland?" Owen guessed.

> Not as much as you might think. **COMPONENTS** are the elements needed to charge up a specific spell. These can include physical ingredients, body movements, activation words, or all three.

"I think I get it," Owen said tentatively. He didn't want the book to think he was too dumb.

> You're not dumb. There are highly intelligent sorcerers who have spent their entire lives pondering this concept and still they do not comprehend it. Of course, they didn't have the assistance of me.

"Are you alive?" asked Owen. He was suddenly reminded of stories he'd heard about spirits trapped in vessels, like genies and **DYBBUKS**. *Wait, wasn't part of Voldemort inside a book, too? What if this thing's evil?*

> I am not evil. Nor am I alive. Think of me as a paper-based computer—filled with information you can access, provided you ask the right questions and earn the answers.

ENCHANTING
DETAILS

DYBBUK (n.)—In Jewish mythology, a malevolent possessing spirit said to be the dislocated soul of a dead person. In 2001, a dybbuk was supposedly found to be haunting a wine cabinet that had been purchased on eBay. The story gives a new meaning to the term "buyer's remorse."

"Yes, ma'am. Or sir. Which one are you?" Owen asked.

> **Neither. I am a book.**

The young man shrugged and continued to read:

> **The third aspect of sorcery, and perhaps the most important, is FOCUS. FOCUS is the supreme control of your own mental attention and acuity, tempered by—**

> **HEY!**

Owen blinked. His eyes had started to wander in the middle of the admittedly wordy sentence. He looked back down at the page.

> **Without focus, NO SPELL YOU ATTEMPT WILL EVER WORK.**

"Okay, jeez," said Owen. "You don't have to get snippy about it."

> **To demonstrate how these three aspects work in concert, let's start with a simple spell.**

"Finally."

On the Mend

Owen turned the page. At the top, printed in a minutely detailed, illuminated text box was his first spell.

A SPELL FOR MENDING

Oh dear.
It appears **somebody broke something**.
I shan't point any fingers, because it no longer matters.
With this **simple enchantment**, you can now **restore** any physical
object that has been **shattered, snapped, severed, cut, busted,
bruised**, or otherwise **rent asunder**.

COMPONENTS NEEDED:

– One {1} **object, broken** –
– One {1} **thimble of salt** –

SOMATIC MOVEMENTS:

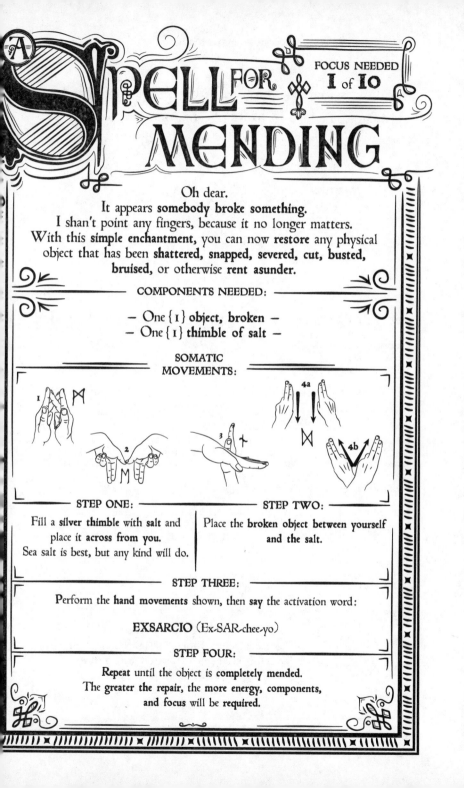

STEP ONE:

Fill a **silver thimble** with **salt** and
place it **across from you**.
Sea salt is best, but any kind will do.

STEP TWO:

Place the **broken object** between yourself
and the salt.

STEP THREE:

Perform the **hand movements** shown, then **say** the activation word:

EXSARCIO (Ex-SAR-chee-yo)

STEP FOUR:

Repeat until the object is **completely mended**.
The greater the repair, the more energy, components,
and focus will be required.

Owen peered at the hand motions. They appeared to be forming some kind of RUNE. As someone who played medieval video games, Owen had seen these before but never realized their true importance.

He went back and read the first step.

> **STEP 1: Fill a silver thimble with salt and place it across from you. Sea salt is best, but any kind will do.**

Owen hopped off his bed and jogged downstairs to the kitchen. The clock read 9:14 p.m. He still had at least four hours before his dad got home from work. Maybe by then, Owen would be good enough to cast the Spell to Rewrite History.

Salt was easy enough to find, but he had no idea if they owned a thimble. Even if they did, the odds of it being made of silver were even more unlikely. Instead, he selected a small silver coffee spoon. *Silver*, he remembered from a video game, *has magical properties. Hopefully what I use for measuring won't make a big diff.* He took the spoon and a saltshaker upstairs.

He tapped what he imagined was a thimble's worth of white grains into the spoon and set it across from him on the bedspread.

SORCERY FOR BEGINNERS

RUNES are ancient symbols that comprise the original language of magic. Forming them with one's hands or fingers will "charge up" the magical energy necessary for a given enchantment. Making a mistake in the movements can cause the spell to fail, create sudden explosions, or simply make one look silly.

STEP 2: Place the broken object between your-self and the salt.

Owen crawled over his bed, grabbing a yellow No. 2 pencil off his desk. He snapped it cleanly in half, arranging it between him and the salt-filled spoon. *This was going to be easy, he thought.*

STEP 3: Perform the hand movements shown, then say the ACTIVATION WORD:

EXSARCIO

(Ex-SAR-chee-yo)

Owen awkwardly bent his fingers into the prescribed positions. *Doesn't seem so hard.*

STEP 4: Repeat until the object is completely mended. The greater the repair, the more energy, components, and focus will be required.

He repeated the hand movements a few times until he felt comfortable. Once he completed a good run, he pointed at the broken pencil and declared in his best sorcerer's baritone: *"Exsarcio!"*

Nothing happened.

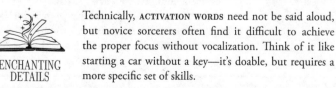

ENCHANTING DETAILS

Technically, ACTIVATION WORDS need not be said aloud, but novice sorcerers often find it difficult to achieve the proper focus without vocalization. Think of it like starting a car without a key—it's doable, but requires a more specific set of skills.

He rechecked the instructions. It did say to repeat until the object was mended. Perhaps he hadn't done it long enough.

He shook out his hands and resumed his SPELL CASTING.

SPELLBOUND

Forty-five minutes later, the bedspread was littered with a dozen broken pencils, and none of them had been mended. Owen had tried breaking the pencils in different places and cutting them in two with a knife. He'd varied the speed of his hand movements, chanted the activation words in a Latin accent he'd learned from YouTube, and even tried singing the spell to various melodies. But there was no change to any of the writing utensils, and now "Itsy Bitsy Spider" was stuck in his head.

He attempted to mend other objects next—a matchstick, a Post-it note, a thread, a corner of the strawberry Pop-Tart. He even tore off a tiny piece of the spell book itself and tried to reattach that.

Nothing worked.

Frustrated, Owen flipped to the back of the book. Perhaps there was another section he could read for a time. Another spell

---

SORCERY FOR
BEGINNERS

Although this book is filled with actual, working SPELLS, it is highly recommended that you DO NOT attempt any of them until 1) you have read all the lessons contained herein, and 2) you receive your Sorcery for Beginners Learner's Permit. Details for acquiring one are explained later, but don't bother flipping ahead. What you see will make no sense at this point.

he could try to take his mind off his current mental block. The Spell to Rewrite History, for example.

The rest of the book, however, was **BLANK**.

The spell he'd seen in Codex Arcanum, gone.

He turned back to the first page. There was the dedication he'd seen in the bookstore, the one that addressed him directly. He flipped ahead. The introduction, T. rex versus robot shark, and the cheeky explanation of the three aspects were all there, in the same order as before. Directly after that was the Spell for Mending, and then—two-hundred-plus pages of white nothingness.

"Where's the Rewrite History spell?" he asked the book. He checked the next few pages, but they were still blank. "Book, I command you to show me the Spell to Rewrite History!"

Nothing.

"Please?" he tried. "That's the only one I really want to do. The only one I *need*. Please, please, *please*!" Holding his breath, Owen turned the page.

A single sentence appeared in the mocking, empty whiteness:

More spells will be revealed when you are ready.

SORCERY FOR
BEGINNERS

Sorcerers have found ways to disguise their spell books since magic was first developed. This is to ensure that only people with the proper training can unlock and cast the spells contained inside. The only drawback is that when someone finds a BLANK book, they have a tendency to destroy it in frustration.

He had hit a wall. The feeling was similar to how he felt upon encountering a difficult video game puzzle. But unlike a video game, he couldn't go online to find out how to get past it. Unless . . .

Another hour later, an exhaustive search of the INTERNET had provided him with no help. There were plenty of websites that discussed magic and witchcraft and sorcery, but they seemed more akin to self-help lessons than real sorcerer training. The majority of them also appeared to have been designed by people with little money and less HTML coding experience. Even more frustrating, there was no mention of *Sorcery for Beginners*, the three aspects of magic, or a Ms. E. Whitmore, bookseller or otherwise.

Owen tossed the spell book across the room. It thumped against the door and landed on the carpet, cover side down. He was about to boot up a first-person shooting game to vent his frustration when he heard the garage door open. His father was home from work.

Owen quickly powered down his computer and scooped the mending spell detritus off his bedspread. He threw it all into a

---

BEWARE THE EUCLIDEANS

In fact, nearly every source of "magic information" on the INTERNET is woefully misinformed. This is for two reasons: 1) the small number of real sorcerers in the world would never publish their hard-won magical knowledge in a place where any dunderhead with a Wi-Fi connection could access it, and 2) when any real information pertaining to sorcery appears online, it is immediately taken down by Euclidean agents.

desk drawer, clicked off his light, and jumped under the covers just as his dad cracked open the bedroom door.

Even though his head was facing the opposite direction, he could feel his father watching him. Did he know he hadn't gone to sleep yet? Could he see the pencil dust on the carpet? Was his parental radar telling him his son was attempting to cast real magic? Owen tried to focus on his breathing, making his chest slowly rise and fall. After what seemed to be an eternity, he heard the door click shut.

The boy rolled over in bed. *Tomorrow morning, I'll go straight to Codex Arcanum. I'll take the book and convince Whitmore to help me make it work, even if I have to turn on the fake tears.*

Satisfied with this plan, Owen closed his eyes and fell into a fitful sleep. In his dreams, he wandered through a wilderness of broken pencils and windblown graphite.

When he woke the next morning, the boy rubbed away his eye crust and stretched his limbs. His hips were still a bit sore from sitting cross-legged so long the night before. He rubbed his joints, turning to where he'd thrown *Sorcery for Beginners*.

The spell book was gone.

Vanishing Acts

A lump settled in Owen's stomach, roughly the size, feel, and taste of a charcoal bowling ball. A quick scan of his floor revealed the book was nowhere in sight. He sprang out of bed, looking underneath the desk, behind the bookshelf, even inside the dresser drawers.

It was well and truly gone.

He dressed himself quickly, his mind racing. *Could someone have followed me home last night and stolen the book? One of those Euclid-people, maybe? Or did Whitmore figure out that I couldn't make the first spell work, and teleport the book back to Codex Arcanum, where she could sell it to someone better?*

Or what if—and this thought was the most unnerving of all—*what if the book left on its own?* If it could guess his name and respond to his thoughts, **GROWING A PAIR OF LEGS** would

Causing an inanimate object to GROW A PAIR OF LEGS, also known as transmutation, is actually quite a complex procedure. It would be much easier to cut off the legs of a living animal, attach those to a book, then cast a spell to animate the legs. It would also be unnecessarily cruel.

SORCERY FOR
BEGINNERS

be child's play. It could at this moment be trotting down the 215 freeway, on its way to a more skillful, deserving owner.

Well, I'm not letting it go without a fight, thought Owen fiercely. This was his first encounter with real, working sorcery, and he needed it to bring his family back together. He needed to unlock the Spell to Rewrite History, go back to four months ago, and tell his mom not to leave. *If that means I gotta ride back toward the store, find the book, and wrestle it to the ground by myself, then so be it.* He grabbed his wallet off the bedside table and ran downstairs.

USE YOUR DADDY

Owen strolled into the kitchen, affecting what he hoped was a casual "I did NOT just lose the world's only working spellbook" manner. His father sat at the table, drinking coffee and paging through a textbook. The teenager grabbed a granola bar from the pantry and a Gatorade from the fridge.

"Goin' for a bike ride," Owen said as he stuffed the items into his backpack. "Might not be back until . . ." He trailed off as he saw the bright cover of the book in his father's hands.

"HEY!" He grabbed *Sorcery for Beginners* from Marcus and flipped through it. The first few pages were filled in, but the rest was still blank. Just as he'd left it last night.

"Interesting book you have there," his father said mildly, sipping his coffee. "Where'd you get it?"

"I bought it," Owen said defensively. "And it was in *my* room. Since when is it okay for people in this house to *steal* things?!"

"Cool your jets. I went up to check on you last night, and it was lying right up against the door. And when I saw the cover, I was . . . surprised, that's all. Didn't know that kind of thing was your cup of tea." He tilted his coffee mug toward the spell book. "**DIFFERENTIAL EQUATIONS**— pretty complex stuff for an eighth grader."

Confused, Owen looked down at the book. There was the title, and the magical graphics, and Whitmore's name. "What are you talking about?"

ENCHANTING DETAILS

DIFFERENTIAL EQUATIONS (n.)—Mathematical equations that incorporate derivatives of a function or . . . I can see your eyes are glazing over. Let's just say they are extremely complex problems that only scientists and building engineers have any use for.

His father stood, dumping the dregs of his coffee into the sink. "Okay, I shouldn't have taken your stuff. Actually, I thought you had nabbed one of *my* old textbooks. Weird that you happened to find the exact same edition."

"Dad." Owen was beginning to feel like the victim of an elaborate prank for a reality television show. "What book do you think this is?"

"*Differential Equations for Structural Engineering.* Same one I had in college. I could practically recite the first chapter." He chuckled.

A mirror for your mind, the book had called itself. For Owen, it was a beginner's guide to sorcery. For his engineer father, it was magic of another kind—the kind he used every day to make steel and concrete rise into the sky. The boy wondered if the book looked different to everyone.

Oh, the questions he had for Ms. Whitmore.

"Right. Well, like you said, it's . . . interesting. Really gives me, like, a window into what you do all day long." Owen stuffed the book into his backpack as he made his way toward the garage door.

"Wait!" called Marcus. "Aren't you gonna call your mom?"

Owen paused. Once she had gotten settled into her new home in Sumatra, Eleanor Macready had attempted to talk with her son every few days on FaceTime. But her cell phone service was often poor, and she frequently got pulled away by local problems. Soon their awkward conversations had decreased to once a week. *But once I cast the Spell to Rewrite History*, thought Owen, *we won't need FaceTime at all to talk. Everything will be like it was. I just gotta make this book work.*

"I'll, uh, call her later," he told his dad. "Anyway, bike ride, see you at dinner . . . bye!" And he was out the door before Marcus could guilt him further.

LOST AND FOUND

Though it was early March and barely half past ten in the morning, the sun was already brutally hot. *Welcome to the desert,* Owen groused to himself as he pedaled down the asphalt bike trail that paralleled South Boulder Highway. *Like Dad says, it's hotter than a volcano sauna, or cold enough to freeze your breath. Everything out here's either crap or crappier.*

It seemed crazy that anyone would choose to live here, much less open a rare bookstore. Especially one in such a low-rent storefront, far from the tourists and rich people on the Strip. What had Whitmore been thinking, coming to Las Vegas? Someone in her line of work seemed more at home in a fog-blanketed, back-alley shop in Edinburgh, Scotland, not jammed between a nail salon and a comic book store in a suburban **AMERICAN STRIP MALL.**

Owen wondered if Codex Arcanum sold other magic books. Surely Ms. Whitmore wouldn't let her rarest and best text go to an eighth-grade boy she'd never met. He wasn't even a star athlete or at the top of his class. *I'm just average,* he thought. *The book she sold me must be pretty average, too. Which means she's gotta have other, even more powerful items for sale.*

ENCHANTING DETAILS

In point of fact, Codex Arcanum has a dozen locations all over the world. The flagship store is situated in Hay-on-Wye, a small village in Wales that has been nicknamed the "town of books." Even though it has fewer than 1,500 residents, there are over thirty bookstores, most selling secondhand and specialized texts.

Owen had his father's credit card—never mind it was strictly for emergencies—perhaps he could return *Sorcery for Beginners* and buy something he could actually understand. Something that would teach him to perform the Spell to Rewrite History by day's end. *Sorcery for Dunces,* he thought sourly. *Perfect for a genius like me.*

The boy turned into the strip mall, already formulating his plea to the bookseller, but then squeezed the brakes on his bicycle so hard, the back tire lifted off the ground.

Codex Arcanum had vanished.

It wasn't simply that the sign had been taken down, or that the inventory had been packed up and moved out overnight, or even that the store had been demolished, leaving behind a pile of rubble. Those events would have been surprising, but explainable. What faced Owen was infinitely more mysterious.

It looked as if the bookstore had *never been there at all.* There was the nail salon on the right, and the comic book store on the left, but instead of a storefront, a door, and a ten-story business filled with thousands of ancient, magical manuscripts, there was only a seam of bricks, barely fifteen **CENTIMETERS** wide. Had

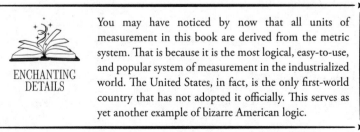

ENCHANTING DETAILS

You may have noticed by now that all units of measurement in this book are derived from the metric system. That is because it is the most logical, easy-to-use, and popular system of measurement in the industrialized world. The United States, in fact, is the only first-world country that has not adopted it officially. This serves as yet another example of bizarre American logic.

the whole place been some kind of illusion? Had Owen walked through a portal to another world?

He dug through his backpack, finding the bookmark Whitmore had given him. There was no address on it, no phone number, no website. In other words, it served no other purpose than to mark one's place in a book. "Great marketing," Owen muttered, shoving it back into an outer pocket.

The boy went into the other stores one by one, asking the clerks if they'd ever heard of Codex Arcanum, or knew of a bookstore in the strip mall, or had seen an old, gray-haired British woman talking in riddles the day before. Each one answered in the negative.

The last place he checked was the comic book shop. The sign above the door told him it was called *Incanto's*. The interior was a combination flea market/purveyor of magic tricks/pile of junk on the side of a highway. Shelves toward the front displayed cheap, prefabricated illusions and how-to guides for stage magic, while plastic-sleeved comics were arranged in bins against the walls. Every other available space was filled with what could only be described as garbage. There were small, crumbling stone statues, crudely made wooden **FETISHES**, and rusted jewelry of

ENCHANTING DETAILS

FETISHES are inanimate objects worshipped for their supposed magical powers or because they are thought to be inhabited by a spirit. Most are completely ordinary, which only proves how great the human desire for guidance is—in the absence of divine instruction, we will bow down before a crudely sculpted rock.

every conceivable design and metal. Owen didn't know what to focus on first.

"Oi! Help you pinpoint something there, mate?"

SOME INCANTO MEETING

The young man peered in the direction of the voice. Behind a large stack of aged wooden boxes was a male, probably in his midforties. His face was covered in a scruff of dark, unshaven whiskers and framed by shoulder-length black hair. Hazel eyes glinted brightly behind thick, black eyeglass frames. The man stood, revealing a generous belly covered in a black T-shirt, which depicted two pieces of cartoon cutlery and the phrase *May the Forks Be with You*. Clearly, a cutting wit was not among his skill set.

"Name's Alec," the man said with an accent that hailed from some working-class British city the eighth grader couldn't place. "This here's my establishment. How can I assist you on this early Saturday morn?"

Owen noticed a poster behind the store owner. It showed a much trimmer, more mysterious version of the man in front of him, in the midst of performing an amazing piece of magic. The title beneath it proclaimed: ALEC INCANTO—WORLD'S MOST LEARNED MAGICIAN!

"Is that you?" Owen said.

Alec glanced behind him, then rolled his eyes. "Yes. And I know I've been a bit generous with the donuts since me glory days;

don't need a reminder. What d'you want?"

"Oh. Uh—I'm looking for a bookstore," Owen said.

"Seems you found it, yeah? What level are you, mate? Intermediate? Advanced? Got some wonderful manuals on close-up magic here." He

Such demonstrations are laughable when compared to real magic.

shoved aside some of the boxes and held up a black ball the size of an American half-dollar for Owen's inspection. He placed it between two of his fingers, wiggled his digits, and quickly multiplied the lone ball into three.

Owen was unimpressed. "Actually, I'm looking for a real bookstore. Like a Barnes and Noble."

"You sure about that?" Alec fanned out a deck of cards, showing Owen they were all random. "Only takes one trick to get bitten by the bug. I was just about your age when it happened to me." He shuffled the cards and cut them. "Saw this bloke perform in the back of a pub. What he did with a deck of cards, it was enough to turn your bleeding hair white. Taught me how to do a **PERFECT RIFFLE**, and I . . . was . . . hooked." He fanned out the deck again, showing the cards were now all hearts.

There was a time when Owen might have been impressed by such a display, but now that he'd seen real sorcery in action,

PERFECT RIFFLE (n.)—A technique used to make a deck of cards look randomly shuffled. Similar techniques include the strip-out, the Hindu shuffle, and various stock shuffling methods. As if such gimmicks weren't appalling enough, magicians also insist on giving all their tricks tacky nicknames.

ENCHANTING DETAILS

multiplying balls and card tricks seemed laughably mundane. "I don't want to learn magic," Owen said. "At least, not the fake-y Vegas kind. I just want to find Codex Arcanum. It was, like, right next door yesterday."

Peeved, Alec pocketed the deck. "Think I'd recall if a competitor muscled in on me turf. Curse them with my considerable powers, wouldn't I? What kind of book were you looking to buy?"

"I already . . . I'm not buying anything," Owen said in frustration. "Are you sure you never heard of this store? Or maybe saw the woman who worked there? Something Whitmore?" He pulled out the bookmark again, showing Alec the text. "Old lady, speaks with an accent, believes in secret wars?"

"Sure, I've seen her. Every time me mum comes for Christmas." Alec handed back the bookmark. "Now, much as I enjoy conversing in riddles, if you ain't gonna grace me with a purchase, then I shall return to my inventory. Feel free to poke around, but if you have any more unanswerable questions, hit up Professor Google, yeah?"

He resumed his inspection of the boxes. Disappointed, Owen wandered farther into the store. He idly investigated the western wall of the shop, tapping here and there to find evidence of a false wall or hasty paint job—anything that would prove Codex Arcanum had indeed been right next door. In this regard, he was disappointed.

"Owen New Guy!"

The boy turned. Perry Spring stepped out of a nearby aisle, wearing a long embroidered green skirt, and a brown corset laced over a short-sleeved white blouse. Her funky purple glasses were the only modern touch. In her hand was a purple velvet bag of brand-new twenty-sided dice.

Inspector Perry

"'Twould appear the gods wished us to meet again," she said cheerily.

"Or it's a dumb coincidence," said Owen sourly.

"Ooooh. Sounds like someone woke up on the wrong side of the MULTIVERSE this morning."

The tiny girl placed the velvet bag on the store counter. "Just these today, Alec."

"Morning, love. Nice to see someone keepin' me business afloat." As the store owner rang up her purchase, she turned back to Owen.

ENCHANTING DETAILS

The MULTIVERSE is the hypothetical set of all possible universes that comprises everything that exists and everything that could exist. Pondering such concepts first thing in the morning would put anyone in a bad mood.

"You ask me, it's kismet," Perry continued. Owen stared back at her blankly. "Destiny? Fate? No human child patronizes Incanto's this early on a Saturday. Am I right, Alec?"

"As ever and always. That'll be $17.95."

Perry handed him a twenty, and once he gave over her change, he went right back to inspecting his pile of boxes.

"He can be a bit rough-edged, but he's secretly nice," Perry explained as she and Owen exited the store. "And his inventory is exemplary. Now then, since the threads of our lives have been entwined by the Norns, what bring-est thee to yonder parts?"

"I'm trying to find the place where I bought this." He pulled the spell book from his backpack.

Her eyes widened. "You got that around here?"

She reached for the book, but Owen instinctively clutched it to his chest. "No. Yes. It's mine."

"Calm down. I'm not gonna club you over the head and abscond with it. I just don't usually see my quote-unquote peers carrying around antique Latin manuscripts." She poked the cover. "And in real leather, too. Fanc-ee."

The book must look different to her as well, Owen realized. "So . . . you can read the cover?"

"*Papa gestare proni ridiculam?*" When Owen simply stared at her, she explained: "That's LATIN for 'Does the pope wear a funny hat?'"

He kept staring. Perry rolled her eyes.

SORCERY FOR BEGINNERS

LATIN was the dominant written language in the fifteenth century. Nearly seventy percent of all printed material from that era was in Latin, so most of the first printed spell books are associated with that language. Be aware, though—casting spells with a Latin accent does little to improve their effectiveness.

"I took an online course over winter break. May I?" She plucked the book from his arms and sat down on the curb. The cover looked the same as always to Owen. But Perry traced the title with a finger, reading completely different words. "*Magicae nam Novitiorum*. Magic for . . . Novices, I think?"

"Beginners." So, unlike his father, who saw engineering equations, Perry saw a guide to sorcery, only it was written in Latin. He suddenly had an idea. "Could you, uh, flip through it? Maybe to somewhere in the back and tell me what you see?"

The girl began turning through the book at random. "It's blank. Is it a gag gift or something?"

He sat next to her, burying his head in his hands.

"Hey, are you okay?" she asked. "You look distraught."

Owen shook his head in frustration. *Why would Whitmore sell me a book that doesn't work? And why does it look different to everyone?* Then another notion occurred to him. *Maybe the enchantment or whatever only works on people! Maybe . . .*

He removed his cell phone from his pocket, turned on its camera, and pointed it at the book cover. On the tiny monitor, there was no textbook cover design, and no English title. Instead, it was as Perry had described—an old leather-bound tome, with gold-embossed letters in Latin. He flipped through the pages, seeing hand-lettered text framed by ornate, beautifully **ILLUMINATED** borders.

ENCHANTING DETAILS

An **ILLUMINATED** manuscript is one in which the text has been supplemented by the addition of decorated letters, borders, and miniature illustrations. Illumination was expensive and time-consuming, frequently incorporating precious materials such as gold and silver leaf, and sometimes taking decades to complete a single text. Makes one appreciate the abundance of illustrated books available today.

"Impressive," said Perry, peering over his shoulder at the phone screen. "Is that like an app or something?"

"No. Yes." *I gotta be a little careful here. If everyone knows I have a magic book, they'll take it away.* "You think you could translate it?" he asked her casually. "The Latin, I mean. Can you read it?"

The girl studied him suspiciously. "I suppose. Trish is the real aficionado. Trish Kim, she's seneschal of our local SCA chapter. The boss," she explained when Owen's face went blank. "We could show it to her. I was actually on the way to our weekly war meeting. You're welcome to accompany me."

"Lead the way." He stood, sliding the book back into his backpack. At this point, Owen would have partnered with Bryan Ferretti if it meant figuring out the Spell to Rewrite History.

ANALYZE THIS

It took them twenty-five minutes to ride their bikes to SCA's meeting place. From the moment they left Incanto's, Perry badgered Owen incessantly about every detail relating to his antique book and his mysterious "phone app." The eighth grader tried to lie, but her tsunami of questions quickly drowned his resolve. By the time they reached the freeway, she had gotten him to spill everything about his visit to Codex Arcanum, from meeting Euphemia Whitmore to the nature of the spell book. Once she knew it was magic, she made him stop his bike and demonstrate how it worked. The eighth grader asked it a question, then grinned as Perry watched it answer him. She checked the book for hidden screens and micro-cameras, eventually coming to the same conclusion he had the night before: it really was enchanted. Rather than worry about Perry knowing his secret, Owen found he was glad to have someone with whom he could discuss things. Especially when it was someone clearly more familiar with the ways of sorcery than he.

"It makes perfect sense the store disappeared," she babbled excitedly as they pedaled down South Boulder Highway. "Think about it. If you were a purveyor of magic guides, people would hound you endlessly unless you found a way to stay camouflaged. You said there were tons of books in there, right? That means tons of enemies."

Owen was less physically fit than Perry, so he was obliged to talk between panted breaths. "So you think—you think . . . they're all magic?"

"No offense, but you don't seem like the yarn-spinning type. The details are too easy to disprove, too specific—if you were lying about being a sorcerer, you'd just say you could fly or change into a dragon or something. You wouldn't fashion *props*."

"Thanks . . . for that . . . I guess."

"I mean, it's incredible! Knowing there's magic out there, it changes *everything*. All the bad things in the world—dictators and poverty and child abuse—we could fix all that, Owen. Real world problems, solved with sorcery."

He rubbed sweat from his eyes, feeling a little guilty that the only thing he cared about using the book for was rewriting history. "If we . . . can get it . . . to work," Owen reminded her, still panting for breath.

"Of course we can," Perry said confidently. "What Whitmore told you, about magic being forgotten but not gone? That makes sense, too. It's the same reason no one knows phone numbers anymore."

"I don't follow." In fact, he felt that way about most things she said.

"Think about it. We have smartphones now. All those numbers we used to have memorized—our friends, family, local library—now they're all available at the touch of a button. So our brains lost that skill. That's probably why you couldn't make the mending spell work—you're too present-day. We simply have to return you to a medieval mindset, and you'll be casting spells like a Level 20 Sorcerer Supreme."

"You really think . . . SCA . . . can do that?"

"Probably more than you'll like," she admitted. "These guys are fun, but they can be moderately intense."

Getting Medieval

"ZOUNDS! Who is this modern jackanape that dares trammel upon our sacred ground?"

Owen and Perry stood before a group of four middle schoolers. They were in an open area just southeast of the Dragonridge golf course. It was literally deserted—five large, sand-beaten rock pillars jutted from the empty, sandy ground on every side of them, creating the impression that they were in the palm of a massive stone hand. Small painted figures, a large battle map, and piles of gaming paraphernalia were placed in the shade of one particularly thumb-like rock column. Whatever SCA's other talents might be, they'd chosen a cool spot for their meeting.

ENCHANTING
DETAILS

ZOUNDS (interj.)—An exclamation used to express anger, surprise, or indignation. Literally a shortening of "God's wounds," which doesn't really make sense either, but sounds suitably shocking.

The young Korean American woman who had spoken stepped forward, frowning. In the normal world, she was Trish Kim: a tall, strongly built thirteen-year-old with chin-length black hair, but here in the desert of Dragonridge, she was the seneschal of all she surveyed. She wore a tunic over metal chain mail, black leather gloves, and a red velvet cape. The result, while absurd, was surprisingly intimidating.

If you're going to practice sorcery,
why not have a pleasant view?

Perry knelt before her, indicating for Owen to do the same. "If it please m'lady," the tiny girl said, "I invited this pilgrim into our lands. While his garb may be strange to the eye, he brings with him an object of great power and mystery. He requests our assistance to decipher it."

Trish folded her arms. Behind her, the three other members of the group looked at each other with expectant glee. They were clothed respectively as a ranger, a female knight, and a medieval lady-in-waiting in a Cinderella-esque dress. They were well versed in their leader's penchant for monologuing.

"Assistance?" sputtered Trish. "May I remind you, *herald*, we have quite a full day before us, which you have already delayed with your tardy arrival. Rather than granting boons, I should be dunking you in boiling pitch!"

"Oh, come on," said Owen. "I've got, like, a real thing I need help with, not some fake role-playing narrative."

"Silence, knave!" cried Trish. "Who dost thou think thou art? Surely a king or emperor, to address our royal person so boldly. Dost thou even hail from this region? Methinks your impertinent face is unknown to us."

"How long do we have to keep this up?" Owen muttered to Perry.

"Uh, he's new to these lands, m'lady," the tiny girl said. "Moved here but two weeks ago. Now can we drop the medieval-ese?"

The ranger, a skinny Indian American boy, stepped to the seneschal and whispered in her ear. Owen recognized him as the younger kid Bryan had been harassing in the gym equipment room. *Feels like it's been days since then*, Owen thought to himself, *but it was only yesterday*.

"Really? What a bunch of dill-holes," Trish said upon hearing the ranger's words. Then she remembered herself. "I mean, such a display of cowardice is verily . . . Whatever, those guys suck. Tried to shake down our meetings a couple of times—you believe that?" She jerked her head toward the ranger. "Ravi told me what you did for him. Any enemy of Bryan Ferretti is a friend of ours. We apologize, and bid you welcome to the Shire of Dragonridge."

She held out a gloved hand, and Owen shook it. Trish removed her metal helm. "Now, what's up? We still have a whole battle to plan, and the heat out here is getting ridic."

"It's this book I bought. I can't read it, and Perry thought you guys might be able to help." He pulled *Sorcery for Beginners* from his backpack. The five members of SCA crowded around.

"Nice," said Trish. "We're all big linguistics and coding nerds here. You mind?" After a moment of hesitation, Owen handed over the spell book.

"Cool," the seneschal said, flipping through pages. "Is it like a Japanese manga, or what?"

"So you see it differently, too?" Perry said excitedly.

"Of course I can see it, dude," said Trish. "It's in my hands."

"But you said it's a manga. Ravi, what do you see?"

The skinny kid poked the cover. "Looks like one of those illustrated guides, the kind they put out for big action movies."

Perry turned to the female knight and lady-in-waiting. "Julie? Moe Moe?"

They replied the book resembled an encyclopedia and a thicker version of a CliffsNotes guide. As before, only Perry could see the title in Latin. Everyone, like Owen, could only read up to the mending spell.

"Okay, now check this out." He had been resistant to this idea, but Perry had assured him the members of SCA would do their utmost to help him decode the guide, especially if they knew what it really was. The young man cleared his throat. "Book, is it okay if these guys help me learn sorcery?"

The response quickly appeared on the blank page after the Spell for Mending:

> **Of course—provided Perry, Trish, Ravi, Moe Moe, and Julie all swear to defend magic just as you did.**

The five middle schoolers made exclamations in a decidedly non-period manner.

"It's magic," Perry informed them happily. "Real, working *magic*."

Practice Makes Practice

After that, of course, Owen had to go over the whole story a second time. But by the end of it, the SCA members had already begun to tackle the problem.

"If a camera can see through the disguise spell, a scanner probably would, too," offered Ravi. "We could scan the whole book and then Google Translate it."

"Might not be that easy," Trish said, studying a phone picture of the mending spell page. "These descriptions are in Latin, but what I can read looks all jumbled up. I think it's in code."

"Even more reason to go digital," said Ravi. "Run it through some image recognition software and *bazzam*! The computer'll crack it in seconds."

"*If* we can unlock more spells," said Perry. "It says right here, more pages will only appear when we're *ready*. We won't be able to use any of them until we complete the first one. Or, more specifically, until Owen does."

"Like leveling up in **WORLD OF WARCRAFT**," agreed Julie, the Caucasian, curly-haired blond girl in knight's garb.

"Why me?" complained Owen.

"Well, the book is dedicated to you," Perry said mildly.

"Yeah, but I didn't know what I was signing up for! If I knew this was gonna be, like, some magic SAT prep class, I wouldn't have bothered."

"Actually, some of these movements look more similar to Tai Chi," said Moe Moe, holding her peaked princess hat while she peered at one of the photographed spell diagrams. The other kids looked at her blankly. "It's a Chinese martial art? Used for defense and health benefits? My grandma does it on Sundays

ENCHANTING
DETAILS

Invented in 1994, **WORLD OF WARCRAFT** is a massively multiplayer online role-playing game, or MMORG. It currently boasts over eight million members worldwide, and its addictive nature has led to the lowered GPAs of many a middle school student.

with a few other Thai ladies. Nobody?" A couple of them shook their heads.

"I don't care if we're doing the Robot, so long as we can make one of 'em work," said Trish. "Come on, let's help Owen give this first one a shot."

They quickly scavenged sticks, breaking one in half. Moe Moe had a few packets of salt in her lunch bag, which they poured inside the silver spoon Owen had brought from his house, and set beneath the wood. Then, at Perry's suggestion, the six middle schoolers sat in a circle, stick, spoon, and salt in the center.

Trish nodded. They all began to try the hand positions, which took some time to figure out. Once they had those down, they started to chant: *"Exsarcio, Exsarcio . . ."*

The words washed over Owen, but something felt different this time. A crackle seemed to form in the dry desert air, like the tang of electricity before a thunderstorm. He could feel the hairs on his arms rise. The ground seemed to thrum beneath him, vibrating in time to the drumbeat of their voices. It was going to work this time, he could feel it—

And then Julie sneezed loudly. Moe Moe dropped her hands, and the electricity dissipated.

"Julie!" Trish said. "What gives?"

The girl looked away. "Sorry, it's just . . . This is sorta lame."

Moe Moe nodded in agreement.

Trish scowled. "What's lame is that it was just about to work! Couldn't you guys feel it?"

Only Perry nodded. The others looked guilty, or worse, bored. Moe Moe checked her phone.

"Hey." Trish's eyes flashed. "Are you guys seriously telling me you have a real magic book in front of you, and you don't think it's *cool*?!"

"Maybe it's magic," said Ravi. "Or maybe it's **NANOTECHNOLOGY** and gibberish."

"It's not gibberish," Perry said. "*Exsarcio* is Latin for *restore*."

"How 'bout we take a break?" suggested Owen. "I mean, my mind's kind of wandering, too."

"No," insisted Trish. "How about this—we'll say the words, but everyone focus on what they *mean* this time. Picture that stick snapping back together."

They joined hands and began to chant the spell again. This time the effect was almost instantaneous. The hair on their bodies rose. A soft lavender luminescence began to glow at either end of the broken stick. Seeing that, they increased the volume of their words, urging the wood to mend—

And with a *snick*, the two halves of the stick snapped together.

"Holy ship," breathed Trish, but she did not say *ship*.

ENCHANTING DETAILS

NANOTECHNOLOGY, or the manipulation of matter on an atomic and molecular scale, is often featured in science-fiction stories, but in present day, it's still mostly in the research stage. But don't worry—there's plenty of existing technology to get paranoid about, such as surveillance drones and genetically modified hamburgers.

Perry grabbed the stick off the ground, inspecting it. "There's no scar or seam," she said, passing it to Owen. "It's like it never happened."

"Holy *ship*, you guys," Trish said.

Owen gently bent the stick. Perry was right: the wood was, if anything, harder than it had been before.

"Do you know what this *means*?" Trish was so excited, she began to pace back and forth. "Forget Harry Potter, forget MERLIN; the real wizards are right here. We just did magic, you guys. Us!"

Perry broke a slightly larger stick in half and dropped it in the sand. "Scientific method," she said. "We have to prove it wasn't a fluke. Let's go again."

ENCHANTING DETAILS

MERLIN (976–1142 C.E.) was a renowned medieval sorcerer who has been incorporated into several ancient tales of fiction. Once, while casting an incredibly difficult spell of prognostication, or looking into the future, he was interrupted. The enchantment backfired, causing him to forever see future events as the past. Not only did it drive him insane, but it made him quite difficult to converse with at parties.

THE DISCOVERY PANEL

It was no fluke. Less than thirty minutes later, they had mended five more sticks of varying widths and lengths. Then they split into groups of two and did a few more.

After another fifteen minutes, Perry and Trish could do it by themselves.

They discovered a few things as they worked:

THING #1: The farther the pieces were from each other, the harder it was to mend them.

"Think about it," said Perry, for what Owen estimated was the ten thousandth time that day. "If it's reconnecting the stick on a molecular level, the farther away the molecules are, the harder it is for them to find their buddies. I wonder if you could 'mend' two unbroken sticks together, though?"

A few attempts later, they had proved you could. This raised several unnerving possibilities, until Ravi suggested they try mending a stick to a rock. The middle schoolers were able to conjure a purple flash, but nothing happened.

"That's kind of a relief," said Owen. "No Frankenstein-ing a bunch of mismatched things together."

"Like attracts to like," agreed Perry.

"Bet you could chop off someone's hands and reattach 'em on the wrong side, though," Trish said with a creepy leer.

"Gross," said Moe Moe.

THING #2: If the broken pieces were placed at an angle, the seam would heal in that position.

"So not a good idea to attempt this on broken bones," Ravi said. "You could end up with permanent duck feet."

"Or Egyptian arms!" Trish grinned, bending her arms sideways like a hieroglyphic figure.

THING #3: Touching the object seemed to increase the spell's potency.

Moe Moe nodded wisely. "My cousin's a masseuse, and she says there's, like, a ton of energy in the hands."

This was the sort of thing Owen would normally have rolled his eyes at, and he began to do just that, but Perry tapped her chin thoughtfully. "If there's magical energy in everything, it must be in us as well. Any sort of physical connection probably increases the **POTENCY** of a given spell. That's why holding hands worked so well."

SORCERY FOR
BEGINNERS

Physical connection does indeed increase the POTENCY of magic. This has led some sorcerers to believe that being naked makes for better spell casting. Not only is this utter bunk, but it can lead to quite an awkward situation if anyone walks in on you.

"Our bodies conduct electricity," Ravi agreed. "I guess the same holds true for magic."

THING #4: The spell seemed to require more focus the more they used it.

"You think it's a concentration thing, like the book says?" speculated Trish, trying to mend a broken twig without saying the words. A purple luminance shimmered a few times around her fingers, but never took shape.

Perry flipped through the first pages of the spell book. "It says here some places have more energy than others. Maybe the more spells you cast in one place, the more energy you DRAIN from it. Like a tank of gas in a car."

"I wonder if there are any magic dead spots," said Julie.

"Try my grandma's house on a Saturday night," joked Ravi.

The others laughed, but Owen rubbed his forehead. A dull pain was beginning to bloom behind his eyes. He couldn't tell if it was from casting too many spells, or simply forgetting to eat lunch. "Well, I feel pretty dead," he said. "How about we take a snack break?"

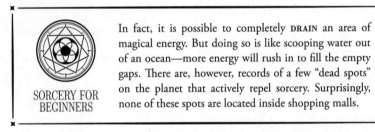

SORCERY FOR BEGINNERS

In fact, it is possible to completely DRAIN an area of magical energy. But doing so is like scooping water out of an ocean—more energy will rush in to fill the empty gaps. There are, however, records of a few "dead spots" on the planet that actively repel sorcery. Surprisingly, none of these spots are located inside shopping malls.

Trish tossed him her lunch bag. "Here you go, PB&J. Now let's see what else this book has to offer."

"Actually, I think Owen's right," Perry said. "We shouldn't push too hard on our first day."

"Are you nuts?" said Trish. "We have a *magic spell book.* Mending sticks is great and all, but I wanna shoot lightning bolts from my fingers."

"Yeah," agreed Julie. "Maybe there's a spell in there for getting better grades in math."

"Or making GIRLS LIKE YOU," said Ravi a bit too quickly.

Or rewriting history, Owen thought.

Perry angrily grabbed the book off the ground. "Are none of you paying attention? We can't use the other spells until the book shows them to us!"

Owen shuffled his feet, trying to dispel the guilt he felt. "We could rip out the pages, though. Just to see what happens."

SORCERY FOR BEGINNERS

LOVE SPELLS are by far the most sought-after area of sorcery, and also the most useless. No other type of magic is so prone to backfiring, regret, and expensive legal action.

"Yeah," said Ravi. "There's gotta be a way to X-ray them or something. We snap a pic with our phones, run it through a few Photoshop filters, and see what comes up."

"Come on, Perry," chimed in the others. "Let's give it a shot."

"*Great* idea, Perry," spoke another voice. "In fact, why don't you show us all your magic spell book?"

The middle schoolers looked toward the speaker. Five figures stood at the top of a sandy hill, gazing down on the SCA meeting. Their bodies were silhouetted by the sun, but Owen recognized the nasal, sarcastic voice instantly.

It belonged to Bryan Ferretti.

DOLLARS AND NONSENSE

The orange-haired thirteen-year-old strolled down the smooth red rock. He casually lit a cigarette and inhaled.

"Will you look at this?" said Bryan, exhaling a cloud of carcinogenic idiocy. "I thought the nerds all went to the library on weekends."

His four cohorts chuckled. One of them, a dark-skinned sprinter with thick, angular leg muscles, called out: "Yeah, dorks. How come you didn't text us an invite?"

"Good question, Abu," said Bryan. "Last weekend, you guys were near all those houses under construction. Today, you come back here without telling us? I mean, it took us almost forty minutes to find you. Gotta work on those PR skills."

"You weren't invited," said Perry, her eyes flashing with anger.

Bryan opened his mouth in mock offense. "But we had such a good time last weekend. And you guys were so generous with your *donations*."

Trish nervously cleared her throat. "We're not doing this again, Bryan. There's plenty of room out here. You guys can just . . . go somewhere else."

Low chuckles came from the rest of the bullies. "But we reserved this place," said Bryan. "Called up the Department of Deserts, and specifically asked them for the dorkiest, dumbest meeting place they had. They made us put down a deposit and everything. How much was it again, Abu?"

"Ten bucks apiece," said the big teenager, cracking his knuckles for effect.

"So that's . . ." Bryan looked blankly at the other four bullies.

"Fifty," Abu whispered.

"Fifty bucks," said Bryan. "Nonrefundable. Tell you what, though. Cause I'm such a nice guy, you give us back the deposit, we'll be on our way."

"Make it fifteen each," said a heavyset Caucasian teenager from behind him. "I wanna get a milk shake at Sonic."

"My bad." Bryan held out his hand toward Trish. "Jeremy wants a milk shake, so it'll be . . ." He looked to his cronies, but now they all looked blank.

"Seventy-five," said Perry. "It's basic multiplication, guys."

"Thanks, nerd," said Bryan. "Seventy-five it is."

To Owen's surprise, several members of SCA actually began to reach for the money in their pockets. Maybe it was because he'd finally cast a real SPELL, or maybe it was because he was tired of running from these guys. Whatever the reason, Owen took a step forward.

SORCERY FOR BEGINNERS

Many novice sorcerers begin to feel rather confident about their fighting abilities once they've got a SPELL or two under their belts. It is best to avoid this feeling, however. Even the most skilled spell casters can be defeated with a well-timed punch to the nose.

"Trish is right," he said, trying to keep his voice even. "We were here first. We're not giving you any money."

RITE OF REFUSAL

The smile stayed frozen on Bryan's face, but his eyes went cold. "You really don't get how this works, do you, new kid? You think cause you got away from us yesterday, the rules don't apply to you today?"

Owen looked to the other middle schoolers. Perry nodded to him—*Go on, we'll back you up.* "The thing is, they sort of don't." *I hope.* The young man cleared his throat nervously. "Not anymore."

"*Ooh-hoo.* Okay." Bryan turned to the other bullies. "Guess we just have to pack it up, guys, and—"

Suddenly he ran at Owen, his strong legs closing the five-meter gap in little more than a breath. Before the boy could react, Bryan socked him in the solar plexus. Owen bent over, gasping for air. The other members of SCA jumped. Bryan nodded to Abu, who shoved Owen to the ground. He placed a sneaker on his head, keeping the boy's face pressed into the sand.

"Stop that!" screamed Perry. She ran toward them, but Jeremy restrained the tiny girl with one arm.

Bryan squatted next to Owen. "Maybe you're slow, so I'll explain it to you again," he said, his nicotine breath foul on the boy's face. "There's only one rule here—mine. What's it gonna take for that to sink in? Huh?" He flicked Owen in the forehead with his finger.

Owen glared. "Cut it out."

"Or what, you'll cast a spell on me? With this?" To the horror of the SCA members, Bryan plucked the spell book off the ground. "*Sorcery for Dummies*," he read, seeing his own version of the title. "Sounds perfect for you morons." He turned to the first page. "*Warning: If you're reading this, you have entered a world of magic and danger.*" He giggled, not realizing the words had changed when he read them. "You dorks really think you're gonna be Gandalf, don't you?"

"We'll give you all the money we have," said Trish. "Just leave Owen's book alone."

"Oh, it's *Owen's* book," said Bryan. "Well, then I suppose we should give it back to him, right, guys?"

"It would be the ethically proper thing to do," Abu said, grinding his shoe into the side of Owen's skull.

Bryan flipped through the spell book. "Tell you what, new kid—I'll give it back to you, only you gotta *beg* me for it."

The Cro-Magnons laughed. *Don't do it*, Owen told himself. *You know you can't trust a thing this thug says.* Just to make sure, though, he pressed his lips together.

Bryan grabbed one of the spell book's pages and ripped it out. Perry gasped audibly. "I didn't hear you," said Bryan. "It sounded like you wanted me to stop destroying your book, but your voice was so soft and weak. What'd you say?"

Owen still said nothing.

RIIIP! Bryan pulled another page from the book. Owen struggled, but Abu's foot kept his head pressed firmly to the ground. "Missed it again," Bryan said. "You were saying?"

"Stop!" Perry cried. "You don't know what you're doing, stop it!"

One, two, three—Bryan yanked out more pages, crumpling them in his fist. He held the handful of parchment in front of Owen's face. "I'm gonna hear you say it, new kid," he whispered. "Or so help me, I'll ram these down your throat."

Feeling his neck muscles cramp, Owen forced himself to look up into Bryan's slate-gray eyes. He could see the spell pages in the bully's hand were no longer blank. Owen supposed the enchantment had broken when the pages were disconnected from the book's binding. And that gave him an idea.

"Okay," he said.

Gone 'Round the Mend

Bryan smiled, showing off the brown tobacco stains on his yellow teeth. "I thought so."

Owen beckoned him closer. The bully rolled his eyes but obliged and squatted next to the boy. "I said," Owen began, his hands moving in four strange patterns, "to stop it." He whipped up his left hand and placed it over Bryan's eyes. *"Exsarcio."*

There was a soft whispering sound, like two fingertips brushing against each other. Owen removed his hand.

The mending spell had **SEALED BRYAN'S EYELIDS SHUT.**

"What'd you do?" Bryan said, experimentally touching his face. "What'd you do? I can't open my eyes! *What did you do to me?!*"

He pulled at his eyelids, but it was like trying to open a window that had been painted on a brick wall. He stretched out a blind hand toward the SCA members. Seeing his mummy-like stagger, Moe Moe and Julie screamed. They both ran for their bikes and immediately rode away.

SORCERY FOR BEGINNERS

This is a perfect example of how a spell can be used for unintended purposes. Some of the worst mistakes in the history of sorcery— the Nile turning to blood, the Tunguska blast, leprechauns—are the result of misused enchantments.

"Someone help me," Bryan said. "Guys? Yell out so I know where you are!"

Abu backed away, taking his foot off Owen's head in the process. "The new kid did something to him," Abu called to the others. "You guys, he—"

But Owen sprang to his feet, his fingers forming four rune shapes before he clapped a hand over Abu's mouth. *"Exsarcio,"* the boy whispered.

Abu shoved him away, but the spell had worked again. The big eighth grader's lips were fused together as if sealed by superglue.

"Mmmhh!" he screamed, or rather, attempted to scream. "MMMPPHHH!"

The perils of improper spell casting, illustrated.

The other bullies looked at each other, clearly unnerved by what had transpired.

"Abu?" said Jeremy. "Quit messing around, man."

"We're not!" yelled Bryan, tripping over his own feet. "All of you, come over here and GET HIM!"

The bullies looked at Owen, unsure. He took a step toward them, heart pounding, and was relieved to see them withdraw. "You heard him, guys. Come get me."

He lunged at them, and the three remaining Cro-Magnons turned and ran.

"That's right, run!" Trish crowed. "Your buddies just ditched you, d-bags!"

Abu grabbed Bryan's arm. "Mmmyynn. Hnnheee!"

"Abu?" said Bryan, his voice shaking. "Abu, what'd they do to you?"

"He's mute and you're blind," Trish said. "You jerks wanna go for deaf, too?"

She feinted toward Abu, and the big teen shrank back, pulling Bryan with him. "Lllggg. Nnnnmm!"

But the Mohawked bully couldn't resist getting the last word. "Just wait, new kid!" he called, stumbling over a rock. "When my dad finds out **WHAT YOU DID TO ME**, you're gonna wish you were dead. Just wait!" Then they staggered over the top of the rocky hill and were gone.

SORCERY FOR
BEGINNERS

Using magic, especially without fully understanding how it works, often has drastic consequences. It's important to depict the reality of this up front, lest novice magicians think spell casting is all rainbows and transmuted puppies. To learn sorcery is to court incredible, unexpected, and near-constant danger. It can be fun, but is not recommended for the irresponsible.

REACTION SHOTS

Trish chuckled, whacking Owen hard on the back. "Dude, that was *awesome*. You were like a real sorcerer, with the curses and the—" She made the sound of a lightning zap. "Bad-*ass*."

But now that the bullies were gone, a semi-sick feeling settled in Owen's stomach. *What have I done?* he thought miserably.

What if Bryan and Abu were permanently disfigured? Will I be arrested? Could I go to jail?

"I, um, I should go," said Ravi, hurriedly getting on his bike. He tried to ride off, but his feet kept missing the pedals. "I have, ah, an event. To attend. With my parents."

"What's the matter with you?" Trish demanded. "Those guys have been all over us for weeks, and Owen took 'em out in five minutes. He's a hero!"

"Thanks, Owen," said Ravi. "I appreciate it, really. But I have to . . . Bye."

He pedaled off, fearfully glancing over his shoulder as he went.

"Fine!" Trish yelled after him. "Guess we'll just learn how to be sorcerers on our own, then!" She turned back to Owen. "I mean, right? What's up with them?"

"They're frightened," said Perry.

Owen and Trish turned to look at her. The tiny girl stood apart from them, her lips pressed into a thin line. "How could you *do* that, Owen?"

There was a long, uncomfortable silence. Finally Trish filled the gap: "Uh, did you see what happened? Bryan was gonna destroy the spell book. Abu was stepping on his face. It was self-*defense*."

"I know, but . . ." Perry looked away from Owen, searching for the right words. "We shouldn't be like them. Using magic like that, it's . . . it was WRONG."

SORCERY FOR BEGINNERS

The concept of "right and WRONG" is a topic of much debate among sorcerers. Some argue that any use of magic to bend the rules of reality is bad; others say that spell casting is like any tool—it all depends on how one uses it. When in doubt, follow the Golden Rule of Sorcery: do unto others magically as you would have them do unto you.

Some part of Owen knew she was right, but still he bristled. "You think I can fight off five of those guys with just my fists? Well, I tried that yesterday, and guess what? I nearly got suffocated in an ice chest."

"You see?" Trish said. "It might have been a tad extreme, but Owen ended it."

Perry shook her head. "We have to be better than that. We have to be better than they are."

"It was one little spell," said Trish. "It's not like Owen declared himself Supreme Archmage of Vegas. He put those guys in their place. That's all."

Perry folded her arms, uncomfortable. "What if there are bigger spells in that book? Worse spells? It's like having a nuclear warhead in your backpack. In fact, it's a little terrifying that Ms. Whitmore would sell it to you without any adult supervision or oversight. Using that book . . . it's dangerous."

Trish reacted loudly to this. "You're saying in the same day we find out magic exists and there's a manual that shows us how to do it, you don't want to *use it*?!" She laughed in disbelief. "If we don't, people like Bryan and his d-bag friends will. So we don't know exactly how it works yet; we'll figure it out. And when we do, we'll only use our powers for the forces of good."

"What about Bryan's and Abu's injuries?" the tiny girl replied.

"Well, I personally don't think they deserve it, but maybe the book has a fix-it spell or something. But we can't help 'em at all if we don't read the thing."

Perry turned to Owen. "It's your property. What do you think?"

For the second time in an hour, the boy who preferred to stay in the background had been forced to center stage. He looked down at *Sorcery for Beginners*. The book seemed so benign, and yet there was no denying that what he'd done to the bullies, even though they might have deserved it, had produced scary results. And, of course, there was still the matter of the Spell to Rewrite History. Owen was torn.

"I think Ms. Whitmore sold me this book for a reason," the teenager finally said. "But we need to use it the right way. We'll do some research and hold off on casting any more spells until we're absolutely sure they're safe."

Trish gave a double thumbs-up. Perry looked troubled, but she nodded.

"I suppose it's better if we know where it is," she sighed. "But we should make a vow." She looked at the other two. "We keep this clandestine. No talking about spells or magic or Codex Arcanum to anyone outside of SCA. Agreed?"

✳ ✳

Owen tucked the spell book under his left arm and put out his right hand. "Agreed."

Trish quickly dropped her hand on top of his. Perry put hers on last, her worried eyes connecting with Owen's. The pledge made, the three of them devised a plan. Owen would examine the book, letting them know if and when more spells appeared. Trish and Perry would divvy up and attempt to decode the pages Bryan had removed. They'd all meet again in a few days to discuss their findings. Again, Perry insisted they refrain from doing any magic. Again, the other two promised.

But that, as it turned out, was a vow they soon broke.

CHAPTER 8

BASIC INCANTATIONS

Owen's mind was a whirl of thought as he biked home. It might be months before more spells appeared in the book. He supposed they could rip out all the pages until they found the Spell to Rewrite History, but he felt bad defacing ordinary books; tearing up a rare, enchanted text would be like maiming a cute and cuddly animal. So it was a relief when, after the young man had arrived home, changed out of his sweat-drenched shirt, and made himself a sandwich, he opened *Sorcery for Beginners* to discover a dozen more pages had filled in. His father had left to run some errands, so Owen stretched out on the living room couch to read the new spells. He still felt nauseated about what he'd done to Bryan and Abu, but the book was rather upbeat about the situation:

Well done! You have mastered the first of
TWELVE BASIC INCANTATIONS. The next
eleven, as you'll see, are designed to give novice
spell casters a grounding in the seven different
schools of magic—

ILLUSION—A set of spells that alter the perception of one or many targets.

ELEMENTAL—Spell casting that draws upon the
natural world to create a variety of enchantments.

CONJURING—Also known as summoning, these
spells can cause objects, beings, and even molecules to instantly transport from one location
to another.

PROTECTION—Spells used for defense, healing,
and the warding off of evil.

TRANSMUTATION—Physically changing the
characteristics of objects or beings into something else.

DIVINATION—A difficult and tricky class of
spells, which focuses on gaining information via
magical means.

SORCERY FOR
BEGINNERS

Once a spell caster moves past the level of novice, he
or she often chooses to specialize in one area of magic.
There are two reasons for this: 1) learning all the spells
in just one school can take years of discipline, and 2)
magicians, like many humans, are lazy. But even the
most ungifted sorcerer should be able to master the
TWELVE BASIC INCANTATIONS.

NECROMANCY—The darkest school of magic, Necromancy focuses on spells that alter, control, or revive things that are dead. For advanced sorcerers only.

Excited, Owen flipped to the next page and read:

THE TWELVE BASIC INCANTATIONS

A Spell for Mending

A Spell for Reversal

A Spell to Cure Light Wounds

A Spell for Unlocking

A Spell for Binding

A Spell to Increase Strength (Level 1)

A Spell of Suggestion

A Spell to Shield Oneself

A Spell to Repel Enemies

A Spell to Detect Magic

A Spell to Nullify Magic

A Spell to Glimpse Future Events

Crap. No Spell to Rewrite History yet. The eighth grader inwardly sighed. *At least I won't have to translate or decode anything for a while.* Detail work, you'll remember, was not his strong suit.

✳　✳

Besides, it appeared the eleven new spells would keep him plenty busy for the immediate future. They involved hand gestures, activation words in various languages, and even complex diagrams. Yes, he had promised to call Perry and Trish when more spells appeared, but it wouldn't hurt to spend a little time familiarizing himself with the new pages first. Plus, it was too hot to head directly back outside.

Owen settled into the cool, air-conditioned comfort of the living room sofa and began to read.

Call for Help

It was only a few hours later that his cell phone buzzed. Owen was in the midst of trying to mimic the uncomfortable finger positions required by Step 5 of **A SPELL FOR UNLOCKING**. He shook out his aching digits and checked the number. He didn't recognize it, but it had a Las Vegas area code. Before they'd parted ways, Owen and the girls had traded contact information, but he'd forgotten to enter any of their names into his phone.

"Hello?" he answered.

"Dude, thank God. It's Trish!" the girl shouted. "Can you hear me?!"

"Plenty," Owen said, holding the phone away from his ear. "What's up?"

SORCERY FOR BEGINNERS

UNLOCKING spells have a variety of uses. They are also among the oldest of enchantments. Evidently, getting locked out of the house was a problem even the ancients had to contend with.

"I am. Slight issue, nothing major, but, uh . . . I need you to get over to my place, pronto."

"Why are you yelling?" said Owen.

"Because I dropped! My phone!"

"So pick! It UP."

"I can't. I'm kind of, well . . . it's easier if I just show you. Can you come over? Please? Before my mom tucks—uh, comes up to say good night?"

He paused. "Were you going to say *tucks you in*?"

"No."

"'Cause it sounds like your mom still tucks you in." Owen was enjoying himself.

"Dude! Are you gonna help me or not?"

Owen still had some homework he'd been putting off, but he didn't much like homework. "Sure. Can you text me your address?"

"Uh . . . no. Just write this down."

She shouted out the name of a street two neighborhoods east of Owen's. Fifteen minutes later, the boy was biking through the quiet suburb. If it weren't for the street names, the housing development would have been identical to his own. Owen found Trish's home, a two-story imitation Cape Cod with a carved wooden sign hanging from the porch that read: THE KIMS.

Owen rang the doorbell. A little melody played, and a plump, cheerful Korean American woman in her late forties answered. Seeing such a regular suburban mom reminded Owen that his own mother was somewhere in Sumatra at the moment, building tree forts or whatever for orangutans. And her son, Owen had no doubt, was the furthest thing from Eleanor Macready's mind. It was such a depressing thought that when Mrs. Kim asked if she could help him, it took Owen a moment to remember why he'd come.

"I'm, uh, a friend of Trish's," he finally managed. "From school."

"Oh. Well, she's in her room, doing homework."

She led him upstairs, through a hallway lined with family photos. Several of them appeared to have themes, such as "Nerds in White Polos" or "Goofball Cowboys." Trish was scowling in every one. Owen was starting to understand why the SCA seneschal had anger issues.

When they reached Trish's bedroom, Mrs. Kim knocked on the closed door. "Trish, honey?" she called out. "Your friend Owen is here!"

She turned the knob and opened the door, but it quickly slammed shut. Trish's voice came from within: "God, Mom, give me a second! I'm just . . . changing my shirt!"

"Okay, okay," said Mrs. Kim. "Owen, honey, can I get you something to drink? Soda? Tea?"

"He's fine!" said Trish. "Can you just leave us alone, please? We have important studying to do. No distractions!"

Trish's mom narrowed her eyes suspiciously, but evidently there had been a recent discussion about the importance of personal privacy, because she backed off. "Okay, then. You two let me know if you need anything."

Flying Lessons

Once Mrs. Kim had gone back downstairs, Owen knocked on the door. "All clear. Are you dressed?"

"Of course, gross," came Trish's voice. "I just said that to get rid of her. But when you come in, promise you won't . . . laugh or anything, okay?"

Owen agreed and turned the knob. Inside was a typical preteen girl's room—movie and comic book posters, a messy desk, a shelf full of medieval-themed action figures, a pile of dirty clothes, a rumpled bed. And above it all, in the far upper corner of the ceiling and upside down, was Trish.

She was floating.

Owen couldn't help it; he laughed. The girl looked like a lost balloon up there, bouncing around as if she'd been let go on a windy day.

"Nice. Thanks a lot, jerk," said Trish. "Exactly what I asked you *not* to do. Now lock the door before my mom comes back."

Owen did so. "You used one of your spell pages, didn't you?"

"No, I suddenly invented the technology they use for hoverboards and I put it all over my feet. Of course I used a spell page! Now, can you help me get down?"

Owen grabbed Trish's hand and tried to pull her back to the floor, but the balloon metaphor was apt. Whatever the force was that was keeping the girl aloft, it was more powerful than he was. Even hanging from Trish's arms had little effect.

"What if you jumped?" he suggested.

She ran a few steps and kicked off, but she quickly slammed back into the ceiling. "Dude, it's like my legs are repelling off the ground."

"Maybe the spell inverted your weight," said Owen.

"Whatever. You gotta find some way to Command-Z this."

"Actually, that's a good idea." Owen took the book out of his backpack and began leafing through it. "What spell did you use, anyway?"

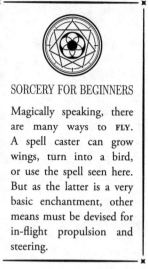

SORCERY FOR BEGINNERS

Magically speaking, there are many ways to FLY. A spell caster can grow wings, turn into a bird, or use the spell seen here. But as the latter is a very basic enchantment, other means must be devised for in-flight propulsion and steering.

"It was for FLYING. At least, that's what Google Translate said. It didn't work exactly great. I think I'm only floating from the knees down. It kinda hurts."

"Why didn't you try it out on an object or something first?"

"Because I'm an idiot, okay? Now search faster."

Owen found the page he was looking for. "Here we go. A Spell for Reversal."

"Hey! You were supposed to call us when more spells showed up!"

"Says the person who magically tried to be Superman." He read the description aloud.

"Got it, got it, got it," Trish said. "Let's do this."

Owen scanned the page. The hand gestures seemed fairly complex, and the activation word was in Latin. "'*Annullare.*' What does that mean?"

A Spell for Reversal

If you're reading this, odds are **some spell you cast** has gone
terribly, terribly wrong.

Don't worry; plenty of novice sorcerers have been in your position.
This incantation, when performed properly, will **REVERSE the
effects of another spell**, provided there are no wards, protections,
or active counter-spells in place.

COMPONENT NEEDED:

– the subject of the spell you wish to reverse –

SOMATIC MOVEMENTS:

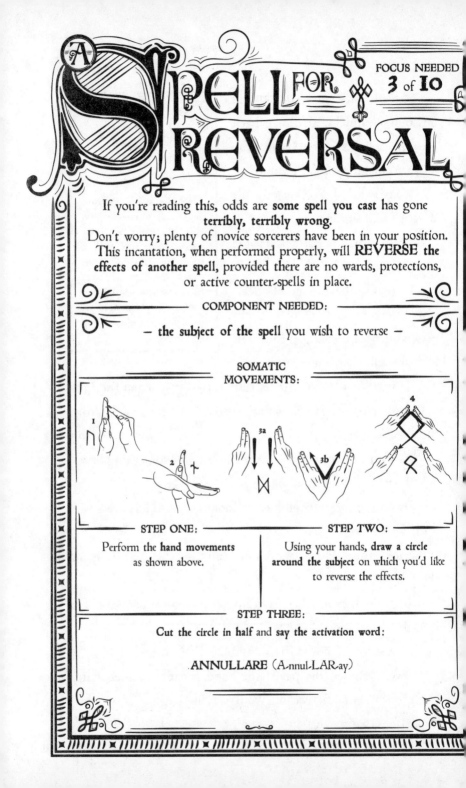

STEP ONE:

Perform the **hand movements**
as shown above.

STEP TWO:

Using your hands, **draw a circle
around the subject** on which you'd like
to reverse the effects.

STEP THREE:

Cut the circle in half and say the activation word:

ANNULLARE (A-nnul-LAR-ay)

"Uh, it's like 'repeal' or 'cancel,' I think. And it's pronounced *Annul-LAR-ay*."

Owen flexed his fingers, then arranged them in the spell's first position. "Ready?"

"Actually, can you give me a few minutes to freshen up?" She scowled. "Yes, I'm ready!"

Owen bent his elbows, curling his fingers to draw four separate runes in the air. Then he swept his arms in a large circle that included Trish and the surrounding area, and chopped a diagonal line across it with his right hand. *"Annual-larry!"* he said incorrectly.

Nothing happened.

"Annul-LAR-ay," Trish reprimanded him. "Man, are you terrible at this."

"I never took Latin," Owen reminded her. He retried the hand movements, chopping the air and shouting, *"Annul-LAR-ay!"*

A hinge popped off the closet behind the girl.

"That's something, at least," she said. "Maybe tighten up your hand-circle a little bit. And aim better."

Owen did so. *"Annullare!"*

This time, the window **UNLATCHED** and flew upward.

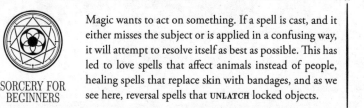

Magic wants to act on something. If a spell is cast, and it either misses the subject or is applied in a confusing way, it will attempt to resolve itself as best as possible. This has led to love spells that affect animals instead of people, healing spells that replace skin with bandages, and as we SORCERY FOR see here, reversal spells that UNLATCH locked objects. BEGINNERS

"Are you even looking where you're casting?" complained Trish. "And roll your *R*s; it sounds more Italian."

Owen scowled, sweeping his hands angrily. *"Annullarrrre!"*

Trish's belt buckle unsnapped and shot across the room. The force of the spell made her skid across the ceiling and toward the open window. Her hand grabbed ahold of the curtain, but her legs went outside. She hung there for a second, half in the room and half out, her feet suspended two stories above the ground.

"Sorry, sorry!" said Owen.

"Nice job, dingbat," Trish hissed. "Now get me—"

But the curtain ripped free, and she flew out of the room.

It is a good idea to danger-proof your area before practicing spells.

I'LL FLY AWAY

"Trish!" Owen whisper-shouted. He ran to the window and leaned out. Several feet above him, the seneschal hung upside down, desperately clutching the rain gutter.

"This isn't some video game where you have infinite lives. Get it right!" she said.

"You know, I've only been doing this for a day," Owen reminded her. But he squared off, beginning to charge up the spell again—

When Trish's fingers slipped from the gutter. She sailed up into the night sky like a bubble, her arms pinwheeling wildly.

"Owen!" she softly screamed in a panic.

"I can't cast it now; you'll fall!" he whisper-screamed back.

"If you don't cast it now, I'll land on the Moon!"

Owen knew she was right; her body was already floating over the neighbor's yard. He exhaled, trying to **FOCUS HIS THOUGHTS** on the word *CANCEL.* He bent his elbows, crooked his fingers into rune-shapes, and drew a circle around Trish's ascending figure. Then he karate-chopped it asunder and said in a commanding tone:

"ANNULLARRRRRRE!"

SORCERY FOR
BEGINNERS

More than anything else, the strength of a sorcerer's FOCUS determines the power of a given spell. There are records of magicians whose focus was so great, they managed to cast enchantments despite poor timing conditions, a lack of spell components, and the fact that they were being chased by life-threatening monsters.

There was a soft *pop*, like a cork being pulled from an old wine bottle, and Trish tumbled to the ground from four stories up. Her falling body disappeared behind the neighbor's hedge.

No, no, no, thought Owen as he ran downstairs and out the front door. *I've hurt another kid. That's three in one day. I'm like a magical serial killer!* He reached the neighbor's yard, hopped over a wooden gate—

And nearly collided with Trish. She stood before him, soaking wet, the water of her neighbor's pool rippling right behind her.

"That . . . was . . . *awesome*." She grinned.

Owen sagged in relief. "Don't do that," he whispered. "I thought you were a pancake, or at least severely—"

"Who's out there?" called a voice from inside the house. "I'm getting my five iron!"

"Shoot, it's Mr. Monty," Trish said, pulling Owen back into her yard. She winced, rubbing her shins. "Ow, ow, ow. Feels like a million pins are stabbing my legs."

"At least you're alive," Owen said. "Perry's right; this is way too dangerous. No more spell casting until we figure out what we're doing."

Trish swept her wet hair out of her eyes. "Fine, fine, fine. I swear—on my very painful feet—that I am done-zo with magical experimentation."

Unfortunately, saying such phrases only seems to guarantee the opposite will occur. Which of course it did, as early as Monday afternoon.

The Notorious O.W.E.N.

From the moment Owen entered his homeroom on Monday morning, he was worried. Worried about what he'd done to Bryan and Abu; worried that they had told their parents exactly how he'd done it; worried that the adults would, at any moment, burst into the middle school, policemen in tow, and cart Owen off to prison for illegal use of sorcery.

Instead, what greeted him created a wholly different sort of anxiety.

The students of his homeroom stared as he entered. Whispers flew behind Owen's back as he took his seat. A curly-haired girl snapped a picture of him with her phone. His homeroom teacher, Mr. Hall, gave him a disapproving glance. On Friday, he had been anonymous, another new student in a school of 750 middle schoolers. Today, he was notorious. It wasn't until lunch that he understood why.

He was standing in the food line, next to a freckled seventh-grade boy with glasses. Owen reached for a plate of beef Stroganoff, glancing briefly at his neighbor. The freckled boy's eyes went wide, and he nearly spilled his lunch tray.

"Whoa, you're him," he said. "The new kid, right? Owen Something."

"Macready," said Owen, concerned where this was going. "Do I know you?"

"Awesome," said Freckles. "I mean"—he leaned in conspiratorially—"nice job."

"Doing what?"

"You know, kicking butt. Taking names." Seeing Owen had no idea what he was talking about, he pressed on: "Putting Bryan and those d-bags in their place, *kemosabe*."

Crap. Evidently, one of the kids at Dragonridge had blabbed about the demonstration of sorcery that had occurred over the weekend. Given the lack of restraint she'd shown on Saturday night, Owen suspected Trish. *I told her and told her not to say anything.* His stomach tensed. "What, uh, what did you hear?"

"Just that you took care of business, son. Sent Bryan and Abu to the ER. Hi-yah, yah!" Freckles did a few sloppy kung fu moves.

The knot in Owen's stomach twisted tighter. "Do you, uh, know what happened to them? Did they have to have . . . surgery?"

"I don't know. Nobody's talked to them yet. But who cares? Those guys were total knobs. The whole school owes you!"

Owen felt more like a criminal than a hero. He quickly paid for his lunch and sat in an isolated corner of the cafeteria. Perry didn't own a cell phone, so he texted Trish, whose lunch wasn't until next period. (NOTE: the following misspellings and poor grammar are, sadly, theirs.)

Hey, **Owen wrote.** Did u say anything about what happnd Saturday?

Almost immediately, his phone chimed with the response: Of course not! **Then:** Which thing are you talking about?

Bryan & Abu, **Owen wrote back.** Everyone knows they went to the ER!

Oh, that. Me say nada. But it's cool—everyone thinks ur a hero, dood!

What if they tell on us? **Owen texted back.** How do we explain what happened?

They didnt even come in tooday, **Trish replied.** And what r they gonna say, we used MAGIC? ☺ Weez all gud, dood. **Then:** But CALL ME if anythg happns!

Her misspelled words did not ease the tension in the young man's stomach. He soon grew tired of the other students sneaking glances at him, and ate the rest of his lunch alone in the quad. As he chewed, he watched the wind conjure up dust devils from the dry, baked earth, and waited for the authorities to arrive.

A MOST DISTURBING LIMOUSINE

But as the school day progressed, it became clear police officers wouldn't be storming into the middle school to slap Owen in handcuffs. There were no calls for him to go to the principal's office, no sudden, grim appearances by Marcus Macready—even the whispers about Owen himself died down. Gradually, the knots in the boy's stomach began to untangle. By the time the final bell rang, he was almost feeling normal again. *Maybe Bryan didn't tell on me after all,* he thought, allowing a bit of hope to enter his thoughts. *Maybe the Spell for Mending wore off, and everything's fine.*

As the other students streamed toward buses and parents and various after-school activities, Owen began to pedal his bike home. It wasn't until he was past shouting-for-help distance from the middle school that he noticed the limousine. The black vehicle cruised about half a block behind him, at a pace even the most law-abiding car operator would categorize as leisurely. Owen tried to get a look at the driver, but the windows were all tinted black.

His stomach promptly tied itself into a **GORDIAN KNOT**. *He's probably just looking at houses,* the eighth grader tried to convince himself. *That, or he fell asleep at the wheel. No worries.*

ENCHANTING
DETAILS

The original **GORDIAN KNOT** was so twisted and intricate, it was supposedly impossible to untangle. When Alexander the Great (356–323 B.C.E.) was challenged to unravel it, though, he took out his sword and sliced it in half. From that point on, brash, rule-ignoring rogues have been inexplicably admired by society.

To test these theories, Owen turned down a random residential street. The limousine followed. *Not asleep, then. But it could still be a coincidence.* It would take three more turns at least to determine if the car was aping his movements. Unfortunately, Owen had come to a cul-de-sac, and he had no choice but to turn around.

He pedaled hard toward the limo, trying to get a glimpse of the driver through the tinted windshield. Except there was no driver. The front seat was entirely empty, with a high-tech digital display in the center of the dashboard. Owen tried to get a closer look—

But a door in the rear of the limo opened, blocking the teenager's path. Owen squeezed his bike brakes, swerved, and tumbled to the ground. Wincing, the boy looked up to see who had nearly flattened him.

"If I were you, I'd be more careful," said a silky, educated voice. A tall, trim man in an elegant suit sat in the back of the limousine. His white-blond hair was slicked down like a helmet. His eyebrows were so light in color, they seemed translucent. He removed his designer sunglasses, revealing glittering blue eyes. "A person could get killed riding like that."

"Sorry," said Owen, getting to his feet and going to collect his bike.

"Apology accepted, Owen."

The boy froze. "How . . . how do you know my name?"

"It's my job. My forte, if you will. Please, allow me to introduce myself."

The man stepped out of the car. He was clean-shaven, and his skin gleamed as if it had been recently lotioned. He smelled of expensive cologne. There was a tattoo on his neck that Owen couldn't quite see, and a pin in his smooth silk tie with an insignia: a compass and a torch bisected by a cross. The symbol looked familiar, but before the teenager could place it, the man extended a hand the color of curdled mayonnaise. His fingernails were unusually long, but manicured. "Samson Kiraz. I hear you're the owner of an interesting book."

STRANGER DANGER

Ice water filled Owen's veins. He got to his feet but did not take the man's hand.

Still, the elegant man smiled. The expression did nothing to make him seem friendlier. "As it happens, I collect interesting books. Pay large sums of money for them, too. Perhaps I could escort you home and we could discuss yours."

Owen looked at the empty driver's seat. "Self-driving," Kiraz explained. "The latest technology, totally safe. Of course, should an emergency arise, I can take control. Get in and I'll demonstrate."

"N-no, thanks," stammered Owen. "I, uh, have some things I have to do. Errands. For my dad. In fact, I was just about to call him."

He took out his phone, but Kiraz placed a manicured hand over it. "That seems impolite, considering we just met. You haven't even heard my terms."

"I don't have any books to sell," Owen insisted. "And I don't want my dad to worry."

"Were I you, I'd be more worried about the police learning of your desert encounter with your fellow classmates. Sent to the hospital, I heard." Kiraz clucked his tongue in faux disapproval. "But should you sell me your book, there would be no reason for me to involve the authorities. I'll give you five thousand for it right now. Just think of all the video games you could buy with that. What do you say?"

Owen didn't bother to weigh his options. Instead, he did the first thing that came into his head. He fled.

CUT TO THE CHASE

Owen hopped on his bike, furiously pumping the pedals. A glance behind told him the limo was already driving after him. Kiraz had clearly taken control of the vehicle, as it was no longer obeying the speed limit. In seconds, the teenager would be impaled on the limo's hood ornament.

He took a sudden right turn into a side yard. It was tougher pedaling through the grass, but at least Kiraz couldn't follow him. He heard the car's engine roar as it sped past, but by that point Owen was into the next backyard.

The eighth grader rode onto the opposite street, pedaling hard while trying to get his bearings. If he kept heading east through the yards, he'd be out of the subdivision in no time. He heard

Even the most skilled magicians find it difficult to outrun a car.

the squeal of rubber, and saw the limousine round the corner at the end of the block. Owen pedaled into another yard. He dodged patio furniture and a trampoline, then he cut across another street. He rode through a flower bed, finding himself at the border of the housing development. It was surrounded by a six-foot-deep drainage ditch, like a moat around the subdivision. On the other side, a busy main road led to a three-story shopping mall.

Owen hopped down into the drainage ditch. This being the desert, it was mostly dry at the moment. Rather than go up the opposite side, the boy walked down the length of it, staying low until he came to a small, impassable pipe. He crept up the hill, peering over the edge of the ditch in both directions—

And there it was. Parked on the side of the main road, less than half a kilometer back. The self-driving limo. It had exited the housing development and was now lying in wait for him.

Were Owen to leave the ditch, Kiraz would run him down immediately. Were he to stay, he would eventually be found. There was no other way to put it.

He was trapped.

PHONE A FRIEND

Owen racked his brain. *If only Trish or Perry were here. They're smart and tough and resourceful. Just yesterday, hadn't Trish humble-bragged that she'd staged sixteen successful military campaigns? True, they had been fought with miniature figurines on plastic battlegrounds, but it's still more action and strategy than I've ever seen.*

The thought of Trish twanged a chord in his memory. What was it she'd said in her last text?

Call me if anythng happns.

Terrible spelling, but he got the point. The boy yanked out his phone and dialed.

"Speak, mage."

"Trish! It's Owen," the young man whispered.

"Dude, I know; it's a cell phone. Where are you? It's, like, super noisy there."

"I'm in a ditch." He quickly summarized his situation. "And now I'm stuck here. Whoever this Kiraz guy is, he's got the road staked out."

"We need more brain cells on this one. I'm gonna conference in Perry." A few beeps and another explanation later, all three middle schoolers were on the same phone line and the same page.

"Hmmm. Quite the persnickety quandary," the tiny girl said with perhaps a bit too much relish. "Do you suppose he's a Euclidean?"

That *was the symbol on Kiraz's tiepin*, Owen realized. *Same as the* INSIGNIA *in* Sorcery for Beginners. "Yup. He's definitely one of them. Does this mean I have to fight him? I don't know any spells. I'm no defender of magic."

"Perhaps he doesn't know your full identity," suggested Perry. "If he did, I assume he would have shown up at your house."

"Well, he's gonna know where I live if I can't get rid of him," Owen replied.

"I suggest we call the police," Perry said. "Explain you're being followed by a creepy stranger."

"And he's supposed to hang out for twenty or thirty minutes in a ditch?" questioned Trish. "He'll be a sitting duck. What we need is a distraction."

"That would be more expedient," Perry conceded. "Owen, can you give us a summary of your inventory?"

The teenager looked through his backpack. "Not much. Pencils, papers . . . the spell book, but there's only those twelve basic spells." After Trish's near-fatal mishap with the flying spell, he'd sent an email to the other members of SCA, coming clean about the new pages that had appeared.

"One of those spells must be able to help," said Perry. "Read the list to us?"

Owen flipped through them. "There's the Spell for Mending, Spell for Reversal, Spell to Cure Light Wounds, Spell for Unlocking, Spell for Binding, Spell to Increase Strength (Level 1), Spell of Suggestion—"

"Pause," Perry interrupted. "Read that last one."

Owen sighed, but did so.

Owen noticed something at the top of the page. "The spell requires an eight-out-of-ten focus. There's no way I can pull that off out here. It's hot, I'm tired . . . and did I mention *I'm in a ditch*?"

"Man up," Trish barked. "Do you want the Euclideans to get the spell book?"

"I concur," said Perry. "The first priority is to get you and the book safely home. Then we can concern ourselves with next steps."

"Say I'm able to do this," said Owen. "What do I suggest to him?"

Trish spoke up first. "Make him think his house is on fire. Or that he just drank poison and needs to go to the doctor. Or that he has to really, really pee!"

"Or," added Perry dryly, "you could simply make him think he saw you riding in the opposite direction."

"That's good," Owen admitted. "Nice and simple. I'm sure I'll find a way to screw it up."

A Spell of Suggestion

An age-old problem:
you need something from someone, but they simply
will not cooperate. You could charm them, or threaten them,
or even ply them with cash, but this spell allows you to skip all that.
Properly cast, this enchantment will **place a suggestion in the mind
of a single living subject** for a period of up to one hour.
But a **word of caution: stupid, embarrassing,
or suicidal suggestions** will be regarded by the subject
in the same way **as if no magic were involved.**

COMPONENT NEEDED:

— a living subject —

SOMATIC MOVEMENTS:

STEP ONE:

Make sure you're **within eight
meters** of your desired subject,
and that you have a **clear line
of sight** to their **face/head.**

{ Note: more **advanced sorcerers** may cast
at **greater distances.** }

STEP TWO:

Form the somatic movements as
illustrated above, **repeating**
until you have a **strong charge**
built up.

STEP THREE:

Speak your suggestion aloud, keeping
it to a simple line or two.

{ A tip: the simpler the suggestion,
the easier it will be to follow. }

STEP FOUR:

When you're ready, **cast your spell**
toward the **subject's head** for it to take
effect.

NOTE: The suggestion will wear off either **when it is fulfilled,** or when **one
standard hour** has gone by.

"We'll stay on the line for moral support," said Perry. "And to assist with any technical aspects."

Owen read over the page. "Crap. The spell says I need to be within eight meters of my subject." Owen began jogging back toward the limousine, keeping his head low.

JUST A SUGGESTION

Once he was within the **REQUIRED PROXIMITY** of Kiraz's limo, he quickly glanced over the edge of the ditch. The driver-side window had been lowered, and the white-blond man sat behind the wheel, scanning the road with a small pair of binoculars.

"Okay, he's in his car," Owen whispered to the girls.

"Good," Perry said. "Now get the image of yourself riding away fixed strongly in your head."

Owen obeyed, tracing the spell's hand movements while he attempted to picture Perry's description in his head. This was more

SORCERY FOR BEGINNERS

There is a REQUIRED PROX-IMITY for the Spell of Suggestion only because Owen is a beginning sorcerer. Were he more skilled, he would be able to cast a suggestion on multiple subjects without even seeing them. The greatest example of this was performed by the Chinese emperor-magician Han Wudi (156–87 B.C.E.), who enchanted an entire invading army into believing they had left a fire burning in their hearths. The soldiers immediately rode off to make sure their homes had not burned down, and Emperor Han avoided a long and bloody battle, all without having to leave the comfort of his throne room.

difficult than it seemed, as the image kept getting shoved aside by visions of himself locked within increasingly scary prison cells.

"It's not working," he said after a minute or two of mental strain.

"Well, it won't if you give up that quickly, dingus," said Trish. "Stick with it."

Owen took a deep breath and closed his eyes. As his hands formed the runes, he pictured himself riding north down the main road, the black limousine receding behind him. *You're convinced you saw me ride north*, he thought to himself. *You're absolutely, positively . . . ugh, give me a break. Why would he think he saw me? It's a totally flat, open area around here. I'm no good at creative stuff like this. Even my mom doesn't think I'm special. No wonder she ditched me for a bunch of monkeys.*

Even though his fingers had begun to tingle, Owen broke off the spell. "Forget it. I'm just gonna run."

"Owen, no!" said Perry. "You can do this, you only have to—"

But the eighth grader shut off his phone and stuffed it into his backpack. He pushed his bike back down the ditch and peeked out again. The limo was about fifteen meters behind him. Kiraz was looking in the opposite direction. Owen would just wait for a gap in the traffic, sprint across the street to the shopping mall, and he would be home free.

A few moments later, he saw his opening. He scrambled up the side of the ditch, his shoes slipping on the dry, loose dirt. But he managed to get his bike up on the road with only a moderate amount of trouble. He began to jog across the road, confident the Euclidean had not seen him—

And then the limousine's tires spun. It pulled off the sandy berm, cutting a tight U-turn and causing another car to slam on its brakes. *So much for home free,* Owen cursed silently.

The eighth grader pedaled down into the parking lot of the busy shopping mall. He sped through the spaces between cars and dodged shoppers. Still, the limo kept pace with him.

Owen turned down a row of parked cars, seeing a big pickup truck backing out of a parking space. The young man slowed until it was blocking most of the lane, then zipped around it. Kiraz slammed his horn, but for the moment he was blocked.

Owen took the opportunity to cut through an alley behind the mall. When he emerged in another parking lot, he was confident he'd lost his pursuer. He biked out of the west entrance to the mall and made his way home, looking back over his shoulder the whole while.

By the time Owen reached his neighborhood, he no longer felt like he was going to vomit. He'd call Perry and Trish, and they'd help him figure out what to do. *Maybe there's another way to unlock the Spell to Rewrite History. We'll start by tearing out all the pages of this dumb book. I'll find it, cast it, erase everything that happened in the last few months, and get my mom back. So what if I haven't "earned" it? That didn't stop Trish from casting the flying spell. True, she screwed it up, but maybe things'll go better if we all work together. And once the spell's done, what happened to Bryan and Abu will be wiped away, too.*

Confident in this plan, Owen put his bike on the front porch and unlocked the door to his house. He was about to head into the kitchen for a Gatorade when something made him stop.

A large, strange man was sitting on his living room couch.

Chapter 10

HOME INVASION

The stranger was in his late forties, typing on an iPad and looking completely at ease in Owen's house. He wore a perfectly tailored dark purple suit, several jewelled rings, and a thin gold chain around his thick neck. Even under the layers of fabric, it was clear he had a powerful, muscular frame. His bald head gleamed in the dim light of the living room.

Seeing Owen, he held up a finger. The teenager scanned the room, startled to see another large man perched silently in the corner. He, too, wore an expensive suit, though his was black. His white-blond hair was trimmed in a short, spiky crew cut. Dark sunglasses covered his eyes, and his expression was stony. He gave off the impression of a man who had once been a football player, or a mercenary, or both.

The man on Owen's couch finished tapping on his iPad and snapped it closed. His dark eyes looked the teenager up and down. "So you're Owen Macready," he said, obviously unimpressed.

"Who are you?" demanded Owen. "How'd you get in here?"

"Please. I wouldn't be where I am today if I allowed myself to be stopped by a simple locked door. Virgil Ferretti," the big man said, getting to his feet and holding out a broad, olive-toned hand. "I believe you met my son, Bryan."

Owen was too afraid to move. He worried the big man would crush his fingers like pretzel sticks, or grab him by the wrist and take him straight to the police. Ferretti didn't seem to mind. He smiled, revealing two rows of perfectly white, over-sized teeth.

"From what I hear, you and my boy had a pretty epic throw-down. I'm sure you'll be glad to know he can open his eyes again." Once more he bared his teeth, but it looked less like a smile now.

Owen swallowed. "My dad's gonna be home from work any minute," he said nervously. Behind him, the blond bodyguard stepped in to block the front door.

Ferretti shook his head. "We called your dad's supervisor. Marcus Solomon Macready is working 'til two o'clock this morning, which means we

Wealthy, powerful, and ignorant—a dangerous combination of traits

have"—he regarded his large, very expensive watch—"just over ten hours until he realizes you're gone."

The teenager said nothing, mostly because the air in his lungs seemed to have vanished. "Kidding," laughed the big man. "If I wanted to abduct you, you'd already be bound and gagged and inside the trunk of my Mercedes."

This statement did not make Owen feel better. A thousand years went by, or possibly thirty seconds. Again, Ferretti looked Owen up and down, a sideways smirk playing over his face. The boy squirmed, feeling as if he were trapped in a petri dish beneath a massive, cologne-scented microscope.

"What?" he finally blurted out.

"Bryan's wrong," Ferretti said. "He called you shrimpy. I wouldn't go that far myself. A little undersized, maybe, but you're more . . . average." His upper lip curled into a sneer at the last word.

"I know I'm average. So what?"

"So, it intrigues me. How a thirteen-year-old kid who gets straight Bs in school, has no interest in science, no famous chemists in the family—it intrigues me that you were able to do what you did to my boy."

"How did you . . . how do you know all that?"

"'If you know your enemy and know yourself, you need not fear a hundred battles.' That's SUN TZU. *The Art of War.*"

Ferretti walked to the bar cabinet, opened a bottle of Marcus's Scotch, and smelled it. Shrugging, he filled a glass with two fingers of amber liquid. He took a sip, mildly surprised by the quality.

"Want some?" Ferretti said when he noticed Owen staring at him.

The boy shook his head.

"Not a Scotch fan, eh?"

"I'm thirteen," Owen said.

"Never too young to appreciate a single malt." He took another sip. "But okay, enough small talk. What'd you do to my son?"

SORCERY FOR BEGINNERS

SUN TZU (544–496 B.C.E.) was an ancient Chinese military general, strategist, and philosopher. The ideas he set forth in *The Art of War* are so profound, they are still studied today by soldiers, people of business, and those wishing to become prom queen.

GUILT RIDDEN

Owen's stomach lurched at the sudden shift in conversation. "I, uh . . . I don't know what you're talking about?"

"Take it easy; you're not in trouble. Not yet, anyway. From a purely objective view, what you did to Bryan was pretty freaking original. Most kids get in a fight, they just punch, kick, and so on. But you? You sealed my son's eyes shut. I mean, how does someone even do something like that?"

"It, uh . . . it was an accident?" Owen said weakly.

"There are no accidents. That's another little saying for you. And it's why we're having this conversation here, not in some police interrogation room downtown. I think what you did to Bryan, however disturbing and uncalled for, is an opportunity. I think we can help each other, Owen."

The young man was shocked. "Help each other?"

Ferretti pursed his lips, annoyed. "You keep repeating what I say, and we're gonna be here a long time. But to answer your question, yes. If you cooperate, I won't press charges. Even though I incurred thousands of dollars in hospital fees to restore Bryan's face."

Owen tried to suppress a nervous laugh, and Ferretti threw his Scotch glass across the room. The boy instinctively covered his face, but the glass smashed against the wall. The teenager was stunned. No adult had ever thrown anything at him before.

The man pointed a thick, tan finger. "You don't laugh, you little turd. Aggravated assault, that's what they'll charge you with for starters. One to six years in prison. Add on possession of hazardous materials, reckless endangerment, criminal conspiracy, and you'll spend the rest of your school years in juvie, fighting off a lot worse than my boy."

The smile was long gone from Owen's face. But one word had jumped out at him. "Wait, what hazardous materials? What are you talking about?"

In response, Ferretti opened his iPad and turned it toward the eighth grader. Onscreen was a picture of Bryan, with his eyes sealed shut. Owen's stomach clenched queasily. *Looks scarier than I remembered.*

"The doctors, they said they'd never seen anything like it. Their best guess was an invisible sealant, ten times stronger than superglue." The big man flicked through more photos, which got progressively more comedic as Bryan's eyelids were pulled on by one doctor, then several doctors, and finally six doctors, three orderlies, and a particularly large male nurse.

"They finally had to laser his eyes open. Lucky for you, there's no permanent damage. But you're still in big trouble, kid." He sat back, letting that sink in. "Unless . . ."

Owen swallowed. "Unless what?"

"Unless you give me what you used on him," Ferretti said coldly.

"I didn't use anything," Owen said semi-truthfully. "I just—"

"Cast a magic spell? Bryan told me. All the money I spent on private tutors, and the kid still thinks Harry Potter's a documentary." He snorted in derision. "Look, I know he's running wild. His mother, she's been . . . out of the picture since we divorced. But I'm not here to punish you for his shortcomings. I want to reward you."

The boy was suspicious. "How?"

"Well, that's what we're here to figure out." Ferretti pressed his thick fingertips together. "In every negotiation, there's give-and-take. You give . . . or I will take."

"Is that Sun Tzu, too?" Owen said.

"No, that's me." Mr. Ferretti leaned forward, his dark eyes glinting like bullets. "Look at your position. No corporation, no

LLC, no registered patents. You got zero contacts in the medical supply or pharma industries. If you keep whatever this is a secret, I'll simply hire some science nerds to reverse-engineer your little adhesive. Might take a few weeks, maybe even a month or two, but in the end *I'll* be the one who sells it. And you'll be the one who goes to jail."

He handed the iPad to his bodyguard. "Or we could save all that time and trouble. You sell me the formula, and I'll forget this whole thing. All you gotta do is cash the check."

Poor Bryan, Owen couldn't help thinking. *His mom's gone just like mine, and all his jerk dad can think about is a business opportunity.* Then he remembered the bully threatening to shove the pages of *Sorcery for Beginners* down his throat. There was no way he could let either of the Ferrettis get their hands on the magic guide book. He'd already seen what could happen when one or two spells went wrong. What if someone like Ferretti had access to the entire book? It could be a world-altering, mass-produced, chain-restaurant-on-every-corner nightmare. The teenager decided to play dumb.

CAGEY MATCH

"There's no formula," Owen said. "I just pushed him away, and it . . . happened. I don't know how. But that's it, I swear."

Ferretti studied him. Owen tried to meet his eyes, making his face as innocent as possible. Then the big man's face broke into a real grin. "Not bad, kid," he said. "Not bad. Couple a years, you might be a real poker player." Then his smile vanished. "But right now, you suck. You don't wanna fess up, fine. I'll give you a few days to mull over your position." He pointed a muscular, gold-ringed digit. "Look me up on Google, call your lawyer, then get your affairs in order. Because the next time we talk, I expect the truth."

Blondie opened the front door, and Ferretti walked out. On the bottom step the big man paused to put on a pair of expensive sunglasses. "One more thing. You tell your parents or teachers or authority figures of any kind about our conversation today, and I'll hear about it. The chief of Las Vegas PD is a good friend. We play squash. And I guarantee you he'll take my word over that of some punk teenager."

He continued down the driveway to a black Mercedes town car parked across the street. The bodyguard gave Owen a creepy salute as he held open the door for Ferretti. Then he got behind the wheel and they drove off. Once their car had turned down the street, the eighth grader ran upstairs and turned on his computer.

He typed "Virgil Ferretti" into Google, and immediately dozens of articles came up. Owen scrolled downward. The phrases "suspected criminal," "Mafia ties," and "**RACK-ETEERING**," whatever that was, seemed to appear quite a bit. He clicked on a few articles, his heart

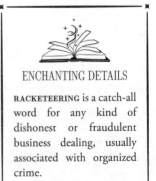

ENCHANTING DETAILS

RACKETEERING is a catch-all word for any kind of dishonest or fraudulent business dealing, usually associated with organized crime.

thumping against his ribs as he scanned the words. "FBI investigation." "Never convicted." "Extremely dangerous." He shut off his computer screen in a panic. *All the people I could have used magic on, and I pick this guy's son? Idiot. What am I gonna do? What am I gonna DO?*

Eventually, his pulse managed to back down from heart attack levels. *Okay. At least I'm not in this alone. And I still have* Sorcery for Beginners. Taking a few calming breaths, he picked up his phone and called Perry.

"It's me again," he said when she answered. "Yes, I got away from the Euclidean guy. But our situation with the spell book? Waaaay worse than we thought."

Emergency Meeting

Owen, Trish, Perry, and Ravi convened the next day after school. They had invited Moe Moe and Julie as well, but the young women had given clearly fabricated excuses about homework deadlines and kidney operations. Perry tried appealing to their logic and Trish threatened them with medieval torture devices, but finally they admitted they wanted no part of "that dangerous magic crap." And so, the Dragonridge Shire gathered in Henderson Middle School's science lab minus two of its founding members.

Once they were all inside, Perry locked the door. Today, her hair was pulled back in a tight ponytail. She wore a T-shirt with an illustration of atoms spelling out the word "Google," a knee-length, polka-dotted skirt, and a purple candy bracelet. "Did anyone follow you here?" she asked Owen.

"I don't think so," he said. He was wearing clothes as well, but his outfit did not merit description. "I heard Bryan and Abu won't be back for a while, and I didn't see Kiraz or Blondie on the way to school this morning, either. That's what I call Mr. Ferretti's driver," he explained to the others.

"Not to stress you out, dude," Trish said, "but there are, like, remote-controlled surveillance drones the size of insects these days. He doesn't need a bodyguard to follow you."

"There are drones spying on us?" asked Ravi. "Nobody told me anything about drones."

"We don't know there are drones," said Perry. "But it behooves us to be cautious."

As she pulled down the blinds, Owen set his backpack on one of the black tabletops. He'd spent so much of the day looking over his shoulder, he had developed a crick in his neck. To think that he couldn't even see his pursuers now made every muscle in his body tense up.

"Did anyone find anything out?" he asked, trying to loosen the knot in his neck.

"Nada," said Ravi, who had been in charge of Internet research. "Nothing on a Codex Arcanum bookstore, E. Whitmore, or a book named *Sorcery for Beginners*."

"I decoded my page," said Trish. Of course, she'd cast it as well, but she and Owen had elected to not tell the others that detail just yet. "Fed it into an online translator. Most of the writing is LATIN with a simple substitution code. You know, *K*s instead of *A*s, pretty easy to crack. It's a, um, flying spell."

ENCHANTING DETAILS

Even though it is considered "dead" today, many modern languages (Italian, French, Spanish, and English, to name a few) have a basis in LATIN. And yet it is no longer taught in most schools.

They turned to Perry, who'd been in charge of analyzing the detached spell pages themselves. "Well, I uncovered plenty," she said. "Can you bring the book over here, Owen?"

INFO DUMP

Perry led them to a little work area that included a microscope, Bunsen burner, petri dishes, and several jars of liquids. "Mr. Hall lets me work in here after school, provided I clean up. I did some tests, and the results are unusual."

"Enough tests," said Trish. "What we need to do is learn the rest of these spells so we can defend ourselves from these d-bags."

"The person most likely to get shot by a gun is its owner," Perry replied primly.

"But we don't have guns; Ferretti does." This was from Owen. "I googled him, and the guy is seriously connected. Not only does he own a couple of casinos in Nevada, he was investigated by the FBI. They think he gets his funding from the *Mafia*."

"We can't take on a real gangster," said Ravi. "We haven't even learned algebra."

"Sure we can," Trish said. "Cause we have the most important thing on our side—Bryan's dad doesn't know magic exists."

"But Kiraz and the Euclideans do," Perry reminded her, flipping open *Sorcery for Beginners*. "I did a little googling of my own, only I focused on magic books. First, the good news. Turns out there's a reason this looks different to everybody. Really powerful spell books have **PROTECTION ENCHANTMENTS** placed on them. Heat spells to burn intended thieves, locking spells that can only be opened with a secret word, and disguise spells, like this one." She tapped the book. "It's a magical security system."

"So . . . even if these guys got ahold of the book, they wouldn't be able to use it?" asked Owen hopefully.

"Maybe. But if they've been fighting sorcerers for five hundred years, they might have figured a way around that. But now for the bad news."

She removed her torn-out page from a large Ziploc bag. "I translated and decoded my page last night, too. Like Trish said, it was Latin with a simple substitution code."

"What's the spell?" asked Trish, still clearly hoping for something they could use to battle enemies.

"A spell for duplication, but that's not the point. You see these illustrations on the side?" She indicated the detailed

SORCERY FOR
BEGINNERS

The strength of an object's PROTECTION SPELL usually corresponds with its value, much like security systems for houses. Enchantments, however, tend to degrade over time, and must be recast on a regular basis to maintain their full potency.

borders around the edges of the page. They all nodded. "If you look at them through a microscope, the designs are filled with hidden runes. At least, they look like runes. I researched all over, checked every lexicon discussion board, and as far as I can tell, these are from a language nobody knows. Possibly it's the LAN-GUAGE OF MAGIC."

SORCERY FOR BEGINNERS

Perry is absolutely correct. There are no records of how the LANGUAGE OF MAGIC was first discovered, but knowledge of it was passed down for generations, until some not-so-bright humans decided to copy it down. Their appalling mistakes in the copying process led to the formation of ancient Sumerian, which is both a frustratingly simple and simply frustrating language. Thankfully, vocal tradition kept the proper magical runes around until they could be correctly transcribed.

Ravi squinted at the page. "So what are they all doing there?"

"I haven't been able to translate them yet, so I don't know," said Perry. "But if they are magic, it means there are spells and enchantments hidden everywhere in this book. Spells upon spells upon spells. Think about it. Anytime we say one of these incantations, it could be altered somehow. Twisted. And not necessarily for the better."

Trish and Owen looked at each other. They certainly had experienced some unexpected side effects with the flying spell, but bringing that up now would only make Perry more worried.

"And there's something else. Observe." The tiny girl lifted her spell page off the table, then tore it in half.

*An excellent example of how to properly
combine sorcery and science*

Paging Perry Spring

Both Owen and Trish cried out in surprise. But Perry ignored them, ripping the pieces a few more times and placing them in a metal tray. Then she grabbed the Bunsen burner and used it to ignite the paper.

"Hey!" said Owen, starting forward.

Perry held him back with a hand. "Watch," she said.

The fire enveloped the scraps of parchment, but it did not seem to consume them. Instead of turning black and ashy, they crackled and sparked with a purple ENERGY. There was a blinding flash, followed by a shotgun-loud *crack*.

SORCERY FOR
BEGINNERS

Magical ENERGY can appear in a variety of colors, but purple is the most common. Because of this, the color purple has come to symbolize mystery, magic, and is often associated with royalty. Not because royals are more magical than commoners, but because they would prefer that to be the case.

When the red and purple spots cleared from their eyes, the teenagers saw the fire was gone. In its place was the spell page, whole again and unharmed. Perry placed it back on the table, using an apple from her lunch box to hold it down.

"Bad-*ass*," breathed Trish.

"I tried shredding it, boiling it, even coating it in acid," said Perry. "Every time, it reconstitutes itself. Look at this."

She placed the page under the microscope, focusing the magnifying barrel. She motioned for the others to take a look.

Through the lens, the page looked like a big, interconnected web of sticks. But whereas most paper atoms are inert and lifeless, these glowed. Purple blobs of light moved along the molecules at various speeds.

"Cool," Ravi said. "It's like a fiber-optic network."

"Now look closer," Perry said, turning the magnification barrel.

Owen again bent over the microscope. Zooming in tighter, he could see the glowing lights actually had structure. In fact, they resembled—

"Are those the *runes*?" he asked in disbelief.

Perry nodded grimly. "Spells upon spells upon spells. And we have no idea if they're good or bad."

MAGIC MORALITY

"Magic isn't good or bad, dude," said Trish. "It's like science, or guns, or McDonald's French fries. It's all about how you use 'em."

✳ ❁

"So if there's a spell of destruction in there, you're telling me that could be used for good?"

"Absolutely. Say you had a bucket of toxic waste. What if you could destroy it? Zap it into nothingness with magic? That's good."

Perry shook her head. "What if **CONSERVATION OF MATTER** still applies? You vanish a bunch of toxic waste, it's gotta go someplace. The moon? Another dimension? Our bedrooms? The point is, we don't *know*."

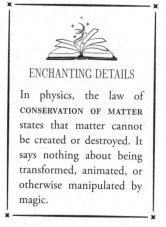

ENCHANTING DETAILS

In physics, the law of CONSERVATION OF MATTER states that matter cannot be created or destroyed. It says nothing about being transformed, animated, or otherwise manipulated by magic.

"So . . . what do we do?" Owen said.

Trish picked up the book. "I say we learn the rest of the spells ASAP. Maybe there's something in here for, like, a memory wipe. We zap all these guys following Owen, and boom—no more problem."

"Actually, there's something even better," Owen said, flipping to the back of the spell book. "I saw it right before I bought this thing—A Spell to Rewrite History. I haven't been able to read it since then, obviously, but if we tear out the page—"

He flipped to the back of the book and did just that. But unlike the others, no spell appeared. "I don't get it," the boy said, inspecting the parchment. "It was on this page; I'm sure of it. Why is it still blank?"

As if in answer, a single sentence appeared:

This spell will only appear when you are ready.

Trish gave a low whistle. "That book is one harsh taskmaster."

Perry took the page from Owen, placed it back in its proper spot, and shielded her eyes from the ensuing purple flash that reconstituted it. "We can't keep messing around. Everything I've read about these books says they're unpredictable and dangerous."

During this whole argument, Ravi had been studying Perry's detached spell page. In the center was a large diagram encircled by runes. Below it, one word was written in a different language from the rest.

SORCERY FOR BEGINNERS

Not every spell requires hand movements or components to be cast. Some can be executed with a diagram or a single uttered **WORD**. This is actually where the phrase "curse words'" originates from—one-word jinxes that have devastating effects. Because of the high degree of danger associated with these enchantments, very few magical curse words are still in use.

"Hey! I know this." Ravi pointed to the **STRANGELY WRITTEN WORD** in the spell. "These letters, they're actually Greek, not Latin. My grandfather showed me how to read this stuff. Ἀντίγραφο," he said slowly.

"No, no, no—" Perry shouted, but she was cut off by a loud *POP!*

The apple resting on the page jumped. The eighth graders looked at it, or rather *them*, because where there had been a single piece of fruit, there were now two.

Apples to Apples

The four middle schoolers simply stared for a moment.

"Did that just—" Trish began, but there were more popping sounds—*POP! POP!* Four apples now stood on the desk.

"It's not stopping," said Ravi. "Why is it not—"

POP POP! POP POP! The four apples had become eight. Several rolled onto the floor. "They're not duplicating; they're *multiplying*," said Owen. "Grab that garbage can!"

Ravi and Trish ran over to the plastic 150-liter can. As they dragged it across the classroom, there was another series of *pops*, and the eight apples became sixteen. The teenagers bent to collect the fruit and dumped it in the garbage can, but before they could get them all, sixteen turned into thirty-two. One replicated right in the palm of Owen's hand, smacking into his forehead. He threw them both in the half-full can before it happened again.

"That is some very aggressive fruit," he said as Trish slammed the lid on top. "But I think that's all of them."

"Good," Perry said. "Now we need a method to turn it off."

"What about the *cancel* spell?" Trish reminded them.

Owen nodded, bending his elbows and tracing a circle around the jittering trash can. He took a deep breath, making the required hand movements and letting the word CANCEL loom large in his mind—

"*Annullare!*" he said, making sure to roll his *R*.

The popping sounds ceased. Owen prodded the plastic can with his toe. It did not move. Trish lifted the edge to peek inside—

And the lid exploded into the air. Dozens of apples spilled forth, like lava from an erupting volcano, multiplying at an even greater speed than before. *Pop pop pop pop pop pop* filled the air almost continuously now.

"It's a reversion spell," Owen remembered. "It can only undo one apple at a time."

Trish bit her lip. "Okay, so we only have to cast it . . ." She scanned the room, trying to count apples on her fingers. The popping noise made it difficult to think.

"There are over six hundred of them by now; forget it," Perry yelled, somehow able to keep a running tally. "We have to find another spell!"

Owen picked up the book, flipping through the twelve basic incantations. Beside him, the apples had formed a considerable pile. Several bounced off his back as they popped into existence.

"Okay, here's something," he said, pointing to A Spell to Nullify Magic.

"I am terrible at art," said Owen.

Perry peered at the drawing. "Piece of cake," she said, grabbing a few erasable markers from the whiteboard and tossing them to Owen, Ravi, and Trish. "Nobody uses chalk anymore, so these will have to do. Everyone follow my lead."

EXSCULPA OMNES MAGICAE

Quickly, Perry sketched a large circle around the perimeter of the room, going over the desks and kicking aside multiplying apples when necessary. Owen and Trish pulled out several dissection trays, arranging them end to end so they could draw the straight lines needed for the diagram's seven-pointed star inside them.

Ravi yelped as more apples popped into being right next to his head. By now, the entire floor of the lab was covered in fragrant red fruit, making it difficult to even walk.

"Toss me the book," Perry called to Owen. He did so, and she went around the drawn circle, carefully copying the runes. Trish and Owen held back apples as she worked. Ravi had withdrawn to one of the desktops, his knees hugged to his chest.

Suddenly, the doorknob to the lab rattled. "Perry?" said an adult male voice outside. "Are you in there?"

"Shoot, it's Mr. Hall," the tiny girl whispered. "He always comes by to lock up. Don't let him in!"

A SPELL TO NULLIFY MAGIC

Worried about **secret enchantments?** Regretting the **effects** of a spell you just cast?
Don't want any **visiting sorcerers** to show up in a **magical disguise?**
Well, this spell is perfect for you. Simply copy the **diagram below,** say the **activation words,** and anything magical within the drawn circle will **VANISH!**

COMPONENT NEEDED:

– chalk –

STEP ONE:

Draw the diagram shown here in **CHALK.** You can expand it to fit any space you like; only remember to **keep the elements in proper proportion.**

STEP TWO:

Have **each sorcerer** present **stand at the poles of the** circle. If there is only one, stand at the northernmost pole.

THE FOLLOWING DIAGRAM:

STEP THREE:

In unison, **chant** the activation **words:**

EXSCULPA OMNES MAGICAE (EX-scul-pa OM-nehs maj-I-KAY)

WARNING: This will work on **ANY** magical items, apparel, or spell books— including this one—within the circle, so **take caution** when casting!

Owen dragged the empty garbage can over to the door. He could hear a set of keys rattling on the other side. He turned the can upside down and kicked a pile of apples underneath it. The interior quickly began to fill up, effectively barricading the door.

"What's going on?" said Mr. Hall. "Are you all lighting firecrackers in there?"

Owen ignored him and ran back to the tiny girl. "How much longer?"

"Almost there," she said, chewing on her upper lip as she copied the runes into the border of the circle. There was a *thump* as Mr. Hall shouldered the door.

"Okay, but FYI? We might not have that kind of time," Trish said.

WHACK! Mr. Hall had now resorted to kicking. "Perry Spring. Open up now or it's a detention."

"I can't get a detention on my record," Perry said in distress.

"It won't matter if you're smothered by apples," shouted Owen, shielding his face from the rapidly multiplying fruit. "Hurry up!"

"Right, sorry. We . . . are . . . done." Perry drew the last rune on a table and made sure to set the spell book outside the circle. "Now we stand at **OPPOSITE POLES**."

SORCERY FOR BEGINNERS

Silly as it may seem, certain spells have more potency if the caster is facing a specific direction. Modern sorcery research suggests it has something to do with the innate connection between magical energy and the Earth's magnetic **POLES**.

Owen scanned the science lab. "Seriously?" The apples were now knee-deep in the room, numbering in the thousands and covering most of the diagram. Owen, Perry, and Trish waded through the pile, sweeping fruit aside to check the runes. Ravi stayed on his table, wincing at every apple *pop*.

"Here we go!" said Perry. She planted her feet at the north end of the diagram, protecting her face as apples popped into being around her. "The other poles should be there, there, and there. Hurry."

Owen half walked, half swam through the

No matter how scary the situation, a sorcerer must maintain good focus.

ocean of red fruit. It was rather like traversing a child's ball pit, if said ball pit were filled with multiplying projectiles that had the potential to end your life. Across the room, Trish grabbed Ravi and dragged him to the east pole. He whimpered and flinched, but stayed in place. Then she took big, leaping strides to the western end of the lab and found her position.

The apple piles were now up to their armpits. Mr. Hall's yells could barely be heard over the thunderous popping.

"Ready?" Perry shouted. "Count of three."

"What happens if this doesn't work?" Owen yelled back.

"Apple eating contest?" joked Trish.

Owen raised his arms and counted down: "One . . . two . . . I forgot the activation words," he realized.

"Cheese and rice!" Perry cursed. She leaned over the book again, making sure to keep it outside the nullifying circle. "It's not as if we're under pressure here or anything. Here! *Exsculpa omnes magicae.*"

"Got it. Everyone got it?" said Owen. The apples were now at Ravi's chin. Perry nodded to Owen. He took a deep breath. "One . . . two . . ."

"*EXSCULPA OMNES MAGICAE!*" they all shouted in unison.

There was a soft *whoosh*, and the lab was empty again. All four teenagers stumbled, their bodies no longer buoyed by an ocean of fruit.

The door to the lab swung inward, knocking aside the now-empty plastic garbage can. Mr. Hall stood there, looking down at the marker runes beneath his feet. His bearded face was sweaty from the effort of trying to break in. He looked back up at the eighth graders, who were as surprised as he.

Only Owen had the presence of mind to feign innocence. "Oh, were you trying to get in?" he said blandly.

The young sorcerers could not contain their relieved laughter.

Then There Were Three

Thirty minutes later, Mr. Hall finally released them. Once he'd done an exhaustive search of the classroom and realized there was no evidence of any real wrongdoing (other than the marker on the floor and desks, which thankfully wiped right off), he grudgingly agreed to let them go. Ravi immediately took off, saying Moe Moe and Julie were right—he wanted no more part of any magical multiplying-fruit death traps.

Owen, Perry, and Trish looked at each other. They were under a tree near the school's empty baseball diamond to avoid the sun. "Ravi might be a coward, but his argument is not without merit," Perry said. "The longer this spell book's around, the higher the probability that one of us will get seriously injured. Maybe even killed."

Trish folded her arms. "You think Whitmore would just let anybody join her magical army? It's like the book says on the first page: this is a test. We give up, we don't bother to learn the spells, and we'll fail. Bye-bye, sorcery."

Perry paced back and forth, her sneakers kicking up clouds of dust. "I wish there was an authority figure with whom we could discuss this. A dispenser of **ADVICE**." She looked up, her eyes bright. "What about Whitmore? She said Codex Arcanum was there to help, right?"

Owen shrugged. "I guess. But she didn't seem super enthused about it."

"We can at least try. May I see the book, please?"

SORCERY FOR BEGINNERS

Centuries ago, it was common practice for experienced mages to take on an apprentice. In exchange for advice and guidance about magic, the acolytes were tasked with collecting spell components for their masters, cooking, and performing varying levels of housework. Once spell books became more available, the tradition began to fade. Nobody wants to do another person's dirty laundry, no matter how magical it may be.

He took it from his backpack and handed it to her. After checking to make sure there was no one nearby, the tiny girl clutched the book in both hands and held it out before her. "Ms. Whitmore," she intoned in a serious voice, "we seek assistance from the Codex Arcanum. Will you grant us your counsel?"

Nothing happened. Trish rolled her eyes and grabbed *Sorcery for Beginners* out of Perry's hands. "You gotta be more forceful with people in the service industry." She rapped on the cover with her knuckles. "Yo, Ms. Whitmore! You in there? Your how-to guide's all janked up and we need you to fix it. Hello?"

She flipped through pages, then shook the paperback as if a tiny version of the bookseller might fall out. "Great idea," she said, tossing the book back to Perry.

"Owen, perhaps you should make an attempt." The tiny girl offered it to him.

He was embarrassed, but took the book in his hands. "Hello," he said, then cleared his throat. "Hi. Um, Ms. Whitmore, if you can hear this . . . we need some help."

Again, nothing happened. He held it out to Perry, but she gestured for him to continue. He sighed, holding the cover to his face like a telephone. "Can you please help us? We have questions." When there was no response, he gave the tiny girl an "I told you so" shrug, and went to place *Sorcery for Beginners* back in his backpack.

"Plnnss strmph yrn kyrstn." A muffled voice spoke from somewhere inside the guide, making the book thrum like a cell phone on vibrate.

The three eighth graders reacted. Owen spun the book around, but couldn't determine from where the voice had come. There were no speakers or screens that he could see. "Uh, can you repeat that?" he said into the cover.

"I said, 'Please state your question.'" The voice was louder this time, female, and clearly originating from the back cover. Owen flipped the book over. There was a description of the contents, a short-yet-impressive biography of Euphemia Whitmore, and a woodcut-style illustration of the author. Nothing that could project a voice.

Then her portrait spoke.

Not-So-Frequently Asked Questions

"Well?" it said, causing Owen to nearly drop the how-to guide. It sounded exactly like the bookseller. "I may be a drawing, but I don't have all day, you know."

"Uh . . ." said Owen, looking to the other two for help. They were both as surprised as he, but Perry recovered first.

"Are you the real Ms. Whitmore?" she said curiously. "Is this book some kind of magical FaceTime screen?"

"The *real* Euphemia Whitmore is far too busy to spend her days answering the questions of prospective sorcerers," said the portrait, inspecting its two-dimensional nails. "She conjured me to act as her **FAMILIAR**, should readers of this volume need additional assistance."

SORCERY FOR BEGINNERS

FAMILIARS are projections of a sorcerer's personality and knowledge at the time of enchantment. They are usually contained in the bodies of animals, but they can be conjured to reside in any being or object. Since they are effectively a copy of a person, however, one must be careful about where they place them. A familiar locked up somewhere with little human interaction or mobility will likely not be in the mood to offer help.

"Like that paper clip that used to show up in my dad's old Word program," said Trish. "'It looks like you're writing a letter.' You're not the boss of me, Paper Clip."

"I can leave, if you like," said the drawing of Whitmore.

"No no no!" said Perry. "We definitely require assistance. Can you tell us anything that Ms. Whitmore could?"

"That is the whole purpose of my existence. Though very few candidates have ever made use of me."

"To be fair, we didn't even know we could," said Owen. "Sometimes your help guide needs a help guide."

"Yeah," put in Trish. "The title says *Beginners*, but a ton of this stuff is super tough."

The portrait sniffed. "No one said sorcery was meant to be easy. If it were, everyone would do it, especially the Euclideans. Please state your question."

Owen looked at the young women. He'd forgotten exactly why they wanted help. "I guess . . . we don't know how to proceed. We've already got a Euclidean and a gangster coming after us, but we can't get any of the spells to work right." *And especially one in particular*, he added silently.

"I'm afraid that is not a question," said the portrait primly.

"How do we learn more spells?" Trish demanded.

"How does one learn anything of value?"

"Practice and effort," responded Perry immediately. The illustration inclined its head.

Owen couldn't resist a groan. "But don't you have anyone who can help us? Trainers, wise men, Yoda-types?"

"The resources of the Codex Arcanum are stretched thin as it is. We are fighting a global war, you know, against an enemy who greatly outnumbers us. We are recruiting as many new candidates as we can, but we lack the numbers to personally supervise them all. That's why I created this guide."

"So there are a bunch of other sorcerers-in-training in the world?" said Trish in excitement. "How many?"

The illustration looked off-page for a moment, as if calculating, then spoke. "Seventeen candidates currently possess copies of *Sorcery for Beginners*."

"There are seventeen of these out there?" said Owen in disbelief. "How come I've got two separate guys targeting mine?"

"Well, you did use magic on Ferretti's son," Perry reminded him.

"Indeed." The portrait nodded. "And as I said, the Euclideans have a vast worldwide network. They have been trying to get ahold of the spells in this book for over five hundred years. Thus far, they have not succeeded."

"Oh, no pressure, then," said Owen sarcastically.

"If you've got seventeen current candidates, how many full-fledged, adult sorcerers do you have?" asked Perry.

"Globally?" For the first time, the illustration looked embarrassed. "Only around four hundred and twenty-five. Many of those have abandoned or forgotten the arcane arts. Sorcerers, I'm afraid, are an endangered species."

"So this whole thing, it's like a competition?" Trish scowled. "First kid to learn all the spells gets a spot on the team?"

"Don't be absurd," said the portrait. "Our aim is to recruit as many young spell casters as possible, not sow discord among our own. Most candidates, however, fail to reach the final examination."

Both Owen and Trish turned away from the book in frustration. Ever the calm one, Perry took the book in her hands. "If you want as many sorcerers as possible, then shouldn't you offer more guidance?"

The illustration sighed. "We do our best. Even so, most young people today never reach the end of the book. I believe it has something to do with your generation's need for instant gratification. Your task is to learn these spells. If you'd like help, you are certainly welcome to seek it out on your own."

"Yeah, that'll go over well," snorted Trish. "'Excuse me, Mr. or Mrs. Adult Authority Figure, can you teach us to be sorcerers? We're totally not cray-cray.'"

Owen, however, began to chew on his lower lip. This was something he did when deep in concentration. "What if we asked someone who has experience with these kinds of things? Someone who already knows a lot about magic."

"A real sorcerer." Perry nodded. She turned to the book. "Can you give us the name of one?"

"I'm afraid not," said the illustration. "Those who would be useful are far too busy with greater Euclidean threats at the moment."

Perry began to pace again. "What about someone more on our level? Think about it. If there are four hundred and twenty-five certified sorcerers in the world, there have to be some who never made it to that level but still have a working knowledge of magic."

"Well, we're in the right city for it." Trish gestured toward the 15 freeway, which was only a half kilometer away. A row of billboards led all the way to the Strip, and every other one featured a self-proclaimed ILLUSIONIST, magician, or supposed expert of the arcane. Seeing their cheesy pictures gave Owen an idea.

"Actually," he said, "I might know the perfect person."

ENCHANTING
DETAILS

Las Vegas is the self-described "Magic Mecca" of the world—home to enough professional ILLUSIONISTS that one could attend a different magic show every day of the year. Why anyone would submit oneself to such torture, however, is a more pressing question.

CHAPTER 13

Stage Patter

"Now, ladies and gentlemen, the time has come for my most difficult, most shocking, most *deadly* bit of magic."

The magician crossed the stage to a dais, on top of which was a pile of treated wood. Shoulder-length jet-black hair framed his pale face. His small mouth was encircled by a pointed, freshly shaved gray-and-black goatee. He wore a ridiculous sequined black vest, no shirt, and tight black leather pants. Around his neck was a bone amulet with a rune carved into it. The overall impression was quite different from when Owen had first seen him behind the counter of Incanto's. On this Wednesday afternoon, before a crowd of 150 in the dark Flamingo Casino theater, Alec Incanto was using his stage persona.

"Hundreds of years ago, people feared magic," he continued, his usual Cockney tenor transformed into a regal British baritone. "Anyone practicing the 'dark arts,' be they witch or warlock, was burned at the stake." He twisted his hand, a bottle of lighter fluid seeming to appear from nowhere. As he continued, he squirted the flammable liquid into the pile of logs.

"But what they failed to realize," he said as he circled the dais, "is that **MAGICAL ENERGY** cannot be destroyed. It simply moves from body to body. Thus, killing one magic-user only created another."

Owen, Perry, and Trish watched his performance from the second row. After some Internet research, they had discovered Alec not only owned Incanto's, but he still put on midsized magic shows all over Nevada. More importantly, he was a true historian of sorcery, having written several well-reviewed but low-selling books on the subject. His stage show, however, made it clear why he needed to sell comics and dice to kids. Owen stifled a yawn.

SORCERY FOR BEGINNERS

What Alec says here is not true. MAGICAL ENERGY may permeate every living thing, but it does not, in and of itself, create magical beings. This would be akin to the ocean creating a fish, or wind creating a bird. Living creatures make use of the magical energy that surrounds them, not vice versa.

"Today," cried Alec, "I will demonstrate that despite their efforts, magic is not gone. I dedicate this next illusion to the thousands of accused who died so horribly. Their spirits may have left this earthly plane, but their legacy remains. Ladies and gentlemen, if you have sensitive stomachs, I urge you to leave now."

Cheesy suspense music was piped through the speakers. Alec climbed the kerosene-soaked dais, standing against a wooden pillar. A bored, bikini-clad assistant came out onstage, chewing gum while she bound the magician with thick ropes.

"I, Alec Incanto, will accomplish what the magic-users before me could not," he said as his assistant tied him up. "I will be consumed by fire and emerge unscathed, like the **PHOENIX** of old."

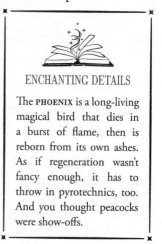

ENCHANTING DETAILS

The **PHOENIX** is a long-living magical bird that dies in a burst of flame, then is reborn from its own ashes. As if regeneration wasn't fancy enough, it has to throw in pyrotechnics, too. And you thought peacocks were show-offs.

"Probably a trapdoor gag," whispered Trish, who had gone through a magic phase a couple years before and had spent the last hour dissecting how all Alec's tricks worked. "Fake fire in front, he drops through the floor, then shows up somewhere else. Supes cliché."

"This is no trick," said Alec as if he had heard the girl. "I will not attempt an escape. I will stand firm, letting the fire burn until it has torched the ropes off my very skin. Again, this is not for the faint of heart. Would someone in the audience like to be my executioner?" Hands shot up, and the magician nodded toward the side of the theater.

Alec's assistant brought up an old lady in shorts and a Hawaiian polo shirt. She was handed a flaming torch.

"Total **SHILL**," Trish muttered to Owen. "Probably the one who opens the trapdoor."

"Hello, madam," said Alec. "Do I have your word that you will not waver?" The old lady nodded. "And you will not fling

ENCHANTING DETAILS

SHILL (n.)—An accomplice to a swindler, whose purpose is to either excite a crowd or create the illusion of randomness. They may know the basic nature of a trick, but the details of how it is accomplished are often kept from them.

the burning torch into this very nice crowd?" She nodded again, laughing. "Very well, love. If I do perish, I hope you've got a good lawyer."

The audience chuckled, and Trish rolled her eyes. Alec nodded, and the woman dropped the torch into the pile of wood at his feet.

THE TOWERING INFERNO

Flames immediately shot upward, making several people closest to the stage recoil. Even in the second row, Owen could feel the heat of the fire on his face.

The assistant spun the dais, showing that fire surrounded the magician on all sides. His clothes began to smoke. They could smell the burning fabric, but true to his word, Alec didn't budge.

And the flames rose higher, igniting the ropes that bound the magician to the pole. Fire sizzled against his bare skin. The magician winced but made no sound.

"That's impossible," said Perry. "Even if he was coated in flame retardant, he'd have to feel that."

"Maybe it's CGI?" Trish suggested weakly.

Other members of the audience had begun to worry as well. There was a dull murmur as they all began to wonder if something had gone wrong.

"Someone help him!" cried the lady who had thrown the torch. "Put out the fire; do something!"

The heat was really pouring off the stage now. Alec's body could barely be seen behind the flames. Perry grabbed Owen's arm tightly.

"What if it's not a trick?" she said, her eyes wide and terrified.

A man in orderly scrubs ran onstage. He had a fire extinguisher in his hands, and had just leveled it at the pyre when a voice rang out from inside the flames:

"Halt!"

The man paused. Alec's voice was confident and calm over the roar of the fire.

"I told you, the flames would

not harm
me. Because
I . . . am
. . . REBORN!"

As he said
the last word,
the flaming
ropes split and

As fake magic tricks go,
this one is rather impressive.

fell to the side. Alec leapt down from the pyre, now clad in a bright orange silk robe. He raised his arms, and the audience erupted into applause. They got to their feet, still clapping, and Owen and his friends joined them.

"You know how I think that one works?" Owen shouted to Trish over the roar of the crowd. *"Magic."*

PARKING LOT PITCH

Fifteen minutes later, the eighth graders stood in the pool area of the Flamingo Las Vegas Hotel & Casino. The vegetation around them was lush, green, and looked rather out of place in the central courtyard of the steel-and-glass building. There was, however, a large colony of actual flamingos in an open enclosure, which at least gave the middle schoolers something to look at while they waited for Alec.

"Right then," said the magician, lugging a wheeled cabinet as tall as him out of a hotel exit. His accent had returned to a reedy, working-class Cockney. He had also, thankfully, changed from the revealing orange robe into cargo shorts and a T-shirt. The bone amulet around his neck and some eyeliner were all that remained of his show persona. He smacked the equipment cabinet. "You lot wanna chat, you're gonna have to help me push this beast to my chariot out back. Go on, she ain't gonna bite."

Owen and Trish each grabbed a corner and began to push the heavy wheeled cabinet through the pool area. Perry jogged ahead so she could talk to Alec.

"Sorry to bother you after a performance," said Perry, "but we simply couldn't delay until tomorrow. Fascinating show, by the way. Very informative."

Alec grunted, trying to light an electronic cigarette. "Yeah, well, most of these quote-unquote *performers*, they don't even know their magical history, do they? Bloody leeches, on the lookout for a quick buck."

They arrived at a gate, which he kicked open but neglected to hold for Owen and Trish. It swung back and collided with the cabinet, nearly knocking them over.

Alec crossed the small parking lot and opened the rear door of a dented white van that had seen better days. The logo of his store was painted on the side, along with contact information for performance bookings. The inside was filled with crumbling antique boxes, cheesy magic kits, and a rack of corny stage costumes.

"You kids today—it's all about *now-now-now*, innit?" he said, indicating they should lift the heavy equipment cabinet into the back. Trish and Owen grunted as they obeyed. "Everything on demand. But I'm not a monster. Give you five minutes, then I'm off to bury me face in a deep-dish pizza."

He removed from his eyes a pair of blue-tinted contacts as Owen and Trish nearly broke their spines boosting the cabinet. Once it was inside the van and they had caught their breaths, Owen was elected, via unspoken eye signals, to begin their sales pitch.

He cleared his throat. "Well. The thing is, we, um . . . we found something."

"Technically, we bought it. Or Owen did," Perry added. "But it's ours. Legally."

"Right," said Owen. "And we were wondering—well, we need to figure out—"

"We need a magician to help us learn real magic," Trish blurted.

"Let me stop you right there, kids," said Alec. "Once a month, I get some plank in me store with a treasure map, or puzzle box, or key that unlocks the Great Grand Blabbedy-Blah. I'm gonna tell you what I tell them—figure it out yourself. Trust me, it's loads more fun. Mmm-kay?"

"This isn't like that," Owen assured him. "We already figured it out. Mostly. What we need help with is . . . training."

"Supervision," put in Perry. "Someone with experience who can . . . advise us."

"About this!" said Owen, taking the spell book out of his backpack.

"You bought a book," the magician deadpanned. "Well done."

"Look inside," said Owen. He opened it, flipping through the pages.

Instead, Alec checked his watch. "And . . . that's five minutes. Tell your friends about the show, yeah?"

Trish stepped in front of him. "But it works," she said. "The spells, the magic, it's way better than the hacky stuff you were doing in there. It's *real*."

Alec's face darkened. "Now your time really is up. First rule of favors, kid—never insult the person you're asking."

The magician pushed past the girl, grabbing the rear door of the van. Desperate, Owen grabbed a coffee mug out of the back and threw it to the ground. It bounced off the warm asphalt, but didn't break.

"Tantrums, wonderful," said Alec. "You gonna slash me tires next?"

"You'll see; just give me one second," said Owen. He grabbed the mug off the ground and threw it down again, with the same result. "What is this made of, steel?" he said in frustration.

"Okay," said the magician. "Time for me to call security."

With one hand still on Owen's arm, he took out his cell phone. He didn't see Perry step forward, making a series of complicated, swirling gestures. Her fingers left faint trails of purple light in the air. Then she pulled a barbecue lighter from her pocket, clicked it on, and intoned in Latvian:

"Atklāt visu burvju!"

She blew on the flame, which detached from the lighter and expanded into a globe of transparent golden light that grew larger and fainter as it radiated outward. Everything the energy wave passed through—parked cars, the objects in the van, Alec himself—briefly vibrated. Then a golden light began to shine from three objects—a wooden boomerang in one of the van boxes, the spell book, and the bone amulet around Alec's neck.

Revealing Magic

Everyone turned to Perry, showing varying degrees of surprise. The tiny girl blushed. "I thought learning A Spell to Reveal Magic might come in handy," she said. "I mean, it is one of the Twelve Basic Incantations."

Alec took the boomerang out of its box, inspecting it on every side. By now, the glow had almost faded. "What'd you use to do that then, some kind of bioluminescent algae? Phytoplankton? Did you break open a bunch of glow sticks?"

"It's magic," said Owen. "Real magic and a real spell. But we need help learning more."

Alec laughed, a high-pitched, desperate sound. "Real magic. I've spent me whole life and every dollar I had looking for real magic, and you know what I found? A couple of half-enchanted trinkets, that's it." He tossed the boomerang back in its box. "Nobody knows how they work. Nobody knows how to replicate 'em. These things, they're anomalies at best."

"Is that what your necklace is?" Trish asked, indicating Alec's bone amulet. "An anomaly?"

Alec quickly buttoned up his shirt. "That's mine," he said. "And I went through a bloody great deal to get it. Which, it sounds to me, you did not do for this book. Tell you what, though." He pulled a checkbook from his pocket. "Two thousand's a FAIR MARKET RATE, but it's a solid trick. Give you twenty-five hundred if you tell me how you did it."

Perry looked at Owen. "He doesn't believe us."

A Spell to Reveal Magic

Say you wish to **avoid a deadly spell-trap,** or locate an enchanted object. You could test everything in a given area with a stick or a small animal, but that might take hours and result in lots of vaporized sticks and animals. Instead, I suggest using this spell. Once cast, it will **illuminate any traces of magic, enchantment, or charm** within a ten-meter radius.

Just be sure to pay attention, because the effect only lasts **a few seconds.**

COMPONENTS NEEDED:

— fire —
— blown glass —

SOMATIC MOVEMENTS:

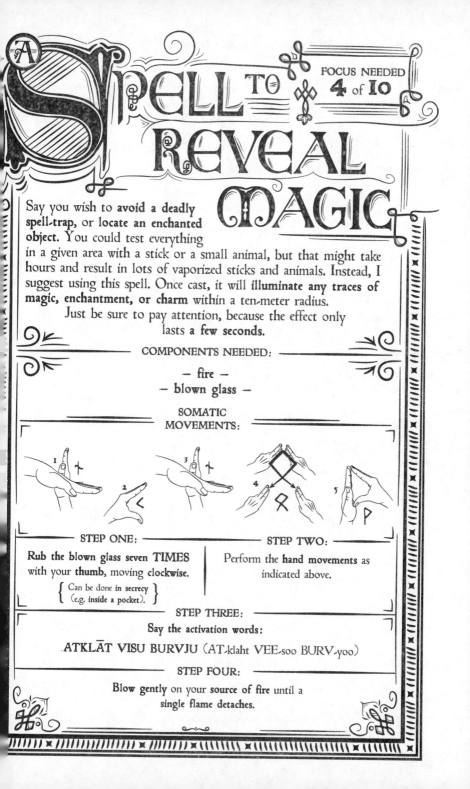

STEP ONE:

Rub the blown glass seven TIMES with your **thumb,** moving **clockwise.**

{ Can be done in secrecy (e.g. inside a pocket). }

STEP TWO:

Perform the **hand movements** as indicated above.

STEP THREE:

Say the activation words:

ATKLĀT VISU BURVJU (AT-klaht VEE-soo BURV-yoo)

STEP FOUR:

Blow gently on your **source of fire** until a single flame detaches.

ENCHANTING DETAILS

Buying magic tricks is standard practice for even the most experienced illusionist. After all, one can't be expected to look good onstage, learn sleight-of-hand, and be creative all at the same time, can they? The only problem with purchasing illusions is that the nature of the trick can always be exposed. Because of this, there is a strict taboo in the magic community against revealing secrets.

Owen nodded. He removed a stone club from one of Alec's boxes.

"You like the cudgel?" the magician said. "Over eight hundred years old, that is, but I'll throw it in, *gratis.*"

Instead, Owen brought the cudgel down on the coffee mug. Finally, the ceramic shattered, sending pieces all over the parking lot.

"Fine then," sighed Alec. "Act like bloody hooligans. Maybe the conservatives are right about all the violent video games you lot are into."

Owen ignored him, sweeping the pieces of the mug into a pile. Then he removed a salt packet and the silver spoon from his pocket and placed them next to the broken shards. He began to move his fingers through the air.

"Bit late for cleaning up, innit?" Alec said sarcastically. "You blew your goodwill. Now if you'll excuse me—"

"*Exsarcio!*" Owen yelled.

There was a purple flash of light, and the ceramic pieces snapped into position, forming a shallow dish with a handle attached. As an abstract art piece, it was fine, but its days of holding coffee were now past.

"You see?" said Trish. "We don't know what we're doing, dude."

Alec gaped at the strange object. He picked it up off the ground, using his fingertips to look for hidden grooves and seams. The ceramic was as smooth as if it had just come out of the oven.

"How did you . . . " he said. "I mean, that was . . . Do it again, yeah?"

And so Owen did it again. He smashed the cup and mended it twice more. Each time, it looked less and less like a coffee mug.

"It's like there's this whole other aspect we don't understand," agreed Perry. "We can manipulate the components and the words, but the magic energy itself . . ."

"It's wild," said Owen. "And we really need to learn how to control it."

Alec sank to the floor of his van. His face had gone pale and his eyes were distant. On the whole, he seemed to be taking the revelation that his view of the world had been upended fairly well.

"Yo, Alec!" Trish called, clapping her hands in his line of sight.

The magician blinked, as if waking from a dream. "What is it you want? I mean, explain to me . . . exactly . . . what you would like me to do here."

"Help us," said Owen. "How do we increase our focus? What are we doing wrong? How do we protect ourselves?"

Alec swallowed. He nodded rapidly. "Proper training, yeah. Step by step. Do it up right this time."

"What do you mean, 'this time'—" Perry began, but the magician cut her off. He laughed, a real laugh this time, and jumped to his feet.

"You know how long I've been waiting for this? Come along, kids; pizza is on me."

Pizza Download

Alec drove them to a restaurant that sold Chicago-style pizza, demanding to know how they had acquired the spell book. As they ate, the eighth graders told him about Codex Arcanum, Trish's mishap with the flying spell, Owen's encounter with Kiraz the Euclidean, and the demands of Virgil Ferretti. It turned out Bryan's father needed no introduction. Once Alec heard the casino owner was involved, he took charge of the situation.

"Right," he said, wiping mozzarella cheese from his goatee. "If you've got these guys on your six, we need to find some spell that'll make 'em forget they ever laid eyes on you. What are our options?"

"There's one that might work," Owen said, flipping to the Spell to Rewrite History. "But the page is still blank for me, and—"

"We have to unlock it," interrupted Perry, ripping out the page so Alec could read the message.

The store owner peered at the words *This spell will only appear when you are ready*. "A bit vague, innit?"

"I think we have to learn the spells in order, then do some kind of magic final examination," Owen said. He explained how the Twelve Basic Incantations had unlocked once they'd mastered the mending spell.

So Alec turned back to the beginning of the book, making Owen go over each of the twelve enchantments. They retired to a deserted corner of the restaurant parking lot, but when the magician attempted them himself, the spells had no effect. This clearly frustrated him, but Perry reminded him it was getting late, and that they had school the next day. Alec grudgingly agreed to call it a night, ordering them to meet him outside the middle school the following day.

Gray Matters

But to their surprise, when the magician showed up on Thursday afternoon with his van, it was not to begin their training. Before they cast another spell, he said, there were questions that needed answering. He drove them to a lab at the University of Las Vegas, the city's primary college campus. There he insisted that each of the teenagers get an MRI. Owen went first. He lay in a large tube while a female neuroscientist named Veera scanned

ENCHANTING
DETAILS

Magnetic resonance imaging, or MRI, is a medical imaging technique used to see the internal structures of the body. MRIs are more detailed and less dangerous than X-rays, but they are also incredibly expensive. Of course, both techniques are positively primitive when compared to, say, the Intermediate Spell to See through Things.

his brain. She was in her early thirties and hailed from Negombo, Sri Lanka. Her dark hair was cut in a hip feathered bob, and she wore cute cat-eye-shaped glasses. Alec had assured them on the drive over that Veera "owed him big time" and would keep their secret safe.

Once they had a picture of Owen's normal brain activity, Alec fitted the boy with a neural monitoring helmet and had him cast the mending spell on a broken pencil. As he did so, Veera could be seen pointing at the monitor and exclaiming to Alec in excitement.

She had the boy cast the spell a few more times to confirm. Then the girls were scanned and observed, and the neurologist reacted the same way. As the eighth graders watched, Alec and Veera had a muffled but clearly heated conversation, which included several comparisons of their MRI scans to one Alec had done on himself earlier in the day.

"What do you think's going on?" Owen said to the girls.

"Whatever it is, **HOUDINI** ain't happy," Trish replied as Alec kicked a chair into the wall.

SORCERY FOR BEGINNERS

Though not a true sorcerer, Harry HOUDINI (1874–1926 C.E.), was an acclaimed magician and escape artist who campaigned strongly against Euclideans and did much to expose those who sought to sully the reputation of magic. Had he lived longer, it is possible that many more people today would be inclined to learn sorcery.

Finally, the magician calmed down and emerged from the observation room. "So . . . it appears as if . . . for reasons currently unknown . . ." —here he glanced darkly at Veera— "there is a particular arrangement of neurons in your brains that adults, myself included, do not possess."

"Actually, they most likely atrophied," Veera explained. "Our brains are wired to pick up any number of languages at birth, for example. But once a specific tongue is introduced, learning others becomes increasingly difficult. Even impossible."

"No *wonder* Whitmore is **RECRUITING KIDS**." Trish nodded.

SORCERY FOR
BEGINNERS

The fact that only children can learn sorcery, while frustrating on multiple levels, does have one clear advantage—children believe in magic. Most adults, even after they've encountered real spell casting, still manage to find some boring rationalization—temporary insanity, liquor, exhaustion—for what they saw.

"So . . . adults literally can't cast spells?" Perry said.

"I need to do a lot more testing, get a larger sample, but . . . short answer? No, adults can't perform magic. At least, not like you kids can," said Veera, glancing at Alec. "Unless an adult developed and maintained these neurons when they were young, or found some kind of . . . **ELECTRONIC-WORKAROUND**. In fact, if you kids would let me do a few more scans—"

She broke off as Alec exhaled in frustration and paced the room. "But . . . that's good, right?" said Owen. "It means even if Ferretti or the Euclideans ever get the spell book, they won't actually be able to use sorcery."

BEWARE THE EUCLIDEANS

Finding a way to understand and defeat magic with technology has been the primary goal of the Euclideans for the last fifty years. Computers, and their massive processing capabilities, have gotten them close to the first part, but they're not quite there. Yet.

"Wrong," said Alec. "All it means is, *I* can't learn how to use magic. Ferretti, he could just get his kid to do it, or hire a bunch of underage Cambodians, or build a machine to stand in for the missing neurons, whatever. I do not have access to those sorts of resources. I am just a regular magician who apparently will never get the chance to do real bloody magic!" He stormed out of the room, letting the door slam behind him.

The middle schoolers looked at Veera, confused. "He's had a hard day," she explained. "Imagine searching for something your whole life, then finding it, then realizing you can't use it. It's tough."

"Oh please." Trish rolled her eyes. "Our lives are in danger; he needs to suck it up."

Trish stomped out of the room, Owen and Perry trailing behind her. They caught up with Alec at the elevators. "So that's it?" Trish accused him. "You can't use sorcery, so you're not gonna help us?"

"Not much point, is there?" Though it was already illuminated, the magician pushed the elevator call button several times. "I mean, nothing in it for me other than possible harm and plenty of jealousy."

"But that's so selfish!" said Perry indignantly. "Human beings wouldn't progress at all if we didn't help each other out."

Alec gave up on waiting for the elevator and started striding down the hallway toward the stairwell. The middle schoolers jogged after him. "I don't care about progress, do I?" he informed them. "I care about my store, and my act, and preventing me skin from being removed by Virgil Ferretti and used as a throw rug."

"But, but you've dealt with stuff like this before," Perry pleaded. "You've taught magic workshops, studied ancient texts . . . you're an *adult*. We need you." Trish and Owen nodded fervently.

"Sorry, kids. I don't care how many sorcery texts you have. You ain't gonna convince me to take on a known gangster with nothing more than me good looks."

"We can do sorcery," Owen reminded him. "We'll protect you."

Alec laughed bitterly. "I've seen you do sorcery, mate. Pass." He pushed open the door to the stairwell. The movement of air through the opening sounded like the moan of a sad, mournful ghost. "But best of luck to youse, yeah? Try not to get killed."

He started down the stairs. The door swung shut, the echoing boom of its closing like a period at the end of a very emphatic sentence.

STOPPAGE

Half an hour later, the three eighth graders huddled in the shade of a bus stop on the edge of UNLV's campus. They had waited in Veera's lab for ten minutes or so, hoping Alec would change his mind and return, but soon it became clear that he really had ditched them. Veera's repeated requests for more brain scans began to weird them out, so the middle schoolers left to find the nearest public transit stop and a bus that would take them back to Henderson. Twenty minutes and three visits to the transit website later, they were no closer to deciphering the bus schedule.

"Okay, I think this might work," said Perry, moving her finger across the complicated chart of times and vehicles. "I think if we take the number 113 to the 202 to the HDX . . . we still won't be anywhere near home." She sat back on the bench, dejected.

"Forget the buses already," said Trish angrily. She had alternated between pacing back and forth and practicing the mending spell. Currently she was pacing. "Who else are we gonna get to help us? It's been almost three full days since Ferretti threatened Owen. He's gonna come back."

"Maybe we should ask a cop or something," said Owen. "Someone with weapons experience."

"You wanna involve the police?" Trish stared at the young man as if his hair were on fire. "Just the fact that this book exists, breaks, like, fifteen laws."

"I don't know, okay? Alec's right: we don't have the resources to fight these guys."

✳   ✳

Perry sat up straight, her eyes focusing on something in the distance. "We might have something else, though." She nudged Owen, pointing out a van that was approaching the bus stop.

It pulled to a stop in front of them, dingy white with a familiar store logo on the side. The vehicle's owner rolled down the passenger window, revealing a goateed face and shoulder-length hair.

"Just remembered there aren't any buses from 'ere back to Henderson," said Alec Incanto. "And I'm not one to leave a group of kids totally unprotected."

"So you'll help us?" said Perry, jumping to her feet. "You'll teach us how to do the spells?"

Alec sighed. "Bloody Cornwall all over again, innit?" he muttered to himself. Then to the eighth graders: "Yes. I will be your Yoda. But on one condition, yeah? I won't teach ya this stuff so you can use it against people, improve your love lives, or show off. I will only do it so you lot can finish learning the spells in the book and take your final exam, whatever that is. We got a deal?"

Perry was almost bouncing up and down with excitement. "Deal."

Owen nodded. "Yeah. Agreed."

They looked at Trish. "So . . . we don't get to use magic?" she said suspiciously.

Alec rolled his eyes. "Yes, you can use it. But you can't go around acting like a magic superhero and drawing attention to yourself. It's too dangerous. The only way I help is if we keep it a secret."

The seneschal scowled, folding her arms. "Fine. Guess I'd rather learn magic and not use it than not learn it at all."

"Wonderful," the magician said sarcastically. "Now hop in before someone thinks I'm trying to kidnap you lot."

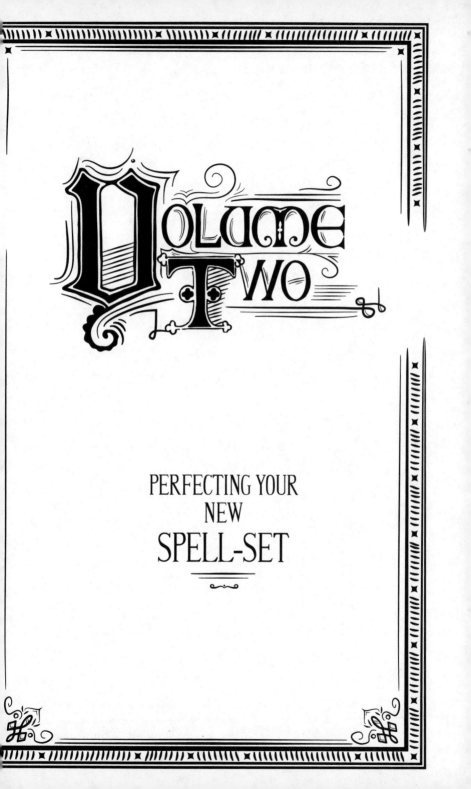

Volume Two

PERFECTING YOUR
NEW
SPELL-SET

CHAPTER 14

PLANS OF ATTACK

Owen stepped forward. His fingers clumsily traced runes in the air. He raised his hands, lifted a cup of water, then dumped it on his head.

"*Ósýnileika!*" he yelled in Icelandic. His hands shimmered and went briefly transparent. But as soon as he moved, they popped back into being. Owen shook the water off his head in frustration. A few meters away, Trish and Perry groaned. For someone who'd introduced them to the world of magic, Owen didn't seem to have much of a KNACK for it.

SORCERY FOR
BEGINNERS

Magic is like any other craft. It can be taught, but some people have more of a KNACK for it than others. People with natural rhythm and dexterity, such as musicians and dancers, tend to be particularly good at the hand movements. More intellectual types excel at memorizing activation words and spell steps. But, as the saying goes, all the natural talent in the world can't replace hard work. (Though that was most likely said by someone with zero natural talents.)

"No, no, no," said Alec, crossing the warehouse. They were in a large, private building on the outskirts of town that the magician used to store items for which he didn't have shelf space in Incanto's. This "overflow inventory" could have easily filled four or five such magic shops, or one medium-sized garbage dump. He and the eighth graders were surrounded by shelving units filled with magic-related equipment and supplies, but Alec had set up a practice area on one end with gym mats and attack dummies. The building was two stories tall and mostly metal, so his words had an impressive echo. "You can't force it, remember? Your body's like a conductor for the energy. Let it flow through you."

"I don't feel like I'm conducting anything," the boy muttered.

"It'll come," said the magician, taking him by the wrists and guiding him through the hand movements. "You just gotta get outta your own way, d'you know what I mean?"

Instead of doing that, Owen reflected on the events of the last few days. After Alec had agreed to teach them, he drove the eighth graders to his warehouse. Once they had cleared a satisfactory practice space and shaken the spiders from Alec's gym mats, he began to train them in earnest.

Alec proved to be a natural teacher—patient but firm, with a keen love of the subject. Under his guidance, the teenagers mastered the Twelve Basic Incantations by dinnertime on Thursday. Once Owen successfully cast **A SPELL TO GLIMPSE FUTURE EVENTS** and saw a tea-leaf image of Trish dropping a can of

SORCERY FOR BEGINNERS

Divination, or using magic to see the future, is the most tricky of the seven schools of sorcery. For starters, **FUTURE EVENTS** are constantly subject to change, which makes it very easy to misinterpret visions. Secondly, most people don't really want to know what's going to happen to them, so divination is often ignored by those who need it most.

Pepsi two minutes before it happened, over sixty more pages appeared in *Sorcery for Beginners*. They included incantations for manipulating the elements, for affecting the emotions of others, and for transmuting objects. Some spells required hand motions, some called for long recitations, some had extensive lists of rare components. Worse, each seemed to be more complicated than the last.

On Friday, Alec picked his apprentices up after school, drove them to the warehouse, and drilled them on as many spells as they could handle until dinnertime. He had suggested they call in sick to school so they could practice more, but Perry refused to lie and Owen didn't think his brain could handle it. Even three or four hours of magic training left him exhausted. He struggled to recall activation words, confused the order of spell steps, and his hand movements were clumsy and slow. By Saturday afternoon, he'd only been able to master eight more spells, while Trish and Perry had completed at least double that amount.

"Think of spell casting as a dance," Alec suggested when Owen was struggling with **A SPELL TO CONJURE LIGHTNING.** "Your body and hands need to move to the rhythm of the

SORCERY FOR
BEGINNERS

SPELLS FOR CONJURING LIGHTNING, ice, water, or fire are among the easiest in the Elemental school. This is because the spell components—heat, electricity, and moisture—are all around us, pretty much anywhere on the planet. Now, try to conjure water on Mars, and you'll have a rather tough time of it.

incantation. Imagine yourself in a thundercloud. Electricity forming all around you. Then the hand movements—once, twice, thrice, then hold for a beat—and snap your hands thusly." He demonstrated, yelling in Latin: *"Fulgur venire!"*

Naturally, nothing happened. But when Trish and Perry imitated him, blue electricity shot across the room, scorching the metal wall of the warehouse. Owen's best attempt, however, only caused a few sparks to sputter from his fingers.

"You'll get it," Perry said kindly, quickly whipping through the hand movements until electricity crackled on her open palm. She stretched the blue energy between her hands like a

*Most high-level magicians use spaces
such as this to store spell components.*

A SPELL TO CONJURE LIGHTNING

You've heard the phrase "**lightning fast**"? With this spell, you can make those words a reality. Follow these steps and you'll be able to **conjure an electrical charge** out of **thin air**. The resulting **bolt** can be **thrown at potential attackers, held as a defensive shield**, or **used to restart a dead car battery**. NOT recommended for use in rainstorms or at pool parties.

COMPONENTS NEEDED:

— none —

SOMATIC MOVEMENTS:

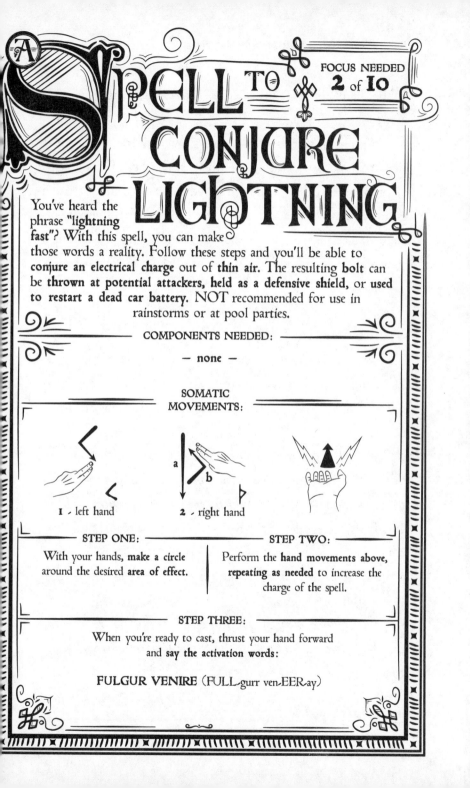

1 - left hand   **2** - right hand

STEP ONE:

With your hands, **make a circle** around the desired **area of effect**.

STEP TWO:

Perform the **hand movements above**, **repeating as needed** to increase the charge of the spell.

STEP THREE:

When you're ready to cast, thrust your hand forward and **say the activation words**:

FULGUR VENIRE (FULL-gurr ven-EER-ay)

rubber band, then let it disperse. "Perhaps elemental spells just aren't your bailiwick."

In point of fact, both girls had shown an affinity for a particular kind of spell casting over the past few days. Perry excelled at protection spells, as they involved a lot of complicated diagrams and concentration. Trish was better at fighting magic—elemental attacks, increasing her speed and strength, anything as strong and aggressive as she was. But Owen—his talent had yet to emerge.

VISIBLE FRUSTRATIONS

Even after a half day of practice, Owen was a complete mess. He could no longer recall any of the spells from memory, he mispronounced every activation word, and his thoughts drifted constantly.

Alec patiently moved Owen's hands through the positions of the invisibility spell. *Like I'm some kind of stupid puppet*, the teenager thought bitterly. *Which I guess I pretty much am.* Perry and Trish had made themselves vanish twice already, but Owen could barely make his fingernails see-through for longer than a moment or two. Every time he tried to focus, he thought of his mom.

They had spoken that morning on FaceTime. It had been ten days since her last call, the longest stretch since Eleanor Macready had left for Sumatra.

"You wouldn't believe how difficult things are over here," Eleanor had told Owen a few hours earlier. He could see a moon-lit, rainforest-covered mountain outside his mom's wooden hut—Sumatra was fourteen hours ahead of Las Vegas. "Even making a cup of tea is a hassle. No electricity, no reliable Internet. Meanwhile, the logging companies have top-of-the-line genera-tors and T1 lines running twenty-four seven. It's criminal."

The young man nodded. It had been just over a week since he'd purchased *Sorcery for Beginners*. He was feeling much closer to unlocking the Spell to Rewrite History, but he didn't think Eleanor would believe him if he told her he was learning magic. He had an idea for how she might be able to contribute in another way, though. "So, I was thinking this week. About how things ended up like this. And I was wondering, if you could go back and fix things, when would you go to? Six months, maybe?" *Nearly two months before mom and dad broke up*, Owen mentally confirmed. *Plenty of time for them to stay together.*

"What do you mean by *fix things*?" Eleanor's glance strayed to the side. *Probably reading emails*, Owen thought sourly, but he plowed ahead.

"You know, like, with you and Dad. How far back would you have to go so, you know, we could all stay in Cleveland?"

"Oh, honey." Now she was looking at him, but her expres-sion was sad. "What's done is done. Me and your dad, we love you, but you know we're not getting back together, right? We had our time together, but it's over."

"No, I know that, but like, hypothetically. *If* you could go back, *when* did everything kind of . . . go bad, or whatever?" *Just give me the day. Give me a date and time, even a rough estimate, so I can rewrite history to make sure none of this ever happens.*

But Eleanor leaned forward. "Owen, listen to me. What happened with our family was inevitable. Even if you could get in a time machine and somehow magically fix things, this still would have happened. I needed to see the world. To be on my own. To take part in world-changing, important work."

"You could still do that. We just need to go back and keep everyone together, then we can go wherever you want. I have a way to do it, Mom. See, I found this—"

"Oh, you've gotta be kidding me!" interrupted his mother.

Owen paused. "No. I really do have a way; it's just, it requires some more work, and I'm not sure when—"

"No, honey, not you. I just got an email from this logging company. They promised me they wouldn't clear-cut a portion of the orangs' habitat, but they just filed a work order to do it first thing tomorrow morning." She started typing, shaking her head. "Unbelievable. Do you know how much damage this will do?"

"Yeah. The thing is, I just need a time to focus on. Then I can—"

"I'm sorry, hon, I can't continue to talk about this right now. But believe me, you will be okay. You'll get through this. You've always been a fighter, even if you don't realize it." She took a break from typing to make eye contact with him. "You understand, right?"

✻ ✳

Owen sagged. *And here I thought the Spell to Rewrite History would fix everything. That I could just wave my magic book around and things would go back to how they were. What a dummy.*

"We'll talk next week. You can tell me about this imaginary time machine of yours then. Okay? Kiss kiss kiss!" Before he could respond, she hung up.

The conversation had been playing through his head all morning. Everything he'd gone through in the last week was for nothing. What was the point of him learning all these spells, of rewriting history itself so his family could be back together, if she'd rather be in Sumatra?

"Knock, knock," said Alec, dropping Owen's hands. "Anybody home? You even attempting to make an effort here, mate?"

"Yeah," the boy said defensively. But as the magician stared him down, Owen looked away. "Okay, no. But it's only cause these dancing finger moves are so *dorky.*"

Trish snorted derisively. "You think I like this pansy crap? Please. But I suck it up and do the work cause of the *payoff.*" Her hands quickly but choppily formed a few runes, then she thrust a hand forward and barked a phrase in ARABIC. A blue spout of

SORCERY FOR BEGINNERS

Enchantments tend to originate in areas of the world where they are most needed. So rain and water spells hail from ARABIAN climes, while wind and navigation spells come from seafaring lands. Ice magic, bizarrely enough, comes mostly from Iceland. I suppose if you name your whole country after the substance, you can't get enough of it.

water shot across the warehouse, dousing a much-abused practice dummy.

"Exactly," said Alec. "Don't think of it as dancing. It's simple
physical coordination, like you need in any sport."

"Yeah, well—maybe I'm not physically coordinated. Maybe
I'm not cut out for any of this." The boy kicked a box of E-Z
Escape brand handcuffs.

"You keep thinking that, and it's gonna come true, mate.
You gotta climb out of your own head. Perry!" he said. "Can you
show Mr. Negativity how to do it with confidence, please?"

The tiny girl stepped forward. She adjusted her funky purple
glasses on her nose apologetically. Owen folded his arms. *Perry
might be smart and strong-willed and as honest as Abe Lincoln, but
confident? Come on.*

The tiny girl placed a shimmery moonstone about the size
of her thumbnail on the floor. Her hands swooped gracefully
through the air, fingers forming runes, then circling them. Her
movements were fluid, sure, and strong. It was like she was conducting a symphony in the air. She brought her palms together
over her head, dumped out a vial of water, and said in Icelandic:

"*Ósýnileika.*" The water bloomed into ribbons of shimmering, translucent light, wrapping around her limbs and attaching
to her torso like wet paper. She spun around once, and vanished.

"You see?" Alec said. "She's not all up in her head about
being smart or stupid or whatever it is you got mucking up your
attic. Trish—how about you give it a shot?"

A SPELL FOR INVISIBILITY

We've all had a moment or two when we **wished we could disappear**. With this spell, you can do exactly that. You (or a subject of your choosing) will be **wrapped in a transparent coating undetectable** by anything except spells to reveal magic. Just remember to not make any sounds or bump into things, as that tends to spoil the effect.

COMPONENTS NEEDED:

– One { 1 } **vial of water** –
– One { 1 } **moonstone, charged** –

SOMATIC MOVEMENTS:

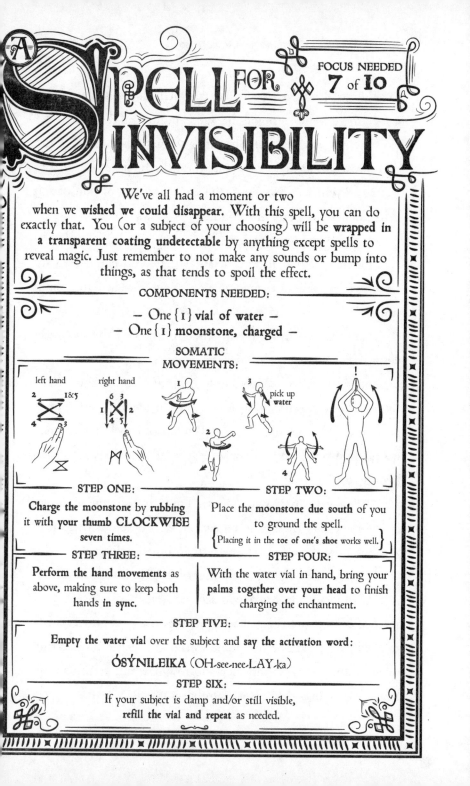

left hand   right hand

pick up water

STEP ONE:

Charge the moonstone by rubbing it with **your thumb CLOCKWISE seven times.**

STEP TWO:

Place the **moonstone due south** of you to ground the spell.

{ Placing it in the toe of one's shoe works well. }

STEP THREE:

Perform the hand movements as above, making sure to keep both hands **in sync.**

STEP FOUR:

With the water vial in hand, bring your **palms together over your head** to finish charging the enchantment.

STEP FIVE:

Empty the **water vial** over the subject and **say the activation word:**

ÓSÝNILEIKA (OH-see-nee-LAY-ka)

STEP SIX:

If your subject is damp and/or still visible, **refill the vial and repeat** as needed.

The girl lumbered over. She frowned, dropped the moonstone, then went through the same motions Perry had. Her movements, however, were staccato and sharp, like punches and jabs thrown at a brick wall. But when she upended her vial of water and yelled, *"Ósýnileika!"* the same shimmer of transparent light cloaked her body in seconds.

"Yeeeah!" she whooped, probably pumping an invisible fist.

"Excellent," said the magician. "Perry, you could do with tapping into some of that aggression. Now, Owen. How about you give it another try?"

"Can we just move on to something else?" the teenageer whined.

"No," said Alec. "We've only been at this for three days. Anytime we hit something a wee bit challenging, you wanna pack it in. Well, no more, mate. There isn't a spell in this book we haven't glanced at by now. What you need to do is quit being bloody *lazy*."

"What if I can't?" said Owen. "I'm only thirteen years old. I'm not special. There're seventeen other people out there with this book; let them fight off Ferretti and the Euclideans."

"Do the spell right now," Alec said. "Don't think about it; just do the motions. Make yourself invisible."

Seething, Owen began to form the runes. Who were they to decide how hard he should be working? It was his book; they were lucky he was letting them borrow it at all. His fingertips began to tingle with the now-familiar FEEL OF MAGIC.

SORCERY FOR BEGINNERS

Experienced sorcerers will not only FEEL their bodies tingle when they access magical energy, but also they can sense the castings of other magicians in this way as well. Hence Shakespeare's witches: "By the pricking of my thumbs, something wicked this way comes"—*Macbeth*, Act IV, Scene 1.

But then he heard Perry and Trish, who were still invisible, whispering to each other. *Am I doing something wrong?* he thought. *Do they also think I'm being lazy? That I'm too ordinary to deserve the book? This whole thing's pointless.*

He dropped his hands. The tingling left his fingers.

"What happened?" said Alec. "You nearly had it; why'd you stop?"

"Can we please just do something else?" Owen said. "There's a time-stopping spell; why can't we look at that?"

"Because this ain't about any one spell, innit? This is about you." Alec peered down at the boy. "What is it, someone told you you weren't good enough? Filled your head with a bunch of defeatist, aim-for-the-middle rubbish that created this great mental block?"

"No. I mean, she didn't say that exactly, but she—" Owen stopped himself, his eyes burning with frustration.

Perry put an invisible hand on his shoulder, making him jump. "It's okay. We all have emotional obstacles to overcome. When my dad died, I couldn't do homework for two months."

"Yeah, dude, just unload already," came Trish's disembodied voice from his other side. "We're on the same team here."

Owen shrugged off Perry's see-through hand. "Wrong. You guys are only here because *I* invited you."

"Cause you had no idea what you were doing," retorted Trish. "If it weren't for us, you'd still be throwing broken pencils around your bedroom."

"So you do think you should have the book instead of me. You do think I don't deserve it."

"No one's saying that," Alec said quietly.

Owen walked over to the spell book and slammed it shut. "Maybe I should just sell it to that Euclidean guy," he continued. "I mean, clearly I'm a crappy sorcerer, so why not make a little coin while I can, right? Whitmore herself even said most people don't finish this dumb thing."

"You can't be serious!" said Perry, CASTING OFF the invisibility spell and walking toward him. "You've witnessed firsthand what the book can do; it's immoral and selfish to give away that kind of power."

"Why?" said Owen, sliding the book into his backpack. "At least the Euclideans know what to do with it." He began walking toward the exit of the warehouse when he felt an invisible hand on his chest.

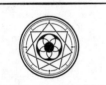

SORCERY FOR BEGINNERS

Enchantments can be CAST OFF in a variety of ways—performing the components of a spell in reverse, using so-called "undo" spells, or simply allowing a spell to fade away over time. This can get a bit trickier when using magic that affects one's memory or the flow of time.

"Dude," came Trish's voice. "You are acting like a super d-bag."

Owen's fingers formed the simple runes for the BINDING SPELL. He grabbed her invisible wrist. *"Immobiles,"* he said.

He could hear the girl's limbs lock up. Then she toppled over, hitting the gym mat with a heavy *thump*.

"Oi!" Alec yelled. "Not cool, mate. Get back here and help her up. Hey!"

Owen's face burned with shame, but he did not stop. He opened the door to the warehouse, wincing at the sudden blast of heat. But he kept going, walking down the street and angrily wiping at his eyes.

He failed to notice the black town car lurking at the end of the building.

SORCERY FOR BEGINNERS

One of the Twelve Basic Incantations, A SPELL FOR BINDING is mostly used for so-called "household" magic—fixing loose cabinets, reattaching roof shingles, or mending a thrown horseshoe. Used more aggressively, it can lock a person's limbs together or fix them to a location until the spell caster chooses to release them.

Chapter 15

Closing Arguments

"That was incredibly selfish," Perry said, jogging after Owen. "Not to mention unlike you. Trish could have been seriously injured!"

The young man kept walking. He was ashamed of what he'd done, but he was still too angry to admit it. He glanced back, seeing that a visible, unbound Trish had also exited the warehouse. "She looks fine to me."

"That's beside the point. We can't let our EMOTIONS bamboozle us into using sorcery on each other. We have to be better than that."

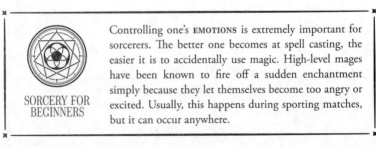

SORCERY FOR BEGINNERS

Controlling one's EMOTIONS is extremely important for sorcerers. The better one becomes at spell casting, the easier it is to accidentally use magic. High-level mages have been known to fire off a sudden enchantment simply because they let themselves become too angry or excited. Usually, this happens during sporting matches, but it can occur anywhere.

"It's easy for you, isn't it? Moral, intelligent, never-do-wrong Perry. Not everyone's like you, okay? Most people aren't, in fact."

Trish caught up to them. "Doesn't mean you get to act like a D, dude. So you've gotta practice a bit harder than us. Man up and do it."

Owen rounded on them. "Don't you guys get it? Learning all these spells won't change a thing. Even if we unlock them all, and I manage to cast the Spell to Rewrite History, it won't matter. My mom will still wanna leave."

The young women looked at each other, finally understanding what was bothering their new friend. Perry was about to respond when the black Mercedes town car pulled up next to them. The doors opened, revealing Ferretti's blond, crew-cutted bodyguard and Samson Kiraz. The Euclidean smiled in greeting.

"Hello again, young Mr. Macready. You should have accepted my terms." He looked over at Perry and Trish. "I'm sure he told you all about me and Mr. Ferretti's bodyguard." Blondie gave a creepy wave.

"You two work together?" said Owen in disbelief.

"Ours is what you could call a more recent alliance," said Kiraz. "Now, I know you three are probably thinking about running or calling for help. But if you get in the car, this procedure will proceed much more smoothly. Either way we'll end up with the same result."

Owen looked up and down the street. The area was filled with anonymous storage facilities, their metal walls shimmering in the afternoon heat. It being Saturday, they were the only people on the block. *He's right. Calling for help would be pointless. But there are other options. I might not be a good sorcerer, but at least now I have a few spells to protect myself.*

During his hesitation, both adults removed black, gun-like devices from hip holsters.

TASERS.

The eighth graders looked at each other. They had been practicing their shield spells since Wednesday, but none of them had yet been able to stop a projectile.

"Good. Now take a step toward me," said Kiraz. "Slowly. No sudden moves, and keep your hands where we can see them."

The middle schoolers did as they were told. Owen racked his brain for an attack spell that could take out both men at once, but his mind was currently preoccupied with wondering how painful it would feel to be electrocuted.

"What, um, what do you want?" the boy said, trying to stall for time.

"Just to chat," said Kiraz. "But since I informed my new partners you can't be trusted . . ."

He removed three zip ties from his suit pocket. Keeping the Taser pointed at Trish, he reached for her wrists—

ENCHANTING DETAILS

While they offer a far more preferable method of subduing people than, say, sawed-off shotguns, TASERS can still be quite dangerous. Since 1999, it is estimated that 148 people have died in Taser-related deaths. So if you want to knock someone unconscious, smelly gym socks might be a safer bet.

"Miyah jariya," the girl whispered in Arabic, and thrust her hands upward. A spout of water materialized from nowhere, pummeling Kiraz in the face with such force, he was knocked back a few steps. Perry took off running toward Alec's warehouse.

Trish, meanwhile, began to form the runes for the invisibility spell. Before she could finish, Blondie pulled the trigger of his Taser. Two wires shot out, attaching to the girl's torso. Her body vibrated. Her eyes rolled back into her head and she screamed angrily, crumpling to the ground.

Kiraz shook the water from his eyes and pointed his Taser at Perry's retreating back. He fired. The wires stuck her right between the shoulder blades, and she, too, dropped into a screaming, twitching pile.

Both men turned to Owen. Hands shaking, the boy began to form the runes for his old standby, the mending spell. The adults walked toward him, their faces shining with anticipation. They were less than a meter away when Owen completed the runes. He took a breath to shout the activation words—

But the blond man slammed the butt of his Taser into the base of Owen's skull. The boy dropped to the ground, his eyelids fluttering closed.

SORCERY FOR BEGINNERS

If a spell is charged up but somehow canceled before it is cast, the magical energy that would have been used is not lost. It simply returns to the surrounding environs, much like scooping out a handful of seawater, then depositing it back into the ocean.

"Children today," Kiraz said to Blondie as Owen slipped into unconsciousness. "So insolent."

A Captive Audience

Owen awoke in a dark room. A throbbing pain radiated from deep inside his brain. He was sitting in a metal folding chair. When he attempted to move, he discovered his wrists were tightly cinched behind him via plastic zip ties. Almost immediately after that, he discovered he needed to pee.

To distract himself, he looked around the room. A thin beam of light shone from underneath the door, allowing the boy to get a rough idea of his surroundings. Perry and Trish were tied up and in chairs to either side of him. Both of them were awake.

"Oh, thank goodness," whispered Perry. "We were worried you had a brain clot or something."

"Where are we?" said Owen.

"Don't know," said Trish. "Thing One and Thing Two put a couple of smelly bags over our heads. And thanks to Blondie, I feel like a piece of microwaved bacon."

Now that his eyes had adjusted to the darkness, Owen was able to take in the room. Cheap metal shelves lined the walls, stacked high with cardboard boxes and plastic containers of condiments—salt and pepper, ketchup refills, canned pickles. In one corner was a utility sink with a mop and bucket. An inexpensive folding table and an empty plastic chair faced him. All in all, not a very scary place to be held captive.

And yet, he and the teenage girls were terrified. *No idea where we are or what time it is,* thought Owen. *Even if Alec decides to go looking for us, which doesn't seem like his style, he won't know where to begin. I'm such an idiot.*

He strained at his bound wrists in frustration. *Why did I leave the warehouse alone like that? And with the spell book in my backpack, no less. The spell book!* A second glance around the dim room told him it and his backpack were nowhere nearby. *It's over, then. Not only are we all going to die, but my stupid immaturity led to the loss of the* **MOST POWERFUL MAGICAL OBJECT IN EXISTENCE.** *Great job, Owen.*

Salt water burned his eyes, but he shook it away. "Guys, they took my backpack. What do we do?"

"Careful. They might be listening," Perry muttered through closed lips.

"I hope they are," said Trish. "Then I can tell them what PANSIES they are for Tasing a bunch of KIDS!"

"Knock it off," whispered Owen. "They could come in here any second; we have to make a—"

He stopped as the electronic lock to the storage room beeped. As the door opened, Perry whispered, "No magic. Play dumb!"

SORCERY FOR
BEGINNERS

Actually, this volume is far from the MOST POWERFUL MAGICAL OBJECT IN THE WORLD. It is not even the most powerful spell book. That honor belongs to *Die Unaussprechlich,* an extremely advanced, dark grimoire that only two or three sorcerers have read and survived to tell about it. If Owen thinks Codex Arcanum would sell a text of that caliber to a teenager for a mere twenty dollars American, then he is grossly mistaken.

The overhead light turned on, making the three eighth graders squeeze their eyes shut. Three adults strode in—Blondie, Kiraz, and Virgil Ferretti.

GRILLED MIDDLE SCHOOLERS

The big casino owner sat in the chair across from the children. His thick, strong fingers sported several gold rings, each one imbedded with a large precious stone. He wore a light beige suit, perfectly tailored, with no tie. His shiny blue silk shirt was unbuttoned enough to show a broad, tan chest devoid of hair. The other men flanked him, their faces thrown into shadow.

"Owen Macready," Ferretti said in his deep, commanding voice. "And friends. It's been a few days."

"Already?" said the boy in feigned surprise.

"Let's not kid each other, kid. My guys have had you under surveillance since we met. Aw, don't look so offended. I'm a businessman. I have a right to know which way the wind is blowing." He got up from his chair and knelt in front of Owen, inspecting him like a banker checking for counterfeit bills. "I know you haven't been to a lawyer, a notary, or even an accountant. I also know you didn't use some kind of chemical on Bryan."

"We're all minors," Perry said nervously. "Imprisoning us here is illegal and morally bankrupt and—"

Ferretti held up a hand, silencing her. "Let me save you the time, small fry. I don't care. I've had guys buried in the desert simply cause they mouthed off to me. What I do care about is *this*."

He stood and snapped his fingers. Blondie tossed him Owen's backpack. The casino owner took out *Sorcery for Beginners*.

"All week, Bryan wouldn't shut up about this thing." He smiled at them confidentially. "Frankly, I don't pay much attention to what my son says on a day-to-day basis. Mind-numbing, superficial nonsense, most of it. But this, he wouldn't let go. The new kid's magic spell book."

Ferretti jerked his head toward Kiraz. "Then this Ivy Leaguer approaches me on Wednesday, and tells me everything my idiot son says is true. That sorcery is real, and he's part of some **SECRET SOCIETY** to get rid of it. He offers to partner up with us, even shows me some classified videos of people supposedly doing magic." Ferretti shrugged. "Naturally, I think it's all a scam. Special effects, CGI. I tell

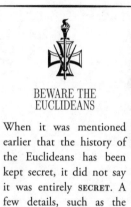

BEWARE THE EUCLIDEANS

When it was mentioned earlier that the history of the Euclideans has been kept secret, it did not say it was entirely SECRET. A few details, such as the purpose of the society and their basic tenets have been allowed to slip out. Otherwise, how would they recruit like-minded individuals?

him we'll get back to him. But then I have my guys ask around, and you know what they find?"

"That you're too lazy to do your own work?" Trish said.

The casino owner pursed his lips. Then he lunged forward, grabbing the eighth-grade girl's upper arm. He lifted her and the chair several inches off the ground, his fingers digging painfully into her bicep. He pulled her close, his cold, unsmiling eyes mere centimeters from hers. "Do not. Mouth off. To me." He dropped her. Trish's chair bounced and hit the concrete wall, but she shook it off.

"Where was I?" said Ferretti as if nothing had happened. "Right, research. So my guys, they found that these Euclideans aren't a bunch of hippy-dippy WICCANS. They're the real deal. Tons of dark money, fingers in all kinds of pies. I'd be stupid to turn down that kind of partnership. But the whole *sorcery is real* thing, it still doesn't sit right with me. I call back my new friend here, and tell him I need proof. Something I can see with my own eyes."

ENCHANTING DETAILS

WICCANS are practitioners of Wicca, a modern religion based on pagan witchcraft. It was created in 1954 and draws upon a variety of ancient pagan symbols. While many Wiccans believe in magic, and even use some of the proper forms for sorcery, any spells they cast are purely accidental.

"Turns out, adults can't do magic. Convenient, right?" He tapped *Sorcery for Beginners*. "But he says if we can grab this, which to me looks like a book called *Legal Loopholes for the Career Criminal*, we could get you kids to give us a little demonstration. So here we all are." He dropped the book on the card table. "Time to do some magic."

Their secret was out. *Maybe I can grab the book from him,* Owen thought frantically. *Scoop it off the table, run far away, and bury the magic manual somewhere the casino owner and the*

Euclideans will never find it. He was just starting to puzzle out how to begin such a plan when Perry did something completely out of character.

She snorted.

"And you, like, fell for that?" she said in a contemptuous, sarcastic voice completely unlike her own. "Dude, if sorcery was real, don't you think we'd be, I don't know, using it right now? We'd flick our wands and zip-zap outta here."

Despite their dire situation, the change in her personality was so striking, Owen nearly laughed. He covered it with a cough at the last moment.

Ferretti smiled as well, but the expression did not extend to his eyes. "You sure this is how you wanna play it, small fry? Cause I got no problem shoving you around, too."

Owen picked up her lead. "No, she's right. The stuff I used on Bryan, it's, um, this fake skin my cousin invented. Like movie makeup. I wasn't supposed to use it on anyone, but I did. And the book, it's just got a . . . fancy cover. Like a video screen."

Ferretti studied them. He looked at Kiraz, who shook his head. The casino owner turned back to the middle schoolers, baring his blinding white teeth. "Been working on your poker tells, I see. But you still ain't good enough." He motioned to Blondie. "Start with Miss Mouthy," he said.

ORDEAL BY WATER

The bodyguard lumbered over to Trish. She tried to duck away, but he dragged her, chair and all, to the utility sink and began to fill the mop bucket with water.

"Another thing my guys came across during their research," said Ferretti, not taking his eyes off Owen. "The Puritans, they had this great TEST for determining if somebody was a witch or not. Called it 'dunking.' See, they'd drop her in a river, and if she floated, she was a witch and they'd put her to death. If she drowned, she was innocent. It's what we in the casino biz call a win-win."

Blondie turned off the faucet. He positioned the brimming bucket right in front of Trish. "Now, all I want is proof that this book works. You do that, and I'll let you all go home right now. You don't, and Mouthy here gets to show me she's not a witch."

Perry and Owen looked to Trish. She gulped, but shook her head. Ferretti nodded to Blondie. The mercenary grabbed Trish's head, pushing it down toward the bucket—

"We don't know anything!" Owen said. "Yes, there's magic. All right? It's all true. But we can't make any of the spells work. So you don't have to drown her."

ENCHANTING DETAILS

The sixteenth- and seventeenth-century authorities developed several like-minded "TESTS" to determine a witch's guilt. Other favorites included stretching the accused on a rack, enclosing them in coffins filled with spikes, or forcing them to drink poison to see if they would save themselves. It is no wonder that the period which followed these atrocities was called the Enlightenment.

Ferretti held up a hand, and the mercenary paused. Trish's face was almost touching the water. She struggled, but Blondie held her where she was.

"What do you mean, you can't make it work?" Ferretti said icily. "You made it work on my son."

Quickly, Owen began to formulate a plan. "That was an accident," he said. "We . . . I didn't know what I was doing. I'll prove it, I swear. Just please take her away from the bucket."

The casino owner nodded to Blondie, who yanked Trish upright.

"Show me," Ferretti said.

"Owen," Trish growled. "Tell this spray-tan oombah to stick it up his—"

Blondie clapped a big hand over her mouth. The seneschal struggled, but her words were muffled. The casino owner motioned for Owen to continue.

Behind his chair, Owen began to trace runes in the air with his fingers. "The book is about magic," he said, trying to make his voice thin and whiny. "But the spells, they're too hard to figure out. So far we've only been able to do the . . . the one I used on Bryan."

Ferretti's eyes narrowed. "Bullshit."

"No, he's totally right." Perry's voice quavered in fear, but she maintained her new persona. "We didn't tell you because it's, like, sooo embarrassing." She even managed to roll her eyes as she said it.

There was a long pause while the casino owner studied them. Then Ferretti barked out a laugh. The other two men joined in. "Will you get a load of these two?" he said. "I should make you both pit bosses at my poker tables. Coupla card sharks, the both of you. But I'm calling your bluff." He jerked his head toward Blondie.

Again, the man shoved Trish back toward the bucket. She turned her head this way and that, using all her strength to resist him, but he had 150 pounds and the fact that he was a maniac on his side. *He really is gonna drown her,* thought Owen desperately. *Do something. Do something NOW.*

Trish's forehead touched water—

"Okay!" shouted Owen. Blondie froze in place, a grim smile on his face. "I'll do it. I'll show you sorcery is real. But I need the book," said the young man. Despite the zip ties on his wrists, he increased the speed of his finger motions, **BUILDING UP THE CHARGE** of the spell.

SORCERY FOR BEGINNERS

Repeating the hand movements for a given spell without saying the activation words will indeed increase its potency, or **CHARGE**. However, it can also cause a spell to replicate multiple times, affect several different subjects at once, or be cast before you are ready. Which result occurs is determined by the strength of the caster's focus.

"Owen, no!" said Trish, but Blondie clapped a hand over her mouth again.

Ferretti met the young man's gaze. He picked up *Sorcery for Beginners* and carried it over to Owen. "Tick tock, kid."

Owen glanced back at Trish, whose head was still just above the water. She shook her head, her eyes wide. He was fairly confident his plan would work, but if it didn't, he hoped she could hold her breath. Next, he made eye contact with Perry, inclining his head slightly. "Turn to page forty-three."

Ferretti sighed, but he did so, his hand holding the page open. "You don't give me some proof, pronto, and I'm dunking her just for fun."

"You want proof?" said Owen. *"Αντίγραφο."*

INFINITE-RING CIRCUS

Pop-pop-pop! Exact replicas of the three rings on Ferretti's left hand—the hand touching the **DUPLICATION SPELL** page—flew upward, striking him in the face. Ferretti dropped the book like it had bit him. There was a pause as all three men looked down at it. Then the rings on Ferretti's hand duplicated again—*pop-pop-pop!*—and shot into the air like kernels of corn escaping a hot pan. The casino owner stumbled backward, struggling to pull the multiplying jewelry off his fingers.

"What the hell did you do?" he said. "Turn it off, turn it off!"

In response, Owen snapped his hands together at the wrist and spoke a word in Latin: *"Ignis."*

SORCERY FOR BEGINNERS

DUPLICATION SPELLS, if not cancelled or contained, have the potential for great destruction. They have led to several historical catastrophes, including the "eruption" of Mount Vesuvius in 79 C.E., the Tunguska blast of 1908 C.E., and the proliferation of the Furby doll in 1998–2000 C.E.

A tiny blue fireball puffed into the floor, but it was enough to melt the plastic zip ties that kept him bound. The boy leapt across the room toward Blondie, forming hand motions along the way. Though Owen didn't have his silver spoon, on the shelf above the man's head was an industrial-sized **BOX OF SALT**.

The mercenary reacted quite fast, considering the circumstances. He shoved Trish's chair aside and fumbled for his Taser. He actually managed to pull it from his holster by the time Owen reached him, but it was too late. The boy clapped a hand on his face.

"Exsarcio," he said.

The muffled shout of surprise told him the spell had worked. Blondie's eyes and mouth were now sealed shut. He reached blindly for Owen, but the teenager shouldered him into the sink. The big man's butt went into the bucket, sloshing water over the sides. Owen severed the zip ties binding Trish with another fireball, then pulled her to her feet. She was shaky, but looked okay.

Perry, meanwhile, had been charging up a spell of her own. Kiraz pointed his Taser, but the tiny girl spun her chair around, revealing a big ball of lightning in her palm. *"Fulgur venire!"* she cried.

SORCERY FOR
BEGINNERS

Many spell components, such as SALT, can sometimes be found quite abundantly in nature. Before casting any enchantment, the novice sorcerer would do well to scout the area first, as hidden deposits of certain components will drastically (and unexpectedly) increase the effects of a given bit of magic.

The bolt of blue electricity sizzled across the small room, striking the Euclidean directly in the chest. He slammed against the wall, limbs twitching and clothes smoking.

Ferretti watched this all play out, his eyes lit by a wild, terrifying joy. "It's real," he whispered. "It's really *real.*"

With one arm still supporting Trish, Owen grabbed the spell book off the floor. Perry scooped up his backpack. Ferretti blinked, regaining his senses. He held out a hand to stop the eighth graders, but gold rings continued to ricochet off his fingers. One cracked one of the casino owner's fake teeth, making him curse in anger. Owen clutched the book to his chest, turning the doorknob to the storage closet—

And he was slammed against the door by a heavy arm. Ferretti flipped him around, jamming his forearm into the teenager's throat. The man had several ring-sized welts on his bald head, and his carefully pressed clothes were now rumpled and sweaty.

"I want. That book," he hissed, his breath hot and garlicky on the boy's face. Trish and Perry pulled at Ferretti's arms, but it was like trying to bend a stone statue. In the background, gold rings continued to bounce off the floor and multiply.

Red spots bloomed in Owen's vision. Fingers fumbling, he clutched a page in the spell book, tore it in half, and closed his eyes.

CRACK! A bright blast of purple light exploded right in Virgil Ferretti's face as the book mended itself. The casino owner staggered backward, temporarily blinded.

Perry had the door open before Ferretti could regain his sight. The three eighth graders stumbled down the windowless concrete hallway. Owen kept a tight hold on *Sorcery for Beginners.*

A *"ringing"* example of using an enemy's trappings against him

"Which way?" gasped Trish as they came to a fork in the hallway.

"Left," said Owen. He began to pull them down the corridor, but Perry resisted.

"What about the rings?" she said, looking back at the storage room. "If we allow them to keep multiplying, they may injure someone."

"Let's worry about that when our lives are no longer in danger, huh?" said Trish, yanking her down the corridor. At the end was a set of double doors. These they burst through.

Before them spread a brightly colored maze of flashing slot machines, gaming tables, and muscled security guards every thirty feet.

They were in the middle of a casino.

Beating the Odds

The eighth graders surveyed the massive gambling area. It was late on Saturday afternoon, and the place was teeming with patrons playing various games of chance. At first glance, Owen couldn't tell which casino they were in, nor where the exits might be. This last bit of information was not surprising; all casinos are specifically designed to keep people from leaving. There was at least one good bit of news, though—

"I guess we're still in Vegas," he said. "Do you guys recognize this place?"

"All casinos look the same," snarked Trish.

"There's an exit sign," said Perry, pointing to the left.

"And there's one there," countered Owen, pointing to the right.

"Welcome to Vegas," Trish commented dryly. "It's probably just two ends of a circular hallway that spits you right back out into the casino."

"Shoot, I almost forgot!" Perry said. She formed a few runes, then laid a hand on the double doors. *"Immobiles."*

The doors shimmered briefly and sealed themselves. Her action was not a moment too soon. They heard someone try to open the door from the other side, then pound on it with his fists.

"That should hold off Ferretti for a second." The tiny girl smiled.

"Nice," Owen said. "But we can't stand in the doorway. Come on." He strode off toward the exit sign on the left. Perry and Trish followed.

Soon, they were lost in a sea of colorful, distracting slot machines. Every one of them had flashing lights; loud, catchy melodies; and inexplicable thematic designs. The overall effect was engineered to make people forget they were funneling money into a metal box.

Patrons sat at several of the machines, their eyes glazed as they pressed buttons and watched the distracting video screens. Not one of them looked up as the children passed.

"It's like Day of the Living Dead," Owen said.

"Your analogy is apt." Perry's voice was unusually bitter. "When I was younger, my dad would bring me to these places on weekends. I was made to stay in the car and read while he went in to 'drop a few coins.'" She frowned, remembering. "Sometimes it'd be six or seven hours before he came back."

"Jeez," said Owen sympathetically. "How'd you go the bathroom?"

"I learned to control it. Also, on the plus side, I learned French in under—"

Trish suddenly grabbed her arm, cutting her off. "Enough Flashback Friday. Goon at three o'clock." When the other two looked around in confusion, the seneschal gave up and pointed. Two rows over, a muscular security guard in a suit pressed a finger to the radio receiver in his ear, then began scanning the sea of slot machines.

Owen pulled the girls behind a big blue machine that was currently unoccupied. It featured, coincidentally, a magic theme. "Welcome, wizard!" the video screen boomed, seeming to recognize a potential customer. "Come cast your spell!"

"We should get hats like that," Trish mused, studying the cartoon sorcerer's pointed cap.

"Shh," Owen said. "Maybe he didn't see us."

But as they peeked through the machines, they saw the guard touch his earbud again. He nodded and began walking directly toward them.

EVASION OF THE BODY SNATCHERS

"What the eff?" said Trish. "How'd he spot us?"

Perry pointed a finger upward. Directly overhead, a black plastic bowl was imbedded in the ceiling. In fact, there seemed to be one every ten feet. Security cameras.

"Those *cheaters*," Trish said with feeling.

"Back this way," Owen said.

He and the girls retraced their steps through the slot machines, staying low so they wouldn't be seen. None of the patrons glanced up. The kids were nearly out of the row when Owen saw two more security guards converging on them.

"We're trapped," he said.

"Says you," said Trish, her hands already karate-chopping runes in the air. "No way am I getting Tased by these nimrods again."

A blue fireball bloomed in the palm of her hand. Perry grabbed her wrist, blocking the sight with her body and extinguishing the flames with a hand motion. "We're in the middle of a public establishment in *broad daylight*. You can't use magic here."

"Psssh. Like any of these zombies will notice."

"Of course they will! Not to mention the dozens of cameras right above our heads."

"You have another bright idea how to get past three" —Trish glanced over her shoulder— "make that *four* security guards the size of gorillas?"

Her observation was correct—they were now surrounded on all sides. In less than a minute, they and the spell book would be back in the hands of Ferretti. They needed to take action, now.

"Owen, tell her," Perry said desperately. "Ms. Whitmore said it was imperative that we keep sorcery a secret."

The boy scanned the casino floor. The guards were only a few meters away now.

"Use your magic!" shouted one of the wizard slot machines. "Cast a spell!"

"Shut up!" Owen said to it. "God, I can't concentrate with these stupid—" Then he stopped himself. "Actually, follow my lead."

He jumped on top of a chair, making himself as visible as possible. "Ladies and gentlemen!" he shouted over the din of machines. One or two patrons looked up at him, annoyed. He forced himself to put on his most winning smile. "Ladies and gentlemen, your attention please. To thank you for stopping by the casino today, I and my assistants"— he yanked Perry and Trish to their feet—"will now perform for you the most amazing, the most incredible, the most **STUPEN-TASTICAL** feats . . . of . . . *magic!*"

ENCHANTING DETAILS

STUPEN-TASTICAL is a portmanteau, or a combination of two real words into a new, made-up word. Stage magic has a long tradition of using portmanteaux to impress audiences. *Alakazam, presto, open sesame, hocus pocus,* and *bibbity-bobbety-boo* are all examples.

THE SORT-OF AMAZING OWEN

He opened the spell book, tearing a random page down the middle. There was a bright purple flash, then the paper was whole again. A few people applauded politely. Several more stopped to watch the impromptu show. As Owen had suspected, the many distractions of Las Vegas made even real sorcery appear to be nothing more than a street performance.

The guards hesitated, whispering into their lapel microphones for further instructions. The boy knew he didn't have long. He ignored Perry's frantic stares and cleared his throat.

"Ladies and gentlemen, I'm not going to waste your time with a bunch of silly tricks. I'm, uh, gonna move straight to the big finish." At the other end of the gaming floor, he saw three men quickly exit a set of doors. One of them was Virgil Ferretti. He'd finally managed to get the multiplying rings off his fingers, but he did not look happy about it.

Owen placed a hand on Perry's and Trish's heads, nearly knocking them over. "Behold! I will now perform an illusion so complex, it has never before been attempted. Come closer, please." To his surprise, several of the tourists obeyed. There was now a solid buffer of patrons between the guards and the eighth graders. The young man knew they had one shot at this.

"What I am going to do now," he said, trying to keep his voice confident and strong, "is make both of my assistants *disappear*—at the same time! Right?" He said to the girls, hoping they understood.

Perry nodded, immediately forming the runes for the invisibility spell. She elbowed Trish, who quickly followed suit. Owen glanced back at Ferretti. The casino owner was only ten meters away now. His steely eyes were fixed on Owen.

The teenager looked down, seeing his friends were nearly done. He had to speed this along. "And . . . ABRACADABRA, alakazam, blah biddy blah—"

ENCHANTING
DETAILS

Though it has become something of a joke, the word ABRACADABRA actually has its origins in real spell casting. Literally meaning "I create what I speak" in Hebrew, the word was primarily used in the casting of mirages and glamours. These days, however, no sorcerer can utter it without getting a few giggles.

Owen grabbed two discarded glasses of water and dumped them on the girls' heads. In unison, they clapped and vanished.

The crowd broke into applause. The guards took a step back in shock, speaking rapidly into their mics.

An invisible hand tugged on Owen's pants. "Now what, smart guy?" Trish whispered. They were still right beside him.

"Take the book and run," Owen said out of the corner of his mouth, handing it over. It disappeared under Trish's invisible shirt. "I'll catch up with you."

The hand let go of his pants, so Owen could only assume the girls had obeyed him. Another glance told him Ferretti was now five meters away. The maze of slot machines and the gathering crowd had slowed him only slightly.

"Thank you, thank you!" the boy said, turning back to the crowd. "And now, my final piece of sorcery. But please, before I go, remember to thank your casino staff today. There are several fine men right in this crowd, in fact, who are here to keep you safe. Go ahead and thank them. I know they look scary, but it's okay. While I prepare my spell, shake the hands of these wonderful, upstanding gentlemen. Go on."

Several people in the crowd turned to do so. Burdened by the weight of social politeness, the guards had no choice but to respond. It gave Owen a moment to focus on the enchantment he needed to cast. He tried to ignore the fact that he'd never successfully pulled it off.

He swept his arms through the air. The fingers of his left hand drew one set of runes, while the fingers of his right drew another. It was difficult to keep both hands working independently of each other, but he finished with no mistakes. The eighth grader circled his arms again, beginning the second set of movements. In his peripheral vision, he could see the guards moving toward him, but he couldn't worry about that now.

He completed the second set. Now for the hard part. Owen entwined his hands, spun, and connected the whole series in his mind. His fingers tingled with magical energy. He knew he'd finally gotten the spell right. There was only one more step. He grabbed a discarded glass of water.

"Osýnileika," he breathed, and dumped it on his head.

A cold, thick substance trickled down his scalp. It quickly spread down his cheeks, nose, and lips. The guards stopped in surprise, and the crowd applauded again. It would be easy for Owen to slip out of the casino now. He hopped off the chair—

And thick, strong fingers clamped onto his shoulder. Fingers that belonged to Virgil Ferretti.

"Isn't he wonderful, folks?" the casino owner said. "But unfortunately, this young man forgot that children aren't allowed

In case it wasn't clear:
casting spells in public is NOT recommended.

on my gaming floor." He grinned. A triangle-shaped chip was missing from one of his fake front teeth.

Owen looked down. His body was still visible. Apparently, the spell had only made his head transparent. He began to form another spell—

But Ferretti wrapped his huge hand around Owen's fingers. "Ah-ah," he whispered. "I'm not falling for that again." He turned back to the crowd. "Okay, show's over! Please go and enjoy one of our other fine entertainments." He nodded for the guards to disperse the gamblers.

Owen struggled, but the big man held him tightly. The teenager could neither fight him nor cast any magic WITHOUT HIS HANDS. He had no idea how to save himself.

"Help!" a voice screamed from right beside him. Perry. She'd never left and was now doing a terrible impression of Owen. "This big man's touching me. Stranger danger, *help*!"

Several people turned to look. Whether it was a criminal instinct or some long-ingrained fear of eyewitnesses, something

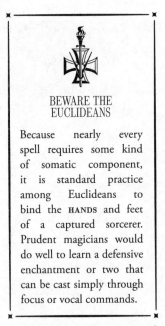

BEWARE THE EUCLIDEANS

Because nearly every spell requires some kind of somatic component, it is standard practice among Euclideans to bind the HANDS and feet of a captured sorcerer. Prudent magicians would do well to learn a defensive enchantment or two that can be cast simply through focus or vocal commands.

made Ferretti actually release Owen. He raised his hands into the air for all to see, as if to say, *See? I didn't do anything.*

Maze Runners

That moment was all they needed. "Follow me!" Owen said. He scrambled on top of the slot machines, running toward the exit. Two of the guards leapt toward him, but an invisible Trish pushed a chair into their path. Down they went, their tailored suits becoming entangled with each other.

Owen reached the end of the row and hopped down. "You guys still with me?" he said.

"Duh," Trish's voice panted beside him. "Someone's gotta make sure you don't get killed."

"Straight ahead," said Perry. "We'll cut through the gift shop."

They ran through the crowded casino, two invisible girls and a headless boy. They cut around slot machines, wove their way through the crowded gambling tables, and dodged cocktail waitresses. They were greatly aided by the fact that, when people saw a headless boy hurtling toward them, they tended to scream and get out of the way. Ferretti and his broad-shouldered guards had a more difficult time navigating the casino floor. Soon, the eighth graders had a comfortable lead on the adults.

At long last, they spotted a sign that read Street Exit. Daylight shone just beyond it. They followed the arrow, running through a gift shop filled with Las Vegas paraphernalia.

"Here," said Trish. A baseball hat floated off a rack and into Owen's outstretched hand. "This way you're not the Headless Horseman."

"We'll pay you back!" shouted Perry to the shopkeeper.

The teenager secured it on his head, now looking slightly less terrifying. They pushed their way through a big revolving door and found themselves in the midst of the **FREMONT STREET EXPERIENCE**.

The three-block area was crowded with tourists. Overhead, a 460-meter-long digital canopy projected a flashy, colorful light show. It was such an impressive display, Owen himself stopped for a moment. Perry and Trish cast off their invisibility spells, flickering back into existence. A few passersby did double takes, but thankfully no one took a picture or fainted.

"Now what?" Trish asked. "We're still in the middle of a high-speed foot chase here, remember?"

"We have to navigate a way out of this crowd," said Perry.

ENCHANTING
DETAILS

Fremont Street dates back to 1905, when the city of Las Vegas was founded. In the 1990s, a section of it was reconceived as the **FREMONT STREET EXPERIENCE**, an outdoor pedestrian mall that was part of a campaign to make Vegas more family friendly.

Examine Your Zipper

Owen scanned the street for options. Not only was it clogged with people, but also there were sales kiosks, street performers, and small carnival rides every half block. One attraction in particular caught the young man's eye—a large metal scaffold rising four stories above the crowd. The platform on top was just a few meters from the brightly flashing video canopy. But what really drew him in was the big sign at ground level that read Fremont Street Escape! A bit on the nose, perhaps, but beggars, especially outnumbered ones on the run, could not afford to be choosey.

"This way." He and the girls began threading their way through the dense crowd.

Ferretti and his guards exited the casino moments later. They saw the eighth graders retreating, and simply began shoving tourists aside to continue their pursuit.

"How will climbing to a place of no escape help us?" Perry asked when they had reached the base of the scaffold. There was a small fenced-off area right beneath it, and a sturdy metal staircase that led to the top. An instructor was showing a few people how to put on safety harnesses.

"Just follow my lead," Owen said as he hopped the fence. He immediately began running for the stairs.

"Hey!" shouted the instructor, a guy in his twenties with shaggy hair. "You can't go up there without a ticket, bro!"

The three middle schoolers ignored him and began to climb the stairs. Trish paused at the bottom, chopping a few runes in the air and extending a hand.

"*Frysta,*" she said in Icelandic. A thick white sheet of ice crystallized on the lower steps. The instructor running toward them slipped on the ice patch, landing hard on his butt and cursing.

"Toughen up!" the girl called, and continued after Owen and Perry.

By now, Ferretti had made it to the fence. He hopped over and shoved the instructor aside. The poor guy slipped again, bruising his rear a second time. Ferretti reached the staircase, hopping over the ice sheet.

Two flights above, Trish caught up to Perry and Owen. "Pick it up!" she said, pushing them in the back. "Tony Soprano's right behind me, and he looks *pissed*."

Moments later, they reached the top of the scaffold. It was a thin platform, about three meters by ten meters. Two long cables stretched off to their left, all the way down Fremont Street. The only other adornments were two dangling harness latches, obviously intended for—

"*Zip lines?!*" Perry said in terror. "That's your plan??"

"It's not like we can actually fly in front of all these people," Owen reasoned. "Grab on."

Trish was game, but Perry hung back. "We don't have safety harnesses. And I'm . . . I'm not so comfortable with heights," she confessed.

Owen looked back. Ferretti was only one story below, his powerful legs quickly moving him up the staircase. His breath whistled through the chipped hole in his veneers.

"No time to debate," Owen said. "Grab on!"

He ran forward, tugging Perry with him. She screamed, wrapping her arms around his neck. He caught hold of the harness latch, and he and Trish stepped off the platform. They shot forward just as Ferretti reached the top. The big man lunged, but his fingertips only grazed the heel of Owen's sneaker.

Then they were flying down the length of the zip line, four stories above the crowds of Fremont Street. The video display above them erupted in colorful designs. On either side, the neon lights of the casinos flashed and blazed. Perry's fearful scream became a whoop of celebration.

When in doubt, use your
surroundings to assist you.

"I stand corrected!" she shouted. "This is rather exhilarating!"

"You're—crushing—my windpipe!" Owen choked.

"Whoops! Sorry," she said, readjusting her hands.

The three of them drew near the opposite platform, four whole blocks from where they'd left Ferretti. Another zip line attendant was sitting in a chair, absorbed in his phone. He blinked in confusion when the eighth graders touched down.

"Hey," he said uselessly as Owen and the girls ran past. "Where's your . . . face?"

"Forgot about that," said Trish, tracing the runes for the undo spell. *"Annullare."*

Owen's head flickered back into being. The middle schoolers ran down the staircase, spotting a line of taxis. They hopped in the back of the closest one.

"Take us to Henderson," Owen panted. "Fast as you can, please."

War Meeting

"We're buggered," said Alec.

Owen, Perry, Trish, and the magician sat at a wooden picnic table in a small neighborhood park near Owen's house. On the taxi drive back to Henderson, the middle schoolers had called their magic trainer. They recounted the tale of their abduction, Ferretti's alliance with the Euclideans, Trish's attempted drowning, and their subsequent escape from the casino. After uttering some very colorful British swear words, he agreed to meet with them at a public place near Owen's house. Marcus Macready was at work, so Owen knew his dad was safe for the moment. For the last hour, they had been discussing battle tactics and watching the streets for approaching mercenaries.

"We still have the advantage," argued Trish. "They didn't get the spell book, and they don't know how to use sorcery."

"News flash: these men are sociopaths," Alec said. "Blokes like them steal and hurt without a care in the world for other people, don't they? They've killed people over a little bit of money. Imagine what they'll do for a bloody great **BOOK OF MAGIC**!"

"Dude," said Trish. "Can you dial it down a notch?"

ENCHANTING
DETAILS

In fact, there have been entire wars fought over **BOOKS OF MAGIC**. The Third Crusade (1189–1192 C.E.) was a religious war against Muslims, but it truly began because King Richard I wished to acquire a particularly strong codex of Coptic spells from the sultan Saladin.

"Dial it down?!" he exclaimed. "They know who you are, and they know where you live. They're probably on their way here to put our heads in a carpet bag!"

"First off: gross," said Trish. "Second: I'd like to see those non-magic-using d-bags try." She twisted her hands in the air, creating a **BLUE FIREBALL** in the palm of her hand.

"Burning the park down? Not gonna help," said Owen, grabbing her wrist. Trish grumbled, but allowed the fireball to flicker out.

"I think we need to contact the authorities," Perry said crisply. "No offense to you, Alec, but we're nowhere near learning all the spells, and it's imperative we protect ourselves. If

SORCERY FOR
BEGINNERS

Elemental spells can be combined with other enchantments to create a stronger effect, such as adding a strength spell to a wind spell to make a cyclone. Combining two elemental spells, however, is not recommended. While magic makes anything possible, the laws of nature tend to get testy when, say, FIRE and water try to inhabit the same space.

Ferretti sent men with Tasers to abduct us today, who knows what he'll send tomorrow."

"Agreed," said Alec vehemently. "I don't care if it's the local SWAT team, SEAL Team 6, or a bleeding traffic cop, but it's time to call in the professionals."

Trish folded her arms. "Assuming they believe us. What if Ferretti and the Euclideans come after us before then? How do we protect the book?"

"We don't have to hold them off forever," Owen said. "Just until the police show up. Then we give 'em the book and this whole thing is out of our hands."

The other three looked at him in surprise. "So you're just gonna give up?" demanded Trish. "Hand it over and forget sorcery exists?"

"We were kidnapped today. You were nearly drowned. Like Perry said, there's no way we can learn all these spells before they come after us again." He flipped through the book, confirming there were at least fifty spells they hadn't even attempted yet. There were also around twenty pages that were still blank. Unfortunately, the Spell to Rewrite History was among them. "We're kids, not soldiers. Maybe one of the other seventeen people who have *Sorcery for Beginners* will be able to defeat the Euclideans, but for us, it's best to hand this off to someone who can really protect it."

Perry and Alec nodded soberly, but Trish folded her arms. "And how do we know we can trust them? Ferretti's friends with the chief of police. How do we know he just won't give him the spell book?"

"Ferretti and the Euclideans have millions of dollars. Trained security guards. Weapons," Perry reminded her. "There are only four of us. Owen and Alec are right; we have to trust that law enforcement will do the right thing."

Trish opened her mouth to protest, but Alec cut her off. "It's three to one, yeah? I don't doubt your bravery, but I'm pretty sure you don't wanna die over a ruddy book."

Trish pushed away from the table and angrily went to sit on a swing. Owen took out his cell phone. "Who wants to call 9-1-1?"

EMERGENCY CONTACTS

Getting someone to help them, though, was more difficult than they expected. First, the 9-1-1 operator thought they were playing a prank. When they insisted they had been abducted and threatened by Ferretti, she informed them that, since it was not a pressing medical issue, they had to contact the Henderson police station.

She connected them, but that office had closed at 5:00 p.m. They googled more agencies until they found a twenty-four-hour police station in downtown Las Vegas. Owen had to repeat the story several more times to various officers and departments until they were finally transferred to a Lieutenant Lutian. Once more, Owen explained what had transpired, only omitting the part that the book was magic.

"I'm not sure I follow," said the police officer. "Why would this Ferretti go through all that trouble for a book? Why not just buy his own copy?"

"Because it's very rare and special . . . and does that matter? He kidnapped and Tased us," Owen tried not to yell, knowing it wouldn't help their cause. "I'm not pranking you or anything. This guy is dangerous, and we are very worried he will come after us again. Can you please send someone to arrest him?"

"I believe you, but before we can detain anyone, we need you to fill out a full statement. Can you have your parents bring you down to the station?"

Perry and Alec shook their heads. "We'd rather stay where we are and protect ourselves. Can you send someone out to my house?"

"Let me see." He heard the lieutenant tapping on her computer. "I guess I could spare . . . Yeah, we've got a black-and-white on patrol we can send around, about fifteen miles from your location. Should be there in thirty to forty minutes."

"Thank you." Owen reiterated his information, then hung up the phone in relief.

While he'd been talking, Perry and Alec had been looking through the pages of *Sorcery for Beginners*. "Look at this." The tiny girl showed the book to Owen, indicating a series of spell pages. "A whole new chapter of protection spells just appeared. It's like the book knew we needed help."

"That's kind of creepy," said Owen. "But let's see what we got."

Protection Details

"A Spell to Repel Enemies," the eighth grader read.

Alec looked over the required components. "Elk antlers . . . pearls . . . don't make it bloody easy, do they?"

"We can expand the circumference, though," said Perry, tapping the diagram. "Protect a whole house."

"We'll need a lot of animal milk for that," Owen pointed out. "We've only got about a gallon of two percent in my fridge. And where are we supposed to find elk antlers?"

"Actually," Alec sighed, "I have a box of those at the warehouse. Pearls and moonstone, too. Magic and fantasy nerds love their cheap gemstones, don't they? I could grind up the moonstone in my rock pulverizer."

"Perfect," Perry said. "But we should have some secondary protections in place, as well."

They flipped through the rest of the new chapter. There was an enchantment that could detect impending danger, one that could create a mirror image of the caster for a short time, and the aforementioned Spell to **STOP TIME**. One glance told Owen it was even more complicated than the Spell to Repel Enemies.

SORCERY FOR
BEGINNERS

Enchantments that profess to alter time do not actually affect the **FLOW OF TIME** itself. Rather, they create a bubble inside the time stream, in which a person, object, or even a small village may move at a different speed. So time creeps on its petty pace for all involved; it is simply perceived in different ways.

A Spell to Repel Enemies

Siblings getting into all your private things? Parents nagging you to finish your homework? Enemies laying siege to your ancestral keep? Worry no longer. Once you've **drawn this protective circle** around yourself, **no one wishing you harm will be able to enter.**

It's extremely time-consuming, but worth it.

COMPONENTS NEEDED:

- essence of **moonstone** -
- **charged pearls {4}** -
- unpasteurized **animal milk** -
- **elk** or **deer antlers** -
- **chalk** -
- **quartz** or **mica** dust -

STEP ONE:

Cast a **Spell to Increase the Potency of Magic** over the assembled components.

STEP TWO:

Using the chalk, **draw a circle** of desired circumference. Use a protractor if needed.

STEP THREE:

Sprinkle the essence of **moonstone** evenly in the chalk border.

STEP FOUR:

Place one charged pearl at each of the **magnetic poles.**

STEP FIVE:

Using the antlers, **draw the following diagram** inside the chalk circle, making sure to **position the lunar symbols** to reflect the time of year:

continued on next page

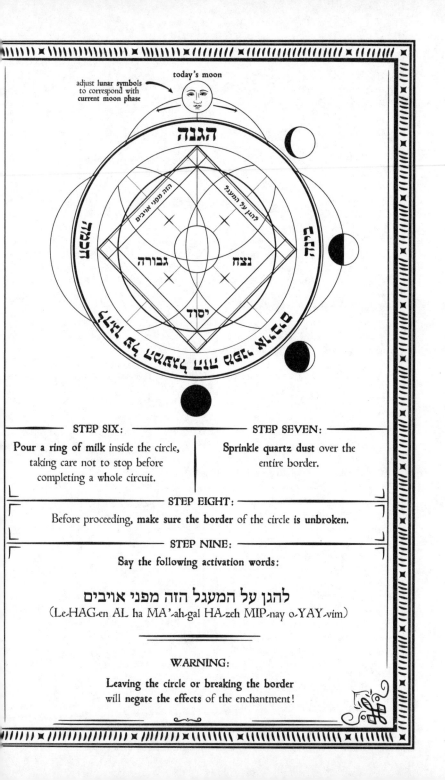

adjust lunar symbols to correspond with current moon phase

today's moon

הגנה

הזה מפני אויבים

להגן על המעגל

נצח   גבורה

יסוד

להגן על המעגל הזה מפני אויבים

STEP SIX:

Pour a ring of milk inside the circle, taking care not to stop before completing a whole circuit.

STEP SEVEN:

Sprinkle quartz dust over the entire border.

STEP EIGHT:

Before proceeding, **make sure the border** of the circle **is unbroken.**

STEP NINE:

Say the following activation words:

להגן על המעגל הזה מפני אויבים
(Le-HAG-en AL ha MA'-ah-gal HA-zeh MIP-nay o-YAY-vim)

WARNING:

Leaving the circle or breaking the border will **negate the effects** of the enchantment!

Trish leaned forward, though. Once they had discovered the new spells, she left her swing and rejoined them. "Yaaaassss. If we're stuck playing defense, at least we get to do it *Matrix*-style."

"Maybe *you* can," Owen said. "There's no way I'm gonna be able to cast any of these."

"We'll work together, dummy." She punched him in the shoulder, nearly knocking him over.

"And it's just a precaution," said Perry. "Hopefully, the police will get to your house before we have to use any of this. Alec, if you could go get the moonstones and whatever else we need, we'll go to Owen's and set up our defenses. Owen, your dad probably won't let us spend the night, right?"

The young man turned a little red at her suggestion. But he cleared his throat. "Um, well—would your mom let me spend the night at *your* place?"

"Of course not," the tiny girl said matter-of-factly. "So we only have a couple hours to prepare."

DOME SWEET DOME

Alec drove the kids to Owen's house in his white van. It was dinnertime, so the street was quiet. The sun hung just above the western hills of Las Vegas, painting the sidewalks a cheery orange.

"Looks clear," said Trish, jumping out of the van. "Maybe all our awesome spell casting scared the Euclideans off."

Perry was more cautious. "Or maybe they're regrouping for a counterattack."

"Then let's set up our defenses," said Owen. Once they made sure his house was empty, they waved good-bye to Alec and began prepping their spells of protection.

When Alec returned from his warehouse ninety minutes later, though, the police had still not arrived. They gathered in Owen's finished basement, where there was furniture, a pool table, and relative privacy for casting spells. At the magician's insistence, the middle schoolers called the station but were told that Lieutenant Lutian had gone home for a family emergency.

"What about the officers who were on their way over?" demanded Owen.

"They were reassigned," said the new lieutenant, a gruff man with a nasal voice. "And your case was officially ruled a prank. Unless you kids want to be brought up on charges, I'd stop calling this department."

Owen cursed. "The Euclideans got to you, didn't they? Did they blackmail you? Or did they just cut checks to the whole police force?"

"Better watch your mouth, sonny. From what I read in your report, it sounds like Mr. Ferretti let you kids off easy. I wouldn't push your luck." Then he hung up.

Owen stared down at his phone. He knew, of course, that a small number of police officers had been known to break the law, but it was still shocking to see it play out before him.

"Did I mention we're buggered?" asked Alec. "Because we are. We're buggered."

Even Trish was taken aback by this turn of events, but Perry kept her head. "Our plan is still sound. First thing tomorrow, we take this book straight to the Henderson police department."

"What good will that do?" said Trish. "The cops just hung us out to dry!"

"There are thousands of police officers in Las Vegas. They can't *all* be on the Euclideans' payroll."

Owen nodded. "We go there in person, prove the book works, then refuse to leave until one of 'em helps us out."

"They don't open for another thirteen hours, though," Alec reminded them. "What exactly do we do until then?"

"Protect ourselves," Owen replied. In fact, they had already managed to make some progress on that front since the magician had gone to gather supplies. As usual, Perry had proved the quickest study, unraveling the complicated steps and timing of the protection spell, while Owen relegated himself to rounding up and organizing what spell components he had.

Trish, meanwhile, had decided to tackle the time-stopping enchantment. She complained loudly and often about how infuriating it was, but had kept pushing forward in her steady, bulldozer-like way. Just before Alec returned, she had managed to enchant the grains of sand in a ninety-second **BOGGLE TIMER**.

Time enchantments on TIMEPIECES are actually quite a clever way to keep track of how much of the spell's energy a sorcerer has used. Just make sure to choose something fairly reliable—spell casters who have enchanted sundials found themselves unable to use them in the middle of the night.

SORCERY FOR BEGINNERS

"It's a limited-use item," she told them all. "But it works. Check it." She turned the timer upside down. In the space of an eye blink, the furniture of the basement was rearranged and the billiard balls spelled out a vulgar word on the pool table felt.

"Trish!" Perry admonished her. "We need to save that for the Euclideans."

The big girl rolled her eyes. "Calm down, Mom. We still have seventy-eight seconds of freeze time left. Be lucky I didn't pants you."

Alec stepped between them. "Before we get to that, maybe you lot can help me with the heavy stuff."

The four of them trooped out to the magician's white van, scanning the street for any strange vehicles. "Feast your eyes," Alec said, opening the back of his van to reveal bags of gem dust, antlers, and various spell ephemera. "Got everything we need, plus a bit extra. But let's try to move things along, yeah? The protection spell's gonna take a while, and I don't want Owen's dad to come home from work to find a weird adult skulking about the house."

The spell did take a while, but after seventy-five minutes of painstakingly surrounding Owen's entire house with a circle of chalk, sprinkling that perimeter with moonstone dust, and figuring out the position of key constellations in the night sky, the only step that remained was to invoke it. The incantation was written in **HEBREW**, but as always, *Sorcery for Beginners* provided a helpful phonetic pronunciation.

ENCHANTING
DETAILS

There is a whole subset of Jewish mysticism, known as Practical Kabbalah, which concerns the use of magic. It is strongly limited to so-called "white magic," such as HEBREW spells of healing, protection, and the well-known golem, which is a figure made of clay that can be brought to life to do a sorcerer's bidding. Unfortunately, once a creature has life, it begins to get its own ideas about how it should spend its time.

After some quick calculations by Perry, they found the center of the circle in the living room, and the three teenagers held hands. It was almost time for Perry and Trish to head home, so they needed this to succeed.

"Ready?" Alec asked them. "Repeat after me: מפני אויבים להגן על המעגל הזה."

"להגן על המעגל הזה מפני אויבים," said the teenagers.

"להגן על המעגל הזה מפני אויבים," he repeated.

"להגן על המעגל הזה מפני אויבים," they echoed. He gestured for them to continue. Owen and the girls closed their eyes, envisioning a clear, impenetrable dome descending over the house. A few repetitions later, and a shudder vibrated through the floor. The eighth graders broke off.

"Was that it? Did it work?" Trish asked.

They went outside to check, walking to the chalk border. The moonstone dust sparkled in the moonlight. Alec extended a toe past the line of protection. When it encountered no resistance, he hopped over, taking care to not disturb the diagram.

"Only one way to test it," said Owen. He tossed Perry a yellow Wiffle bat. "Try to hit me."

The tiny girl raised her eyebrows, but hefted the plastic cudgel. She reared back, swung it at Owen's arm—

And stopped about ten centimeters from his torso. The Wiffle bat was clearly over the chalk line.

"All that work," moaned Trish. "I can't do any more ASTRONOMY CALCULATIONS tonight."

"Maybe it knows you're not an enemy?" Owen guessed.

"Allow me," said Alec. He took the bat from Perry, making eye contact with Owen. "Don't take this the wrong way, mate."

Then he swung the bat at the eighth grader's face. Unlike Perry, though, the magician didn't hold back. Owen threw up his arms to protect himself—

And there was a low *clang*, like the strike of a massive gong. The Wiffle bat had rebounded off the invisible barrier. A translucent purple ring spread out from the point of contact like ripples in a pond. Alec's arms were still shaking from the impact.

"Cool," said Owen. He hopped across the border, and they took turns swinging the bat at each other's faces. Each time, it was stopped by the protective spell. They switched to thrown objects—balls, bricks, Marcus Macready's golf clubs—Owen even launched himself at the girls, elbow extended. Each time,

SORCERY FOR
BEGINNERS

Occasionally spells will require you to calculate where constellations or ASTRONOMICAL bodies are in relation to your current global position. There are charts on the Internet to assist with this, but there's no real substitute for waiting until the sun goes down and looking into the night sky.

the attacking object was repelled as if it had struck a thick trampoline.

"You think it'll stop bullets?" Trish asked breathlessly. She'd just done a flying kick at the barrier and been knocked on her butt.

"Let's hope we don't have to find out," said Alec. He turned to Owen. "Well, looks like you're buttoned up, mate. Now we gotta go do the same thing to the girls' houses before their parents get home."

They began to pack up their gear. "We'll be back first thing in the morning," Perry assured Owen. "Then we'll all go to the police together."

Trish punched him on the shoulder, grinning. "Don't look so worried, Macready. If you need rescuing, just holler."

The girls got in the van, and Alec stepped gingerly over the protective border. "I'll text you if there's a problem, yeah? In the meantime, practice your shield spell and try to get some sleep. Hopefully by breakfast tomorrow, this'll all be over."

The boy nodded. "What about you? You can't cast any spells to protect yourself."

Alec grinned. "They don't know I'm involved, do they? You just keep practicing, mate, and don't lose sight of that book. This'll all be over soon." But as he got into his van, his smile was replaced by a worried expression. Owen opened his mouth to ask about it, but the magician shut the door of his van and drove off.

A Spell to Shield Oneself

While there are plenty of magical counterattacks and enchantments of protection one can use for defense, **sometimes the situation warrants a quick block.** This spell will **conjure a magical barrier** between your hands that **can block anything,** be it sorcerous or not. Just make sure you get the timing right.

COMPONENTS NEEDED:

– none –

SOMATIC MOVEMENTS:

do this series TWICE quickly

then this:

STEP ONE:

Perform the somatic movements as shown above.

STEP THREE:

Repeat as necessary.

STEP TWO:

Once the spell is charged, stretch out your hands and hold for two seconds, like so:

Owen went upstairs and brushed his teeth. He was too wound up to sleep, so he spent the next couple of hours working on the **SHIELD SPELL**. He would toss a tennis ball into the air, then try to put up a shield before it came back down.

SORCERY FOR
BEGINNERS

A SPELL TO SHIELD ONESELF, you'll remember, is one of the Twelve Basic Incantations. There are two drawbacks to the conjuration—the shield only lasts for a couple seconds, and it must be cast while facing forward. Yet another reason why sorcerers should never sit with their backs to a door.

After the twenty-fifth tennis ball had thumped off his skull, he decided that practice wasn't his strong suit. He hid the spell book behind his headboard and curled up in bed, keeping his eyes fixed on the window. The toll of being knocked unconscious, abducted, threatened, chased, and just plain worried finally began to catch up with him. The young man dropped into an uneasy sleep. It never occurred to him that when Ferretti's attack came, it wouldn't take the form of an explosion or a gunshot, or even a burst of magic.

Instead, it came with the sound of a doorbell.

CHAPTER 18

ARRESTED DEVELOPMENT

The doorbell rang at nine thirty the next morning. Owen, exhausted from the previous day's physical and emotional zip lines, was still in the embrace of a deep sleep and failed to notice. Neither did he stir when his father knocked on the bedroom door. It was only when Marcus entered the room and jostled his son's shoulder that the boy finally sat up.

"Hedfan," Owen BLURTED in Welsh. He'd been dreaming about flying in circles over his house. Every time he tried to land, he bounced off an invisible barrier. He was so caught up in the

SORCERY FOR BEGINNERS

Because so many spells only require hand movements and words, using magic in one's sleep can be a real danger. More than a few sorcerers have awoken to find themselves floating over a city, or encased in suffocating layers of sponge cake. To prevent these unwelcome wake-up calls, some advanced spell casters actually strap down their limbs during slumber.

dream that, for a moment, he forgot the events of the previous day. Then everything came rushing back, and he threw off his covers, fully awake and on high alert. "Is someone here?"

"Get dressed and come downstairs" was all Marcus said.

Owen peeked out the front window. A police vehicle was parked out front. He threw on some clothes, texting Trish that the cops had arrived. Then he jogged down to the kitchen.

A female police officer in her late twenties sat at the table, looking small but stern in her crisp dark blue uniform. Her blond hair was slicked back in a tight, no-nonsense bun, and there was a steaming cup of coffee in her hand.

"You must be Owen," she said, standing to shake the boy's hand. "Officer Brenda Biggs, Reno PD. Sorry about the hour; I know it's a Sunday and all."

Relief flooded through the boy. "You came," he said. "After we talked to that lieutenant last night, I was worried no one would believe us."

Officer Biggs and Marcus looked at each other. Then Owen's father pulled out a chair. "Uh, why don't you sit down, son. Officer Biggs has some questions for you."

Owen sat, forcing himself to be calm.

"So, Owen," said the woman, flipping open a notepad. "Where was your father at 12:30 p.m. on Wednesday, February twenty?"

He looked to his father in surprise. Why was she asking about Marcus? And about a day three weeks ago? His father's expression was grim, but he nodded. "It's okay. Just answer truthfully."

"I, uh . . ." Owen thought. There seemed to be no reason to lie. "He was here. And at work, I guess."

"But you don't know?"

The boy looked back to his father. "Well, if it was a Wednesday, I was at school."

"Mmm-hmm." The officer made a note on her tiny pad. "And when did you see him next?"

"Um . . . Thursday morning? He works nights."

The officer flipped her notepad shut. "Looks like our time-line matches up. Does he have someone who can watch him while you're away?" she said to Owen's father.

"I'll, uh, I can make a few calls," said Marcus.

Owen was baffled. "Where are you going? What's happening, Dad?"

Officer Biggs stood. Marcus cleared his throat. "It, um, it seems that a couple weeks ago, someone matching my description robbed a Reno casino."

"What?" Owen said. "That's impossible!"

"They have video footage that confirms it. Officer Biggs drove through the night to show it to me. I have to go with her now and get this all cleared up."

"But that's ridiculous; he—" A terrible thought occurred to Owen. "This casino, is it owned by Virgil Ferretti?" Officer Biggs shrugged, packing up her notebook. "Well, even if it isn't, this footage or whatever, it must be fake. He kidnapped me yester-day. Me and my two friends. He Tased us and tied us up!"

"Calm down, son," Marcus said. "Lying isn't gonna help me get out of this."

"I'm not lying! Call my friends; call Perry and Trish. Ask 'em; they'll tell you. You're making a mistake."

The police officer placed a hand on Marcus's shoulder and he stood. "If there's a mistake, trust me, we will figure it out. But right now, I have to take him into custody."

"To Reno?!" said Owen. "But that's—how far away is it?"

"Seven hours," said Officer Biggs, leading Marcus toward the front door. "Is there anyone else you need to contact?"

"No, his mother's in—she's out of the picture." Marcus turned to his son. "Owen, just stay calm. There's food in the fridge and the emergency numbers are in your phone. I'll get someone to come over tonight. This'll all be over soon."

"No, it won't! This Ferretti guy, he wants a book I bought. It's like a how-to manual for magic that actually . . ." He trailed off, realizing the only thing he needed to complete his crazy story was a tinfoil sorcerer's hat.

The two adults didn't even break stride. Officer Biggs opened the front door, marching Marcus down the driveway. Owen watched, helpless, as his father was loaded into the backseat of a Reno squad car. Marcus Macready lifted a hand, and then the vehicle drove away.

Directly behind it was a familiar-looking black Mercedes town car. Its rear door opened and out stepped Virgil Ferretti.

BREAKFAST ORDERS

"Morning, kid," he said with a wave. Kiraz nodded imperiously from the front passenger seat. "Looks like Daddy's on the wrong side of Johnny Law. And it's not even ten o'clock yet." He smiled, showing his cracked tooth had been fixed sometime in the last eighteen hours.

"What do you want?" Owen said.

"Seriously? All the questions you could ask right now, and you go for the one you already know the answer to." Ferretti shook his head. "You wanna be boring? Fine. You give me the spell book, and I'll dial up my friends in Reno. Get this egregious error with your pops all tidied up."

Anger bubbled inside Owen like a boiling cauldron. Ferretti had attacked, all right, but he'd used the most benign, ignorant pawn possible. Officer Biggs didn't even know she was being used, so she'd been able to cross the protection barrier. She probably even thought her actions were *helping* Owen.

"Wouldn't think too hard," the big man said. "It's a long drive back."

Still, the boy did not respond.

"You want me to sweeten the deal?" asked Ferretti. "Okay. You don't give me the book, and you're the next one that gets arrested. I got two witnesses who'll testify *you* stole that book from *me*. I got video footage of you running out of my casino. And I got friends in the department. The same friends who put your little kidnapping call last night down as a prank."

Ferretti's ten steps ahead of us, Owen realized. *He spent every minute of the last eighteen hours preparing to steal back the spell book. All I did was put a circle of chalk around my house and sleep. I didn't even* **LEARN** *the shield spell.*

He did, however, have one or two magic items in his basement.

"It's upstairs," he said, attempting to look defeated. "I'll go and get it."

SORCERY FOR BEGINNERS

If you haven't noticed by now, there are no shortcuts to **LEARNING** magic. Even a well-written, easy-to-read guide such as this one still requires a certain amount of study and practice. Becoming an elite mage? That could literally take a lifetime.

"Two minutes," said Ferretti, holding up his phone. "I have the PD on speed dial."

Owen walked back inside, feeling the casino owner's eyes bore into his back like lawn darts. Once the door closed behind him, his phone buzzed with a text message from Trish: Dood, we r out back.

He went to the kitchen and opened the patio door. Trish and Perry were waiting, breathless from riding their bikes over so quickly. "Trish called me," the tiny girl explained. "Was Ferretti able to cross the protective circle? And where are the police you texted us about?"

"He hasn't tried," Owen said. "And the cop, she showed up to arrest my dad. Ferretti set him up somehow. Now he says if I don't give him the book, they're gonna take me in, too."

❋   ✳

Perry raised her eyebrows, impressed. "On some level, you have to admire him. He's evil, but very well prepared."

"He's a black-hearted, unchivalrous *cheater*," said Trish. "Ten seconds with him on the field in single combat, that's all I want."

"Later," said Owen. "What do we do now?"

"Well, you can't give him the book," Perry said crisply.

"You think?" the boy snapped. "But if I go to kid prison, they can take as long as they want to look for it."

Trish cracked her sizable knuckles. "Let 'em try. We can **HOLD 'EM OFF** as long as we need to."

"Or we could try to destroy it somehow," Perry said. "If we do it right in front of him, then nobody will have it."

"But then what happens to my dad? To us?" Owen's thoughts were racing. "Ferretti won't stop until he gets what he wants. So let's give it to him."

He briefly outlined a plan that had been forming in his mind over the last few seconds. Once they all agreed, he ripped the duplication spell page out of *Sorcery for Beginners* and then placed the book on top of it. The three of them stood in a circle around the magic help guide.

"Αντίγραφο," they said in unison.

ENCHANTING DETAILS

The longest magical fight in history took place on the island of Crete. From 1648–1669 C.E., Venetian sorcerers prevented sixty thousand Ottoman troops from entering the city of Candia by casting a variety of protection spells, glamours, and wards. The city eventually fell due to the loss of a warship and low supplies. Even the best magicians need to eat.

THE CLONE WARS

A minute later, Owen opened the front door. *Sorcery for Beginners* was clutched tightly in his hands. Perry and Trish stood behind him. Virgil Ferretti smiled when he saw them.

"We'll give you the book," said Owen. "But after that, we're done. You bring my dad back, and I don't want you bothering any of us ever again."

The casino owner held out a hand. "First let me inspect the goods."

Owen walked to the edge of the protective circle and tossed the spell book into the middle of the street. Ferretti didn't even bother to pick it up. Instead, he motioned to the black Mercedes. Kiraz got out, pulling a tall, too-skinny man stringy gray hair from the back. The man blinked in the sunlight. He looked as if he'd been living underground for years. His skin was red and tender, as if he'd recently been power-washed. His mouth was gagged and his hands were locked in a sturdy steel box stamped with the **EUCLIDEAN LOGO.**

Kiraz removed the gag and steel box, and the Thin Man shuffled to pick up *Sorcery for Beginners.* He timidly stroked the cover, as if handling a small, fragile animal. Kiraz

BEWARE THE EUCLIDEANS

As in any war, there have been prisoners taken on both sides of our centuries-long conflict. When sorcerers capture a EUCLIDEAN, they use magical means to erase their memories after interrogation. Our enemies are not so kind. Sorcerers have been held captive for years, tortured for information, even experimented upon like animals.

handed him a jeweler's eyepiece, over which the Thin Man muttered a few words before fitting it to his eye. He opened the spell book, flipped through a few eyepiece filters, then slowly shook his head.

"Shoot. They know it's a copy," said Owen.

"No," said Trish. "That was such a good idea!"

Ferretti smacked the spell book out of the man's hand. He gestured toward Owen's house. The teenagers couldn't hear what he was saying, but the big man was clearly angry.

The Thin Man again shook his head. He tried to explain something, miming a circle with his bony hands, but Ferretti rudely shoved him aside. He strode toward the house. His rage was so malevolent, the teenagers instinctively shrank backward.

Then Ferretti hit the **PROTECTIVE BARRIER**. He stumbled backward as if he'd run into a brick wall. Seeing the chalk outline at his feet, he tried to kick but found his feet were blocked in a similar manner.

Ferretti barked out a disbelieving laugh. "You see?" he said to no one in particular. "You see what I'm dealing with here? Tell him to knock it down," he ordered Kiraz.

"The thing is, uh, this diagram. This diagram is like nothing I've seen," the man said in a high, reedy voice.

SORCERY FOR BEGINNERS

The best aspect of **PROTECTION SPELLS** is that they are effective against any enemy, no matter the level of magic mastery. However, the more experienced a mage is, the more likely they will know of alternate ways to circumvent such enchantments.

"You want 'em to toss you right back to where you came from?" Ferretti roared. "No? Then knock it down. NOW."

The Thin Man licked his lips. He nodded and shook his head several times, muttering to himself as if having an internal argument. Then he began moving his hands through the air. His fingers and arms were tattooed with runes. The Thin Man's long, pale digits traced symbols the teenagers immediately recognized.

"He's a sorcerer," Perry said. "An *adult* sorcerer. Where did Ferretti locate a real ADULT SORCERER?"

"You ask me, it looks like the Euclideans have been keeping him prisoner," said Trish grimly.

As if hearing them, the casino owner stepped forward. "You like my new hire, kids? Another perk from our Euclidean buddies. Helped us clean up that replicating ring problem you almost destroyed my casino with yesterday. Now he's gonna help me get past whatever this is. Then we're gonna find the real book and take it."

Trish made a few hand motions, conjuring a ball of electricity in her hand. "You try it, Baldy, and you're gonna regret it."

Ferretti sneered. "Watch it, Mouthy. You're not the only one with magic on your side now."

SORCERY FOR BEGINNERS

As has been mentioned earlier, there are around 425 ADULT SORCERERS in the world, but each of them learned to cast spells as children. Unfortunately, those who do not keep up with the training soon find themselves forgetting how to use their abilities.

At that moment, the Thin Man placed a hand under his chin and blew. A small but strong funnel of wind spiraled from his mouth. It made contact with the chalk circle. The border held at first, but the mag-ically amplified wind kept pressing on the invisible wall, soon blowing away the runes and moonstone dust. It was a simple thing, but effective.

Seasoned sorcerers can draw upon both spell knowledge and life experience.

"Oh no," Perry wailed. "It's not an attack—it's a conjur-ing spell. The circle's only designed to protect us from enemies, not weather."

The chalk ring was severed. Purple energy flickered all over the transparent dome, then vanished with a low *thrum*. Ferretti extended a hand over the chalk border and grinned.

The circle of protection was **BROKEN**.

ENCHANTING DETAILS

One of the most well-known examples of BREAKING a protective barrier occurred during the battle of Jericho, and has been catalogued in the Bible's Book of Joshua. According to legend, the walls of Jericho were impenetrable. But Joshua's army marched seven times around the city, blowing an enchanted ram's horn at the end, and as it says in the song, the walls came tumbling down.

Chapter 19

FREEZE TAG

Virgil Ferretti strode up the driveway. His powerful frame was evident even underneath the layers of his cream-colored suit. "There are no rules anymore, kids. Just people who have access to magic, and those who don't."

He pulled an object from his pocket. Even from three meters away, the kids could see it was a snub-nosed revolver. "He has a gun," Perry said, her voice shaking. "Owen, he has a real gun!"

The boy didn't wait for the man to aim it. He reached into his pocket and pulled out the Boggle timer Trish had enchanted. Then, making sure his friends were **WITHIN A METER**, he turned it upside down.

SORCERY FOR BEGINNERS

This particular time enchantment creates a sphere with a radius of three **METERS**, inside of which anything and anyone will be able to move normally, while the rest of the universe is frozen. As such, it is not recommended for large groups.

Everything around them **FROZE**. Ferretti was caught in mid-step, his tanned, meaty hand in the process of raising the pistol. Behind him, the Thin Man stood like an emaciated scarecrow and Kiraz scowled. Across the street, two ravens were paused in mid-flight.

The weirdest part was the silence. No birds called to each other, no cars sped down the distant freeway, not even a rustle of wind blew past. The lack of sound was deafening.

The three teenagers looked at one another. "It worked," said Owen, wincing as his voice broke the quiet.

ENCHANTING DETAILS

Using magic is not the only way to affect the flow of TIME. Scientists have proven that our perception of time can be greatly affected by our experiences. Traumatic, scary, or boring events seem to slow time down, while happy experiences seem to go by too quickly. Some have even speculated that the afterlife is nothing more than our final moment of perception, stretched out to an infinite length. It's a nice idea, unless your last moment is, say, being eaten by a school of piranha.

"Do I know how to enchant something?" said Trish with a smile. "Or do I know how to—"

"We have less than seventy-eight seconds to get out of here," Perry reminded them. "Let's not waste it gloating."

Staying tightly together, they grabbed their bikes off the porch. Moving through the thick, still air was difficult, akin to walking through a heavy snowdrift. It even took an effort for Owen to shoulder the backpack that held the real *Sorcery for Beginners*.

"Better grab this," said Owen, trying to pull the revolver from Ferretti's hand. But whether it was some aspect of **FROZEN TIME** or whether the man's grip was that strong, the gun did not come away easily. Owen tried to yank it out with both hands, and when that failed, he braced a foot on the casino owner's thigh. He then gave a mighty tug.

SORCERY FOR BEGINNERS

FREEZING TIME turns people quite literally into statues. While this makes them easier to avoid, moving or changing the position of a full-grown adult is like trying to adjust a six-foot-tall, ninety-one-kilogram stone sculpture. It is best undertaken with power tools and furniture dollies.

There was a sharp, crisp *snap*, akin to a twig breaking, and the revolver came free, tumbling into a shrub. Owen stumbled backward, noticing Ferretti's index finger was now pointed at an unnatural angle. Before he could fully parse what that meant, his butt connected with the concrete driveway. The Boggle timer fell from his pocket, and the enchanted sand stopped flowing.

Time, and sound, resumed.

Ferretti immediately grabbed his broken finger, screaming in rage and pain. He saw his gun was gone, and Owen sitting on the ground a few feet from him. It didn't take an Einstein-sized intellect to deduce who had done this to him.

He leapt for the boy, his big hands extended.

Owen shielded his face—

And once again, time froze.

The casino owner was stopped just over three meters from him, his hands outstretched and his face twisted into a mask of rage and desire. Perry and Trish stood just behind Owen, the Boggle timer in Trish's hand.

"From now on, let's try not to lose the enchanted object, huh?" suggested the seneschal.

"Thanks," Owen said as he got to his feet. "I didn't know it would be so hard to get the gun away from him."

"Explanations later," said Perry quickly. "Since we are literally on a ticking clock."

"Right," remembered Owen. "I had an idea about that."

He took the timer from Trish and held it sideways, so the flow of sand slowed but didn't stop. Ferretti began to move forward in slow motion. His eyes swiveled toward the teenagers, facial muscles very slowly forming an expression of surprise at what, to him, was their bizarre, sped-up behavior. But by slowing time instead of stopping it entirely, Owen gave them a large enough window to collect their things and mount their bikes.

"I'll ride with you," Perry said to Owen. She stepped onto the pegs jutting from his rear wheel, hooking her arms through the straps of his backpack for balance. Despite the situation, the young man felt himself blushing at her close contact. "We'll need someone in a position to cast spells."

"And why should it be you?" Trish demanded.

"Because I'm the best spell caster and the worst bike rider," the tiny girl explained matter-of-factly, securing her purple glasses. "And we don't have time to dither."

Owen and Trish started to pump the pedals of their bicycles. Riding through the still, slow air was even more difficult than walking through it. But they fought through the resistance, and soon built up a bit of forward momentum. Once they were a few houses down the block, Owen again turned the timer in his pocket upright. He thought saving a few seconds of freeze time might come in handy. He and Trish shot forward, the change in speed nearly causing them to spill.

Behind them, Ferretti tumbled to the grass. But the big man quickly recovered, getting to his feet. The cheerless, animal grin returned to his face. He ran back toward his car, pulling the Thin Man and Kiraz with him. The Mercedes leapt forward, leaving behind a strip of burned rubber.

A SUNDAY DRIVE

"Here they come!" Perry called.

The sunroof of Ferretti's car opened. The Thin Man stood up, his stringy gray hair streaming from his head like the tail of comet. He looked almost giddy as his long fingers began to twist through the air.

Perry watched him, puzzled. "It looks like he's casting a—turn left!" she suddenly screamed.

Trish and Owen obeyed, just as the Thin Man thrust a hand forward. A GREEN FIREBALL left his hand, blowing up a wooden mailbox that stood right where Owen's head had been.

"These guys are serious!" Trish shouted.

"The golf course," Owen said between panted breaths.

Elemental spells can take on different COLORS depending on the caster. Some have speculated this is a reflection of the magician's diet, their mood at the time of casting, or even their spiritual aura. Whatever the cause, knowing your personal hue is key, lest you conjure anything that clashes with your outfit.

SORCERY FOR
BEGINNERS

The teenagers cut through a set of backyards. Two streets over, an eighteen-hole golf course bordered one side of the subdivision. It was a strange sight in the middle of the arid landscape—lush green fairways, perfectly manicured, surrounded on every side by parched brown desert.

Owen and Trish pedaled toward the boundary fence. Whoever was driving Ferretti's town car had no qualms about following them through private yards. The Mercedes drove right over grassy lawns, turfing flower beds and crushing the occasional child's toy. Within seconds, it was less than two meters from the teenagers. The Thin Man twisted his hands, muttering as he prepared another spell.

"They're gonna run us down!" yelled Trish.

"I have an idea!" Perry shouted back. She spun her wrist, crooked her fingers, and said in Czech: *"Otevřít!"*

The unlocking spell caused the town car's front HOOD to pop open. The metal covering shot upward, effectively blocking the windshield. The vehicle swerved, skidded across the grass, and came to stop.

Blondie got out of the driver's seat and slammed the hood back down. His eyes, which Owen had magically sealed shut

SORCERY FOR BEGINNERS

Creativity can be one of the most useful tools in a sorcerer's arsenal. Using a simple spell in an unexpected way, such as Perry unlocking the car HOOD to block their vision, is often better than casting a stronger, more complicated enchantment.

the day before, were still red and puffy from where they'd been lasered open. He appeared to be none too pleased about his new look.

"Pedal faster," advised Perry.

Owen and Trish complied. The golf course stood just ahead, two fairways stretching off to either side. Despite the heat, there were several golfers on each hole.

"Which way's . . . the station?" Owen gasped, wiping sweat from his eyes.

Trish checked her iPhone. A blue line traced the shortest route from Owen's house to the Henderson police station. It was only one and a half miles away, but between them and their goal was the Dragonridge Country Club, the 215 freeway, and a snarl of twisty residential streets.

"Northwest," Trish panted. "But first we gotta get through the golf course."

Fore!

They coasted down a gravelly hill, pedaling through an open gate in the fence and onto the eleventh-hole fairway. It was much easier biking over the close-cropped grass than it was navigating the backyards. For a moment, Owen actually thought they'd lost Ferretti.

Then the black town car crested the hill and accelerated onto the golf course. Chunks of turf flew up from the manicured fairway.

"The golfers are not gonna like that," Trish commented.

The Thin Man stood in the open sunroof, his eyes closed as he prepared a new spell. Spittle flew from his lips as he whispered the incantation over and over. Whatever magic he was preparing, it was powerful. He thrust out a skeletal hand.

A pillar of hard sandstone burst from the ground just in front of Owen. He swerved, barely missing the obstacle.

"He's using EARTH ELEMENTAL ATTACKS," Perry informed them.

EARTH ELEMENTAL ATTACKS work by summoning swaths of the surrounding land, then transmuting said swaths into a more weaponized substance. Changing dirt into stone is one example. Such spells are also useful for traversing dangerous areas, saving people from quicksand, and relandscaping one's backyard.

SORCERY FOR BEGINNERS

"Oh, how'd you figure that out?" Owen said sarcastically.

Again and again, the Thin Man thrust out his hands. More stone obstructions exploded from the ground. Owen and Trish slalomed through the barriers, grazing the columns of rock once or twice but managing to stay upright.

"We're getting creamed out here!" Trish shouted.

"Go toward the lake," Owen said.

In between the tenth and eleventh holes was a long, thin reservoir with a spray fountain in the center. The teenagers steered toward it. Ferretti's Mercedes followed. Nearby golfers jumped out of the way, yelling at them in annoyance.

"Perry, can you get us across?" Owen said between breaths.

The girl turned her head, taking in the approaching lake. "Give me a minute." She pulled the spell book from Owen's backpack, attempting to block out the surrounding chaos while she flipped through pages. Trish and Owen, meanwhile, pedaled hard toward the water hazard. The town car drew closer.

"You don't have a minute," Owen said. The lake was less than ten meters away.

"Got it," said Perry, quickly scanning A Spell to Increase the Potency of Magic. She took a good look at the hand positions, then stuffed the spell book back into Owen's pack. She leaned over, ripping a few hairs from Trish's scalp.

"Hey, what gives?" the big girl complained.

"Trust me, it's a compliment," said Perry. Clutching the hair and closing her eyes, the tiny girl cycled her arms through the air. Her fingers left purple trails of light.

Owen glanced back. The town car was so close now, he could see the Thin Man's bloodshot eyes. He was charging up another spell of his own.

"Anytime now!" the boy shouted. The edge of the water was a meter away.

A SPELL TO INCREASE THE POTENCY OF MAGIC

What's that you say? It's not enough to learn real, working spells; you want them to be **bigger and more impressive?**
I shouldn't be surprised—it seems like nothing is valued in the Western world unless it is the largest possible version of itself. Very well—who am I to stand in the way of a young sorcerer's greedy, ungrateful desires? With this spell, you will be able to **maximize the effects of any other spell.** Just remember: the more powerful the enchantment, the more difficult it is to control.

COMPONENTS NEEDED:

— the **hair from** any **strong animal** —
such as a bull, elephant, or lion

SOMATIC MOVEMENTS:

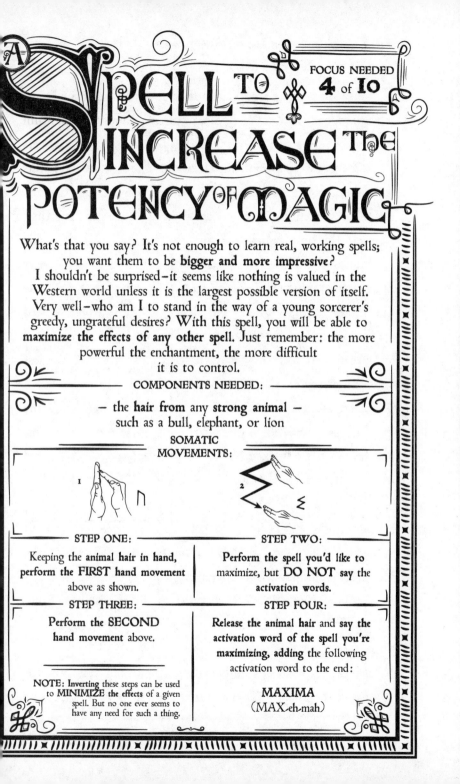

STEP ONE:

Keeping the **animal hair in hand**, perform the **FIRST** hand movement above as shown.

STEP TWO:

Perform the spell you'd like to maximize, but **DO NOT** say the **activation words.**

STEP THREE:

Perform the **SECOND** hand movement above.

STEP FOUR:

Release the **animal hair** and **say the activation word** of the spell you're maximizing, adding the following activation word to the end:

MAXIMA
(MAX-eh-mah)

NOTE: Inverting these steps can be used to **MINIMIZE** the effects of a given spell. But no one ever seems to have any need for such a thing.

Perry slipped her arms out of the backpack and turned herself around on the bike pegs. She pointed a hand right in front of them, uttering two words: *"Frysta maxima!"*

ICE CRYSTALS bloomed in the water. They spread across the thin lake, creating a narrow, frozen bridge strong enough to hold the bikes. Owen and Trish pedaled straight across, their tires slipping a bit on the slick surface.

The town car's brakes squealed. The vehicle fishtailed, ripping up the close-groomed grass, but it was too late. Its rear tires hit the ice. The magically frozen water cracked, dropping the tail end of the Mercedes into the lake.

The rest of the ice broke apart just as Owen, Trish, and Perry reached the other side. They looked back, catching their breaths and laughing.

SORCERY FOR BEGINNERS

ICE is the most versatile of all the elemental states, able to form weapons, housing, bandages, even armor if need be. Underclothing is recommended if creating the latter, otherwise the benefits of protection may be overwhelmed by the side effects of frostbite or hypothermia.

"Good job, Perry," said Owen appreciatively. The tiny girl met his eyes and looked away, smiling but embarrassed.

"*Ice* try, dum-dums!" Trish called to their pursuers. Both Perry and Owen gave her a withering glance deserving of such a pun. "Come on, that was a solid burn."

But Ferretti and the others weren't finished yet. Blondie gunned the engine, rolling the car back and forth until they were out of the reservoir. The town car might have to drive the long way around, but it would still reach the teenagers in minutes.

"Man, do I hate this guy," Trish said with feeling.

Goin' Biking on the Freeway

Owen double-checked Trish's phone. The police station was only half a mile away, but the 215 still lay between them. The map program wanted them to bike a half mile west to a pedestrian bridge, but if they did that, Ferretti would easily catch up to them. If they went straight across the freeway, however, there was a chance they could reach the station before the casino owner. The only problem was the endless river of speeding cars that separated them from their goal.

"Let's go," Owen said.

Within a few minutes, they had reached the 215 on-ramp. Cars whizzed past at 112 kilometers per hour (roughly seventy miles per hour for any American readers) on both sides.

"Um, Owen?" said Perry. "Tell me you're not doing what I think you're doing."

"It's just a few feet to the other side," he yelled over the noise of the cars. "If we can get there before Ferretti shows up, he'll have to drive down to the next on-ramp and all the way back. I've got a couple seconds of sand left in the timer. We'll slow the traffic down and go for it."

Trish grinned. "Kick-ass."

Perry glanced back, seeing the Mercedes was less than two blocks away. "It would appear we have no choice."

They faced the freeway, and Owen turned the timer sideways.

The speeding cars slowed to blurry, snail-paced blobs. The sudden shift in sound was louder than a shotgun blast. The teenagers pumped the pedals, working hard to build up speed in the thick, still air. Their legs burned as if they were biking up a steep, muddy hill, but they soon reached the freeway's concrete median.

They heaved their bikes over the barrier and resumed their seats. Perry stood on Owen's pegs, her hands around his waist. They had just begun to pedal when the LAST GRAINS OF ENCHANTED SAND fell.

The world resumed. Sound exploded like a nuclear detonation. Cars that had been slow-moving blurs were now whipping past on either side of them. Horns blared. The resulting gusts of wind nearly knocked them flat.

"Now what?!" Perry yelled.

Owen looked back at the on-ramp. Ferretti's town car was already there, having seen them ride onto the freeway. The casino owner pointed at the boy from a back window. His Mercedes accelerated, beginning to merge across the four lanes of traffic. Once they reached the median, Ferretti and his hostage sorcerer

---

SORCERY FOR
BEGINNERS

There are obvious pros and cons to using ENCHANTED OBJECTS. On the upside, an object does not require any memorization or casting effort. On the downside, it can be used by non-sorcerers, become misplaced/stolen, or, as we see here, simply be used up at a critical moment.

could simply run up the concrete lane to them. Owen figured they had a minute at most to reach the other side.

"We have to keep going," he said.

"What?!" said Perry. "Those cars are going seventy miles an hour."

"They'll stop for us," the boy said firmly.

Slowly, he pushed his bike forward, desperately waving a hand. It took a few moments, but one by one, the oncoming cars began to stop so they could cross. It did not prevent several of them from using their horns.

"Sorry! Sorry," Owen said as they began to push their bikes across the now-clear freeway. Once they reached the other side, there would be no way Ferretti could follow them. They'd have plenty of time to reach the police station, prove to the cops that sorcery worked, and this would all—

The sound of screeching tires cut through his thoughts.

The world slowed, but this time it was not the result of any spell. It was the boy's own heightened senses, which had alerted him to the small but important detail—a 1,360-kilogram car was heading straight for them. The driver, who was texting on her phone, had failed to notice every other vehicle on the freeway was stopped until one second before. She stomped on her brake pedal and began to skid on melted rubber toward the eighth graders.

Owen could tell she was going to hit them. His survival instinct kicked in, and he ran forward, pulling Perry along with him.

Trish obeyed a different call. She dropped her bike and faced the oncoming automobile. Her hands and fingers chopped through the air. Then she sank to her knees, spreading her arms as if pulling a piece of taffy. A sparkling gold, translucent oval stretched between her fingers. The shield spell.

Her timing was not a millisecond too soon. Immediately after she cast it, the car collided with the golden barrier. Its front bumper flattened as if striking a steel wall. The headlight shattered and momentum spun the vehicle sideways. Its rear tires lifted off the ground, then came back to earth and shuddered to a stop ten meters away.

Spell casting under this kind of pressure
shows the spirit of a true sorcerer.

"Whoa," breathed Trish. She stood, grinning at Owen and Perry. "Did you guys see that? I just beat up a speeding—"

SCREEEECH. A high-pitched squeal cut her off. All three middle schoolers swung their heads toward the sound—another oncoming car.

Trish only had time to blink before it struck her. There was a sick, heavy *thump*. Her body spun into the air, hit the concrete highway, and tumbled for three or four meters. From that moment on, she lay still.

THE HARDEST PART

There's a reason it's called a waiting room, thought Owen. *What else is there to do in a hospital? Either you're healing, you're killing time, or you're killing time while you heal.* He looked around the Henderson Hospital emergency room. *Yeah, there may be magazines to read, and a TV to watch, but let's face it—the only thing people can really do here is wait. Wait for someone to tell you how badly injured your friend is. Wait for the guilt to go away. Wait for your enemies to arrive and finish what they started.*

Perry sat beside Owen, furiously paging through the spell book and writing in one of her spiral notebooks. They had not spoken or looked at each other in two hours. That was when the paramedics had informed them that Trish's right femur was broken. The kids had told the hospital staff that they were being stalked by a group of adults, but the paramedics told them to wait (again, that word) until the police arrived to take their statements. When they asked if their friend would be okay, the eighth graders were informed that Trish had a concussion, but she should be fine.

Still, Owen was sure that Perry blamed him for Trish's injury. *How could she not?* he said to himself. *I certainly blame myself. I was the one who brought them both into this situation. I was the one who suggested we run from Ferretti, who insisted on crossing the freeway to reach the police station, who showed them the stupid spell book in the first place. And all because I wasn't skilled enough to cast a simple mending spell on a broken pencil.*

Of course Perry couldn't stand to look at him.

So while she spent the time paging through *Sorcery for Beginners*, he had been texting Alec. He told the magician what had happened with Ferretti, that Trish had broken her leg, and which hospital they were in. He asked several times what they should do next. Owen himself had no idea. Ferretti and the others had disappeared when the freeway bystanders dialed 9-1-1, but the boy knew they'd be back. Simply handing the book to the police no longer seemed the wisest course of action. The men they were up against were rich, amoral, and had a sorcerer working for them. Owen could stash *Sorcery for Beginners* on the moon, and the Euclideans would just cast a spell to bring it back. He texted this to Alec as well, but again received no reply.

Just as Owen was beginning to believe their erstwhile mentor had abandoned them, Alec walked through the hospital entrance. His face was pale and waxy and there were dark circles under his eyes. It was clear he hadn't slept the previous night.

Perry ran over and hugged him. The magician stood there for a moment in shock, then patted her briefly on the back. "Where have you been?" she demanded. "We had to evade the Euclideans by ourselves. Ferretti had a gun!"

Trish's parents looked up at this, so the magician took the two teenagers aside. "Owen told me. Incessantly and in great detail. You still got the book, then?"

"Right here," said Owen, lifting his backpack.

"Good. You need to bring it and come with me."

"What about Trish?" said Perry.

"Listen to me," said the magician. "The Euclideans didn't try anything at the freeway because there were too many witnesses, but they will come here. And if they got one **IMPRISONED SORCERER**, I'm sure they can round up more."

The girl frowned. "You two can't abscond with the book and fight them by yourselves. For starters, I'm the only one who knows how to cast any spells!"

"We're not casting spells," said Alec. "We're gonna get rid of the bloody thing once and for all."

"How?" Owen asked. "Every time Perry tried to destroy a page, it just reconstituted itself."

BEWARE THE
EUCLIDEANS

Once our enemies are aware of a magic-user's existence, they will do anything to hunt him or her down and neutralize their abilities. For many spell casters, the best way to avoid this is to cut ties with anything that might lead to them being found, such as a job, bank account, or permanent residence.

Alec nervously stroked his goatee. "Yeah, I've been mulling on that one. Veera—the neuroscientist from UNLV, you remember her—she told me about this thing called the Z Machine. Uses X-rays to create conditions of extreme pressure and temperature. We're talking up in the range of around three and a half billion degrees Fahrenheit. Now I don't understand how it works, but a temp that high is enough to melt diamonds, yeah? We chuck the book in the Z Machine, flip the switch, and kablooey. Let's see it reconstitute from that."

"What about my dad?" said Owen. "And Trish, and all of us? What'll the Euclideans do when they realize we've made it go kablooey?"

The magician met his eyes. "There are at least seventeen other copies kickin' around, right? Let 'em go after one of them."

"So we just shift this mess to someone else?" Perry shook her head. "That seems lazy. Not to mention *wrong*."

"Owen." Alec placed a hand on the young man's shoulder. The magician's eyes were filled not with accusation, but regret. "I want sorcery in my life as much as you do, mate. I do. But . . . perhaps it's better if *we're* the ones who forget about this."

Owen turned away, looking out a waiting room window. Even after everything he'd been through in the last week, now that they were talking about destroying *Sorcery for Beginners*, getting rid of it forever, he found himself hesitating.

"Couldn't we take it to the police?" Owen said desperately. "Once they see what it can do . . ."

Alec shook his head, anxiously rubbing the bone pendant around his neck. "Little problem there. I, uh, went to see my local constable this morning. The bugger tried to arrest me on sight. Some nonsense about my immigration papers being invalid. Needless to say, I pulled a few tricks and exited the premises. But the Euclideans, they've got **CONTACTS EVERYWHERE**. They will never stop hounding us until they have the book, or we prove it's gone forever."

BEWARE THE EUCLIDEANS

All authorities, be they law enforcement, government, or religious organization, are inherently distrustful of sorcerers. The centuries-long propaganda campaign of the Euclideans has seen to this, depicting spell casters as shifty, thieving murderers in league with the Devil. Granted, there have been a few like that, but there are Euclideans who fit that mold, too.

Owen bit his lip. "If we destroy it, that's it. Our chance to do something important, to be special, is gone."

The magician ran a hand through his long hair. "I know, mate. Believe me, I know it more'n most people. But sometimes, to truly protect something, you gotta make sure no one else can ever get to it."

He was right, of course. Owen knew that. But why had Whitmore shown them the door to a greater world, a magical world, if they were simply meant to slam it closed? It made no sense. But if there were any other options, he couldn't see them.

The young man stood. "Perry, could you stay here and keep an eye on Trish? When she wakes up, tell her—tell her I'm sorry."

ONCE UPON AN ALEC

"I do know how you feel," the magician said as they drove across town.

Owen did not respond. He sat in the passenger seat of the cluttered white van, numbly watching the dry desert landscape pass. They had snuck out the back entrance of the hospital and driven in circles for a while to make sure the Euclideans weren't following them. The backpack containing the spell book was clutched protectively on the eighth grader's lap.

"I might not be able to do sorcery like you lot, but I've known it was real since I was your age," Alec continued. "The stage show and the tricks I peddle in the store—those are just a way to pay rent. Real magic, that's been the focus of me whole life. Discovered it when I was fourteen. My parents were having what they called 'relationship issues,' so they shipped me off to an aunt's in CORNWALL—that's on the southern tip of England—for summer holiday. She had a creaky old cottage on the coast, filled to the brim with odds and ends. Completely bats, but a proper sorceress, she was. Practiced Wicca before it was fashionable and everything.

"Anyway, soon as I arrived, she set me to sort through all her things. Figure out what was broken, what she could sell, and so

---

ENCHANTING DETAILS

Located at the southernmost tip of Great Britain, the county of CORNWALL is bounded on three sides by water, has a population of 536,000, and is best known for its bleak coastlines, fishing, and an indoor greenhouse called the Eden Project, which resembles a housing development from a science-fiction film.

on. So one day, there I am, rummaging through the attic, when I come across this box."

A half-smile played on his face as he merged onto the freeway. "Pretty little thing. Clearly old. About the size of a jewelry box, and yay deep." He spread his hands ten centimeters apart. "It sort of vibrated when you touched it, almost like it had a pulse. Found out later it was carved from rowan wood, which is used quite a bit in magical items.

"Weird thing about this box—it had no hinges, no lock, no way of opening it at all. But there were these intricate carvings done up on the lid and the sides—runes, you'd recognize 'em as now. And

Young Alec's life would never be the same.

after, oh, half a day of banging it around, I finally realized you had to hold down a few of the symbols to open it. This hidden drawer popped out, and inside were five gold coins."

Owen frowned. "That's it? How is that magic?"

"Wait for it, yeah? At the time, England was still on the pound sterling. I couldn't very well go around slinging gold doubloons at people, so I set aside the coins for my aunt, put the box on a shelf, and moved on to other things.

"When the next day rolled around, I'd forgotten about the box entirely. I was back up in the attic, digging through this pile of creepy old tintype photos, when what should my wandering elbow bump into, but the money box. It fell to the floor, and I heard something clink inside. Now I was positive I'd taken the coins out, so I unlocked it, opened the drawer—and there were five gold coins."

He paused to let the revelation sink in. "Five *new* gold coins?" Owen asked.

"Five new ones," the magician confirmed. "Found the ones I gave her the day before in a coffee tin. Naturally, I didn't tell her straight off the box had spit out five more doubloons. First, I had to test it."

All That Glitters

Alec turned the white van off the freeway and headed east. "So over the next week, I became a right little scientist. Checked the box every half hour to see when it would produce more money, and wrote the results down on a little piece of graph paper. Five coins every twenty-four hours, it turned out. I took the box to some local pawnbrokers and had 'em estimate its age. Four hundred years old was the average, even though it looked brand-new.

"Couple weeks later, I had a stack of seventy gold coins. I knew the bloody thing was magic. Now, I wasn't the sort that good stuff generally happened to. Picked on a lot, I was. Bullied.

Bit on the tubby side. Basically, I'd stopped believing there *could* be magic in the world."

His eyes got a far-off look. "But now there it was, staring me right in the face. Proof that magic was real. That there might be something bigger out there than me."

"And here we are again," Owen said, brandishing the backpack. "You still want to throw it away?"

"Patience, mate. My inquiries about the BOX—and they were not, shall we say, discreet—they drew all kinds of folks to Cornwall that summer. Some were like me aunt, basically good people with a nose for sorcery, but others were like our Mr. Ferretti. Blokes who were out for power and didn't care what they had to do to get it."

Alec sighed. "When I finally told my aunt, she thought like you did—we could just hide the box until the bad sorts went away. So we buried it, somewhere nearby, and put out a story it'd been lost in the ocean."

Owen's hopes rose. If Alec had done something like this before, perhaps they could try it again. "And? Did it work?"

ENCHANTING DETAILS

Enchanted money BOXES, wallets, and pouches were quite the rage in the seventeenth century. Thieves and cutpurses wandered the countryside, so the prepared traveler would do well to invest in such a magic storage device. There were drawbacks, of course—the amount of cash that would spawn was usually small, and once removed, it would take at least a full day or two for the gold to reappear. Worse, if the bandits realized your billfold was bewitched, they would often kill you out of frustration.

"People like that, like the Euclideans—if they want something, they keep after it. No matter the cost to anyone." His hands gripped the wheel until his knuckles turned white. "These blokes, they found my aunt and tied her to a chair. Then they stuck burning matches under her fingernails until one of us told 'em where the box was hidden. Four matches. That's how long it took me to spill me guts."

Alec turned up a road that led to a collection of large houses overlooking the city. Owen was too caught up in the story to pay much attention. "It wasn't your fault," he said. "You were fourteen; you couldn't do anything to stop them."

"You can always do something," the magician replied. "What I did was lead these men to where we'd buried the box. I told them where to dig it up, despite my aunt's protests. And when they pulled the box from the ground, she attacked 'em."

The magician smiled sadly at the memory. "Three grown men with guns, and she threw herself at 'em like some kind of lunatic badger. They were surprised, but they got over that right quick. One of 'em took out his gun, and he shot her in the stomach."

Alec's eyes were wet, but his voice was hard and bitter. "And you know what I did? I ran. Left the box, left my aunt, bolted straight back into town and told the police everything. Course, by that time, it was too late. She ended up in a wheelchair for the rest of her life and we never saw the box again. I've been looking for it ever since."

BEWARE THE EUCLIDEANS

While there are some MAGICAL OBJECTS still left in the world, in the nineteenth century, the Euclideans began an initiative to find and eliminate all enchanted items. They were largely successful. Those that could not be destroyed were locked away, but the location of this magic hoard is one of our enemy's best-kept secrets.

Silence filled the car. After a long moment, Owen spoke. "If you knew it was the wrong thing to do, why are we doing it again? Why aren't we fighting these guys like she did?"

"I didn't say it was the wrong thing." The magician looked at him. "I said I ran. Maybe it weren't brave, but it's the reason I'm alive today. I ran, and I spent the next twenty-three years tracking down MAGICAL ITEMS and keeping them away from men like that. Life ain't the movies, mate. Heroes? Usually get killed right off. It's the cowards who make it all the way to the end."

He turned the white van into a gated driveway. An expensive camera and buzzer were imbedded in the stone wall. Beyond the tall steel bars, Owen could see a large, modern home of concrete and glass, with a perfectly manicured desert garden out front. Beyond it, the city of Las Vegas shimmered in the early afternoon heat.

"Where are we?" the young man asked. "I thought the Z Machine was at UNLV."

"Actually, that's in Albuquerque," Alec replied. "But don't worry—we're getting rid of that book before anyone else gets injured."

The gate silently opened before them. The magician drove forward into the circular stone driveway. Several polished, expensive cars were already parked in the roundabout. Owen turned to see the metal bars close behind them.

"What are you doing?" he asked Alec.

The magician turned off the car. This time, he was unable to meet the boy's eyes. "What I have to," he said quietly. "What I've done many times before. Surviving."

The front door of the house opened. Owen saw a tall, skinny man with stringy gray hair and a shorter, well-dressed man walk onto the driveway. The Thin Man and Kiraz.

Alec had driven him straight to the Euclideans.

ENTRAPMENT

Owen turned to his trainer, stunned.

"They gave me no choice, mate," Alec said. "They grabbed me last night, after I dropped the girls at their houses. Threatened to burn down me shop, you understand? Everything I have—poof. Gone. Ferretti, he just wants the book. If we give it to him, all this will go away and we can get on with our—"

The eighth grader didn't wait for him to finish. He kicked open the car door and ran for the steel gate. It had already closed, but he twisted his fingers, forming the runes he'd been struggling to learn for the past week. He didn't have time to second-guess himself or wonder if he was worthy; he simply **EXECUTED THE SPELL** and thrust his hand at the gate.

"Otevřít."

There was a loud *click*. Unfortunately, that was all that happened. The spell, you will recall, was for unlocking only, not opening.

SORCERY FOR BEGINNERS

This event illustrates why focus is so important to sorcery. Once one has learned a spell and mastered its somatic components, the only obstacle to a successful casting is the sorcerer's mental acuity. And nothing focuses the mind like a healthy dose of life-threatening danger.

Owen grabbed the thick steel bars and pulled. The gate barely moved. The boy planted his feet and pushed, but only succeeded in moving the heavy barricade a few centimeters.

Behind him, the Thin Man clucked his tongue. "Foolish fly," he said in a high, wheezy voice. "No point in flitting when the spider's web reaches everywhere."

Owen strained to push the steel gate wider. The Thin Man crooked his fingers in front of him and extended a hand. A burst of lightning shot toward the gate. Owen dove to the ground. The energy bolt sizzled past his head, singeing his hair and striking the steel bars of the barrier. They crackled with electricity. Were he to touch them now, he would become a human lightning rod.

He glanced at his pursuers and saw that Kiraz was pointing some kind of long-barreled rifle at him. Before Owen could even get to his feet, the Euclidean fired.

Again, the boy reacted. He brought his hands together, fingers forming runes. He pulled them apart—

And a long, silver tranquilizer dart bounced off the translucent, golden oval between his hands. At last, Owen had successfully cast the shield spell, but he didn't stop to congratulate himself. Instead, he scrambled to his feet and ran down the length of the perimeter wall.

"There's no point in fighting, Owen," Alec called. "Just hand over the book and they'll leave us alone. They promised!"

Owen wasted no breath answering the back-stabbing magician. He scanned the yard, sizing up his options. The section before him sloped downward toward another concrete wall, ten feet high and impossible to scale. In between was a desert garden—manicured gravel paths, clusters of large cacti, and squat, thorny bushes. To his left he could see the corner of a pool, with an infinity edge overlooking the distant city.

He ran toward the pool. He cut around the cacti, skidding on gravel. Behind him, he could hear the familiar sizzle of a fireball whizzing toward him. He ducked instinctively. The head of a cactus just past him exploded, coating the boy's face with bitter plant material and needles.

Owen spat and kept running. Mentally, he began flipping through *Sorcery for Beginners*. If there was no way for him to escape, perhaps he could at least send away the book. He knew there was a spell for increasing strength—if he cast that, maybe he could throw *Sorcery for Beginners* into outer space, or at least to California. He then recalled that spell required **SEVERAL MAJOR COMPONENTS**, among them the hairs of a strong animal.

SORCERY FOR
BEGINNERS

Sorcerers don't wear robes because they're stylish. The average magician's robe has at least three dozen pockets and pouches sewn on the inside, all for stowing spell **COMPONENTS**. After all, one wouldn't want to find oneself trapped in a desert garden, with no way of casting spells.

Teleportation, then. There was a page they'd briefly examined but never attempted that promised the ability to move objects through space. Owen just needed a few minutes of quiet so he could read it and memorize the complex hand motions—

Another fireball sizzled toward him. This time the boy did a baseball slide across the gravel. The green missile struck a scrubby manzanita bush, igniting the bone-dry twigs.

Owen stood back up, knowing he was kidding himself. He had possibly thirty seconds until he was wounded, incapacitated, or cornered by the Euclideans. He needed something fast. Something surprising. Something that would give him a little breathing room. If only there was a way he could disappear—

But there was. The spell for invisibility—why hadn't he thought of that earlier? True, he hadn't been able to make it work yet, but the pressure of getting caught and/or killed seemed to be improving his skills so far. *As soon as I get around the corner of the house,* thought Owen, *I'll find a place to hide and cast the spell. All I need is some water from that awesome pool.* He put on a burst of speed—

WHAMMM. A thick, muscled forearm connected with his nose. Bright red spots exploded across Owen's vision. His legs went out from under him. The backpack slipped from his shoulder. He hit the ground, which had the regrettable side effect of replacing all the air in his lungs with burning coals. The **PAIN** was so intense, for a moment it literally paralyzed him.

SORCERY FOR BEGINNERS

Since sorcerers spend so much time in the pursuit of intellectual studies, they tend not to be the most physical of specimens. It's a good idea for every novice magician to block out a few hours each week for exercise and self-defense lessons. One doesn't want all their years of spell training to be defeated by a simple punch.

A pair of expensive sneakers crunched across the gravel toward him. A freckled hand reached down, plucking Owen's backpack off the ground. Then a familiar, upside-down face loomed over him. Bryan Ferretti.

"Hey there, new kid," the older boy said. "I wasn't sure I'd ever see you again, since my dad made me go to military school after our little desert encounter. But here you are." His eyes, Owen noticed, had puffy pink lines of scar tissue instead of eyelashes. The effect was bizarrely humorous, but neither teenager was in a laughing mood.

"See, my dad needs someone who can actually cast the spells in this book of yours. A kid." Bryan grinned, exposing his yellow, tobacco-stained teeth. "Which means it's *your* turn to get experimented on."

He smiled, and then he socked Owen in the gut.

TASKED FORCE

Alec was right. So thought Owen as he looked around the interior of Virgil Ferretti's mansion. *There was no way we could have ever beaten the Euclideans.*

He stood in the central living room, an expansive two-story space with five-meter-tall windows overlooking the city. The house had been transformed into an impressive command center. One whole wall was covered with monitors. Several people sat at high-tech workstations, scrolling through web pages, analyzing gigabytes of text, and studying video surveillance footage. Owen realized with a start that many of the images featured him. Some, in fact, had been taken as recently as a few minutes ago—showing him unlocking the main gate, using the shield spell to block Kiraz's tranquilizer dart, and looking quite the klutz as he dodged spells. The observers were clearly excited by his actions, rewinding the footage several times and pointing out various details.

In another area, three older scientists with enchanted eyepieces examined piles of antique fetishes and artifacts. Most they cast aside, but a select few were sealed into plastic containers. Beside them, two more analysts pored over stacks of ancient texts. A large see-through display stood before them, translating reams of runes that looked identical to the ones in *Sorcery for Beginners*. Beyond them, a professional chef could be seen preparing dinner in the kitchen. Every one of them wore the Euclidean insignia somewhere on their body.

It had been slightly under twenty-four hours since the boy had escaped the casino, but in that time Ferretti and the Euclideans had assembled this entire task force on magic.

The Euclideans may have impressive resources,

The casino owner entered the room, having changed into a trim gray suit, a costly maroon shirt open at the collar, and his usual overabundance of gold jewelry. His index finger had been reset and taped in a splint. Owen instinctively started to form a spell, but Bryan yanked him back by his hair.

"Uh-uh, new kid," he whispered into the boy's ear. "You try any of your magic crap, and I'll seal your mouth shut the old-fashioned way—with staples."

but sorcerers will always have more style.

"There he is!" boomed Ferretti, his voice immediately causing the hubbub of the room to go silent. The big man strode toward Owen, his too-white teeth blazing against his tanned, leathery skin. "The boy who discovered the wonderful book that'll change the world. We can't tell you how grateful we are to you for bringing it to us."

He stopped in front of Owen and Bryan, holding out his hand. As usual, Owen saw the casino owner's wide, manufactured smile did not extend to his eyes. Bryan, eager to please, took the spell book from Owen's backpack and passed it over. Owen reached for it, but Bryan yanked his head back again.

Ferretti held the book up for everyone to see. "Here it is, as promised—the ROSETTA STONE of magic. They tell me it looks different to everybody. But you take it apart"—he ripped out a page and held it aloft—"and its true nature comes through." The members of the task force murmured to themselves in quiet awe.

Ferretti tossed the paperback to Kiraz, who in turn handed it to one of the analysts, a gray-haired man in his fifties. "I want a full breakdown within the hour."

The man nodded, jogging back to the page examination table. The others crowded around, pointing out various details as the book was dissected.

Ferretti jerked his head. "Come on. I'll give you the dime tour."

The teenager resisted, but Bryan kicked him sharply in the ankle and propelled him forward. As they walked through the crowded living room, Ferretti pointed out various work areas.

ENCHANTING DETAILS

The ROSETTA STONE (created in 129 B.C.E.) is an Egyptian rock that had the same text chiseled on it in three different languages. It was the single most important artifact to modern understanding of Egyptian hieroglyphs, and as such, has now become a generic term for any object that unlocks a complicated subject.

"Some of these guys are Euclideans, but we have a couple new hires, too. Right here's our surveillance team." The big man indicated a half dozen people before the wall of monitors. "Not only have they been tracking you, but they're currently scouring the globe for any other magic users. Turns out there're hundreds—a few of 'em right here in town. The Euclideans have a whole watch list. Only problem is, sorcery seems to have a weird effect on the adult brain. The ones they have in custody, they're a little cuckoo for Cocoa Puffs." He nodded toward the front of the house, where the Thin Man was repeatedly tapping the wall with his hands, which were once again enclosed in the steel box.

Ferretti beckoned Owen and Bryan to the next work area. Quickly but efficiently, Euclidean scientists were ripping apart *Sorcery for Beginners.* One cut the pages from the book's binding with a scalpel, while another placed them between two plates of clear plastic. These were handed to the bearded men at the rune table, who scanned, translated, and examined them through microscopes.

"This here's our nerd herd," Ferretti said. "The top minds in linguistics, chemistry, old books. I don't even know what this guys does," he added, nodding toward the gray-haired man who'd caught the book.

The gray-haired man cleared his throat. "I have PhDs in particle physics and astro—"

"Did I tell you to talk?" barked Ferretti. "Long as you're in my house, I want you Euclideans to show me some respect. Are we clear?"

The gray-haired man looked to Kiraz, who gestured for his underling to do what Ferretti had said. The doctor nodded and turned back to his computer.

"Where was I?" said Ferretti. "Right, the nerds. As you can see, I worked out a deal with our new friends. Convinced 'em to take a different approach to this whole sorcery thing. Where I come from, if you got something powerful and strong, you don't keep it locked up in a safe. You *use* it."

"So what?" Owen said. "You're gonna cast spells against all the other gangsters?"

Bryan smacked the back of his head. "You heard what he said, new kid. Don't speak until spoken to!"

Ferretti held up a hand. "Take it easy." He smiled at Owen. "My son, he's eager to help, but sometimes he doesn't think. He's working on it, though. Aren't you?"

Bryan looked away, sullen. "Yeah, Pop."

FUTURE VISIONS

Ferretti refocused his attention on Owen. "Vegas, that's small potatoes. After these guys"—he jerked his head toward Kiraz—"told me their history, I realized magic is global. It can affect everyone. Sorcery could revolutionize medicine, stop poverty, end wars—provided it's in the right hands."

Owen made a face. "Let me guess. Your hands."

Ferretti pointed to the city outside the window. The massive casinos of the Strip could be seen from the living room. "Look at how terrible things out there have gotten: crime, terrorism, people marching in the streets. Not just in this country, but everywhere. Democracy has failed, kid. People are divided. Now more than ever, the world needs a leader. A strong leader. Someone who's ready to do what needs to be done. Someone with true power."

Owen laughed. He couldn't help it. "You wanna use sorcery . . . to what? Become president? That's your big plan?" He laughed again. A few analysts look over nervously. "Out of all the things you could do, you pick the most boring. All those spells will really come in handy during conference meetings." He turned to Kiraz. "Did you guys put him up to this?"

The slick Euclidean walked over to stand beside the big man. "We support Mr. Ferretti's vision one hundred percent."

"Yeah, I'll bet. Especially since he's paying for everything. Congratulations," he said to the casino owner. "They're totally scamming you."

Ferretti grabbed Owen by the upper arm, his fingers digging into the eighth grader's bicep. "I don't get scammed, kid. That book over there—it's an express lane to anything you want. Maybe I wanna become the Steve Jobs of magic, or command an army of sorcerers, or just run the friggin' world. Whatever it is, with that thing, I'm gonna be able to do it. And all you're gonna be able to do is watch."

He was just crazy enough to try, Owen could see that. And now that the Euclideans were apparently embracing sorcery, the casino owner had all the support he would need. Still, there was one factor keeping Owen from complete despair.

"Adults can't use magic," he reminded them. "How are you gonna do any of that with something none of you can use?"

"Ah-ha. That is where our final team comes in." Still holding his arm, Ferretti led the eighth grader to three more people in lab coats. There were several blueprints of what looked like a suit of armor spread out before them. "According to the Euclidean neuroscientists, there may be a way to bypass the old noggin. Something about using neural implants to **REROUTE BRAIN ACTIVITY** into an external power source. I'm told they're already using similar techniques to treat strokes and what have you. Bottom line? It won't just be kids getting to use magic anymore."

ENCHANTING DETAILS

Neural implants are not just used to treat strokes, but also Parkinson's disease, depression, and epilepsy. Using an implant to commandeer the area of the BRAIN responsible for magic is, unfortunately, not so far-fetched.

Owen's heart dropped. He imagined the events of the last few weeks played out on a global scale. *Ferretti and the Euclideans could hex anyone who disobeyed them*, Owen thought miserably. *Laws will be meaningless. Governments will crumble. The world will be ruled by bad guys.* There was only one way to describe it.

"That sounds . . . horrible," the teenager said.

The casino owner shrugged. "Sure, things might get messy for a while, but folks will survive. The smart ones, the connected ones . . . but don't worry, the secrets in that book will be more protected than the nuclear codes." He put a heavy hand on Owen's shoulder. Ferretti's finger splint dug into his skin. "Magic's gonna be in real good hands."

"It wasn't meant for you," Owen said quietly, then raised his voice to the room. "Call it what you want, but everyone here, all you Euclidean scientists and experts—you're just thieves."

The members of the task force heard him. Most chuckled or rolled their eyes, but one or two looked away uncomfortably. Ferretti responded by taking out his billfold. It was thick with hundred-dollar bills and cinched with a twenty-four-karat gold band. The casino owner thumbed through the stack of cash until he found a twenty. He pulled it out, tucking it into Owen's shirt pocket.

"There, now it's a legitimate sale. Keep the change."

Consolation Prize

Alec volunteered to drive Owen home, but Kiraz insisted on going with them. The reason was clearly not to keep the magician company, because the two adults said not a word to each other the entire way. The silence was awkward, but at least it gave Owen time to think. There must be a way he could get back the spell book. Anything he considered, though—sneaking into Ferretti's compound, using magic to attack the task force, tweeting to J. K. Rowling for help—fell apart due to the simple fact that he was thirteen years old. There was no way he, or even he and Perry, could take on a whole team of adult Euclideans. They had the police in their pocket, they had security, and now it looked as if they had a way to use sorcery, too.

It was dark by the time Alec's white van stopped in front of Owen's house, and he still hadn't come up with a viable solution. Kiraz grabbed the eighth grader's arm.

"Best for you to return to status quo," he said softly. His blue eyes glittered like ice. "If we have to visit you again, it will not be friendly."

"I'll walk him to the door," Alec said stiffly. Kiraz released Owen and went back to tapping on his iPad.

Once they were a few feet from the vehicle, Alec spoke in a pained whisper. "I know you don't believe me, but I really did do this to keep everyone safe. The Euclideans would have never, never left you alone."

"And you think they will now?" Owen replied. "Once they figure out how to cast spells, how long do you think it'll be until they get rid of all us *witnesses*?"

"There ain't any call for 'em to do a thing like that. We keep our heads down, stay out of their way, and get on with our lives. Hate to break it to you, mate, but this is how the world works. The good guys don't always win, and evil doesn't always get punished. The only thing folks like us can do is get by the best we can."

"Yeah, well, this? Is nowhere near your best."

Alec winced as if Owen had punched him. But he nodded. "One day, maybe, you'll understand. I only hope you never have to make the choices I did." He untied the bone amulet from around his neck, pressing it into the boy's hands. "I don't know if this'll help or not, but any magic I have, twenty-five years of research and study and God knows what all—it's right there in your hand. Whatever you do, don't take it off."

The boy looked at the amulet, refusing to meet the magician's eyes. Alec opened his mouth as if to say something else, but then he changed his mind and strode back to the car.

Once the white van was gone, Owen let himself into his house. The place was a wreck—holes had been knocked in the walls, the carpet had been ripped up, and every drawer had been opened and emptied. Clearly, the Euclideans had sent their task force to search and demolish the house while Owen and Perry had been in the hospital. The teenager knew he should clean up, but right then it felt like the perfect place to wallow in his bad feelings.

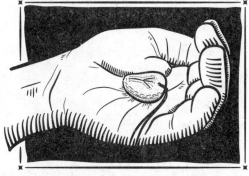

Alec's Amulet of Protection

He swept a pile of drywall off the couch, sat down, and checked his phone messages. There was a voicemail from his father (Call me immediately), a text from Trish (Dood, Im ok, got a cool cast), and several voicemails from Perry (short version: What is going ON?!). He couldn't yet bear to tell Perry or Trish he'd lost the book to the Euclideans, so he dialed his father.

THE 4-1-1 ON DAD

Marcus answered on the first ring. "Owen! Where are you? Is everything okay?"

The teenager felt himself beginning to cry. "They took it, Dad. I tried to stop them, I ran, but—they took it."

"I know they took me, but I'm fine." Before the eighth grader could correct him, Marcus kept going. "Listen. This thing in Reno, turns out it was a big mix-up with the surveillance footage. They released me an hour ago. I rented a car and I'm driving back home now."

Owen hung his head. Now that the book was gone, there was no way he could tell his father why he'd really been arrested.

"Look, I know things have been rough with us," Marcus continued. "I know I haven't really been there for you, and I've been working too much, but I promise, starting tomorrow, I'm gonna do better. Okay? We're gonna get back to normal."

The teenager laughed bitterly. *Normal.* For a little more than a week, Owen had been anything but that. He'd cast spells, run from criminals, stood up for others. He'd been extraordinary. He had, for the first time in his just over thirteen years, *lived.* It had been scary and exhausting and painful, but it had also been thrilling. And the worst of it was, his father was right. From now on, all that would be a memory.

"Owen?" his father said. "You still there?"

"Same as always," his son muttered.

"Well, look. I'm still probably six hours away. Why don't you order a pizza? Get whatever you want; just put it on the credit card. We'll talk first thing in the morning before you go to school, okay?"

"Sure, Dad." He hung up. That his father still believed a pizza could fix things only highlighted how much Owen had changed in the last weeks. Before finding the spell book, he'd been a boy—a lazy, self-centered child who only cared about his own pain. Now, he was something else. What exactly, he wasn't quite sure yet.

He only knew he was alone.

Hope Springs Eternal

As if someone outside had heard his thoughts and wanted to prove him wrong, the doorbell rang. Owen ignored it, so whoever it was switched to knocking. A lot of knocking. Which, after another minute, turned into pounding and kicking.

"What?!" Owen shouted. He strode toward the front door, not caring if it was Ferretti or Alec or the Publisher's Clearing House Prize Patrol with an oversized million-dollar check. "What?! What?! WHAT?!"

It was Perry Spring. Her ponytail had gone frizzy and she was out of breath from her assault on the door.

"About time," she said, pushing past Owen. She stopped when she saw the state of his house. "Whoa. I assume this is not the result of spring cleaning."

"Euclideans." Owen began to collect broken picture frames off the floor. "They were looking for the book."

"But they didn't find it, right? Because you and Alec got rid of it, right? You guys put it in the Z Machine and atomized it into nothingness. Right?"

✳ ✳

The look on Owen's face was answer enough.

"What happened?"

Owen dropped a broken lamp into a garbage can. It made a satisfying, heavy *crash*. "They took it."

Perry blinked. "But I don't . . . How'd they find you guys? Did they torture you? Is Alec okay?"

The boy took a shuddering breath and told her everything that had transpired in the last few hours. He told her about Alec's betrayal, the Euclidean task force, and Ferretti's plans for becoming the President of Magic. The news he related was horrible, yet it felt strangely better to share it with someone. *Maybe,* the young man thought, *I'm not so alone after all. That's something.*

Once he finished, Perry asked a single question.

"So what now?"

Owen was stunned. "What do you mean, what now? It's over. The Euclideans have the book. They won."

The tiny girl scoffed. "The only reason bad people win is because good people don't keep trying to stop them."

Owen held up his fingers one by one. "We can't go to the police. Telling our parents puts them in danger. Ferretti has our only means of casting magic. Face it, Perry: it's *over*."

"Ferretti does *not* have our only means of utilizing magic." Perry fumbled through her bag. "I thought a SPELL BOOK BACKUP would be wise, so I copied down all the pages I could when we were in the hospital. The diagrams might be a little wonky, but I managed to transcribe over forty enchantments." She held up a sheaf of yellow notebook paper.

SORCERY FOR
BEGINNERS

When acquiring a new spell book, the experienced sorcerer should make it his or her first priority to create several copies of the entire text. These serve as BACKUPS in case of theft, damage, or the spell book's own desire to go elsewhere. Hand-copying is not necessary, but it does help commit the spells to memory.

The boy flipped through the pages, taking in her neat, orderly penmanship. The whole time he'd been sitting in the waiting room, feeling sorry for himself, she'd been hard at work. Making plans. Refusing to give up.

Owen threw his arms around the tiny girl. Perry froze, her cheeks turning rosy. Realizing he was hugging a member of the opposite sex, the young man suddenly backed off. Their eyes met, then they both glanced away awkwardly.

"Sorry," he said. "I didn't mean—"

"No, no, it's fine." She waved her hands, then dared to look up at him again. "It was . . . nice."

Now Owen blushed. The sick, heavy feeling in his stomach had been replaced by an odd, fluttery one. He coughed, shuffling the hand-copied spells.

"These are great, seriously, but even if we did use magic on the Euclideans, they have it now, too. By this time tomorrow they'll probably have an army of sorcerers."

"You're right. We need help." Perry began pacing back and forth in the wrecked living room. "What if we contact Whitmore again? Think about it. She said all we had to do was ask."

"Yeah, but they have the book."

"There must be another way to reach her. I'm sure we're not the first ones to lose it."

"It's not like she's been very—" Then he remembered. "Actually, she did say something along those lines. *In case you need to find us again.* Then she had handed me the book, and the—" His face lit up, and he began to rummage frantically through his backpack. The Euclideans had searched it, of course, but the only things they'd taken were *Sorcery for Beginners* and his various spell notes. Everything else—school papers, folders, office supplies—had been ignored. Perhaps what he was looking for was still there.

"She handed you the what? Hello? I am figuratively smothering in suspense."

Owen's fingers closed on the tiny object. It was still in the front pocket of his backpack, where he'd placed it the day he discovered Codex Arcanum.

The bookmark.

Bookmark's the Spot

The two eighth graders sat on the couch and inspected it. **CODEX ARCANUM,** read the pressed lettering. **Purveyors of the Exotic, Rare, and Unusual.**

"No offense, but that doesn't appear to be super helpful," Perry said.

"If it's anything like the rest of her store, it might have a hidden message or enchantment or something." He ran his fingers along the thick-grained paper and examined the dark,

bumpy text. Just as he was becoming convinced it was nothing more than an old-timey, skinny business card, something
caught his eye. A design, imbedded in the paper. He showed
it to Perry.

"A **WATERMARK**," she breathed. She tilted the bookmark,
trying to find the best angle to view the design. The shapes were
strong, graphic, and decidedly familiar.

"Runes," Owen realized. "It's a message in runes."

Finding a notepad in the living room debris, he quickly
sketched them out. Then they turned on his father's laptop—
thankfully Ferretti's men had left that intact—and navigated to
a rune website. Decrypting codes wasn't the sort of activity the
young man usually enjoyed, but for once Owen stuck with it.
For thirty minutes he and Perry sat in the living room, painstakingly translating the runes one by one until they had a short,
mysterious message:

> **Questions? Concerns? Simply press the button
> and ask for HELP.**

"Great. What button?" said Perry.

Owen picked up the bookmark again, seeing the ornate,
sorcery-like diagram beneath the store's name. It was the only
thing remotely close to a button. Could it be that simple?

ENCHANTING
DETAILS

Modern **WATERMARKS** have been around since 1826 C.E.
They are used to identify a manufacturer's product, or as
a security system to prevent counterfeiting. The marks
are done in such a way that they can only be viewed in a
certain kind of light.

He pressed his thumb to the letters. "Help," he said.

Nothing happened.

"You call that a plea?" Perry said. "Put your back into it, swabbie."

The boy pressed harder, until his hand hurt. "Please. We really, really need assistance here. The Euclideans have the spell book and a whole team of adults, and some of them even know how to do magic, and we have no way of getting it back. We need your help, Ms. Whitmore. We can't do this on our own. Please HELP!"

He shouted the last word, breaking the silence of the empty house. But still, nothing happened. He didn't know why he expected anything different. The old woman hadn't exactly been a beacon of guidance so far; why would she change her ways now? He took his thumb off the bookmark.

WHOOOM.

A loud, concussive sound exploded outside. It sent a vibration through the floorboards, rattled the glass in the windows, and set off car alarms two blocks away. If Owen had taken a moment to ponder, he would have realized he'd heard such a SOUND before—right when Bryan's thugs were about to stuff

---

SORCERY FOR
BEGINNERS

Teleportation by magic is a wonderfully quick way to travel, but also incredibly dangerous. Make the slightest wrong calculation, and you could squish passersby, appear two hundred feet off the ground, or materialize in the center of a mountain. There is also, as we see here, the concussive SOUND of all the air molecules at your arrival point being suddenly shoved aside. This unfortunately prevents using teleportation for sneak attacks.

him into an ice chest. But he did not ponder. Instead, he peered through the living room shades.

Directly across the street, in a previously empty spot between two identical suburban homes, towered a bizarre ten-story building, each level a different style of architecture from the one beneath it. Hanging above the ground-level door was the familiar wood-carved sign.

Codex Arcanum.

THE LIGHT'S ON, BUT . . .

Owen and Perry bolted across the street without even bothering to look for cars. Now that Whitmore had finally shown up, neither of them intended to lose her again. When they reached the building's doorstep, though, the size of the ten-story structure made them pause. Every window in the weird, looming tower was silent and dark.

"Moment of truth," Perry whispered. "Either we get some actual answers . . ."

"Or it was all for nothing," Owen finished nervously. He took a deep breath, raised his hand, and knocked on the door.

It silently swung open at his touch. Beyond, they could only see shadows.

"Ladies first," said Owen.

"You got us into this," Perry hissed, and shoved him inside.

It was just as Owen remembered. Carved wooden shelves soared high into the darkness over their heads; cozy green-shaded banker lamps hung from every corner; and everywhere they looked, there were books. Filling every nook, stacked in cairns on the floor, spilling out of overflowing shelves. And permeating it all, the comforting, musty smell of old paper.

"Wow," Perry said in awe. "I mean, you told me what it was like, but . . . *wow*."

"Yeah," Owen agreed. They moved into the store, looking down the dim aisles. Soon they reached the cashier's area. It was illuminated by a small glass-shaded desk lamp. Behind the small oak lectern stood a life-size sculpture of the mythical creature known as a **KIRIN**. It had a fierce, dragon-like head with two wavy horns protruding from its skull, the squat body and legs of a boar, and the thick tail of an ox. It was slightly over a meter in length, and its flanks were covered in fiery orange, yellow, and red scales. It was so realistic, it almost appeared to be breathing.

Then Owen realized it *was* breathing. This he determined because the kirin turned its great head toward the eighth graders. Then it spoke.

ENCHANTING DETAILS

Known as the qilin in China, the **KIRIN** is a mythical creature greatly admired for its power, wisdom, and propensity for bringing good fortune. A single kirin can live to be one thousand years old and only appears in places ruled by a wise and benevolent leader (even if they are as small as a bookstore). Although fearsome to behold, the kirin only harms evildoers. It can walk across any surface—snow, grass, water— without leaving a mark. All in all, the ideal house pet.

Chapter 23

Wake-Up Call

What do you seek within these shelves? said the beast. Well, *said* is perhaps incorrect, as the kirin's lips did not move. Its words merely appeared and resonated in Owen's and Perry's brains, as if someone had struck a very loud, very clear bell.

"Uh . . ." was all Owen could muster in response.

Speak, child, the animal's voice came again. It didn't hurt, but it had the effect of crowding out any other thoughts in their brains. Also, the child reference was a bit irksome.

"We're looking for Ms. Whitmore," Owen managed. "We need help."

Please wait here, said the kirin. Then it sprang upward into the shelves, galloping straight up the delicate spines of the books without leaving a mark. It disappeared into the darkness above.

"Great, now we have to deal with magical animals, too," said Owen.

Kirins make wonderful assistants,
provided you can convince one to work for you.

"What do you suppose that was?" said Perry. "Some kind of enchanted **CHIMERA** Whitmore created?"

"*He* is a kirin," came a dry British accent behind them. "And his name is Kyle."

Whitmore stepped out from one of the darker aisles. She wore a dusty leather jacket, a khaki shirt, knee-length boots, and flared tan jodhpurs. Despite the dirt, she still managed to look fabulous. In fact, the bookseller appeared to have grown younger, and yet, more imposing since the boy had last seen her.

"Owen Macready. And friend," she said, giving Perry a cursory

---

ENCHANTING DETAILS

CHIMERA (n.)—A beast of Greek mythology that sported the head of a lion, the body of a goat, and the tail of a snake. The term has since come to represent any mythical creature with weirdly mismatched body parts.

glance. "I'll have you know, I was in the midst of a very important magical excavation."

"So that—he—*Kyle* was real?" Perry asked.

Whitmore arched her eyebrow. "This is the question with which you wish to begin? When I have not even had the pleasure of your name?"

"This is Perry Spring," Owen said. "She's, uh, been helping me figure out the book."

"I have a great adulation for your work," Perry said, extending a hand.

Whitmore cocked an eyebrow, but gravely shook the tiny girl's hand. "You are, at least, more polite than your friend was at our first meeting. And to answer your question, yes. Kyle watches over Codex Arcanum when I am indisposed."

"And . . . where were you? Indisposed, I mean," Perry asked.

"RABAT, Morocco. Quite lovely this time of year. But now I am here, so tell me—what can I do for you both?"

ENCHANTING
DETAILS

People go on about Casablanca, but RABAT is the city to see if you ever travel to Morocco. Not only is it the capital of the country, but it also features beautiful oceanfront restaurants, plenty of exciting sports teams, and some wonderful historic sites. But the best activity by far is to eat pastilles in the medina (old town) and watch the locals go by.

DISCUSSION QUESTIONS

Perry and Owen looked at each other. Now that they were standing in front of the bookseller, they had no idea where to begin.

Owen attempted to make a go of it anyway. "I—you didn't—you shouldn't have sold me that book," he finally blurted.

"Nonsense," Whitmore replied. "I have been recruiting sorcerers for a long time, young man. I pride myself on selecting the appropriate candidates. Is there a problem with your purchase?"

"No."

"Was it defective or undesirable in any way?"

"It's not that; it's—"

"Then I fail to see how the fault lies with me. Books, Mr. Macready, are mirrors for our minds. They merely reflect what we bring to them. Therefore, any unhappiness with your situation rests solely on *your* shoulders."

Owen looked down at the polished cashier's counter. The conversation was not going as he'd envisioned. Perry jumped in to help. "The thing is, we had an unfortunate . . . encounter," she said. "With a . . . person. And this guy, he—"

"I lost it," Owen said.

"What's that? I know they don't teach elocution in schools anymore, but it's still no excuse for mumbling."

"I lost. The book," he said louder.

To his surprise, Whitmore merely nodded. "I am aware. But you took an oath, did you not, to protect it at all costs?" The teenager nodded miserably. "Then your task is simple. You must reclaim it."

Perry stepped in. "The thing is, the man who stole it, he's very . . . connected. Wealthy. And now he's partnered up with the Euclideans."

Whitmore shrugged. "A usual ploy of our enemies. Welcome a new member to their ranks, taking care not to tell him too much. Then if things go sour, they cut the strings of their puppet and disappear back into the shadows."

"It's possible they have a different tactic this time," said Perry. "Owen said they're planning to use MAGIC!"

"Don't be ridiculous," the woman said with a sniff. "Such an act goes against their primary system of belief."

"Believe it," said Owen. "There's about twenty of them less than ten miles from here, ripping apart the book and devising a way for adults to cast spells. You should have seen how excited they were."

"A rogue faction." The bookseller sat behind the counter, clearly dismayed by this news. Owen was surprised to see her so

BEWARE THE EUCLIDEANS

Forbidding the use of MAGIC is one of the ten basic tenets of the Euclidean Code. For sorcerers, the primary danger of our enemies learning how spells work was that they would find ways to block or undo our magic. Now that they no longer follow that rule, they are infinitely more dangerous.

rattled. "They have been shielding themselves from magical surveillance of late, and now we know why. A very unfortunate development." She straightened her spine and faced the teenagers. "The volume you know as *Sorcery for Beginners* has been lost and found many times over the last five hundred years, but never has our enemy attempted to use it against us. I fear what this means for the future." She shook her head slightly. "But it does not change the limitations on our resources. You're the ones who lost it; you must be the ones to recover it."

"Can you at least tell us how to do that?" asked Owen. "Maybe give us a hint or something? Even a riddle would be great."

"Or perhaps we could buy another magic book," Perry suggested, scanning the cluttered bookstore. "You appear to have ample inventory."

But the bookseller stared at her coldly. "So you lose an extremely powerful, ancient text, and you want me to hand over another rare magical resource? I think not."

"What about the other seventeen candidates?" Owen said suddenly. "The kids you gave copies of the spell book to? Maybe we can borrow it from one of them. Or we can all join up and fight the Euclideans together!"

"Ah, yes." Whitmore steepled her fingers together, her expression growing more stern than usual. "I'm sorry to report they are no longer with us."

History Repeats Itself (Or Not)

The two young people were stunned. "They're . . . dead?" Perry squeaked.

"Good heavens, no." The bookseller brushed away the idea with a hand. "But the Euclideans found ways, by one method or another, to have them renounce sorcery. So, as per our agreement, their memories have been expunged of all contact with me, magic, and the Codex Arcanum. Not only is our enemy clever, but their reach is long. You, Owen Macready and Perry Spring, are the only candidates left."

Silence descended on the bookstore. "You can't leave it up to us." Owen was growing desperate. "What about the Spell to Rewrite History? The book showed me that even before I bought it. If you've sold dozens of copies, you must have *that* page somewhere. That's the only one we need. We cast it, we can turn back the clock on this whole thing."

The bookseller looked at him over her glasses. "You know as well as I, that spell will only appear when you have earned the right to learn it. Even if I were to show you a copy, your untrained brain would only perceive a blank page." Owen opened his mouth to object, but she held up a hand to silence him. "Perhaps if you finish what you began, that spell will reveal itself to you. But be warned, Mr. Macready—sorcery does not always operate in the manner one expects."

"Are you saying that the spell doesn't actually change history?" said Perry.

"Oh no, it does. But the ramifications of its casting can be incredibly destructive. Especially for one person in particular."

She spread her hands toward them.

"The caster," Perry realized.

Whitmore nodded. "Once the spell has been cast, the selected moment of history is ALTERED for everyone but the sorcerer. For that unlucky person, *both* versions of the past exist as one. Which leads, quite naturally, to a paradox. Especially if the altered moment is from the caster's own personal history."

SORCERY FOR BEGINNERS

In fact, true ALTERATIONS of the past have only occurred three times in the entire history of magic. And for those, we must take the word of the sorcerers who performed the spells, since the rest of us cannot remember a different version of events. Such is the paradoxical nature of tinkering with time: even if you succeed, you will be the only person who realizes it.

The meaning of her words began to sink in. If Owen magically changed history so that he never left the hospital with Alec, or never cast the mending spell on Bryan Ferretti, or never moved to Las Vegas in the first place, it would erase his problems, but there would be a devastating side effect:

"It would make me insane," he said.

Whitmore nodded. "And there are those who, facing despair, have chosen such a path for themselves. But doing so, I believe, is gravely shortsighted. As Martin Luther King Jr. said, 'The arc of the moral universe is long, but it bends toward justice.' Even now, there is still some hope for your success."

"Success?" Owen said bitterly. All this time, he'd been counting on that spell as his solution. It was his fail-safe, his way to fix all the mistakes he'd made since buying the spell book. Now Whitmore was telling him it was nothing more than fool's gold. "We're just kids," he continued. "We're not big, powerful magicians. That book, it's not—I can't—I don't *deserve* it."

A strangled sound escaped his throat, and he turned away in embarrassment. Perry laid a hand on his back. The bookseller watched them over the frames of her glasses, neither pitying nor judging, until he stood upright again.

"Are you finished?" she finally said, not unkindly. "Your words are not only pointless, they are incorrect. You were given the book, and you found this store—twice, as a matter of fact— precisely because you *are* worthy."

Heavy Mettles

Owen and Perry looked up at her in surprise.

"I told you, it was not chance that brought you into my establishment. A series of tests guided you here. The encounter in the gym, the dodgeballs, your escape from the ice chest—all arranged to test your mettle. Then there is the spell book itself, which can only be unlocked by children who are brave, strong, resourceful, and above all, worthy of such powerful and arcane knowledge."

The eighth graders were stunned. "But why . . . why choose us?" Owen said.

"As you know, you are not the first to go through the recruitment process," Whitmore said. "I have been to hundreds of cities over the last decade, tested thousands of children, sold scores of copies of *Sorcery for Beginners* and then been forced to recover them. Do you know how many have come as far as you? How many, in those ten years, committed themselves to the study of sorcery, who did not succumb to laziness or greed, who only used their newfound powers for defense and protection?"

Owen and Perry held their breath.

"Eleven," Whitmore said. "Eleven approved candidates, culled from thousands. So I think you can scrub the notion that you are not special or deserving. You have come this far on your merits. The question now is, will you persevere?"

"Persevere at what?" Perry said. "If you're giving all these tests, what kind of result are you looking for?"

The bookseller lifted her head a bit higher. "I may not look it, but I am no—what's the phrase?—spring chicken."

Owen raised a finger. "I don't think anybody says that."

Whitmore ignored him. "The sorcerers of the world have grown old, and we are searching for our replacements: the next generation of spell casters, who will take charge of and add to the knowledge you see around you." She indicated the surrounding bookshelves. "But we're getting ahead of ourselves. Before you can join our ranks, you must pass the final examination."

"Which is what, precisely?" asked Perry.

Whitmore steepled her elegant fingers together. "I should have thought that was obvious. Retrieve the spell book. How and if you do so—such details are up to you."

"But the Euclideans, they've got millions of dollars, they've got scientists and guns and self-driving cars. How are we supposed to fight that?" asked Owen.

"There is one crucial element they will always lack," Whitmore said crisply. "Sorcery. Whoever may possess the book, you, Owen Macready, were the selected candidate. Sorcery chose *you*. As I mentioned before, the texts of Codex Arcanum pick their owners as much as the owners pick them. *Sorcery for Beginners* recognized something in you. Something, it appears, you yourself have yet to see."

"Which is?" the boy said.

"How should I know?" said Whitmore. "We conversed for five minutes; now you wish for me to explain the meaning of *your* life? I am a bookseller. All I can do is point my patrons toward a particular path. You must be the one to do the work."

"We already trained for a whole week," Perry pointed out. "Owen worked really, really hard. Can't you—"

But the young man cut her off. "No, I didn't. You guys did, but I . . . I just wanted to unlock the Spell to Rewrite History and fix my family. Ms. Whitmore's right. Using that spell on Bryan and Abu, asking Alec to help us, letting Ferretti take the book—I didn't have to do any of those things. I could have fought harder, studied more . . . I could have listened to you, even."

Perry blushed.

"I made an oath to protect it. It's my responsibility. But whatever I do, it's gonna be dangerous. You should hang back," he continued.

The tiny girl rolled her eyes. "As if I'd let you have all the fun. Besides, TWO HEADS ARE BETTER THAN ONE."

Owen faced the bookseller. "We'll get the book back. I don't know how, but I promise to try."

"I'm not allowed to play favorites," said Whitmore. "But between the three of us" —she glanced around, then leaned in to whisper— "I do hope you succeed. And if that occurs, perhaps I'll call on you again. "

"And, uh . . . if we don't?" Owen said.

The bookseller held his gaze. "There are many possible worlds. Let us hope this is the best of them."

Perry and Owen said their good-byes and exited through the front door. The chimes overhead tinkled brightly. They turned, but the tall building had already vanished. The last chime note hung in the air as if it were being stretched across a very long distance. When it finally disappeared as well, Owen and Perry went back inside the Macready home.

CLEAN-UP DETAIL

They decided to order a pizza after all.

As they ate, they took stock of the house wreckage. There was no way to fix all the damage on their own, but they could at least clean up. It was a thought, Owen reflected as he and Perry filled garbage bags, which would have not occurred to him two weeks ago.

Leaving Perry to handle the kitchen, the boy went upstairs to start on his room. Like the rest of the house, it looked more like a garbage dump than a dwelling. Owen scooped up the

SORCERY FOR BEGINNERS

The idiom "TWO HEADS ARE BETTER THAN ONE" was unfortunately taken literally by sixteenth-century sorcerer Urquhart the Undecided (1511–42 C.E.). Finding himself overwhelmed by the process of decision-making, he conjured a replica of his own head and attached it to his shoulders. Rather than make him smarter, however, the procedure only doubled the arguments he had with himself. It also made him far less attractive to his neighbors.

obvious trash bits—bed stuffing, chunks of drywall, old video games that had been cracked—and placed them in his garbage bag. He hung his strewn clothes back in the closet and reshelved his thrown books. He dumped his scattered school supplies inside the desk.

A cream-colored chunk of parchment in one drawer caught his eye. It was hidden under a pile of broken pencils and salt packets—the detritus of Owen's first attempt at spell casting. It had only been nine days ago, but it felt like years.

He fished out the scrap of **PARCHMENT**. He remembered that during his frustration with the mending spell, he had torn out a piece of the spell book in an attempt to fix it. Now it was all he had left of *Sorcery for Beginners*. The rest was locked in Ferretti's mansion, systematically being dissected by the Euclideans. If only he'd had the foresight to rip out more pages, or make copies like Perry had, or at least pay attention to the actual words. He'd been so eager to skip ahead, he hadn't taken time to learn the spells properly. He could barely even recall all twelve of the basic incantations. And this one, tiny scrap of parchment couldn't help him in that regard.

Unless.

ENCHANTING DETAILS

PARCHMENT is made from animal hide, and is far more durable than paper products. It can also be scrubbed and reused; recycled parchments are called palimpsests. Unfortunately, the format was mostly abandoned in the Middle Ages for paper, because the latter was cheaper and faster to produce. But, as with many techniques that favor those two qualities, it was not better.

Unless, by some incredible long shot, it *could*.

A plan began to take shape in his mind. A wild, daring, and decidedly dangerous plan. The kind of plan he probably should have put into action the minute after Ferretti had first approached him. The more he considered it, the more he knew it was what they had to do.

He ran downstairs with the parchment scrap clutched in his fingers. "Perry," he said, panting more from excitement than the short jog. "I know how we can get the book back. But we're gonna need more sorcerers."

Volume Three

FINAL EXAMINATIONS

CHAPTER 24

SALES PITCH

Owen and Perry stood in the center of the middle school's practice gymnasium. It was less than twenty-four hours after they'd spoken to Whitmore. Butter-colored afternoon sunlight streamed through the room's high windows, illuminating tumbling mats, climbing ropes, two basketball hoops, and bins filled with PE equipment. Before Owen and Perry were the three other members of the Dragonridge chapter of the Society for Creative Anachronism. Their expressions were not receptive. Owen had also asked Trish to be there, but she was still recuperating in the hospital and they were short on time.

"Thanks for coming," he said. "I know the last time you guys saw us use sorcery, it was a little . . . scary."

Ravi scoffed. "Scary? Every time my mom opens a jar of applesauce, the smell gives me a panic attack."

A Spell to Conjure Thunder

Elemental attacks are powerful, but there may be times you want to suppress an attacker without freezing, electrocuting, or setting them on fire. Using only the **power of sound**, this spell creates a **concussive burst of energy** that can **shatter glass or knock an enemy off his feet**. It is also quite effective for getting the last word in an argument.

COMPONENTS NEEDED:

– none –

SOMATIC MOVEMENTS:

STEP ONE:

Perform the hand movements as above.

STEP TWO:

Clap your hands once in the direction you wish to send the spell.

NOTE: Clapping at one's own face is not recommended.

"We've gotten a lot better since then," Perry assured them. "We've been practicing, and learning new spells, and . . . well, it's easier if we just show you."

She and Owen faced each other. They'd argued extensively the night before over whether or not to do this, but in the end, their need for help had overruled the other concerns. Besides, Owen could see that Moe Moe and Julie were already rolling their eyes. They needed to get them on board now.

He twisted his hands in the air, fingers forming runes. He heard the girls whispering, but knew he had to block it out. Everything hung on him doing this correctly. He completed the movements and thrust his palm forward.

"Ignis."

An orange fireball hurtled toward Perry. The whispers were replaced by gasps. Ravi stepped forward, but the tiny girl held her ground. She intertwined her hands, crooked her fingers, and spread her palms. A translucent gold shield appeared in front of her. The fireball impacted against it and vanished.

Perry didn't stop there. She powered up another spell, shooting a bolt of blue electricity toward Owen. Rather than block it with a shield, though, he formed a few runes and brought his hands together. A deafening thunderclap shook the gym mats, and a wave of concussive energy spread out from his palms. It broke apart the lightning and knocked over a bin of flag football belts in the process.

The two of them went into a frenzy of spell casting, blocks, and dodges. Owen sent another thunderclap at Perry that shattered the glass basketball backboard, but she quickly cried *"Exsarcio!"* and restored it. She followed that up by casting a river of ice at his feet, but he dispelled the effect with a well-timed *"Annullare."*

For their finale, Owen executed a series of complex hand movements, then threw a handful of sparkly mica dust. Streams of COLORED LIGHT erupted from his fingers. The glamour curled and capered through the gym like see-through, rainbow-colored puppies. The SCA members gaped.

Then Perry stepped forward, charged up an intricate spell, tipped a bottle of water over her head, and said in Icelandic, *"Osýnileika."*

She vanished.

The middle schoolers stared, then burst into a round of applause. Owen caught his breath, looking out at the members of SCA. He could tell from their faces that their small fighting force had just grown by three.

Know Your Enemy

They began practicing that same afternoon. Knowing anyone could walk in on them in the gymnasium, and not

SORCERY FOR BEGINNERS

There are many types of glamour spells, but the most basic is a simple spray of COLORED LIGHT, as seen here. The more complicated and realistic the glamour, the more focus is required.

particularly wanting to get into the whole "sorry to annihilate your world view, but magic exists" issue, the SCA members reconvened at their old meeting place at Dragonridge rocks.

With the rock pillars standing guard, Perry spread out the spell pages she had hand-copied in the hospital. There were forty-three in total, including every one of the Twelve Basic Incantations. Some had blank spots, particularly the enchantments that required complicated diagrams, but it was impressive how much of the book she had managed to transcribe.

"We really appreciate you guys helping us," Owen said. "But before we get started, you should know what we're up against. The spells you see here, they're only about a third of what's in the book. Which is why . . . we need your help to get it back."

"You show me how to turn invisible, and I'll help you clean the toilets in the boys' locker room," said Ravi.

Moe Moe pointed at one of the sheets. "Yeah, what about that Spell to **SUMMON ANIMALS**? Can we start with that?"

"No, the **SPELL TO COMPEL PLANTS**," Julie said, pointing to another sheet.

SORCERY FOR BEGINNERS

SUMMONING spells bring a creature or object to a place of your choosing. The greater your skill, the larger and more powerful your summoning ability. A novice may only be able to call up groups of nearby insects, but a high-level mage can summon magical creatures such as unicorns, dragons, and even huge monsters from other planes of existence. Be warned, though—simply calling a creature does not guarantee it will do your bidding.

SORCERY FOR BEGINNERS

Often used in conjunction with summoning, spells of compulsion bend another entity to a sorcerer's will. Again, skill level will determine how well said entity will obey. COMPELLING PLANTS to trip someone is relatively easy; forcing a human being to injure a loved one is more difficult.

Owen held up his hands. "We'll teach you any spell you want. But we have to go in order. And we need your promise that we can count on you."

"Count on us for what?" asked Moe Moe.

Perry and Owen looked at each other. This, they knew, was the hardest part of their sales pitch. "We have a way to get the spell book back," said Owen. "But when we take it, Ferretti and the Euclideans are going to come after us. They could send soldiers, drones, even other sorcerers. People might get hurt."

The middle schoolers looked concerned. Ravi cleared his throat. "Ferretti, as in Bryan Ferretti? The guy you facially disfigured?"

"That was an accident, and he's fine. We're talking about his dad," Owen said.

"Oh, so even worse," said Julie.

"I heard his dad killed a guy with a stapler," said Ravi.

"I heard he sent someone to the hospital for giving him the stink-eye," added Moe Moe.

They all began to talk at once, relating all the scary gossip they'd heard about the Ferretti family.

"People. People!" shouted Owen, but they ignored him. He charged up a thunderclap and brought his hands together over his head. A loud *CRACK* reverberated over the desert, silencing the bickering kids.

"It's true, Ferretti and the Euclideans are dangerous," he said. "That's why we're not going to take them on until everyone knows how to protect themselves. If you want to leave now, we won't hold it against you."

They looked at each other, but no one left.

"Okay, then," said Perry. "Let's get started."

TRAINING WEEK

They began by going over the mending spell. It came back quickly to the other members of SCA; so quickly that within thirty minutes, each of them could cinch two broken sticks together on their own. Perry and Owen then went over the other Basic Incantations. A couple hours later, the group had mastered two of them.

They met after school every day that week. By Wednesday afternoon, everyone had learned all Twelve Basic Incantations. By Thursday, Trish was able to join them. She insisted on practicing with the others, even though the big blue cast on her left leg made it more difficult to cast spells.

It soon became clear that each of the new sorcerers excelled at specific schools of magic. Moe Moe had an affinity for summoning spells: ordering rabbles of butterflies to block someone's vision or armies of ants to spell her name. Ravi was the best at illusions: creating complicated light shows, auditory hallucinations, even hologram-like copies of the other kids. And Julie excelled at plant magic: compelling the desert flora to respond in ways that no vegetation should be capable. Perry was still the best at protection spells, while Trish remained the resident expert on attack magic.

As for Owen, he finally stopped questioning whether or not he was worthy, and simply focused on his training. Now that his mind was clear, he was able to work in any school of sorcery with relative ease. But his true talent, he found, lay in leadership. Because he'd had such difficulty learning the spells, he knew when to encourage, when to push, and how to break down difficult enchantments in ways that made sense. By the time the sun began to set on Friday, the group could reliably cast over two dozen spells thanks to his tutelage. Owen knew they couldn't risk waiting any longer.

This is it, he thought as he looked over the small team of spell casters he and Perry had brought together. *Time for the big speech. You've faced worse in the last month; you can do this.* He cleared his throat. "Everyone? Hey." None of the SCA members heard him. "HEY!"

One by one, they came over. "Thanks. You guys have all done great work this week. But every day the Euclideans have the book, they're getting stronger. Tomorrow morning we're taking it back."

The middle schoolers looked at each other—some excited, others anxious. "We'll meet here at 10:00 a.m. We don't know how they'll respond when we take it, but no matter what happens, you guys are ready to defend yourselves."

✳ ✳

They said good night. Trish hobbled over to Owen and Perry, her blue cast caked in dust from their practice.

"'Once more unto the breach, dear friends,'" she QUOTED with a grin. "You really think these noobs are ready?"

"They're better prepared than we were in the casino," said Perry. "Provided they remember their training."

"They'll remember," said Owen. He did not add that their plan would be a resounding failure if they did not.

All's Well That Mends Well

The next morning, all six members of the SCA Dragonridge chapter showed up at the desert rock formation. They had debated making their stand elsewhere, but the desert had the advantage of familiarity, secrecy, and isolation. There were no innocent bystanders who could be hurt, and no cameras that could record their spell casting for future viral videos.

Owen surveyed the group, half-relieved and half-worried that everyone was there. Trish had suggested they wear their SCA costumes, but Owen and Perry agreed they were too prohibitive for spell casting. Instead, each sorcerer had chosen his or her own version of comfortable athletic gear. As he watched his friends stretch and shake out their hands, Owen sighed. *If they*

ENCHANTING DETAILS

Trish is QUOTING from William Shakespeare's *Henry V*, Act 3, Scene 1. The play is based around the real Battle of Agincourt (25 October 1415 C.E.), during which twenty-eight-year-old King Henry's English soldiers were outnumbered by the French almost six to one. Even so, Henry won, giving hope to underdogs everywhere.

get hurt, it's on me. But I can't do this without them. He spread out a large roll of paper, upon which he'd sketched a battle plan.

"Everyone remember their positions?" The rest of the group nodded. "We don't know which direction they'll be approaching from, so be ready to reconfigure your defenses. Any questions?"

There were none. "Okay then," he said, unable to think of a more rousing speech. "Let's do this."

He removed the scrap of spell book parchment from his pocket. He faced his body in the direction of Ferretti's mansion and tightly clutched the parchment in both hands. He closed his eyes, picturing the spell book in front of him. The magic symbols on the cover. The crisp smell of the pages. The way it made him feel when he opened it. Confident he had it clear in his mind, he nodded to Trish and Perry.

They each placed a hand on his shoulder. One by one, Moe Moe and Julie and Ravi joined them. Once all six were connected, Owen spoke.

"We'll do it together. One . . . two . . ."

Six pairs of hands moved through the air as one. Six voices spoke the words of the mending spell, clear and strong:

"EXSARCIO MAXIMA."

For a long moment, nothing happened. Then the tiny piece of

SORCERY FOR BEGINNERS

Adding a strengthening spell is recommended when casting any enchantment on an object at a distance. Think of it like using an amplifier for sound, or a telescope for viewing.

parchment began to quiver in Owen's fingers. The edges of it shone with golden light.

"It's working!" said Owen. "Keep concentrating!"

What happened next was not seen by any of the middle schoolers. Fourteen kilometers away, in the compound of Virgil Ferretti, sat a gray-haired paper engineer. His name was Dr. Clark Murray, and at that moment he was fitting a plastic-encased spell book page under the lens of an electron microscope. Despite his scientific interest in the project, he was exhausted. He'd been awake for over thirty hours, and Ferretti was an unforgiving taskmaster. He seemed to take particular joy in tormenting Dr. Murray, forcing him to redo test results and chewing him out in front of the others if he made a mistake.

The work conditions were so bad, he'd considered quitting. Unfortunately, he had been promised a sum of money he could dearly use. It had been reiterated several times that if he left early, he would receive nothing. In response to this, Dr. Murray had made it his objective to complete this project as quickly as possible. Hence the decision to sleep less.

One of the spell book pages on the table began to vibrate. He checked his fingers to see if he'd developed a stress tremor. The digits were still. Perhaps the table had hit some kind of sympathetic resonance with the microscope? Surely it didn't put out enough power for that. He checked the power supply anyway, failing to notice that the corner of the responsible page was glowing.

He did, however, notice the entire table was now vibrating. Dr. Murray blinked. Perhaps his tiredness had caught up with him, and he was hallucinating? Slowly, he reached toward the spell page. His dull reaction time probably saved him from several broken bones.

The spell page shot out of the table clamps, rending metal and hard plastic like a hot knife cutting through butter. The case flew across the room, smashed through the twelve-centimeter-thick, earthquake-reinforced living room window, and disappeared into the morning sun.

Dr. Murray stared at the hole. Now he was sure his exhaustion had caught up with him.

"What the hell was that?" Ferretti yelled from the upstairs master suite. He strode out onto the walkway that overlooked the work area, several high-tech plates strapped to his limbs. Dr. Murray was convinced the man hadn't slept at all since acquiring the book. Everyone assumed he was taking stimulants to compensate, because his moods were, at best, erratic.

Seeing the shattered window, the casino owner's eyes narrowed. "Someone tell me right now who broke my window, or I swear—"

His words were interrupted by a deep, ominous *thrum*. Each member of the magic task force turned to the source of the sound. Every spell page, whether it was being scanned by a machine, or analyzed by linguists, or simply locked in the rolling safe Ferretti had purchased, was now vibrating violently.

Down in the living room the Thin Man smiled. "Little fly," he whispered. "Little fly has grown his wings." Then he ducked behind the couch, covering his head with the steel box encasing his hands.

All at once, hundreds of plastic-encased spell pages ripped through the mansion. They tore through brick and plaster, burst through wood and window, and cut through carbonized steel as if it were water. The house was being torn apart from the inside out.

"Grab them!" Ferretti shouted over the massive din. "Don't let any of them go!"

A few of the casino owner's employees were brave or foolish enough to follow his instructions. They reached for the hard plastic containers as they flew past, but all they received for their trouble were bruised or broken fingers. In less than a minute, every spell page and the book's binding had flown into the western horizon. What was left of the mansion now resembled Swiss cheese more than a home.

Still, Ferretti kept his head. "The GPS CHIPS!" he shouted, running down the pitted and bent stairs. "Every case has a chip inside it; now somebody *TRACK THEM!*"

SORCERY FOR BEGINNERS

One of the problems with magic being three thousand years old is that many spells are confounded by modern technology. An object may have all sorts of enchantments to disguise it from human eyes, or prevent it from being found (*Sorcery for Beginners* has both), but as we've seen, such spells can be circumvented with cheap present-day gadgets such as camera phones and GPS CHIPS.

LATE ARRIVALS

Back at the Dragonridge rock formation, things were less exciting. The teenagers had repeated the incantation a few more times, but other than the scrap of parchment vibrating, not much else had occurred in the last two minutes. Ravi even muttered that the mending spell hadn't worked.

Then they heard the unmistakable sound of 340 plastic-encased sheets of parchment breaking the sound barrier. They flew toward the middle schoolers in a spiral, looking from a distance like a massive swarm of plastic-encased bats. Seconds later, they looked more like what they really were— incoming projectiles approaching at a speed of MACH 3.

ENCHANTING DETAILS

An object's Mach number is determined by the ratio of the speed of a moving object to the local speed of sound. Yes, you read that correctly—the speed of sound changes depending on the temperature and moisture of a given area. So while MACH 3 might be slightly different if you're in a rain forest or a desert, rest assured that pretty much everywhere, it is roughly three thousand kilometers per hour. Or to put it another way—very, very fast.

"Hit the deck!" yelled Trish.

The others needed no encouragement. They dove to the ground and covered their heads. Only Owen stayed upright. Wincing slightly, the boy held up the tiny scrap of paper.

Ten meters from him, the first spell page broke free of its plastic housing. The hard material shattered, burning up in the hot desert air. The parchment snapped against Owen's scrap with a flash of golden light. He had just a moment to read the words at the top—A Spell for Mending—before the other pages arrived.

They swirled and swooped and spiralled around the thirteen-year-old. It was like being in the eye of a great hurricane, and yet he felt no fear. This was no random, dangerous act of nature. It was more akin to being at the center of a huge, complicated dance. Only this dance was being performed at three thousand kilometers per hour.

Quickly, the pages cinched themselves together. The stack of parchment grew in Owen's hands, a living thing that pulsed and jumped in his fingers. Soon, all that was left was the heavy leather-bound cover, which sped toward them like a large brown hawk. It wheeled around and braked in front of him, snapping itself into place.

Sorcery for Beginners was whole once more.

The Last Temptation of Owen

Only it was no longer the familiar paperback he had purchased at Codex Arcanum. Gone were the magic symbols that had been on the cover. Instead he held an ancient, heavy volume filled with hand-lettered, gorgeously illuminated pages of pressed parchment. On the front, stamped in a gold gothic font, were the words **Magicae nam Novitiorum**.

Owen flipped through the book, the heady scent of time and wood pulp filling his nose. "Guess it doesn't need a disguise anymore," he said.

"Or maybe you've **EARNED THE RIGHT** to see it how it really is," Perry suggested.

SORCERY FOR
BEGINNERS

While this is a nice idea, the truth is that once the spell book was ripped apart by Ferretti's task force, the disguise enchantment was broken. The same holds for almost any ensorcelled object—if it is damaged too greatly, any spells cast upon it will likewise be removed.

The others got to their feet. They crowded around Owen, pressing close to get a glimpse of the antique text. They touched the thick pages and murmured the names of various spells.

"We should get ready," Trish said, readjusting her grip on her crutches. "D-bag and D-bag Jr. are probably gonna want this bad boy back."

Owen agreed. "How much time do you think we have?"

Perry checked the time. "Twenty, possibly thirty minutes."

"All right, everyone," Owen said to the members of SCA. "Let's get ready for battle."

The middle schoolers sprang into action. After referring to the spell book, Perry drew a ring of protection around the rock formation, pulling components from a bag they'd spent the week filling. Julie enchanted every bush and tumbleweed in the immediate area. Trish drilled Ravi and Moe Moe on their attack spells, while Owen made sure all the pages had indeed come back to them. He flipped to the end, and his breath caught in his throat. On one of the last pages, where for weeks there had been only a blank field of white, was the spell he'd been waiting for. The title was in Latin—*Incantatio Praeteritorum Rescribo*—but as he looked, the letters rearranged themselves on the page until they were written in plain English.

It was the Spell to Rewrite History.

After all this time, it was right in front of him. There were the three illustrations at the bottom, only instead of Owen and his mom, it now showed the teenager facing a line of dark figures. The second panel showed him saying the spell, and the third was the same as before—the boy and his parents back in Rocky River, sitting on a bench overlooking Lake Erie.

A Spell to Rewrite History

Wow. Things must have gotten quite bad, otherwise you wouldn't even consider **casting a spell to change the past.** Do you even know what kind of repercussions such magic has? You could, for example, accidentally alter the course of evolution, or be responsible for the death of millions, or cause yourself to never be born. But let's assume you've already considered those factors, and you wish to proceed anyway. **This enchantment will go back** and **alter a section of the past** to your specific liking. Beware, though—the effects will, most likely, only be noticed by the spell caster. **Choose wisely.**

COMPONENTS NEEDED:

— none —

STEP ONE:

Focus on the moment of history you would like to change. **Recreate it** as **vividly and specifically** in your mind as possible. Sounds, smells, physical sensations— **the more realistic, the better.**

STEP TWO:

Once you have the moment firmly in your **mind,** focus on **how** you would like to alter that moment.

STEP THREE:

Holding the **new moment** in your mind with **supreme focus,** say the activation words:

VELIM PRAETERITA MUTARE
(VAY-leem pray-TARE-ee-ta MEW-tar-ay)

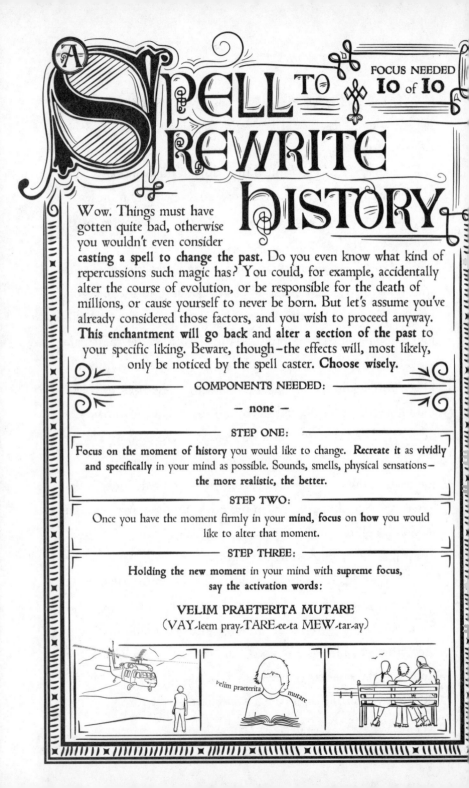

Though it was appealing, the boy knew the last image was false. He could say the spell—ironically, it appeared to be quite simple—but if he did so, he would erase everything he had become in the last month. The new Owen—the Owen who worked hard, stood up for what he knew was right, and had learned to be a leader—that person would be dispelled, possibly to never exist again.

Still, he was tempted. Their future was unsure, stressful, and very likely perilous. The odds of six middle schoolers beating whatever the Euclideans would send their way were pitifully small. He knew that. But after everything he'd seen and experienced in the last weeks, Owen couldn't go back to his old self. He'd spent years acting more dead than alive. Even if he only had a matter of minutes left on Earth, he was going to spend them as a sorcerer.

He ripped the spell page out of the book, stuffing it in his pocket before it could reattach itself to the binding. It was decided, then. He'd protect the book, or die trying.

"Everything okay?" Perry said, sprinkling the last of Alec's moonstone dust on the border of her protection spell.

"I'm good," the young man said. "Just, uh, taking a page out of Whitmore's book."

Hesitantly, the small girl put a hand on his shoulder. "Your mom would be proud of you, you know. What you achieved in the last two weeks, it's pretty special."

"Even if it doesn't work?"

"Especially then," she said emphatically. Then she rose to the tips of her toes and gave Owen a quick kiss on the cheek. Both eighth graders blushed, looking down at the ground.

"Ugh, seriously?" came an angry voice. It was Trish, who had seen the intimate moment and now had her arms folded in disgust. "You guys know we're prepping for a battle here, right?"

"I know, I know," Owen began, then stopped as he felt a vibration in the spell book. He flipped to the back. The final page, which had also been blank this whole time, was filling in. What it revealed was a message, written in runes.

Perry took a piece of notebook paper from her backpack. The two teens had just started to translate the symbols when they heard the approaching sound. Perry's time estimate had been too generous. Only eighteen minutes had elapsed since the pages had flown from Ferretti's house, and the Euclideans were already arriving to take them back. But it was not, as they had all expected, by car.

It was by helicopter.

Chapter 25

Blackhawk Attack

Two helicopters, to be exact. Twin Sikorsky UH-60 Blackhawk models favored by the US Army were approaching. Since the military had recently switched to a newer model, the attack vehicles were available for purchase to anyone with an eight-figure line of credit. The Euclideans had one.

The choppers had appeared low on the northwestern horizon, not exactly an unusual sight for a city that frequently hosted the incredibly wealthy. But as they drew closer, it became clear these vehicles were not en route to photograph the Hoover Dam.

Ravi, who was practicing the hand movements for the shield spell, broke off when he heard the sound of approaching rotors. "Are those coming for us?" he asked.

The others followed his gaze. "They are," Owen said grimly. "Attack positions!"

Each middle schooler performed the hand motions for his or her favorite projectile spell—fireballs, electricity, even a long-range modification to the freeze spell Perry had created. Once they were charged, however, they refrained from using their activation words.

"Wait for it. . . ." Trish said.

The Blackhawks crested the rocky hills. But instead of touching down or flying past the rock formation, they hovered just out of range.

"Why are they hanging back?" Perry whispered to Owen.

"I don't know," he whispered back. "Keep 'em **CHARGED!**" he told the others.

There was a flash from inside one of the helicopters. An object streaked toward them, shining like a meteor. Was it a tracer round? A missile?

No, it was only a flare. But the fact that it was heading straight for Owen lent it some added menace. He screwed his eyes shut—

SORCERY FOR BEGINNERS

Once a spell is ready to be cast, its CHARGE can be held indefinitely, provided that the sorcerer stays awake and maintains focus. The longest holding of a charge is attributed to Maria Guadalupe Luis de Valencia (1581–1610 C.E.), who was arrested for witchcraft. Before having her hands and mouth bound, Valencia charged up a Spell for Destruction, but refrained from casting it until she was brought before the Spanish Inquisition a full five days later. She vaporized the entire tribunal and herself in the process, but to date it is the most impressive display of focus ever recorded.

But the projectile struck an invisible barrier. The flare extinguished, and purple ripples spread over the transparent dome. Immediately, the helicopters banked away.

"Dang it! Now they know we cast a protection spell," Perry said.

"Fire!" Owen shouted.

The middle schoolers thrust their hands forward, shouting activation words. Ice shards, fireballs, and bolts of electricity all shot through the air toward the helicopters, but the Blackhawks had already retreated to a safe distance. Only Trish's fireball reached one of the vehicles, but it barely scorched the thick, armor-plated hull.

The choppers wheeled around, heading straight for the teenagers. "Fire at will!" yelled Owen.

The group began to charge up new spells, but the oncoming Blackhawks caused Ravi and Julie to falter. They dropped to the ground, covering their heads as the attack helicopters approached. The vehicles banked right before hitting the circle of protection. They passed so close, Owen could smell the fumes of engine exhaust. The Euclideans fired no more flares, but they did activate one weapon as they went by—a water cannon, used for pacifying crowds. Only they didn't aim it at the tight knot of teenagers.

They sprayed the line of chalk that encircled the rock formation. The enchantment boundary broke apart under the powerful spray, and the dome of protection evaporated. The

Even Spells of Flight and Protection are no match against military-grade helicopters.

Blackhawks turned again, preparing to touch down. Owen and the other members of SCA were now exposed.

The boy dropped his hands, the orange flames of his fire spell dissipating. He touched the bone amulet around his neck for reassurance. Hopefully Alec was right, and whatever power it had would help protect them.

DEAL OR NO DEAL

"Form a line!" Owen yelled. "Remember to use your shield spells. And whatever comes out of those helicopters, wait until they get closer to attack."

The six middle schoolers pressed tightly against each other. Owen zipped the spell book into his backpack. Trish thumped him on the shoulder, smiling. "Can you believe it? All that time I spent in SCA setting up pretend battles, and now here

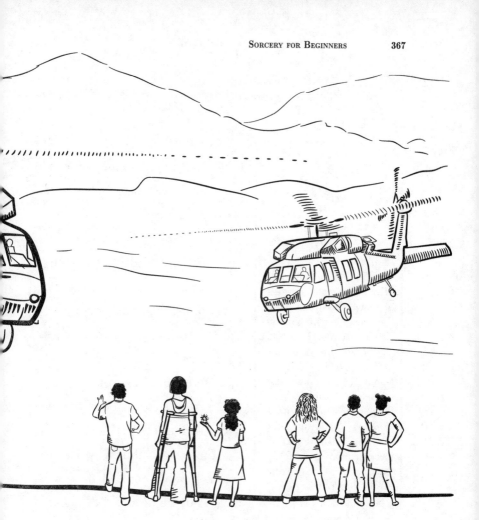

we are, doing it for real. Come on!" she shouted at the landing Blackhawks, already twisting her hands to form a devastating fire spell.

Owen grinned and turned to Perry. Her small face was terrified but determined. "We can take them," he assured her.

"If you're sure, I'm sure," she replied, briefly gripping his hand.

The Blackhawks touched down fifteen meters from the teenagers. Each of them had a white insignia painted on the side—a compass and a flaming torch bisected by a cross. The SYMBOL of the Euclideans.

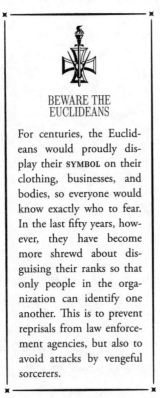

BEWARE THE EUCLIDEANS

For centuries, the Euclideans would proudly display their SYMBOL on their clothing, businesses, and bodies, so everyone would know exactly who to fear. In the last fifty years, however, they have become more shrewd about disguising their ranks so that only people in the organization can identify one another. This is to prevent reprisals from law enforcement agencies, but also to avoid attacks by vengeful sorcerers.

One of the cargo doors slid back. The children tensed, but then only one figure emerged. He wore a clean three-piece suit over his powerful frame.

"Like my ride?" said Virgil Ferretti over the sound of the spinning rotors. "Courtesy of my new friends. Turns out, they're even better connected than I thought."

"We're not giving you the book," Owen yelled back. "You're gonna have to kill us first!"

The other children swung their heads toward him. "Um, excuse me?" said Moe Moe. "No one said anything about *killing.*"

"Yeah, I can't die before I get to first base," Ravi said.

"Just trust me," Owen told them.

Ferretti laughed. "You kids, you only think in black and white. Right or wrong, alive or dead—what you don't realize is, there're plenty shades of gray in between. You don't hand over my property, and there's all kinds of things I can do—painful, permanent things—before I kill you."

He held out his hand. Owen took a step forward. But instead of reaching for his backpack, he quickly bent his fingers and brought his hands together. There was a loud thunderclap, and a wave of concussive force knocked Ferretti into the helicopter.

"Come and take it," Owen said.

Ferretti stood, straightening his suit with a scowl. He made a "go ahead" movement toward the Blackhawks. A dozen men leapt out—massive, muscular men in high-tech riot gear and face shields. The Euclidean logo was on the shoulder of their uniforms, and in their hands were M5 assault rifles.

"Mercenaries," said Perry. "He brought mercenaries."

"Coward!" yelled Trish.

The leader of the mercenaries, a bald, handsome Euclidean whom we last saw in St. Petersburg, leaned in to Ferretti. "You didn't tell us there would be so many."

"So they brought a few friends," said the casino owner. "They're little kids; what's the big deal?"

"If they can all use sorcery, it will be a very big deal." But he assessed the SCA members, then shrugged and pulled down his face shield. "Weapons free," he said to the other mercenaries. "Pacification rounds only."

WHEN EUCLIDEANS ATTACK

The Euclidean mercenaries fired on the middle schoolers. It wasn't gunfire, but a flatter, less explosive sound.

Rubber bullets.

"Shields!" Owen screamed, but he was a beat too late. He and a few others managed to get theirs up in time, the projectiles bouncing off their energy walls. But Moe Moe and Ravi were hit. They dropped down to the sand, howling in pain.

"Attack!" yelled Owen. He quickly charged a fire spell and cast it. An orange ball of flame shot from his hands, slamming into one attacker and knocking him off his feet.

Beside him, Trish had dropped her crutches and conjured a spell for lightning with both hands. Bolts of blue energy ripped from her fingers and struck two approaching mercenaries. They fell to the ground, twitching but immobile.

Perry was not only spinning her arms, but twisting her entire body as well, in a complex pattern Owen had never seen before. Wind began to swirl around her small frame, creating a miniature tornado. Then she thrust her hands toward a cluster of three soldiers, shouting the activation word for a Turkish wind spell—*"Kasırga!"*

A CYCLONE leapt from her fingers, gobbling up gouts of sand and enveloping four of the advancing men. Their bodies spun into the air, the wind tugging the rifles from their fingers.

SORCERY FOR
BEGINNERS

All spells can be adapted to fit your needs. This can be done by modifying the somatic components, increasing the necessary materials, or combining two or more enchantments to create a new effect. Here, Perry has taken a basic wind spell and embroidered the hand movements to create a weaponized CYCLONE.

The whirlwind dissipated, sending the soldiers tumbling to the ground. They lay there, stunned.

"Holy awesome," said Trish. "You've been holding out on us, girl."

"I wasn't sure a modified spell would work," Perry admitted.

But there was no more time for congratulations, as the remaining Euclideans quickly closed the gap. A few were snared by previously enchanted bushes or tumbleweeds, but the rest kicked free of the vegetation and kept coming. Once they were on top of the middle schoolers, the fight became a full-fledged melee. The mercenaries simply shoved or yanked the children aside, clearing a path to Owen and the spell book.

The teenager was in the midst of conjuring another thunder-clap when the head Euclidean grabbed his backpack. He tried to stop the big man from yanking it off, but couldn't break his grip. Thankfully Moe Moe saw what was happening. She bent her fingers, muttering words in Latin as she pointed her hands at the sand beneath them.

"*Impetus!*" she cried. Thousands of ANTS burst from the sand at the bald man's feet. They swarmed up his legs like dark

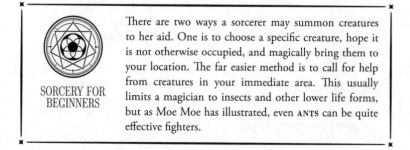

SORCERY FOR BEGINNERS

There are two ways a sorcerer may summon creatures to her aid. One is to choose a specific creature, hope it is not otherwise occupied, and magically bring them to your location. The far easier method is to call for help from creatures in your immediate area. This usually limits a magician to insects and other lower life forms, but as Moe Moe has illustrated, even ANTS can be quite effective fighters.

tentacles, crawling under his pants and biting his skin. This was a man who had kept his cool in all kinds of life-threatening conditions, but even he had his limits. He let go of Owen, frantically brushing his pants and shaking his legs to get the insects off.

The other middle schoolers were occupied with battles of their own. One mercenary swung the butt of his rifle at Ravi's head, but it went through the boy's skull like it was made of smoke. "Sorry," said the human mirage. "Try Door Number Two." The soldier turned, and the real Ravi thrust out a hand.

"Dancez avec la plus belle fille du monde," the boy said in FRENCH. Colored ribbons of light flew from Ravi's fingertips, wrapping around his attacker's eyes. The hardened fighter dropped his rifle, grinned stupidly, and began waltzing through the desert with a dance partner only he could see.

Perry, meanwhile, had been restrained by another mercenary, who turned out to be Kiraz. Unfortunately for him, the man had forgotten to bind her fingers. She quickly formed runes and fired a stream of ice crystals at his feet. His boots froze to the ground, and in his surprise, he let go of the tiny girl. She charged another spell and tapped the Euclidean's chest.

"Immobiles," she said. Kiraz's arms and legs snapped together, and he toppled to the sand like a plank of wood.

SORCERY FOR BEGINNERS

No one knows why so many illusion spells require a sorcerer to speak in FRENCH. Perhaps it's because several of the great illusionists hailed from that country. Perhaps it's because the French coined other terms of illusion such as *mirage* and *diet*. Perhaps it simply sounds nice.

At the same time, Trish and Julie faced the remaining three mercenaries. Julie spread her fingers and spoke a phrase in Portuguese. Tumbleweeds rolled toward the Euclideans from every corner of the desert, sticking against two of the soldiers until they looked more like twig snowmen than seasoned killers.

Trish, meanwhile, had charged her metal crutches with electricity. When the final mercenary got within range, she simply touched him with one of her homemade shock sticks. His body convulsed, but he managed to throw a punch, clocking Trish in the jaw. The big girl crumpled to the ground, dazed. Owen saw the mercenary's eyes and mouth were ringed by puffy red welts, evidence of where they had been lasered open. Blondie.

Blond, Lame Blond

"Don't you touch her!" Owen yelled. He ran at the large man, who turned to face him. He pulled out a stun baton and swung. But the boy was all instinct now, throwing up shields to block every swing of the weapon. He twisted his hands, creating a golden oval in front of him, then he ran at Ferretti's guard like a linebacker.

The shield slammed into Blondie like a brick wall, knocking him back two meters. Owen charged a fire spell, but a hand touched his shoulder.

It was Trish. She'd gotten back on her feet, her cheek already red from where the big man had struck her. "Allow me," she said.

Ferretti's guard snorted. "What are you gonna do?" he sneered. "So what if you know magic? You're nothing more than a big—"

KRRSHH! A powerful jet of water streamed from her hands, striking the big man in the face. He gurgled and choked, trying to block the spray, but it was so **POWERFUL**, it knocked the helmet off of his head. The stun baton slipped from his hand, and electricity coursed

SORCERY FOR BEGINNERS

The more mass an element has, the more difficult it is to conjure out of thin air. Trish creating a jet of water in hot desert conditions demonstrates not only a great deal of focus and **POWER**, but a good deal of stubbornness, as well. But sometimes anger outweighs logic.

through his wet body. His limbs twitched, then he fell into the sand, unconscious.

"Not so fun getting drowned, is it?" Trish said, kicking away Blondie's stun baton.

Owen looked around. Every Euclidean mercenary, save their leader, had been incapacitated, and the middle schoolers had only minor injuries. The boy stepped toward the bald, ant-covered man. The soldier tried to lift his rifle, but it was clear that thousands of ant bites were affecting his concentration.

"I'm gonna make this easy on you," Owen said to him. The eighth grader moved his arms through the air in a series of smooth motions, then he extended a hand at the man's head. "You need to rethink your career choices. Maybe go home and start an ant farm."

The Euclidean's eyes went vacant. He dropped his rifle, staring off into the desert like he had just had an epiphany. "I need to rethink my career choices," he agreed.

Owen's Spell for Suggestion had worked. The mercenary walked off, removing his military gear and absently brushing off ants. He started to whistle a happy tune as he left.

"Dude, you should be a guidance counselor," said Trish.

"You think you've won?" came an imperious voice. It was Kiraz, still struggling against Perry's Binding Spell. His blue eyes were shining with fury. "All you've done is prove us right. Sorcery is dangerous, and the Euclideans will not rest until every last bit of it is under our control."

"Try to come after us," said Owen. "When you do, we'll be ready."

He nodded to Perry, who canceled the Binding Spell. Kiraz got to his feet, brushing sand and ice from his military garb in as dignified a manner as he could muster. Seeing he was outnumbered, he made his way back toward the Blackhawks. He stepped inside the first helicopter and shut the door.

The six middle schoolers looked around the shallow bowl and laughed. "Honestly?" said Owen. "I did not think we would beat a bunch of soldiers in helicopters."

"Of course we beat 'em," said Trish, firing a lightning spell at one of the mercenaries who was trying to get to his feet. He twitched and lay still. "We're *sorcerers*, dude."

Owen grinned, glancing toward the Blackhawks. There was no sign of Ferretti, so maybe he'd finally accepted the spell book would never be his. It was a hopelessly naïve thought, perhaps, but he was thirteen years old. Even though he'd seen much more of the world in the last two weeks, he still believed at heart that people were good, honest, and logical.

So he was more than mildly surprised when three figures exited the second helicopter. They wore no riot gear, nor held any weapons, but Owen immediately recognized each one of them. The Thin Man was in the center, grinning as his long white fingers conjured a spell. To his right was Bryan, who had shaved his orange Mohawk and looked more confident and hateful than ever. And on the left stood Abu. Like Bryan, his magically sealed skin had been lasered open. As a result, his lips were puffy with red scar tissue. His eyes were filled with an intense, fiery rage, and they were focused directly on Owen.

SPELL VS. SPELL

There were no taunts or witty remarks. The three simply went into action. Bryan ran a few steps, casting the thunderclap spell at his feet and launching himself into the air. Abu turned an hourglass timer and bolted at the six middle schoolers, becoming a **SUPER-FAST BLUR**.

The Thin Man stayed where he was, but hurled a massive green fireball at the group of middle schoolers.

"Frysta!" shouted Perry, twisting her fingers and firing ice shards at the fireball. It extinguished in a puff of smoke.

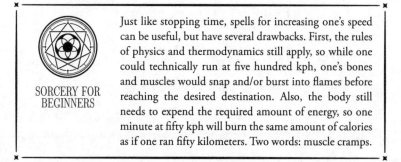

SORCERY FOR BEGINNERS

Just like stopping time, spells for increasing one's speed can be useful, but have several drawbacks. First, the rules of physics and thermodynamics still apply, so while one could technically run at five hundred kph, one's bones and muscles would snap and/or burst into flames before reaching the desired destination. Also, the body still needs to expend the required amount of energy, so one minute at fifty kph will burn the same amount of calories as if one ran fifty kilometers. Two words: muscle cramps.

Bryan landed in the center of the group, his hands crackling with electricity. The impact on the ground made Trish and Moe Moe stumble. Bryan fired blasts to either side, electrocuting both girls at once. Julie and Ravi panicked, running in opposite directions.

"Stay together!" Owen yelled. "Don't let them—"

WHUMP. He was suddenly knocked off his feet, the air in his lungs replaced by red-hot lava. A silhouette loomed over him. Abu. He had punched Owen in the chest at over fifty kilometers per hour.

"Bet you forgot all about me, huh," said the muscular older boy. Up close, his lips looked like puffy hot dogs. "Well, I remember you. Every single time I open my mouth."

Owen rolled sideways, attempting to charge up a spell. But Abu turned his timer again and kicked Owen six times in the ribs in less than a second. The pain was so acute, Owen's eyes unfocused for a moment.

"Imagine how I felt when I got a call from my old buddy Bryan," Abu continued. "And he told me I could get you back for what you did to me."

He knelt, placing his fingers on Owen's eyes and mouth. "Don't worry; it doesn't hurt until after they cut you open. Then it hurts all the time. *Exsarci*—"

BAMMM! A metal crutch connected with the side of Abu's head. Trish stood next to them, her face tight with the pain of leaning on her injured leg. Even though the electric charge had dissipated from her crutches, the force of her swing was enough to send the enchanted timer flying into the desert. If she hoped her hit would knock Abu over, though, she was disappointed. The big kid merely shook his head, yanked the crutch from her hand, and flung it aside. Then he began to conjure another enchantment.

Perry, meanwhile, was going spell-to-spell with the Thin Man. His mad eyes flashed as he sent a wave of earth rolling toward her. The tiny girl held her ground, though, forming a circle with her hands and chopping it.

"Annullare," she commanded, and the mound of sand dissipated at her feet. She pivoted like a dancer, already halfway through the hand movements for her next spell. She flung a glamour at the long-haired man, but he merely **BLOCKED IT** with a shield spell. The rainbow-hued band of light vanished.

"Little Ant must try harder," he said, showing a mouthful of brown, rotten teeth. "My own eyes show me worse visions every day. Wanna see? *Vipera!*" He twisted his fingers, and a bundle of hissing snakes flew from his hands. The tiny girl screamed as they slithered around her legs.

A few meters away, Bryan was making quick work of the other SCA members. He had clearly done little besides practice spells in the time since his father had acquired

SORCERY FOR BEGINNERS

Glamours, and most spells of illusion, can be thrown at targets from a distance. However, the enchantment must make contact with a target's eyes to take effect. If spotted, the incoming enchantment can be **DEFLECTED** by other spells or simply dodged.

Sorcery for Beginners. His movements were choppy, but efficient. He knocked Ravi down with a thunderclap, set Julie's sweater on fire, and blinded Moe Moe with a glamour before she could get back on her feet.

Ravi stood, attempting to charge up an electricity spell, but Bryan simply jogged to his side and socked him in the face. The small boy fell to the earth, dazed. A shadow blanketed him as the bully advanced.

"Let me show you a little something I came up with myself," Bryan said, his fingers forming runes.

Ten meters away, Owen wheezed, trying to force some air back into his lungs. He took stock of his friends. In a few short moments, Ferretti's sorcerers had turned the tide of the fight. Ravi, Moe Moe, and Julie were down; Trish had been knocked aside by Abu, and Perry was unsuccessfully trying to compel the Thin Man's reptile buddies to leave her alone. Within minutes, it would all be over.

Finishing Moves

Abu turned back to face Owen. The big kid grinned, forming a few runes and barking a word in German. His fists changed color, taking on the hue and texture of rock-hard granite. He threw a flurry of punches at the thirteen-year-old. Owen blocked his first volley with shields, but the force of his blows sent the eighth grader sprawling.

Then Abu advanced on Owen. His face was sweaty from the exertion of battle, but he raised his stone hands, grinning.

He was enjoying his new power. He pressed Owen toward one of the rock pillars, throwing punches with abandon. The young man blocked one thunderous fist, then ducked under another. Abu's granite hand smashed through the red rock column right above Owen's head, showering him with fragments of stone.

Abu pulled back his right fist for a big haymaker. Owen knew he couldn't withstand a direct hit. He raised his hands.

"Wait. Why are we fighting?" he said. "I know what I did to you sucks, but if you remember, you were standing on my head at the time. So rather than wailing on each other, how about we figure out a way to fix your face, huh? There's gotta be a spell in here we can use."

Abu cocked his head, pretending to think about that. Then he smiled through what used to be his lips. "Nah. This is more fun." He brought down his fist.

Owen's fingers quickly sketched runes in the air. Instead of dodging the incoming fist-shaped rock, he stretched out his hand and spoke one word: *"Frysta."*

Blue ice enveloped Abu's fist, stopping it midair. It spread up his arm, freezing the moisture all over the big kid's sweaty body, creating a thick, cold shell that rendered the fourteen-year-old an ice sculpture. He blinked in surprise, but that was the only movement he could make.

Perry, meanwhile, had realized the snakes were only an illusion. *"Annullare!"* she shouted. The vipers disappeared, but by that point the Thin Man had reached her. He grabbed the tiny girl by the throat. The fingers of his other hand twitched and curled until blue electricity crackled from his fingers.

"Why are you helping them?" she said, pulling uselessly at his hand. "They're enemies of magic!"

"Five years, they held me," he said, his eyes rolling madly. "The things they did . . . like lightning to the brain. Let me show you."

He lifted the ball of electricity toward her skull. But as his gaunt, grinning face came toward her, a fireball appeared in her hand.

"Sorry," she said, and shoved the flames into his mouth. The electricity vanished from his fingers. The Thin Man staggered backward, clutching his chest. A mad, desperate giggle escaped from his throat.

"Little Ant," he coughed. "Little Ant shouldn't play with—" But he didn't finish the sentence, because a **RIVER OF FLAME** poured from his throat. He fell to the ground, unconscious, gray smoke seeping through the gaps of his ruined, stained teeth.

Nearby, Bryan had nearly finished conjuring his massive spell creation. Purple energy crackled around his fingers as Julie and Moe

SORCERY FOR BEGINNERS

While magic **FLAMES** have some of the same properties as ordinary fire (burning, giving off heat, et cetera), they can also be manipulated in extraordinary ways. Fire sculpting, non-consuming fires, and even fire breathing are all possible when sorcery is involved.

Moe got to their feet. Julie compelled desert roots to ensnare the bully's feet, which was enough to break his spell casting. Bryan cursed, sending a blue fireball at the vegetation. He made a few more gestures and cast a thunderclap right in Julie's face. The girl's head snapped backward unnaturally. Her body skidded across the sand, slamming into a pillar of red rock, and she lay still.

Bryan rounded on Moe Moe. The dark-haired girl shrank from him, but she still attempted to charge up a summoning spell. When she stretched out a hand to cast it, though, he slapped it aside. A follow-up shove knocked her to the ground.

He turned toward Trish, batting aside an elemental attack with a shield spell and forming runes of his own. He pivoted, arms twisting as he charged up his own attack. The cyclone spell. "You ever wanted to fly, nerd? Cause you're about to." He was about to thrust his hands forward when a voice stopped him.

"Excuse me," said Ravi.

Bryan turned, a miniature tornado still funneling in his hands. The skinny boy stood behind him, his clothes covered in dust, and a purple bruise discoloring his cheek. "Didn't you read the book?" he said. "There's an easier way to **FLY**."

He thrust his hands at Bryan's feet and said in Welsh, *"Hedfan."*

SORCERY FOR BEGINNERS

A Spell for **FLIGHT** can be directed at anyone, but only the casting sorcerer can control it. Whether it is used on oneself or another, wearing a parachute is highly recommended.

The bully immediately toppled forward, his feet lifting off the ground. The tiny cyclone in his hands blew apart as he scrabbled at the dry sand. His body floated upward, but Ravi made a hand motion to halt his ascent. Bryan hung upside down, suspended ten feet above the desert floor. Owen, Trish, and Perry joined Ravi.

"Help," the fourteen-year-old pleaded as the sorcerers advanced. "I never learned the undo spell!"

"Good," said Ravi. "Next time you wanna torment somebody, remember what *this* feels like."

He flicked a finger, and Bryan's body shot into the sky. The bully clawed at a rock pillar, but his fingers slipped and he only went higher. "Dad!" he shouted at the Blackhawk helicopters. "Dad, you gotta help me. Daddy!"

The middle schoolers' mirth disappeared. They looked back at the Euclidean vehicles. A shape was indeed emerging from the second helicopter, but it seemed to be more robot than human. Its limbs were covered in thick, biometric plating knit together with wires. Attached to the back was a buzzing generator device. A reinforced helmet with a digital, retina-controlled display shielded the head. In spite of this, the children recognized the face inside the armor.

It belonged to Virgil Ferretti.

Techno Magic

"Very impressive show, kids," said the casino owner. He motioned to the second helicopter, which lifted off and went

to collect Bryan, who was floating in the distance like a lost balloon. Then Ferretti strode toward
the teenagers, the joints of his
high-tech body armor whirring
as he came.

"But I'll bet you don't have
one of these," he said, modeling
the suit for them. "**ANTI-MAGIC
ARMOR.** Another loaner from the
Euclideans. They built it years ago,
but I'm the one who suggested they
add a spell casting database to it.
Why not fight sorcery with sorcery,

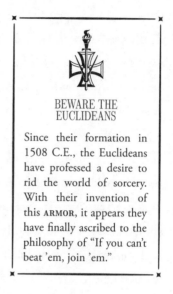

BEWARE THE EUCLIDEANS

Since their formation in
1508 C.E., the Euclideans
have professed a desire to
rid the world of sorcery.
With their invention of
this ARMOR, it appears they
have finally ascribed to the
philosophy of "If you can't
beat 'em, join 'em."

I told 'em? Thanks to your book, we made it happen."

"Is that the final design?" Owen was unimpressed. "Cause it
seems a little rushed."

Trish snorted a
laugh. "Yeah, dude,
you look like a robot
hockey goalie."

Ferretti's
expression darkened.
"This is just a prototype,
smart-asses. Once we
prove that it works, the
Euclideans are gonna

*The worst of science and magic,
personified*

mass-produce these babies. The perfect blend of sorcery and science." He tapped his helmet. "Retinal-operated heads-up display so I can download the steps and incantations to any spell I need. Strength and protection enchantments all over the armor, plus a power source wired directly to my brain. Whole thing does the work for you—watch."

Following the prompts on his display, he moved his arms and fingers in the pattern for an earth attack. The generator on his back hummed to life, and when Ferretti thrust out his hands, a massive rift opened in the sand. The crack in the earth spidered toward the middle schoolers. They dove aside, but the rock pillar behind them broke apart, dropping into the newly formed chasm.

"That's *cheating*!" said Perry indignantly. "You're not learning the spells; you're just letting some computer make the calculations for you."

"It's a digital age, small fry. What you call cheating, I call *progress*. Imagine an army of soldiers wearing these. No country will be able to stand against us." He fixed his steely gaze on Owen. "But we can't do that if a bunch of kids are running around, telling people how to use magic to defend themselves. So I'm gonna need you to give me back my property."

Owen removed *Sorcery for Beginners* from his backpack. Maybe it was the enchantments on the tome, or maybe it was just luck, but somehow it had remained undamaged during all the morning's violence. He touched the gold lettering on the dark leather cover. "This kind of power, it shouldn't be easily given to anyone. It needs to be *earned*."

Ferretti smirked. "What are you gonna do, blow it up? I already know that doesn't work. The spells on the book are too strong."

"But I can make it so it never existed," said the boy, taking a piece of parchment from his pocket. "I can cast A Spell to Rewrite History."

A Spell to Rewrite History

The smile started to fade from the casino owner's face. The other middle schoolers turned to Owen, just as confused.

"You're lying," said Ferretti, frantically searching his heads-up display. "There's no spell like that in the database."

"Because it was hidden," said Owen. "Even if you tear out the page, it won't show up until you've earned the right to see it. But to know that, you'd have to do the actual work."

"Owen, you can't," said Perry. "You heard what Whitmore said."

"Yeah, dude, anytime someone messes with time travel in the movies, it does not turn out well," said Trish.

"He's not gonna do it," said Ferretti. "If he erases the book, then where does that leave him? Just an ordinary eighth grader with a B average. He needs this thing to exist as much as I do."

Owen dropped *Sorcery for Beginners* onto the sand. "Maybe so," he admitted. "But if I'm going to learn magic, I want to do it the right way."

He closed his eyes, forming runes with his fingers and muttering words under his breath. Ferretti started to run toward the boy, but his heavy, high-tech armor made him slow. He had only gone a meter or two by the time Owen raised his arms over his head, clapped, then slammed his open palm into the center of the cover and spoke in Latin:

"**VELIM PRAETERITA MUTARE.**"

There was no implosion, no great rip in the fabric of space. The spell book, the source of all Owen's excitement and doubt and misery in the last two weeks, simply vanished.

Ferretti halted in shock. "You idiot," he said. "You stupid, selfish brat, bring it back. NOW!"

"Bring back what?" said Owen. He honestly seemed confused.

The big man began to cycle his hands through the air. He was charging something big, a combination of spells so complex and powerful, the middle schoolers had never attempted it. Purple energy crackled all around his suit. The man's face turned red from the effort.

"Uh, Owen?" said Ravi. "I think he's really gonna kill us."

SORCERY FOR BEGINNERS

Literally meaning "I wish to alter the past," the words of the activation phrase VELIM PRAETERITA MUTARE are not as important as the intention behind them. The spell caster must hold two simultaneous thoughts in her mind: the specific event in the past she wishes to change, and the new event she wishes it to become. If either thought is not clearly visualized, the spell will fail in spectacular fashion. Usually this results in some form of brain damage to the caster.

The boy still seemed bewildered, so Perry spoke up. "Fighting positions."

SHOWING HIS HAND

But Ferretti didn't cast an attack spell. His automated gloves helped him form runes, and he read a long incantation off his retinal display. The ground trembled beneath them. The casino owner extended his hand and curled his fingers. The pillars of rock behind them bent and cracked, mimicking his movements.

"It's a transmutation spell," said Perry. "A really, really big one."

"Attack," advised Trish. She and Ravi began charging up spells, but Ferretti simply lifted his hand.

The ground lurched beneath them and rose skyward. The eighth graders toppled to the sand, suddenly finding themselves on a stone platform four meters wide. Dirt and desert vegetation fell away, taking Ravi with it. The platform and its surrounding rock pillars continued upward, revealing that Owen, Trish, and Perry were now trapped in the palm of a massive, red rock hand. They were easily five stories off the ground.

"Let them go!" shouted Ravi. He charged up a ball of electricity, but Ferretti now threw back his head and opened his mouth. A sinkhole appeared at Ravi's feet. The boy stumbled backward as a massive rock structure rose from the ground. It moved into the air until it was level with the stone hand. Owen, Perry, and Trish stared. Before them was a ten-meter-high rock replica of Virgil Ferretti's face.

Multiple spells cast together
can have unexpected and devastating effects.

"This seems bad," said Owen.

Ravi aimed another spell at the casino owner, but the man tilted his hand and opened his mouth. Five stories above, the huge rock head did the same. The message was clear—one bite from the casino owner, and the three eighth graders would know how it felt to be a handful of popcorn.

"This is not how I pictured my life ending," said Trish. "I mean, yeah, there were giant monsters involved, but they were way cooler than this."

"What's it gonna be, kids?" said the giant rock face, aping the movements of Ferretti. "You ready to throw your lives away on a book?"

Owen looked at the girls. Their faces were etched with fear, but they knew what needed to be done. The eighth grader held out his hands. Trish and Perry each took one.

"Bite me!" he shouted.

Ferretti gritted his teeth. Five stories above him, the stone head followed suit, spraying the middle schoolers with shards of rock. The casino owner read another incantation off his helmet display. The generator on his back crackled, sending energy coursing through the high-tech suit. The stone hand tilted the kids toward the giant mouth. A light appeared in the depths of the rock throat, an angry red light that carried the stink of brimstone. Owen, Perry, and Trish struggled to hang on, but the mouth opened wider beneath them—

Then the generator on Ferretti's battle armor died. The five-story rock replica went slack. It teetered briefly, then began to tip sideways. The eighth graders experienced a moment of weightlessness, and then the stone hand hit the desert floor with a bone-rattling *thud*. It broke into pieces, throwing Owen, Trish, and Perry into a sand dune. They kicked their way out, spitting sand but luckily unharmed.

"Dude," Trish said. "We could charge admission to something like that."

"Are you nuts?! You're lucky you didn't break your other leg," said Perry.

"Save it," said Owen. He appeared to have recovered some of his mental faculties, perhaps due to his fall from the massive stone hand. "We're not done yet."

RESIGNATION

Ferretti knelt several meters away, his head bowed. Now that his high-tech armor was powerless, it was little better than, literally and musically speaking, a pile of heavy metal. The weight of it had literally forced the big man to the ground.

Behind him, Kiraz stood in front of a helicopter, holding a remote in his hand. "A quite disappointing display," he said in a clipped voice. "But not entirely unexpected. It's clear we need to reconceive this device."

"You turned it off? Why?" The casino owner panted, trying and failing to get to his feet.

"The Euclideans have remained hidden for five hundred years," Kiraz said coldly. "The magical murder of three children would end that secrecy before you could say *nationwide outrage*. Besides, the book is gone."

"I can get it back," said Ferretti. "I'll cast the kid's Spell to Rewrite History or something. Just turn my armor back on!"

The Euclidean pressed a finger to a hidden earbud and nodded. "I've been instructed to inform you that our partnership is concluded," he said to Ferretti. "All databases and security footage regarding this matter have been erased. Do not try to contact us. And you"—he turned to the middle schoolers—"stay away from sorcery. Otherwise our paths will cross again."

He jerked his head, and the rest of the Euclideans boarded the helicopters, carrying or dragging those of their number who were still unconscious. They left Bryan tied to a bush, and the Blackhawks lifted off, disappearing back to wherever they'd come from.

"What'd I tell you?" said Owen to the casino owner. "Easy come, easy go."

Ferretti tossed aside his helmet. Veins bulged in his neck as he slowly forced himself to his feet. "You think . . . I'll let them stop me?" He punched a button on his chest. The heavy armor plates popped open and fell to the ground.

"Dude, you really don't know when to hang it up," said Trish.

Perry stepped forward, holding up Owen's cell phone. "We called the police. Also the FBI, NSA, 9-1-1, and some park rangers. They're already en route, and they're very interested in your use of illegal weapons against children."

Indeed, they could all hear sirens approaching from the distance. The casino owner pulled an automatic pistol from his pocket, pointing the barrel at Owen's chest. "You bring back my book," he demanded. "Now."

The eighth grader slowly raised his hands. "I don't know what you're talking about."

The sirens were louder now. Emergency vehicles squealed to a stop at the edge of the rock formation. Police officers and paramedics emerged, running toward the standoff.

Ferretti pulled back the hammer on his gun. Owen's heart thumped against his rib cage, but his voice remained steady. "You really gonna shoot me in front of all these people?"

The big man's mouth curled. "I'm rich, and I'm powerful. I could stand in the middle of Las Vegas Boulevard and shoot someone, and I'd get away with it."

The teenager swallowed, worried that the older man was right. But he stood firm. "You won't get away with this. For once in your life, you've lost."

The casino owner glared. "I—do not—*lose*."

And he pulled the trigger.

Death Becomes Him

Owen heard no gunshot. He only felt a massive pressure against his chest, like someone had struck him with a baseball bat. He fell backward as if in slow motion. There was no pain. He only felt a dull sense of surprise that a person could be so spiteful. *That's the problem with power,* he thought as he dropped. *Be it magic or technology or money, it only amplifies whoever a person is to begin with. Someone as hateful and selfish as Virgil Ferretti, all he could ever create with sorcery is destruction.*

Then the young man's body hit the ground.

"Owen!" said Perry. She dropped to her knees, taking the boy's hand in hers. Behind her, shock filled Trish's face.

Ravi and Moe Moe ran forward. They brushed past the casino owner, who stared down at the eighth grader as if even he couldn't believe how far he had gone. The pistol dropped from his hand, but not before it was seen by the approaching police officers.

Perry bent over her friend's body. "Please," she whispered. "Please work, please." She pulled down the top of Owen's T-shirt. Underneath, tied around his neck with a black leather cord, was Alec's bone amulet. Carved into it was the rune for protection.

The teenager blinked. He put a hand to his chest, wincing. There was no blood, not even a wound. There was only a bullet, flattened as if it had struck a wall of diamond.

"I knew it," said Trish. "I knew that fire trick of Alec's was fake!"

"It's no trick," Owen said, touching the AMULET gratefully. "It's magic."

Behind them, two police officers cinched handcuffs onto Virgil Ferretti. They shoved him to his knees, sand coating the man's expensive suit. But he didn't protest or struggle. He simply stared at Owen in disbelief.

"But I shot him," he said in disbelief. "I shot him point-blank."

Owen waved good-bye as the police officers read the stunned

SORCERY FOR BEGINNERS

Alec's AMULET of Protection is actually quite famous among sorcerers. It was created by the Native American medicine man Tatunke Iyotake (1831–1890 C.E.), better known by his nickname, Sitting Bull. Wearing the amulet led to his survival during the Battle of Little Bighorn. After his death, it was passed on to his relatives, and has been through the hands of many owners over the last one hundred years.

casino owner his Miranda rights. They shoved him toward a squad car. A mustached lieutenant approached, pushing back the wide brim of his hat.

"You the kids that texted 9-1-1?" he said.

Perry nodded.

"You wanna tell me what happened here?"

Owen looked around the devastated rock formation. Paramedics were tending to Ravi and Moe Moe's minor wounds, while another checked Julie for signs of a concussion. One police officer handcuffed Blondie, while another questioned Bryan. Two more chipped ice off of Abu. The Thin Man, Owen saw, had disappeared sometime during the final skirmish.

But he wasn't worried. If the man turned up again, the boy was confident they could defend themselves. After all, they were sorcerers.

He turned back to the lieutenant. "That depends. Do you believe in magic?"

CONGRATULATIONS!

You have successfully completed the beginner's guide to sorcery. Now that you have a grounding in the basics, you can apply for your Sorcery Learner's Permit, the details for which are found elsewhere in this book. Since this is the new and (I'm told) improved version of the help guide, the spells should have been much easier to understand, and the absolutely true story of Owen's candidacy should have explained the more confusing aspects of learning magic. Also, there is no need for a Final Examination such as the one Owen and his friends endured. Instead, we encourage you to continue practicing until you are called upon to join the fight.

In the meantime, perhaps you'd like to know what happened to our young candidates. Yes? Then let's jump to eight weeks later, shall we?

EPILOGUE

EIGHT WEEKS LATER

It was a bright afternoon in May. Owen, Perry, and Trish were walking home from school. There was still a fortnight left until summer vacation, but they felt as if the holidays had already begun. Trish's leg cast had been removed on Wednesday, and though she still had a slight limp, the doctors were confident she'd make a full recovery. Perry had received an email stating she had won a scholarship to a summer science camp. And Owen had learned, barring any final exam disasters, he would be receiving two A minuses on his report card. They were his first As since grammar school, where (let's face it) one receives top marks merely for sitting still.

Their good feelings were capped by the news that that very afternoon in a Las Vegas courthouse, Virgil Ferretti had been sentenced to twenty-five years in prison after pleading guilty to a long list of crimes.

"I only hope Bryan doesn't want revenge," said Perry. "He looked apoplectic at the trial."

"Dude, he's on lockdown, too," said Trish. "He and Abu are stuck on house arrest until they turn eighteen."

"But they both still know sorcery," the tiny girl said. "What if they decide to tell someone else about it?"

Owen shrugged. "Who's gonna believe them? Without the book, the best they'll be able to conjure up are a few expensive-looking tricks." They had seen this borne out since the fight at Dragonridge rocks. Ravi and Moe Moe had attempted to cast a spell or two in the last months, but without daily reinforcement of the hand movements, their enchantments had fizzled. A stern visit from Owen, Perry, and Trish had convinced them to leave off spell casting until another guide to sorcery was found. The only magic the SCA members employed now was of the imaginary or card game variety.

And as for Owen, he had finally come out of his funk. Instead of playing video games alone every night, he had an active social life with his new friends. Even better, Owen's father had made good on his promise. Marcus had switched shifts at work so he could spend time with his son after school. Dinner conversation had been awkward at first, but the male Macreadys were slowly becoming friendly with each other. A five-day rafting trip down the Colorado River had been scheduled for August, and both father and son were looking forward to it.

Owen still spoke with his mother once a week on FaceTime. She was now in Rwanda, working with mountain gorilla conservationists. She said the primates were even more endangered than orangutans, and the work was fulfilling. She didn't know when she would return to the States, but the teenager no longer resented her for leaving him. He truly hoped she would find something that gave her life purpose. He had already found his. Even if he couldn't be a practicing sorcerer, he planned to spend the rest of his life studying the topic.

"Congratulations, candidates," spoke a warm, elegant voice.

TEST RESULTS

They turned. Behind them stood Euphemia Whitmore, looking unruffled by the Las Vegas heat despite her dark blouse and long skirt. She was as entrancing as always. She inclined her perfectly coiffed head toward the teenagers. "Mr. Macready, Ms. Spring, and . . . Ms. Kim, I presume? A pleasure."

"How did you—" Owen began, then remembered who he was talking to. "So you heard what happened?"

"Indeed. Quite an ingenious plan, 'erasing' the spell book from history in front of everyone. One of the more thrilling FINAL EXAMINATIONS I have witnessed. Of course, if the

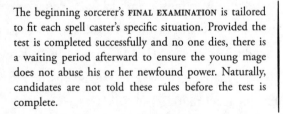

SORCERY FOR BEGINNERS

The beginning sorcerer's FINAL EXAMINATION is tailored to fit each spell caster's specific situation. Provided the test is completed successfully and no one dies, there is a waiting period afterward to ensure the young mage does not abuse his or her newfound power. Naturally, candidates are not told these rules before the test is complete.

spell had truly worked, none of you would remember magic exists. Curious."

Shyly, Owen reached into his backpack, taking out a battered chemistry textbook. A few finger movements and a muttered word, and it transformed into *Sorcery for Beginners*. "I finally figured out the invisibility spell," he explained. "I cast that in my mind while I said the words to **REWRITE HISTORY**. Thanks to Abu being frozen, I was able to get some water on my hand. Even though everyone thinks it was erased from the past,

---

SORCERY FOR BEGINNERS

Astute readers will have realized by now that Owen's casting of the Spell to REWRITE HISTORY could not have worked as we saw here. Had the young man really erased the book from the past, Ferretti and the others would have been unable to recall its existence, too. Were the Euclideans more versed in time travel, they might have realized this, and the boy's ruse would have been discovered.

I like to keep it close by. But we only plan to use the spells when we absolutely need to."

"A most mature decision. And in fact, it appears that need has already arisen. There has been an incident in Scotland. The cryptid affectionately known as Nessie has been trapped by Euclideans."

She paused to let her words sink in. Perry, as usual, was the first to figure it out. "**CRYPTID**? As in *mythological creature*? You're talking about the Loch Ness *Monster*?"

ENCHANTING DETAILS

A CRYPTID is a creature whose existence has been suggested but is regarded as highly unlikely by the scientific community. Examples include kirins, dragons, the Himalayan yeti, and the subjects of many a modern-day motion picture.

Whitmore nodded. "A quite crafty, magical beast. There are, of course, other such creatures around the world, but wrangling them is difficult for those without the ability to cast spells. I was hoping you three could assist us in this matter."

"Hold up, dude," said Trish. "You're saying there're magical beings out there? In addition to all the enchanted objects and spell books?"

"Beings, places, even parallel worlds," confirmed the bookseller. "What do you suppose is contained within all those books in Codex Arcanum? As I told young Mr. Macready, *Sorcery for Beginners* is but one small part of our vast collection. If you were to assist us on this mission, we would, of course, provide you with the proper instruction." She removed an object from her handbag. It was a green-and-silver paperback, its title stamped on the cover in black lettering:

Cryptozoology for Beginners.

SORCERY FOR BEGINNERS

CRYPTOZOOLOGY is the study of animals whose existence has not been proven (or accepted) by the world at large. It is but one of many so-called Arcane Fields, which include Sorcery, Alchemy, Time Manipulation, Paranormal Studies, Inter-Dimensional Travel, and Cryptocartography. Each is deserving of its own easy-to-read help guide, but I do have a life, you know.

"CRYPTOZOOLOGY?" asked Owen.

Ms. Whitmore placed the book in Trish's hands. "You may begin your studies once you have met the others."

"Others?" echoed Perry.

"The Council Arcanum, of course. Before we go any further, you three must be approved, receive your Learner's Permits, sign the necessary death and dismemberment waivers—"

"Who *are* you?" interrupted Owen.

"Codex Arcanum is no mere bookstore," said Whitmore. "It is the library of the Council Arcanum, a worldwide society dedicated to the preservation of powerful and ancient knowledge. Now that you three have proven your mettle, justly and judiciously using your knowledge of sorcery, we would be most honored if you'd join our ranks."

"But we didn't learn all the spells," Owen said.

The bookseller shrugged. "Close enough. Frankly, we need the help. As you saw firsthand, the Euclideans surpass us in both resources and numbers. Owen's ruse put them off for a while, but now they have committed to claiming and using magic for themselves. They will not stop until they succeed. Will you help us stand against them? Will you help rescue Nessie?"

The eighth graders looked at each other, a silent agreement passing between them. Owen turned back to the bookseller and grinned.

"Let's go save a cryptid."

ACKNOWLEDGMENTS

It's difficult to know who to thank with a first novel, since many people have supported my writing in various ways over the years. I will do my best, but since I have a couple decades to cover, I'm sure I will leave someone out. If it's you, I apologize.

First off, thank you to my parents Pam and Len. They didn't choose to have a creative-type son, but they rolled with it. I appreciate all the extra writing classes and literary clubs and story camps you drove me to, and I really appreciate that you never suggested I give up. Sorry my name isn't bigger on the cover.

Thank you to Wade Werner, eighth-grade teacher and my first writing mentor, who stayed after school with me for many days without pay, and to whom this book is dedicated. Sadly, he passed away before seeing these words in print. My very first published story was due to him, and I will never forget his influence.

To my other writing mentors: Julie E. Washington, Joe Scherma, Wendy Macleod, June Mack, Paul Wolanksy, Ami Vitori, and Amy Kane. You all made me a better craftsman.

To my beta readers: Nora McFarland, John Fletcher, Jehu Morning, and Jan Kimbrough. Your notes were invaluable.

Sara Saedi, Paula Yoo, and Laura Hopper were generous with their publishing expertise and industry contacts.

Kellen Kaiser translated the Spell to Repel Enemies into Hebrew for me and watched my firstborn while I wrote this. Any mistakes with the various languages are the fault of me and Google Translate.

Adam Gomolin discovered this book on the Inkshares site while it was still in draft mode, and has tirelessly championed it for the last fifteen months. Adam, I hope to one day have a tenth of your drive and enthusiasm.

Also thanks to the other good people at Inkshares, who have all helped nurture this word-baby to publication: Avalon Radys, Elena Stofle, Angela Melamud, Thad Woodman, Pam McElroy, Kevin G. Summers, Kaitlin Severini, and Mike Corley. You guys are champions.

Thanks to my editor, Staton Rabin, for such thoughtful, expansive notes. You made me take a hard look at my work, and it improved because of your suggestions.

A big "ox ox" to illustrator Juliane Crump, who has been working on this book nearly as long as I have, and handled my unclear descriptions and poor grasp of design with grace and aplomb. You are great at what you do, and I hope to collaborate on many more projects with you.

Thanks to Mike Esola and Howie Sanders at UTA, and Jonathan Shikora at LGNA.

My deepest gratitude goes out to the 255 friends, family, and complete strangers who preordered this book, shared my posts on social media, wrote reviews, and put up with my annoying emails for months on end. Crowdfunding was one of the scariest things I've ever done, but your support made it easy. *Sorcery for Beginners* exists because of you.

Finally, a heartfelt thanks to Juliane, Ronan, and Milo for agreeing to share your lives with me. Every day I'm grateful.

Matt Harry
Los Angeles, April 2017

GRAND PATRONS

Adam Gomolin
Andrew Fisher
Adam Richardville
Brad Kawamura
Candace Lutian
Daniel Hashimoto
Darren Kamnitzer
Eleanor Rank
Elisabeth L. Murray
Eric M. Miller
Erika Bruun Andersen
Glenda Crump
Grey S. Wears
Heath Luman
Jennifer Stone
Jim & Bonnie Garrison
Jones & Jane Dickerson
Joyce Able Schroth
Mandy Richardville
Megan L. Maulsby
Moe Moe Lwin & Odin Shafer
Nora McFarland
Raymund B. Utarnachitt
Todd & Taryn Jirousek
Veera & Tagore Murray

INKSHARES